The Companion

BY THE SAME AUTHOR

The Bacheloress
The Couple

The Companion
Woman in Progress 2

by
Victor Margueritte

translated, annotated and introduced by
Brian Stableford

A Black Coat Press Book

Edited by Peter Gabbani

English adaptation and introduction Copyright © 2015 by Brian Stableford.
Cover illustration Copyright © 2015 Mike Hoffman.

Visit our website at www.blackcoatpress.com

ISBN 978-1-61227-361-7. First Printing. January 2015. Published by Black Coat Press, an imprint of Hollywood Comics.com, LLC, P.O. Box 17270, Encino, CA 91416. Printed in the United States of America.

Introduction

Le Compagnon, roman de moeurs by Victor Margueritte, here translated as *The Companion*, was first published by Ernest Flammarion in 1923. It was advertised as a sequel to the highly controversial best-seller, *La Garçonne* (1922; translated in an edition uniform with this one as *The Bacheloress*). The author's preface reports that *Le Compagnon* had been planned as a part of a couplet, collectively entitled *La Femme en Chemin* [Woman in Progress], and that a preliminary draft of a section of the present novel had been completed before work began on *La Garçonne*. That preliminary draft was published the fifth issue of *Oeuvres Libres* in 1921 as "La Femme en Chemin."

In fact, although about two thirds of the wordage of "La Femme in Chemin" was eventually adapted into the text of *Le Compagnon*, the two stories are very different. The central character of the earlier story is not Annik Raimbert, the heroine of the eventual version, but her sister Paule, and "La Femme en chemin" is essentially the story of her unhappy marriage and rancorous divorce. Annik merely provides her with occasional support and sets for her a good example at the end of the story—an ending which is comprehensively transformed in *Le Compagnon*, where Paule meets a markedly different fate. The author's modifications partly stemmed from the necessity of moving Annik to center stage, together with the requisite number of associated characters to round out and enhance her story, partly from adaptations introduced to link the novel to the story of *La Garçonne* and partly in response to the fierce reaction provoked by the publication of the earlier book—the antipathy of which, involving loud protests against its alleged obscenity, was what had boosted the book to best-seller status.

After the publication of *Le Compagnon*, the author decided to extend the couplet into a trilogy by adding a third volume entitled *Le Couple* (1924; translated in the same uniform edition, as *The Couple*.) Although it would have been perfectly rational to do so, as a means of further exploiting the enormous publicity given to *La Garçonne*, it is also an entirely logical move in artistic terms, given the futuristic rhetoric with which the fervent propaganda for feminism contained in *Le Compagnon* is supported. Indeed, if ever a Naturalistic novel cried out for a futuristic sequel, it is *Le Compagnon*. It was not the first to be provided with one—Émile Zola had added a substantial futuristic sequence to *Fécondité* (1899; tr. as *Fruitfulness*), and Andre Couvreur had followed *La Mal nécessaire* (1899; tr. as *The Necessary Evil*)[1] with the baroque futurist sequel *Caresco, surhomme* (1904; tr. as *Caresco, Superman*)[2]—but *Le Couple* was a more conscientiously detailed supplement in terms of its careful extrapolation of what had gone before, and it owed much of its impetus to the groundwork laid in *Le Compagnon*. There is no other book that so neatly fuses the two separate meanings of the term *roman scientifique* that emerged in the 1870s, one applying to Jules Verne's accounts of technological possibility and the other to Zola's notion of the novelist as a scientifically-scrupulous observer. Without the attempted deployment of Zolaesque insight in *Le Compagnon*, the unique features of *Le Couple* could not have been developed.

Although the ultimate version of *Le Compagnon* transplants the central characters of *La Garçonne* and continues their stories, it does so in a slightly awkward fashion, perhaps inevitable given that *Le Compagnon* is more an exercise in contrast than continuity. Annik Raimbert eventually forms a close and sympathetic relationship with Monique Lerbier, the heroine of the earlier work, but Annik is a very different character: a counter-example of feminist strategy, who never wavers in her convictions, even under the most seductive pressure. Whereas the deeply wounded Monique was driven by

[1] Black Coat Press, ISBN 978-1-61227-253-5.
[2] Black Coat Press, ISBN 978-1-61227-254-2.

trauma to do everything wrong before eventually returning to enlightenment and her true self, Annik never falters in her faith or method, in spite of almost making a false step when, like poor Monique, she is led into illusion by her innocent optimism.

The fact that Annik avoids that false step, and this remains untraumatized, cannot work to the advantage of the dramatic tension of *Le Compagnon*, although the author works hard to make up for this deficit; he retains Paule as a further standard of comparison, a character who does not have Monique's fundamental virtue and resilience, and thus carries her own trauma through to an exceedingly bitter end, providing one of several exemplary alternatives of women who cannot see the feminist light and are eventually crushed in consequence. The plot is further complicated, and perhaps somewhat disrupted, by the introduction of the artist Jean Roussot, whose function is to substitute for the author, in being subjected to a bitter hate-campaign as a result of publishing an allegedly honest exposé of the corrupt mores of post-Great War French morals—in this case a painting entitled *Le Gynandre*, the reordering of the Greek roots by comparison with the more familiar androgyne emphasizing the implication of a woman who resembles a man rather than a man who resembles a woman.

It was probably the author's unrepentant reaction to the fuss kicked up by *La Garçonne*, given the substance in the satirical characterization of Roussot, rather than a desire to pander to the readers who bought *La Garçonne* because they had been assured by the highest authorities that it was obscene, that led him to insert some rather graphic passages into *Le Compagnon* that might otherwise seem gratuitous. The accounts of what would nowadays be called "dogging" in the Bois de Boulogne, a visit to an exceedingly dispirited brothel, and a prim senator's ludicrous sexual fetish are, however, described in more euphemistic terminology than the scenes in *La Garçonne* that some readers found so shocking, and they do not give rise to the charge leveled against *La Garçonne* that

7

the author found most hurtful: that of besmirching the honor of French womanhood. While not discarding the popular Sadeian myth that French convent schools were hotbeds of lesbian lust that corrupted their pupils permanently, *Le Compagnon* does not give the notion anything like the prurient prominence that it had in the earlier novel.

As a result of the process of its composition, *Le Compagnon* is more of a patchwork than its predecessor—and, for that matter, its successor—but the patchwork in question is sewn together with sufficient dexterity not to deflect attention away for too long from the central theme of Annik's brand of feminism and the necessity of its gospel spreading that a better world is to come into being. Modern feminist readers are perhaps more likely to think that cause weakened by the fact that it is being expounded by a male writer than by any purely literary defect, although such readers would probably also be sensitive to the irony of the fact that, in 1923, only male writers could say such things forthrightly. No female writer could have published *La Garçonne*, even in Paris, and it is likely that no female writer could have published *Le Compagnon* either, even if she had consented to censor the blatantly and conscientiously obscene passages. If the authorship of the work renders its protest fundamentally suspect—and it is at least arguable that it should not—that alleged defect is at least entitled to compensating approval on the grounds that it is clearly the work of a sincere enemy of the enemies of feminism, and one possessed of eloquence as well as fervor.

It is frequently the case that the middle volumes of trilogies are incapable of standing alone, being shorn of both the introductory function provided by the first volume and the conclusion provided by the third, but *Le Compagnon* suffers less from that problem than most second volumes, having originally being devised as the introduction to the project, and then redesigned to provide a conclusion, to which the third volume was added as an afterthought. Given that it did eventually become the second element in a triptych, however, it does benefit now from being read as a bridge rather than a

8

terminus, and more as an introduction to *Le Couple* than as a conclusion to *La Garçonne*. As such, it is certainly a useful underpinning for the *Le Couple*, even though the logic of the latter story's development forces feminism to take third place in the final novel's nest of ideologies, behind socialism and pacifism. The detailed development of Annik's character in *Le Compagnon* provides invaluable groundwork for the motivation of her actions in the final novel, and for the assessment of their true significance.

The whole trilogy thus becomes, ultimately, considerably greater than its parts, and *Le Compagnon*—as it always aspired to be—is part of a far larger quilt than its own internal patchwork. Whether or not *Le Compagnon* can qualify as a classic of feminist literature, having been penned by a mere man, it is nevertheless a significant milestone in the development of that literature. It is all the more significant because the problems it analyzes in such detail have not, as the text and its heroine optimistically hoped, been effaced by time, or even greatly eroded. Although muted, they still simmer beneath the surface and behind the mask of a society still corrupted by most, and perhaps all, of the evils to which the trilogy calls attention.

This translation was made from the London Library's copy of the Flammarion edition.

Brian Stableford

THE COMPANION

PREFACE

Habent sua fata libelli, Horace has said. Books have their destiny.

Two years ago, I was working on a plan for a pair of novels—or rather, a single novel in two volumes, *Le Compagnon* and *La Garçonne*, the plan of which I had had in mind since writing *Jeunes filles* and *Prostituée*—when, during the summer of 1921, Henri Duvernois asked me urgently for my collaboration in a periodical that he was founding.

I then wrote a few chapters, rapidly: a first draft of the part of *Le Compagnon* that I intended to write first. The piece appeared in *Oeuvres Libres* under the title "La Femme en Chemin." That was the title under which I had promised myself to assemble the two works.

Then, that first work not seeming to me to be ready as of yet, I modified my project and wrote *La Garçonne* from beginning to end. It was thus that, designed to appear second, that book was subjected to the fires of criticism, combined with those of the society of which it gave too exact a depiction for the latter's liking.

I will amuse myself some day, not without some scorn, by relating the underside of the unique adventure that befell me with that book, of which Hatred and Envy multiplied the success. I do not want to wait until then to thank all of those Frenchmen and Francophiles who wrote to me spontaneously, in the thousands, to express their sympathy: a host of unknown friends, whose letters I have joined to the decree that honored me by dishonorifying me: a document whose stupidity and illegality are so obvious that, in spite of the announcement in the newspapers of 3 January of its imminent publication in *Le*

11

Bulletin des Lois, they dared not print it. I only made acquaintance with it myself five months later, through the intermediary of a commissioner at the Special and Judiciary Delegations. The text, worthy of a Jesuit or Calvinist Homais,[3] will offer diversion to those inclined to laughter in the future.

In the meantime, with regard to *Le Compagnon*—of which I can only say one thing, which is that it is, like all the works I have signed, "a book of good faith"—I am continuing, while enlarging it, the furrow commenced in 1896 with *Le Désastre* and *Femmes nouvelles*.[4]

A few of the characters of *La Garçonne* will be found in *Le Compagnon*. Even if, having become wiser, my enemies do not give it the same publicity, Annik Raimbert will doubtless arouse no less anger than Monique.

A logical consequence of my study of feminine mores, *Le Compagnon* claims, in fact, and loudly, the right to say everything, in accordance with the honest naturalist method to which the poet of *Au Fil de l'heure* is proud of having been able to remain, incontrovertibly, faithful.[5]

Throughout all my work, historic or romantic, I have had only one artistic concern, the Truth, and one ideal, Life. I do not care that I have irritated hypocrites and exasperated the jealous. There is, however, one point that I want to clarify. Worthy people have claimed, and others have repeated in sheep-like fashion, that "I only wrote *La Garçonne* with the objective of making money." It must be admitted that after

---

[3] Monsieur Homais is the self-important apothecary in Flaubert's *Madame Bovary*.

[4] *Le Désastre* (1897) was the first of a four-volume series by the Margueritte brothers collectively entitled *L'Époque*, set during the Franco-Prussian War of 1870, but the later novels were only added some years later. *Femmes nouvelles* (1899) was not part of the set, but was the next novel they published.

[5] The poetry collection *Au Fil de l'heure*, signed by both Margueritte brothers, was published in 1896, and presumably contained their earliest collaborative endeavors.

thirty-eight books, of which one, *Prostituée*, published in 1907, offers similar violences, it is a calculation that I would have been well advised to make sooner! I had no need to wait until my fifty-sixth year to ensure, by the most facile means, an ease that, thanks to my labors, has never been lacking. It is a filthy calumny, which I hurl into the mud in passing, and which I would not have mentioned if I had not always tried not only to conserve in its purity, but also to augment in its luster the glorious name that I have inherited.

As one grows old, the certainty of the nullity of certain foundations and the vanity of certain forms on which social convention is based appears so clearly that, if there is one thing one regrets, it is the excessive brevity of existence, in order to continue working and to work better.

I hope that here, I have taken a step forward.

The heroines that I have attempted to animate thus far—those of *Femmes nouvelles* and *Jeunes filles*, and those of *Le Talion* and *Le Soleil dans la Geôle*, and even *La Garçonne*—were merely unevolved bourgeois women. Except for Monique, who deliberately affirms the absolute right of the Virgin to entire sexual equality, all the others submit, in accordance with their era, to the compromises of the age-old yoke. Annik Raimbert, a sister to Monique in physical liberation, goes further than her in the emancipation of the mind.

Monique stops part way, and, as soon as she can, returns to the natural order, to the point that she is reconciled to the social order by means of a happy marriage. Gently but rigorously, Annik carries her beliefs through to their logical conclusion. The fortune and education of the former were one of the conditions of her fall, as her deep-seated honesty was one of the causes of what some critics have called her redemption. Less exalted, more conscious and better organized, the latter completes the stage of the journey: a stage in which men suffer, in their turn, from the laws they have made. How many lives—especially female lives—will be spoiled before the liberation that Annik anticipates? The road that leads to the

13

future city will have turnings that no one can foresee any more than the precise means of that liberation.

It is thus, by the side of the man she loves, that Annik is not the effaced and submissive companion of yesterday, but marches with an equal stride: the tender and voluntary companion who is heading toward tomorrow. And if she sports in her short hair the cockade of the bacheloress, it is to show that, while remaining a woman to the fullest extent possible, she is also capable of virility.

That is the entire meaning of *La Femme en chemin*, and I hope that certain feminists—I mean those women who pride themselves on being feminists but who are less revolutionary than they claim, or even than they believe—will be more understanding this time.

I have never varied my philosophy, and more than the manner of its presentation, and I would have liked to give *Le Compagnon*, as well as *La Garçonne*, as an epigraph, these lines that I wrote eighteen years ago in *Prostituée*:

"Slave or mistress: when will we cease to veil, of our own accord, the true face of woman under those two masks? When will we understand that she will only cease to be the enemy when we know, by means of honesty and tenderness, how first to make her a friend? When will there finally be equal rights and duties for all human creatures: one sole morality, one sole justice?"

PART ONE

Nature does not know vice;
it is education that invented it.
Camille Mauclair, "De l'amour physique."[6]

I

The bell at the entrance door rang.

In the redoubt that served her simultaneously as a bathroom and kitchen, while she finished pressing the large sponge to her bowed neck, Annik thought: *Paule perhaps? No, she has a key.* As she was naked, standing up in her tub, she did not go to the door, but held the sponge under the water running from the tap in the kitchen sink until it inflated, and then, tranquilly allowed it to run out again over her body.

"How good that is!"

The salubrious caress of the cold water ran like a frisson over the muscular back and chest of the young warrior woman, the abdomen protruding like an ivory shield, and then glided over the full, tapering legs, and sprinkled her arched childlike feet and the agate pink of her round toenails with a rain of droplets.

The doorbell was still ringing.

"*Zut!* Who can it be?"

She shook the brown curls of her short hair, and turned her mutinous face and gilded eyes, with the serious shadow that they took on at every passage of thought.

Still ringing!

---

[6] "De l'amour physique" appeared in Camille Mauclair's *Essais sur l'amour* (1912).

She had decided not to disturb herself. Except for her sister, she was not expecting anyone, or anything. For a start, Sunday was not a day for consultations. Liberty, after a hard week! A desire to run and sing uplifted her: it was a beautiful day! An excursion in the auto, lunch in the countryside…she had to be ready by eleven. Pierre Lebeau would be there.

But the obstinate ringing of the doorbell and a few desperate raps on the door were succeeded by a disappointed voice:

"Annik! Annik? It's me, Cécile—Cécile Hardy… Mérette."

"What! Wait, darling. I'm coming."

Amazed, but even more joyful, Annik leapt out of the tub. Instantaneously draped in a large towel, and leaving large damp patches as she ran over the worn carpet of the studio—which constituted on its own all the rooms of her apartment—she opened the door and drew into a affectionate embrace a woman whose benevolent face was radiant with pleasure. Filially and fervently, she kissed the faded cheeks with tender pecks. Then, stepping back with a burst of laughter, she recommenced: "Too bad! I've made you wet…"

"Let's at least go inside," said the unexpected visitor, also laughing. She contemplated the favorite of all her former pupils, her spiritual daughter, with the pride of her obscure life and the tenderness of her solitary devotion. "Not changed! Morally, at least. As for the rest, who cares? You've grown, Mademoiselle Advocate. I haven't seen you for two years— that's a long time!"

"You could say so."

They filled the vestibule, so narrow that it contained not a single item of furniture.

"Go on," said Annik, "so that I can show you my study…"

With an ample, mischievous gesture, she indicated the room, painted in ocher, in which a few canvases by young painter friends spaced out their bright patches.

"It's magnificent."

"You really think so?"

Content, she pointed to a corner alcove: the divan, the shelves laden with books. "My bedroom." Then, between two old chairs, the black and gold lacquered wooden table, where parrot tulips displayed their indented scarlet petals in a long crystal vase: "My dining room."

Mademoiselle Hardy, in her simplicity as a small town schoolteacher, marveled at everything—not so much because, having been poor all her life, she was unfamiliar with the research of elegance, as because everything touching Annik, and everything that Annik touched, was suddenly embellished.

The young woman had sat down on a corner of the desk—a massive modern art table in maple wood, whose top disappeared beneath heaps of files. Tightening her savage's loincloth around her dangling legs, she said: "What a pleasure it is to see you, Mérette! Explain..."

"You know that when you left Yvelines, I was beginning to prepare for my examinations in order to qualify as a Head-mistress. Well, I've just been appointed—at Versailles. Exactly! What do you say to that? By train, an hour from your Rue Saint-Sulpice. I amused myself with the idea of giving you that surprise."

Annik clapped her hands. Then, moved as if by a spring, she leapt toward the woman who, when she emerged from her mourning, had welcomed her, a little lost orphan, and, in the absence of Paule—her older sister, engaged in her own struggle for existence—had served as her other, educator and friend.

Taking her in her arms, she said: "Dear, dear Mérette. You can't possible know how pleasant it is to know you're there now, to have you so close by."

She had leaned her head on the shoulder that had sustained it so many times, warming with a caress her forlorn-ness, her dreams, and all the anxious tenderness of a young soul, nascent to discoveries and disillusionments...

Today, enthusiastic and strong, armed for the struggle thanks to her "Mérette," she read with emotion in the wrinkles

17

of the face and her maternal eyes the corrosions of time—the time given without reserve to clear the route for young girls, the wives and mothers of tomorrow, in order to smooth their uphill path into the rude future...

Cécile Hardy had grown old—but not in spirit. Her gaze retained the same limpidity, the gush of a pure spring...

In the quick exchange of their memories, Annik revived the years of her early childhood, enclosed in the shop where everything was sold: groceries, clothing, kitchenware—*À la Confiance chez Raimbert*—a musty Limbo through which the pale vision of her widowed mother, always ill, wandered like a phantom...the abrupt deliverance that had been her entry to the school: a hatching, life, the sun revealed...

Mademoiselle Hardy, already an aging spinster, eaten away by the regret of maternity, had kept her after class one evening when the debilitated child, coughing and feverish, was causing her distress... No parents. In the house of the neighbors who had taken charge of her and Paule, for money, when Madame Raimbert had died and the shop had been sold, the two sisters slept together on a mattress in a cupboard. Nourished on scraps, in spite of the monthly payments made by the notary from the three thousand francs of the Raimbert family funds, they were, Paule at seventeen and she at thirteen, as thin as little birds fallen from the nest...

"Oh, you can boast of having acquired new plumage, my child, since the time when you were lamenting because you were all skin and bone!"

"It's been filled in."

"A true woman!" observed Madame Hardy, admiringly.

Annik had raised her head again, and, unwinding their embrace, while she adjusted her towel, she said: "Well, yes, Mérette! Twenty-four years old, since the day before yesterday. And now, it's time that your daughter got dressed...your aging daughter, because, next year, Saint Catherine..."

She had gone to the Provençal wardrobe, whose shiny patina she liked, in which, underwear and garments appeared, carefully arranged.

Having a healthy mind in a healthy body, kept supple by daily gymnastic exercises, being beautiful, she had never blushed at being naked. At Yvelines, Mademoiselle Hardy had brought her up in the cult of cleanliness, the primary self-respect, and in the entire knowledge of natural functions. Thus, while at the nearby religious boarding school, the Annunciation, where her sister had spent three years, the boarders, constrained to hypocrisy, the seed of all vices, simmered in dirt, Annik had grown up innocently, like a free flower.

Without false modesty, she put on her chemise with one of those rapid, harmonious gestures in which she always remained decent.

"You'll excuse me, darling! There's a slight lack of screens. It's because I never receive any visitors here, except for clients.

Mademoiselle Hardy smiled, wagging her finger. "You can't make me believe, made as you are, that there's not the slightest amorous individual in the wings?"

"Oh, there's no shortage of amorous men. No...but if there were anything serious, you'd know about it. My letters have never hidden any part of my life from you."

"Bah! You might, like all your generation, be attached to your single-life independence, but you're still at the age of Arvers' sonnet: *My heart has its secret, my soul...*[7]

"Neither secret nor mystery—or, at least, nothing as yet sufficiently precise for me to be able to talk about it. I can

---

[7] The line from Félix Arvers' most famous poem, "Un Secret," is misquoted; the first phrase actually has "*âme*" [soul], not "*coeur*" [heart], and continues "*ma vie*" [my life] not "*mon âme.*" The line translates as "My soul has its secret, my life its mystery...." The poem goes on to lament, in lachrymose terms, that the object of the poet's affection (Charles Nodier's daughter Marie) did not deign to notice his infatuation. It was enormously popular, and endlessly quoted—to the extent, obviously, that people began to retain the significance while forgetting the precise wording.

scarcely think about it." She stopped and reflected. "No, that's not true; I think about it more and more!" And, before the mute interrogation, she let herself lapse into the tenderness of thought, this time aloud: "No, nothing definitive..."

Many men, in fact, had paid court to her, but only two had pleased her, precisely because they had always maintained, in her regard, a certain reserve: Amédée Jacquemin, the socialist député, a cheerful and good comrade, for whom she had an affectionate esteem, and, most of all, Paul Lebeau, whose character often irritated her but toward whom, by virtue of one of those natural contradictions of the heart, she felt physically more attracted.

Amédée Jacquemin was free, however, and Pierre Lebeau had a long-standing liaison. A liaison, to be sure, that he was ready to break off—at least, he had recently affirmed that to her; otherwise she would not have envisaged for a moment, in her intransigent conception of sexual morality, and her thirst for honesty and reciprocal equality, the possibility of loving him. There was, however, no calculation in that way of being, even less any hidden agenda of marriage.

Annik had seen too many unhappy households attached so passionately to the reprisals of hatred or the compromises of resignation. She had decided, on principle, not to abdicate the liberties and the rights that, so long as she was not married, laws accorded to a woman and a mother: liberties almost equal to those of a man, save for the political rights that she still hoped to enjoy one day. Thus, she would remain her own mistress, and that of her children...

"I'm hesitating between two possibilities. They both have their attractions, but I'm inclining more willingly toward one of them. I've written to you about the help that Monsieur Lebeau has given to me in getting me into the *Appel*, first as a stenographer and subsequently as a private secretary. A stenographer in Paris hasn't a sou! For the scant banknotes that remained of my share of the inheritance after the armistice only lasted—as you know better than anyone—for the first few months after my arrival. One needs accommodation, doesn't one, and to dress oneself, however modestly? And the purchase of a machine...and the search for work, the refusals, the trials, the failures... It's hard earning a living. Especially when one isn't ugly, and wherever one goes, inside and out, whatever one attempts, one bumps into the same refrain: *Screw or starve...*

"And with all that, the law studies, the preparation for the examinations... It takes determination not to chuck in all in. I had that, thanks to your lessons and your aid. Now, thanks to Monsieur Lebeau, I can breathe. The editor of a big newspaper, in Paris—you can't imagine the power! Especially with his talent! It's to him that I owe my first cases. Oh, he's been very good!"

"Or very cunning."

The observation was made with such a bitter hostility that Annik was nonplussed by it. A harsh expression froze Mademoiselle Hardy's features momentarily: an impulse of bitter amity?

Without pausing, Annik continued: "I was so alone..."

"What about Paule?"

"Paule?"

Annik took the turn, glad to avoid the subject of Lebeau by changing the topic of conversation. She could not see sufficiently clearly into her own mind as of yet. "Paule has had enough trouble getting herself out of difficulty to help me. She's has a great deal of it. I'm not criticizing her...and then, as you know, we don't have the same nature."

"Indeed! What's become of her? Still a musician? Her harp?"

"Still, but only in the evenings. Lessons, concerts... By day—one has to eat—she's a model at Mauricette's, the big house of couture."

"What about the famous ambition, marriage?"

"She dreams about it more than ever."

"And in the meantime?"

"She lives with a friend, a sales assistant, also at Mauricette's."

21

"Ah!"

Annik prepared to defend her sister against the possibility of a mocking allusion, but Mademoiselle Hardy, devoid of all malevolence—and not understanding, in any case, that a woman could take pleasure in sensual perversions—had not put any malice into her exclamation. She added: "Poor Paule! She doesn't resemble you. Another one whose education has prepared her oddly for the struggle! A woman who has no vocation but the stewpot and no métier but the harp!"

"To be fair," Annik put in, putting on her shoes, "recognize that between her adolescence, educated in the convent, and mine, fashioned by you...and then again, there was the war! In accordance with their character, people have reacted to it differently..."

"That's true; old people never take that upheaval sufficiently into account. By emptying hearths, and then killing millions of men, the scourge emancipated hundreds of thousands of women at a stroke...and those who didn't have the necessary equilibrium of strength..."

Annik evoked the Terrible Years and their frenzy for life, exasperated by the proximity of death...the furnace of the factories, the promiscuity of the hospitals, the intimate whirling of the dance halls... Personally, she had escaped all of that dementia, having remained under the wing of her instructress until 1917, when, quitting the tutelary refuge, she had played her part in the labor of women and the misery of soldiers. Certified by the Red Cross, she had come to do relief work, replacing, with the ardor of a committed volunteer, some of the original nurses, wearied before the end of their second year: those for whom she had heroically cared—passing from a hospital for contagious wounded men to one for those with facial wounds—knew that the soul of a sister of charity, and an apostle also, was hidden beneath her delicate envelope.

From the child of fifteen that the war had surprised in the middle of her studies, and soon plunged into the midst of hell, a young woman, an adult, had been born, who, from the contact with human distress as well as social fury and imbecility, retained a mystical impetus toward a new order. Whereas Paule had ended up losing her balance, Annik, by virtue of the environment in which she was steeped in a quotidian vision of terrors, had been preserved and hardened. Her tenacious personal work in her hours of repose and her active appetite for sport had brought her, as a new individual, to the edge of amour.

"Paule's like the majority," she observed, "enslaved by prejudice. Marriage, for her, is the gilded chain, at the end of which there's the food bowl and the kennel. How many of us are there for whom the family only exists if there's a bond of election?"

Mademoiselle Hardy looked at her proudly. The schoolteacher saw her again, young, departing for the propagation of her faith: a world regenerated by female liberation. How many evils could be avoided without the satisfied egotism of some and the lamentable flabbiness of others! Oh, if only everyone wanted to unite, after so many horrors, against injustice and misery! Against war, above all, the source and sewer of all crimes!

"Dear girl!" Mademoiselle Hardy murmured.

Annik would be the continuer, would realize what she herself had attempted, fruitlessly, in her good will as a schoolteacher: her impotent dream, always broken against the hostile walls of a society made by men for men.

She held out her hands, which Annik squeezed tenderly.

"You'll never know, Mérette, the extent to which I adore you. You collected me and protected me in frightful days. But for you...! That's why, even though Paule is older than me, I often have the sentiment of being riper than she is for liberty, and that I need to look after her, as if I were the elder. You'll see her—she's coming. We're going to go out, with Monsieur Lebeau, to have lunch in a quiet corner on the Oise. I say *we* because I'm taking you...no, no, no resistance! Today, it's you who have to obey, Mérette. You can tell me afterwards what you think of him."

She was ready, clad in a short straight dress in red crepe, with a floral pattern, a black varnished leather belt, and a large white turned-up collar, which gave her a bold appearance. Not the enticing slyness of the "Claudine"[8] of yore, but a straightforward charm of pure adolescence. She placed an authoritarian hand on the gray head, coiffed in an old fur bonnet in spite of the May sky, the soft azure of which entered through the open window.

"It's yes?"

But Mademoiselle Hardy shook her head. "It's no." And, abruptly making her decision, she went on: "Your Lebeau, in spite of all you've said about him, doesn't signify anything worthwhile to me. You're too young to have known the *Appel* before the war, when it was nothing but a cheap rag. The true Lebeau revealed himself nakedly there: a professional blackmailer, a soul of mud. Yes! It's him, I assure you; it's him who called the Republic "cow-dung" when it left him with an empty stomach…today, now that he's rich, he has only one obsession: the Académie and Parliament; he's changed his coat and his batteries, but fundamentally, he's still the same man: nothing but appetites and hatreds. Intelligent, agreed—but that only makes him more despicable. Oh, people forget quickly in Paris!"

Surprised, Annik remained silent. What insect had stung the worthy Mérette?

"He's done you a service? But you're an incomparable secretary! He's facilitated the first steps for you at the Palais, has he? It's because he hopes that you'll return the favor with others, you can be sure."

---

[8] The protagonist of the early quasi-autobiographical novels of Colette, published between 1900 and 1904, originally under the pseudonym of her husband, "Willy," which seemed slightly scandalous at the time, but now seem charming in their innocent sensuality.

With a hint of mockery, Annik raised her tranquil eyes. "What would be the harm? I know what I can do. I'm an adult."

"I know your ideas!"

"They're yours, Mérette..."

"Mine? Mine...revised and augmented!"

"What! Haven't you always told me that, for women, a good free union is better than a bad marriage?"

"Obviously...but everything depends on the circumstances...for with our backward mores, many risk losing their livelihoods there."

"The weak! Not me."

"So it's not a matter of the principle at stake. Free union? Marriage? Both of them imply the same lottery ticket: a choice. And it's yours, my dear child, that's worrying me."

"Why?"

"I've told you."

"An impression! Is that sufficient for you to condemn a man you don't know?"

"Well..." Mademoiselle Hardy hesitated.

Annik thought that she was about to raise the objection of the *ménage à trois* with the Lourdals, to which the journalist had cynically attached himself. "It's Madame Lourdal, isn't it?"

Mademoiselle Hardy raised a surprised gaze. "No, who's that?"

Worthy Mérette! She was obviously a provincial! Regretfully, Annik was obliged to explain that Lebeau, in the sight and with the knowledge of Parisian society, served the famous couple as a manger.

"You've heard of the Lourdals! Lourdal of the Académie des Sciences Morales et Politiques, the philosopher who, after having written *Le Matérialisme Roi* and married Simone Viale, was converted to the ideas of the day: the saber and the aspergillum.

Mademoiselle Hardy went from one astonishment to another. "Simone? The one who paints all those prettily disgusting nudes—self-portraits, it appears?"

"That's the one. The former wife and model of the caricaturist Viale. In thickening out, she's become, like her second husband, a great thinker. She's the art critic at the *Appel*. But Lebeau is beginning to tire of her..."

"Of the trio?"

"Oh, Lourdal isn't inconvenient. Poor old fellow! He accepts everything. No, of the duo. And I believe that if I wanted..."

Mademoiselle Hardy had a surge of revolt: "Don't do that. If you knew...!"

"What? Now, you no longer have the right to keep quiet. I like him." She shrugged her shoulders. "Anyway, I'm tranquil. If you knew him..."

"You're right; I've never seen him—but I've read enough of him to be certain that I know him better than you do. Anyway, after what you've just told me...listen! Do you remember Rosa, at Yvelines? A tall blonde...a simpleton, but pretty. She came to the school for a while. Yes she did! The daughter of La Blanchard, that housekeeper who had a red birthmark on her face..."

"Ah! I know..."

"Rosa was a housemaid for the Morevals."

"The stepfather of Amédée Jacquemin, the socialist député?"

Mademoiselle Hardy made a gesture of ignorance. "All I know is that the mother presides over the Oeuvre des Asiles du Soir. The old man's a senator, a former Minister and High-Commissioner...the whole works!"

"That's right! Like Pierre Lebeau, Amédée Jacquemin is a good friend of mine."

"He's your other possibility, then?"

"Exactly."

"Well, perhaps the stepson has generous opinions—but his parents..."

"Known! They're redoubtable bigots. In fact, as sectarian skinflints go, there are none finer! All that, of course, under the cover of big words. Honor! And even the Légion d'honneur...for Monsieur de Moreval is some kind of *grand officier*...he was once in the diplomatic service. But I don't see the connection..."

"Rosa was sacked, brutally, on the day when it was perceived that she was pregnant."

"By whom?"

"There we are."

Not for an instant did the name of Pierre Lebeau brush Annik's credulous sentiment with a suspicion. Astonished, she said: "Amédée?"

But a sadness impregnated Mademoiselle Hardy's compassionate features. "No: your Lebeau."

"Him? It's impossible! He has an embarrassment of choice! To have loved that girl!"

Mademoiselle Hardy became grave. "Who mentioned love?" By Annik's emotion, she measured the emprise of the seduction over the young, enthusiastic and sincere soul. At the risk of a temporary suffering, the necessity of a more urgent warning became urgent.

"It's hardly worth the trouble of having been a nurse and qualified in law if you still believe that men aren't all the same! *Screwing*, as you put it yourself—all of them, and as much as they can. Love...that's something else entirely."

"Pierre Lebeau isn't an ordinary man. Him, with that girl! What a joke! It's just a filthy rumor."

"You only have to ask Rosa, if it interests you."

"Inventions! Blackmail!"

"There are accents of truth that don't lie."

"But in the end, how do you know, Mérette? Tell me! Yes, speak! You'd be doing me a service—yes, a great service."

"Rosa told me. One day when she had come to bring him an urgent letter..."

"At the paper!"

"No, at his home…a letter from Madame de Moreval, about a lawsuit…"

"A lawsuit? Hang on…the Oeuvre des Asiles du Soir versus the Compagnie Laitière, perhaps?"

"Perhaps. What's certain is that your Pierre thought Rosa pretty, told her so, and proved it. Yes, right away…just like that, in his study. Undoubtedly he's one of those sick individuals who can't find themselves alone with a woman without passing from sight to desire, and from desire to action."

"Oh, I can assure you that he isn't."

"He must know to whom he's addressing himself! That idiot girl was so silly, and perhaps flattered, that she let him go ahead. As she got a taste for the game, they carried on until she confessed that she thought that she was pregnant. Oh, it didn't drag on. The result…"

"But when did she tell you all this?"

"She came back to Yvelines a fortnight ago—in what a state! Sacked by the Morevals at the first apparent sign, she'd taken her belly from house to house, and then, as no one wanted her anywhere, from sidewalk to sidewalk. In the end, exhausted and consumptive, she fell back on her mother's house, where the money is already insufficient for one. Then I took an interest in the unfortunate…I helped her a little. I even succeeded in getting her a place, but only in exchange for board and lodging, with Monsieur Seuriot, the new butcher."

A whirlwind of images passed through Annik's vision: the incredible stupor…the child-mother on the streets and then discarded…the whole tragicomedy of seduction and abandonment, of feminine weakness and malevolent society. But she felt a surge of revolt.

"If you believe everything she tells you! A delinquent, as you said yourself. Pierre is an easy target."

"No, Rosa's stupid, but she isn't a liar. She kept it to herself for fear of the consequences. She wanted to be married—to marry, with a crown of authentic orange blossoms, an employee of the gas company… Unfortunately, your Lebeau got there first."

With a revolt that astonished herself, for she had often been shocked by some of the journalist's behavior, Annik cried: "You're always the dupe of your generosity! Monsieur Lebeau has too much taste for such caprices, and too much conscience not to act, always, as an honest man. No, no. If he had had a responsible role in this…romance, I'm certain that he would have acted differently."

"Do you know his response to all Rosa's appeals? That she was mad and that if she annoyed him any further—the police!"

The doorbell rang. "There he is!" said Annik, and ran to the door.

"I'll leave," Mademoiselle Hardy declared. "After this, I can't see him… Oh it's Paule…"

II

Preceded by her habitual amber perfume, Paule Raimbert came in, very elegant, bursting into laughter.

"You thought it was him, eh? I've lost my keys, along with my handbag and purse, yesterday, in the Metro. Oh, Mademoiselle Cécile! What a nice surprise! *Bonjour!*"

She embraced the schoolteacher affectionately Although many dissimilarities separated her from Annik, she remained grateful to Mademoiselle Hardy for what she had done for her sister, as she would have done for her, too, if she had not preferred, eight years previously, to attempt the great adventure of setting off alone and poor for Paris, in the middle of the war, with the immediately dissipated provisions of her inheritance, her talent as a musician and her ignorance of all the conditions of life.

In a few words, they exchanged the recent news of their existences: one, that of Mademoiselle Hardy, similar to her spring-like eyes, so luminous and frank that everything was perceptible in an instant; the other so complex and so secret that Paule did not know how to read it herself. With her uncertain gaze, as blue-gray as a slate from which everything is erased, she maintained an enigmatic expression from which something was absent.

With her curled blonde hair, her skin so white that it seemed even milkier by contrast with her black dress, tall and thin enough that she would have seemed emaciated if the fashion were not for straight lines and the tips of two small well-shaped breasts had not raised the silk of her corsage, Paule offered, to the examination of the provincial, a striking contrast with her sister. Only five years distanced them from one another, but between them, under the bridge of their affection, there was an abyss: Paule, bourgeois in her soul, to the point of hypocrisy, in spite of her independent life; Annik, proletarian at heart and displaying her liberal beliefs like a sign.

The doorbell rang again. This time…!

To the amazement of Annik, however, who hastened to answer it—happily expectant of seeing the man from whom she expected love, and fearful that she might find the one that had just been depicted to her—a post office employee handed her a pneumatic dispatch. She recognized the familiar handwriting and nervously removed the rubber band.

"Called away to Lyon…he sends his apologies…bad news regarding his father."

"Shit!" said Paule. "And I turned down lunch with my fiancé…" She swelled with pride. "For I haven't yet told you the big news: Monsieur Martinet's marrying me. He finally decided to make his proposal."

"Really?"

"Congratulations!"

Annik and Mademoiselle Hardy surrounded her with their curious astonishment. And yet, at the happiness that illuminated her elder, the younger sister became anxious with the sentiment of an obscure threat…an instinctive antipathy against the fat man, so common, who was about to become her brother-in-law, or a simple cloud over herself?

This unexpected absence, succeeding that base revelation: Rosa? She shook off her feeling of unease. No, she could not believe it. Pierre was incapable of lowering himself to that bestial brutality, even less of degrading himself subsequently by an evil deed. No, no—impossible! The man she had chosen! Now, she was sure of that, given the reaction that had been produced within her by the unjust accusation. She could not be mistaken to such a degree!

"Do you know what we're going to do?" proposed Mérette. "I'll take you out. There's a midday train at the Quai d'Orsay. Everyone gets off at Vélisy. Lunch at a restaurant in the forest. The woods are full of lilies of the valley. And it will be a jolly first of May anyway."

"Let's go!" Annik and Paule acquiesced. "We'll come back with large bouquets…"

They were already respiring the perfume beneath the resplendent azure.

After the tiring day in the crowded trains, the warm light filtering through the green foliage whose renewal was taking place like an explosion, Mademoiselle Hardy had gone directly home to Versailles. The two sisters, each clutching her odorous bunch of flowers, got down from the tram at the corner of the Rue de Lancry and the Boulevard Magenta. Paule lived there with her friend, Lili.

Weary but happy, they participated in the popular joy, the immense blossoming of Paris in the wellbeing of its repose. A cheerful and childish gaiety, an impression of insouciant release, emanated from the crowd in the process of musing and amusing itself. Its dense columns of ants made their way in slow streams along the broad thoroughfares. There were flower-sellers everywhere, men, women and children: *Buy happiness!*

There was not a single stroller who was not scenting hope in the flowery bells. Along the side streets, people were taking the fresh air on the doorsteps. The very houses were breathing in, through their open windows, the bright softness of the evening.

It was so warm that a mist was tinting the sky with opal. The coming and going of hasty waiters spread an odor of false absinthe over the terraces of the cafés, which extended to the edge of the sidewalk, overflowing with customers. One might have thought them multicolored flowerbeds, with their orchestras hired for the day and their crowds of spectators. Tranquilly seated in families, they were watching the pedestrians file past: the innumerable cortege of bit-part players, invading the roadway.

There were no taxis, just, here and there, drivers on holiday with their wives. They appreciated various private cars as they passed by, in accordance with their makers' names. The human mass opened up in docile fashion at the sound of bells; autobuses and trams were circulating, packed with passengers.

They were continuing their service, under the orders of the Fédération des Transports en Commun, which was only due to be interrupted for one hour, between five and six. Thus they were affirming, at the same time as the principle of their rights, the good will of workers in the service of all.

The international strike having been postponed until tomorrow, in order that the holiday should not diminish the scope of the gesture, it seemed—in spite of the police forces assembled in the Place de la République—so calm was the end of the magnificent afternoon, that the first of May, a veritable ceremony of spring, far from being a symbol of social demands, was solely that of nature at work. It was a festival of the earth and laborious humanity, striving everywhere, from the soil to the bud, from the act to the thought, in the great work of life: not a day of strikes but a truce of everything that was not a communion with natural law.

"One might think that it's the fourteenth of July!" said Paule.

"And more beautiful, celebrating the future rather than the past."

A fever of hope was stirring Annik. Her young blood was beating in her temples: a seething of the universal energy, waves of the great rhythm that impels youth toward the fecund unconsciousness of instinct. To love and create, the ambition of all beings!

Nothing within her attenuated the force of that primordial need of the female, the born mother. Thanks to the vigilant solicitude of Mademoiselle Hardy, her belief had never been falsified, like that of the majority of young women of today, by the absence of parental education, the husband having business to attend to and the wife pleasures or pains. The parlor and salons for some, the hovel and the workplace for others, and the streets for all—Annik had escaped those veritable masters of contemporary formation.

"Damn!" said Paule, as they arrived outside her building. "The buses are stopping—it's five o'clock. Come up for a minute. Lili ought to be there, unless...I haven't seen her for some time. She's upset."

Although she had an antipathy for the sales assistant, Annik, alarmed by the idea of going home on foot, allowed herself to be dragged along. In the corridor, however, the concierge shouted to Paule: "Mademoiselle Lili said to tell you that she won't be back until the day after tomorrow."

"What about the key?"

"I don't have it."

"She hasn't left it with you? That's my luck. I've lost mine."

"Come on," said Annik. "We'll go wait in the café and have a glass of beer. You can sleep at my place. I only have a rendezvous at Madame Broussat's at half past six. Too bad— I'll have to go as I am, with no make-up and dusty.

Paule pinched her lips. For her part, she did not much like Madame Broussat, first of all because she was jealous of her, as her sister's great friend and protector, and secondly because the foundation with which the excellent woman occupied herself at Auteuil—a refuge for unmarried mothers— offended her prejudices. Inclined toward feminine amities by a penchant that dated from her passage through the convent, she could not imagine that one could give oneself to a man without the excuse of conjugal necessity, far less have a child outside the law. That was an inexhaustible source of arguments between herself and Annik. Free union and its risks, Paule affirmed, was a criminal utopia. The burden and the defect of bastardy—one would have to be insane to inflict it on poor children who had not asked to be born!

They sat down at a terrace table in the Boulevard Magenta.

"How hot it is!" Annik sighed.

"It's a pity that Lili wasn't there. You could have put on your make-up at the house."

She shrugged her shoulders. "I have plenty of opportunities to see her, thanks." She held Lili's abnormal influence over her sister against her. Although Paule had always denied, with an apparent vehemence of sincerity, being anything to Lili but a comrade, Annik was convinced that the liaison was preventing her big sister from becoming a true artiste and establishing a life with a man who would love her, instead of marrying that Martinet...

"You're unjust to Lili. She's a good girl...oh, you can smile. For a start, you've never understood me!"

"I love you anyway—that's the essential thing."

"No, people only truly love one another when they understand one another completely."

Piqued, Annik smiled. "Then you'll be very unhappy with Martinet, for even if the mutual 'understanding' that you and Lili have justifies your friendship, I don't believe that, from any point of view, your future spouse and you will be able to understand one another."

"Who can tell? He's less brutal, deep down, than he appears. I domesticated a jackal during the war when I was employed as a laundress at the hospital at Blidah. I even took it to Algiers, in 1918, when I went into the catering service at the Prefecture!"

"Your jackal didn't make the demands of a husband."

"You're stupid," murmured Paule, blushing.

In spite of the successive métiers to which her vicissitudes had constrained her, and the complacencies to which she was habituated—as much by curiosity, at first , as for fear of the consequences of masculine demands—she had maintained a modesty that reappeared at the most unexpected moments. It was thus that she had been able to preserve from the definitive violation that which she imagined she could not lose without sin: her virginity, an illusory barrier of which she was proud, as an ultimate virtue, as well as a supreme means of success.

That aberration had caused her to accept, as a temporary union, setting up house with Lili Brontier, then a model at Mauricette's, when she had entered the house herself as a mender. The strangeness of the cocaine addict, and even her nickname: "Except That" had attracted her immediately. Paule nonetheless judged that marriage—at which she ought to arrive, for want of any other capital, intact—was the sole logical goal of every female destiny. She saw no other exit from the cul-de-sac of her semi-success, and did not like Annik to joke about it.

"I'm not stupid," Annik protested, "but I have a horror of false calculations. At least I'm logical."

"It's just that you annoy me, with your theories. We'll see where they get you! Oh, I know what you think. I'm behind the times! What do you expect? I'm not a conscious and organized revolutionary, like you. I'm impulsive...a neurotic...at least, I'd become one, with the existence it's necessary for me to lead. Oh, without my music...fortunately, it consoles me for everything. It transports me to another world..."

Always, with a stubborn determination, through all her avatars, Paule had returned to that redemptive refuge. Even when, having been promoted to model, at the same time as Lili Brontier had become a saleswoman, she had enough to live on, she had courageously continued giving harp lessons and improving her own skills. Gifted, she had soon progressed to becoming a "name" sought by the best night-spot orchestras.

It was in one of those Montmartre restaurants that Louis Martinet, a broker of fine pearls, had noticed her. He had thought that he could buy a facile pleasure for the price of a dinner and a fake diamond. He had invested days, weeks and finally months, until the "pretentious hussy," whose name was now beginning to figure on the programs of excellent concerts, had finally promised to say yes—but only in front of Monsieur le Maire. In exchange, of course for bidding farewell to couture and merchandising at Mauricette's. As for the music, *bonsoir!* Except in public, Martinet wanted his wife to be his, a true housewife...

"In your place," Annik declared, "I'd hesitate. You know what you're leaving behind, but you don't know what's waiting for you."

Paule sighed profoundly: "Yes: security! No more always trembling for tomorrow! I won't even mention the social consideration...that would make you laugh, anarchist! And yet...to return to normality! A husband, children..."

"A husband you don't love! Children that might resemble him..."

"Yes, but a hearth!"

"A hearth? A chain! The dream of a bearskin! You're selling it, moreover, before having bought it. You'll see at what price!"

That cowardice on the part of the majority of women, their submission to waiting for a man's pleasure instead of earning the money indispensable to existence by their own labor, was one of Annik's great astonishments.

"You're not adding up the balance sheet! Today, you're free. Tomorrow, when married, you'll fall back into dependency. A servant! Not even that: incapable, with no more rights than children or lunatics!"

She resented, in her sister and all their countless other sisters, their blind servility, and their futility, above all: the cause of so many ruinations. Women adorning themselves for men, men stealing and murdering for women...all industries, included that of war, all of that immense modern technology reduced to spinning gold for that pleasure machine!

War! When she thought of what mother had permitted to be done to their sons, when she pictured the death of millions of people, that stupid massacre, in order that pearl necklaces could grow longer and skirts shorter... Were they really women, those mothers who, if they had wanted to, could have raised their children in the worship of life, in the love of work and peace, in the religion of justice? No...recumbent bitches, who only merited, along with their leash, the whip!

She shrugged her shoulders.

"Everyone is responsible for their own happiness. I promise you that I'll try to make mine. Everyone is responsible, too, for their own unhappiness. Be careful that you aren't going toward yours by consenting not to work any longer. At least I'll have warned you... What's happening?"

A rumor coming from the direction of the Gare de l'Est was propagating and swelling. The seamstresses! On strike for a fortnight, theirs was the only trade union that had decided, in response to the employers' lock-out, to hold a public demonstration in addition to the private meeting of the C.G.T. delegations at the Bourse du Travail.

Carrying copies of *Le Peuple* and *L'Humanité* as rallying signals, groups with bright bodices, sprightly hats with four-sou pompoms and poor neat dresses were advancing through the curious lines of onlookers. They were all carrying their bouquets of lilies of the valley, tied up with red ribbons. Hemmed in by policemen, the valiant little troop of a hundred workers were marching in serried ranks, singing to the tune of *Lampions*: "Down with the profiteers! Down!" or "Take your wool to Charenton! Take your trash to Charenton!" Sometimes, when a boor started to abuse them, a chorus of protest went up: "Climb up there and you'll see Montmartre!"[9] The popular song, verses and chorus, unfurled cheerfully, like a challenge. The mocking voices pierced the enormous hum of the City, awakening sympathy in the comprehension of the idlers.

"Poor kids!" said Annik. "They're in the right."

"Not as much as that. Lili could tell you. The more they earn, the more they complain. When I was a mender, I had to be content with my nine francs a day."

"Bread and meat are getting more expensive for everyone. How much do they pay you as a model?"

"You know—seven hundred francs a month."

"And Lili?"

"Fifteen hundred, because her primary interest in is selling."

"The point of view changes."

---

[9] This titular line of a popular song, written by Lucien Boyer, was adopted as an expression to signify the scornful refusal of a proposition. The song itself became known, sarcastically, as "the hymn of the Republic of Montmartre."

Annik felt sincere approval of the seamstresses, using up their youth ornamenting bourgeois ostentation, for derisory wages. The old and new rich, an entire caste of idlers who thought nothing of paying three thousand francs for a dress, screeched like ospreys when the workers, earning just enough not to die of starvation, demanded an increase!

Raising up their frail forms, and smiling as they passed by, the seamstresses were heading toward the Maison Confédérale. By virtue of the fact that the majority, in their bleak poverty, were displaying the grace that is the hallmark of the native Parisienne, their youth, in spite of their servitude, exhaled a loveliness and an insouciant boldness. Annik did not conclude, as Paule did, that they were uninteresting. On the contrary...

The cortege had just turned onto the Rue de Lancry. Squadrons were clearing the Boulevard Magenta all the way to the Bourse du Travail.

"Look! An autobus that's moving! The stoppage is over already. Look...in the direction of the Place de la République..."

"No, the other vehicles aren't moving. It must be some volunteer of the Union Civique, one of those saviors of society—horse-flies![10] Beware of accid..."

She had not even completed her sentence when, trying to avoid one of the groups driven back by the police, the occasional driver lost control of his heavy vehicle. The projectile mounted the sidewalk and, knocking over a street light, plunged into the crowd. There were strident cries, and panic. A wave of stampeding people flooded over the terrace, knocking over chairs and tables laden with glasses, and shoving customers to the ground, pell-mell.

---

[10] *Mouches du coche* [horse-flies] has a particular metaphorical reference derived from one of La Fontaine's fables, referring to individuals who move about uselessly while others work, and then pretend to be responsible for their achievements.

Annik, with her usual presence of mind, had drawn Paule inside the café. The catastrophic noises circulated while everyone fled from the threat of death. Three casualties were carried into a nearby pharmacy. Around the autobus, people hurled abuse at the crusher:

"The one time you work...!"

"Aristo!"

"Swine!"

Blows were about to follow when an eddy agitating the tumultuous boulevard dispersed the crowd.

An irresistible pressure ran along the sidewalk, chasing a confusion of strollers and idlers away from the Bourse du Travail. A confused clamor went up. Suddenly, covering the roadway like a tidal wave, a black whirlwind appeared: a tumultuous chaos of human beings jostled and struck by policemen. They were the union delegations whom, as they left the meeting, the police had invited, brutally, to move along. The collision had been so violent and unexpected that it had immediately degenerated into a brawl and a battle. There were punches, thrusts of canes, and then, almost immediately—the furious policemen having unsheathed their weapons, and dagger-thrusts having replied to saber-thrusts—the workers and the policemen, placid a few moments before, had confronted one another hand-to-hand in re-ignited eternal hatred. Revolver shots rang out. Victims fell in both camps.

Annik saw bloody faces passing by in the disarray of hectic flight. Inoffensive spectators and demonstrators took evasive action as best they could. Stupor astounded them, as did a spirit of revolt, impotent against the savagery, unleashed on all sides.

Pursued by a demented mob with bulging eyes, an old man rushed into the café. They made room for him, but he staggered into Paule. A uniformed policeman in a kepi with a gilded chinstrap caught up with him, and hammered his skull with a massive fist. Others made the floor ring with their iron-studded boots.

"It's shameful" cried Annik, grabbing hold of the policeman. "You, a child of the people…!

"Go wipe your brats!" growled the enraged animal. Shoving her in the chest, he knocked her backwards. At the same time, there was a sharp pain: the impact, on her head, of a blunt object. It was the "child of the people," administering, by means of his truncheon, a lesson in respect for law and order.

Annik fell, unconscious.

III

That same evening, on the road that goes through the thickets of the Bois de Boulogne alongside Longchamp race-course and the Seine, an auto was traveling at low speed.

The headlights illuminated the tarred roadway at a distance, and the trees inclined a magical foliage into the luminous beams. As they passed by, they fanned out to illuminate the undersides of bushes and small trees emerging from the density of the undergrowth.

Warmth made the air heavy in spite of the river, which could not be seen but whose cool black flow could be divined. A silence, a great repose, dying down at such a short distance from the city, descended from a velvet sky, the dark blue of which was speckled, above the hill of Saint-Cloud, by a scintillation of stars, while in the direction of Paris, a confused reverberation filled the spring night with a russet pallor.

"Delightful!" murmured Simone Lourdal, without conviction, while her gaze searched the penumbra that surged forth and disappeared in the glare of the headlights. Beyond the revealed zone, she was trying to pierce the tempting obscurity, the shady attraction of its lairs...

"Delightful!" repeated Pierre Lebeau, churlishly, sitting next to her at the steering wheel. "But I think we're arriving too early."

In spite of the telegram addressed that morning to Annik, and after a scene with the jealous Madame Lourdal, he had not left Paris. Simone and he were alone in the big roadster: no chauffeur to make an inconvenient witness. As for Lourdal, he had gone to Lyon the previous day, where he was giving a lecture on "Freud and the Theory of Sexuality." Toothless and bald, since his conversion, the author of *Matérialisme Roi* could not abide the birth of new ideas, to which his youth had contributed in the times when he was a hairy swashbuckler.

"This is the place, however," observed Madame Lourdal. "You see? The old acacia at the corner of the little path…that's where each auto has to stop. Ronchard explained it to us in detail."

Ronchard, the multimillionaire of the famous Mines de Vingré,[11] so-called Republican shareholder in the *Appel* and, in order to restore equilibrium, reactionary député for the Basse-Seine, was, like Pierre Lebeau and Simone Lourdal, curious for adventures, for the unfamiliar excitement of which lassitude left him incessantly in need. They were blasé individuals who were, out of snobbery as much as corruption, always running after the latest fashionable vice.

For some time, that had been the Saturnalia in the Boise de Boulogne: an excess that not only carried the weight of conversations in after-dinner smoking-rooms but had reached the newspapers—to the point that, in order to deflect attention, Lebeau, a regular at the meetings, had invented the Scandal of the Exterior Boulevards: socialites and artistes went there, he said, to meet up with shady individuals in the vicinity of Ménilmontant. Under the headline, *The Frisson of Murder*, his leader demanded, forcefully, in the name of outraged modesty and in the interests of society, "a good sweep."

The article had excited public opinion. Surprised by threatening letters from a few apaches, which he had exploited to the full, Lebeau had declared the very next day that his conscience, at the service of French health, gave him a duty to

---

[11] There are, indeed, mines in the region of Picardy where the commune of Nouvron-Vingré is located, but the name Vingré was famous for a very different reason, in connection with six soldiers who became known as the "martyrs of Vingré" were shot in 1914 for alleged cowardice, although they claimed to have been obeying an order to retreat. The legal battle to clear their names came to a sensational conclusion in 1921, after which the officer who had denied having given the order was charged with perjury. The author clearly selected the place-name for its symbolic significance.

identify hypocrisies and defects wherever he encountered them.

In the neighborhood of the Allée des Acacias, as in the thickets of Neuilly, which had already provided an arena, before the war, with the stupor of a few prowlers or maniacs, to outdoor amorous frolics, the increasing putrefaction of mores had taken over the entire Bois. Its shadows were now swarming, all the way to Longchamp, with partners and voyeurs: after the thickets, the clearings, where people amused themselves in circles.

The whores of old had been joined by women of all classes: debauched young workers, sales staff from the big stories, who, having finished their day's labor ended up by unwinding there; socialites as devoid of heart as of intelligence with flat stomachs; ever-riotous film stars in quest of new spices; foreigners who came to Paris every year to take their cure of lubricity... Thus, the aberrations of a few individuals had been succeeded by an increasingly-intense competition of actors and spectators in the open-air performances.

A lady-killer in spite of his sausage-shaped torso and smooth jaw, Pierre Lebeau, beneath his mask of generous honesty, had only one goal in life: to enjoy everything as much as possible: a complicated objective, for a soul corroded as much by ambition as vice and ennui.

Simone Lourdal aided him in his quest. A Bulgarian Jewess, with mixed and hot Oriental blood, she was frantic at putting on too much weight, in spite of massages and surgical manipulations, and carefully hid the scars on her skillfully-stretched skin beneath little mahogany curls. Growing old, the artistic editress of the *Appel* hung on to her situation by serving as a vigilant procuress. Obliging friends, scarcely nubile models and actresses in need of publicity—anything was good to retain the fickle salacity of "the Boss."

Thus, the day before, after dinner at the Morévals—a celebration for the rosette of Reichmeyer, one of the proprietors of the Grand Magasins du Tout Pour Rien[12]—Ronchard, relating his latest exploits cigar in mouth, had found an audience enticed in advance.

"No, truly, does the Bois really exist?" Lebeau had thrown out, negligently, while recalling the latest sessions in which he had taken part.

"Oh, it existed," Ronchard had replied, with a disdainful moue, "but there's something better."

"Details!"

"I fear making Madame blush..."

"Artist and painter!" Madame Lourdal had cried. "You're among men—you can go ahead. Everything is pure, in any case, for the pure."

At which Ronchard had emptied his sack of filth, to the exclamations of the Saint-Touch-me-Not: "What horror! And you've fixed another rendezvous? We'll go, won't we, Pierre? You ought to take account of it, like Monsieur Ronchard... Eighteen, there ought to be? That's too many for me... Really? Good people... Oh! The Entraygues and the handsome Max, again, that doesn't astonish me...but Rayot! A former President of the Council...!"

"Well, my dear Madame, doubtless he'll only come, like you and me, to see what's going on. You know, in any case, that he's senile. Politics is a jealous mistress; when one takes too many others, she gets her revenge. Before Rayot, a certain President of the Sénat...and don't forget, finally, the famous sanitarium at Rueil,[13] which can be proud of having played

---

[12] The name, satirizing the advertising of such "five and dime" chain stores as F. W. Woolworth's, translates as "The Department Store of Everything for Nothing."

[13] Le Sanatorium de la Malmaison at Rueil was founded by Louis Bour in 1876; he combined his medical activities with literary and artistic culture, his wife Véra Himidoff founding a notable salon at about the time the present novel was written, whose regulars sometimes took "rest cures" at the sanitarium. Several notable statesmen, and such artists as Maurice Ravel

host, along with other illustrious individuals, to the highest-placed Statesmen. Hasn't our friend Hutier been its most beautiful ornament for six months? It's a case, my dear Lebeau, of applying your famous expression: 'the cow-dung.' It's high time that we Nationalists, with a thrust of the tillers to the right, brought the ship of government into cleaner waters..."

Lebeau recalled, with gentle irony, the expression of reproval and dignity with which, in order to listen more closely, Simone had draped herself, as if with a veil. The author of so many licentious nudes, who had caressed more roundnesses than she had painted! Fundamentally misogynistic, however he delighted in his contempt for all women, especially those he used as playthings.

"Look! There's an auto."

She consulted the time on her wristwatch. Diamonds sparkled on her plump wrist in the light of the little lamp that she switched on above the oil gauge.

"Eleven o'clock. That must be the first of the gang. Switch off the headlights. We'll switch them on again for the agreed signal."

He obeyed, gripped by an equal voyeurism. They remained on watch, one beside the other. Becalmed in the same lassitude, they each ruminated their impatience, she amused by the imminent sensation under unknown lips, he curious for the sight that might, perhaps, stimulate his senses...

The auto arrived slowly, searching the sidewalks and pathways with a mobile searchlight. As it went past, it slowed down even further, directing its raw light at them.

"How many are you?"

"Two."

"Not enough! *Au revoir.*"

And before Lebeau had switched on the lights, the connoisseurs drew away.

---

and Georges Feydeau, had been inmates there in the years immediately preceding the novel's publication.

The warm atmosphere was ponderous. Furtive shadows passed by occasionally, and paused, whispering, before vanishing into the night. Heavy with bestiality, the shadows hung over thickets filled with a confused animation.

"This time!" breathed Madame Lourdal.

Another auto emerged from the direction of the Porte de la Seine. Abruptly, its dazzling lights came on, aspiring the narrow ribbon of the road and the acid emerald of the bushes. To the signal given by Lebeau—headlights lit and then extinguished twice—the accomplices responded with a similar maneuver.

"It's them!"

Before drawing level, the auto, which was rolling silently, switched its lights on full; at the same time, Lebeau darted his exploratory probes. The nickel and varnished red of the Sunbeam[14] were resplendent. It contained three women and three men. Lebeau recognized the Entraygues and Max de Laume. An unknown man, a strapping red-faced fellow, was at the wheel; the Marquis was leaning toward him, with his grandiose appearance of a distinguished woman. In the back, facing Michelle and the handsome Max, were two heavily made-up girls—one brunette, one blonde—laughing in stifled gurgles.

The Sunbeam stopped. The Entraygues and Max de Laume got out at the same time as Lebeau and Simone.

"Fancy seeing you here!"

"My dear friend!"

"*Bonjour*, my dear Monsieur."

Vaguely, Entraygues introduced: "Mr. Jim, my trainer…a pony-trap to try out." He jammed his monocle back into his left orbit and smiled, with the superior air of a great stable

---

[14] The English automobile company Sunbeam merged with the French-based Darracq in 1920, and the company rapidly became famous for marketing luxury limousines as well as racing cars.

owner, momentarily engaged in a small race devoid of interest.

"We weren't expecting you," Max de Laume admitted.

"If someone's been indiscreet," protested Madame Lourdal, "it's Ronchard..."

"Not at all!" said Michelle. "The more the merrier..." She put her arm round Simone's waist, and kissed her.

Since her mother's death, Madame d'Entraygues had reopened the Jacquet salon, modernized, expanded and repainted. Simone Lourdal featured advantageously among the five-footed sheep and the flock of choice quadrupeds—eternal Candidates, and sometimes even Immortals, at any price and on any drums—in the milieu in which Max de Laume was enthroned. The arbiter of literary elegance and political debate, since his success at a by-election in the XVIIth arrondissement, he had entered the Chambre; he had been flattered by an appointment as distributor of the Fine Arts budget, and would soon be the Minister of Public Education and a member of the Académie Française, if one could believe the rumors that he propagated via a few journalistic comrades.

Pierre Lebeau and Simone had climbed back with Michelle into their car, alongside which Max had parked. They chatted tranquilly about one thing and another. The latest gossip unfolded. First of all, Ginette Hutier's divorce; she was about to change Ministers by marrying Ernesto Quorida, the plenipotentiary of the Republic of Honduras. It wasn't Peru, but it represented, all the same, it was said, an annual income of three hundred thousand francs. A fine marriage, and definitive. On the other hand, Simone guffawed on learning that Madame Blanchet—the ex-Bacheloress!—was going to have a second child.

"Two in less than two years! She's going strong...it's a fine thing, repentance!"

"It's not the repentance, it's the horse-riding."

"What?" said Max de Laume, nonplussed.

"Of course! There's nothing like equitation for displacing the organs. A great American physician advised her to take it up."

"You still see her, then?" asked Simone.

"You think so? Madame no longer sees anyone. Fundamentally, she's worth less than her reputation...a bourgeoise! She tried to practice vice, but she's one of those naïve individuals who does everything to excess, and above all with ostentation. She doesn't hide anything, not even the ridicule of displaying her pregnancy to the point of being indecent. Can you imagine that I saw her yesterday at the exhibition of Belgian Art? A belly...and what a belly! It was obscene..."[15]

"Forgive me, my dear friend, if I'm interrupting..."

That was Monsieur d'Entraygues, with his customary urbanity. He declared that he was finding the wait tedious. "What would you say, while we wait for Ronchard to deign to appear, to a little stroll along the bank? Jim would gladly stretch his legs, and these demoiselles are getting bored." He indicated the guests, who were smiling in the most obliging fashion.

"But what if Ronchard comes?" Lebeau objected.

"Don't worry," said Michelle, jumping out and dragging Simone with her, without paying any heed to Max. "He knows the place. He'll understand."

"Well, I'll stay," said Max, vexed at being abandoned in such a cavalier fashion. "A good cigarette is worth as much as your gymnastics."

"You think so!" said Michelle. "You're expecting the unexpected."

---

[15] This implies, working forwards from the calculated chronology of *La Garçonne*, that it is now May 1928 in the time-scheme of the two novels; although Monique could, in theory, have gotten pregnant for a second time after Christmas 1925, when the first novel concluded with her engagement to Blanchet, by May 1927, it is highly unlikely that the pregnancy would show to the indicated extent.

"What? Someone has to guard the cars."

"Yes, my dear, you're right. Good luck."

The group drew away along a small path into the woods. Entraygues and his entourage immediately turned aside, without waiting for the clearing known to Lebeau, for which he was searching.

"Look—it's already occupied."

Intermingled bodies were frolicking there. Simone guided Michelle into one of the free corners. Lebeau followed, entering into the dance with a little concupiscent growl. He had just perceived—there! exactly!—a glistening nudity under a moving coat. He launched himself forward...

And there was soon a general Sabbat; a chain with living links, interchanging, coiling with a bleak frenzy, a cold drunkenness, punctuated with spasmodic gasps....

In the meantime, Max—who was, indeed, tempted more by the unexpected than the common rejoicing—had climbed back into the Sunbeam, his eyes and ears on the alert. A couple suddenly emerged from the shadows.

The woman seemed graceful. They went past slowly, stopped and came back. The man whispered in a thick foreign accent: "You must be bored all on your own?"

"Very."

"We could keep you company for a while."

"Excellent idea."

"And you know, if she pleases you..." He indicated the woman, whom he was holding by the waist.

"Don't inconvenience yourselves. I'll watch."

The unknown woman, very elegant, uttered a brief, shrill laugh. Her perfume—White Rose—embalmed the whole vehicle. Max sat her down inside and proceeded to be "was no inconvenience" to the visible satisfaction of the man. He shared, in a solitary fashion, in the pleasure to which the interjections of his companion testified...

Max savored all the spice of the adventure. Who might these people be? What if, their vice satisfied, they took out revolvers and said *Hands up*?

While the woman got out, tranquilly, he patted the revolver in his own pocket, and then his wallet. He escaped with nothing more than a toothsome anxiety. The crazy pair silently drew away.

When the woman in the sable coat got up, marmoreal in the fur, surprise drew an exclamation from Lebeau. He had just, without any doubt about it, made a more ample acquaintance with Luce Mérac, the star of the Variétés. She moved closer in order to make out his face.

"Oh! Pierre Lebeau. *Bonjour!* How are you?"

He put a finger over his lips and smiled.

"Of course!"

A freemasonry linked the initiates.

By another path, he calmly returned to the auto. Michelle and Simone preceded him, with the most natural air.

They had scarcely rejoined Max de Laume when the latter said: "Here's Ronchard!"

Two lanterns had just pierced the darkness, coming from the direction of the Moulin de Longchamp, so slowly that Lebeau, an expert, declared: "That's not an auto. Two cyclists, I'll wager…and two *flics*. Exactly! Let's chat as if nothing abnormal…"

Their voices alternated, serenely, as if at the hazard of an amicable encounter. Respectful at the sight of the two large luxury vehicles, the policemen, as they went past, darted a glance of consideration at the well-dressed strollers, whose appearance suggested that they were not merely irreproachable, but untouchable.

Sensing that the peril had passed, Max thought it amusing to stop the patrol momentarily. He detached himself from Michelle and stepped away, raising his fingers to the brim of his hat in a military fashion for a condescending salute. He had not been four years an officer in the complement of the G. Q. G.[16] for nothing.

"Pardon me," he said, patronizingly. "You wouldn't have a light, would you?"

He had taken his large golden cigarette case out of his pocket. Slowly, he took a light from the match that one of the policemen, impressed, was holding out to him. Then, magnanimously, he offered them each a cigarette, and thanked them with a "*Merci, mes braves!*"

The two *sergents de ville* returned the salute like soldiers, straddled their bicycles again, and disappeared.

The smiling Lebeau concluded: "Go, good servants! Go somewhere else to ensure order, while we conscientiously hold the candle."

"It's a fact," said the representative of the people, "that d'Entraygues owes us one. It's more than half an hour. I've a good mind to go and see what's become of him. Ronchard will arrive in the meantime. It's necessary to wait for him, since he's the only one who knows where we're going..."

Since the recent manifestations of police, provoked by a few complaints, the metallurgist was one of the prudent individuals who went as far as the edge of the nearby forest to search for a remote spot where—according to one of the favorite quotations of the Marquis, who was as fond of literature as he was of morphine—"one had the liberty to distract oneself in peace."

A short distance away, Max discovered the quartet. The first turning of the path had seemed good to him; without waiting for the propitious clearing, the Marquis, who required a long preparation, had set about savoring without delay the wetness of a pleasure that was multiplied by an appetite for risk. He was one of those unhealthy individuals who can only be animated with the attraction of danger by the idea of being

_____

[16] Grand Quartier Général—the General Headquarters of the French Army during the Great War.

52

perceived. Apparently, Max de Laume brought his sensation to its peak.

D'Entraygues got up and nobly adjusted his clothing. Then, having replaced his monocle, he piped, as if at a weigh-in: "You arrived at the finishing line, my dear."

Jim laughed coarsely, as the bit-part players smoothed their rumpled skirts with little pats. Simone, attracted by curiosity, appeared at the same time, and darted an admiring glance at the trainer, whose broad shoulders had had an effect on her. Jim swelled up, while, certain of being understood, Madame Lourdal resumed the short route to the auto with the lord of the stable, escorted by Max.

"What an ugly woman!" muttered Léa, the blonde.

"It makes you sick," said Fredd, the brunette.

"It could also make one sweat, if one wanted to," concluded Jim.

All three of them, the two dance hall tarts and the former stable hand, understood one another in their scorn of the humble for the "dirty rats" who paid them. However, to the questions they asked him—"Who is he, your fellow?"—Jim opposed a shrewd mutism. He recruited, and he served; that was all. Oh, if he had the misfortune to be sacked one day...but until then, professional secrecy!

"Look," said Fredd, when they reached the road. "Reinforcements. What do you think, my girl?"

"Oh, that one I know," exclaimed Léa. "It's Lili Brontier. A gimlet, and no mistake!"

"If you've got your eye on her...!" said Fredd, menacingly.

But a nudge of Jim's elbow made them shut up. Silently, they took their places again, from which they contemplated, mockingly, the greetings of the new arrivals. A third car, a saloon, had drawn up alongside Lebeau's. Ronchard, after having shaken d'Entraygues' hand, introduced to the group: "Mademoiselle Brontier, alias 'Except that,' a salesgirl at Mauricette's. It's thanks to her that you'll be able to witness,

53

and even take part, Mesdames et Messieurs, in the little party I promised you."

"What about Rayot?"

"What, you don't know? He's been struck down by the commencement of a cerebral congestion at the Finance Committee. In bed—he won't get up again."

Long in the upper body and short in the legs, his hair and beard dyed golden blond, Ronchard hid his native vulgarity behind a fake Henry IV face. By virtue of his rotundity he made a sharp contrast with the tall thinness of his companion for the evening. He extended a majestic arm, as if for a funeral oration.

"What do you expect? That's life!" Changing his tone, he added; "Who loves me, follow me!"

He climbed back into his limousine and manipulated the steering wheel with the dexterity of a man who is used to steering everything, and took the hand of the procession.

The autos traveled at speed. Confusedly, while Max de Laume amused himself in amazing the little group of whores with sibylline considerations, and Michelle, pleased by Lili's androgynous appearance, watched the landscape file past.

The motionless décor seemed to be flying away with a movement so rapid that they reached the perron of a villa lost in a large park without even having noticed that they had traversed the Seine, a village and a wood.

At the noise of their arrival, a lady of the most honorable appearance, under her henna-tinted wig, had advanced onto a porch in order to receive the important guests in an appropriate fashion. Without knowing their names, the Comtesse de Saint-Valentin knew, via Lili Brontier, that they belonged— some of them, at least—to the highest echelon of society.

An enriched adventuress, she had traversed all the echelons, looting from each as she passed everything that she could. Swiss by birth, originally a children's maid, debauched by her first master, then chambermaid to a demi-mondaine, then a bareback rider in the circus, then a Comtesse authentically espoused by a Viennese confidence trickster, whom she divorced for a Baltic Baron, and finally a widow and brothel-keeper in Belgium, she had crowned her fortune during the war, in The Hague, by means of espionage on behalf of Austria and counter-espionage on behalf of France. That guarantee obtained, she had returned to Brussels, had liquidated her funds and bought a château near Liège, and, at the same stroke, the name of Saint-Valentin.

Under the latter label, she had done penitence for three years, receiving the curé and taking holy communion, acquiring a new identity—after which she had rented a magnificent apartment in the Avenue des Champs-Élysées and, under the pseudonym of Madame Laurent, the Villa de Villebon. In the city she welcomed a mixed society part-artistic and part-socialite, for whom she provided gambling facilities, and in the country, she played hostess to anyone at all, once they displayed a few blue banknotes. Alternately Saint-Valentin and Laurent, she lived as a Parisienne in the consideration of everyone, including the police.

She was one of Mauricette's best clients. It was at a fitting at the couturier's that she had met and appreciated Lili Brontier. The saleswoman, gradually let go by Paule, whose impending marriage and evenings taken up by concerts and orchestras occupied her thoughts and her time, had turned to that new association unreservedly. She hardly spent any time in the Rue de Lancry any more, half-installed in the Avenue des Champs-Élysées. An unparalleled beater, and, on occasion, performer, she shared with Saint-Valentin the fees that she brought in, in accordance with the heads and the purses, for Laurent.

It was thus, at the appointed hour, and always under the color of gaming, that practitioners of all the vices met up at the Villa Adrienne for the distraction of a few dilettantes. A hardworking criminal class, richly remunerated, found there, with the price of their supper, more security than in the suburban undergrowth where they normally toiled

"The Bois is becoming democratized," pronounced Ronchard, "only good for the proletariat! Here"—he burst into

55

song—"it's *the rendezvous of noble company!*[17]And then, at least one's at home. Mademoiselle Brontier guarantees anonymity."

He exchanged a wink with Madame Laurent, whose other name Lili had revealed to him.

Disappointed, Lebeau and Max de Laume considered with bleak expressions the hall surrounded by divans and strewn with cushions, where, without paying any heed to the new arrivals, a troupe was cynically enchained in living tableaux.

There were ten performers, naked or draped in bazaar kimonos: four men, one of whom must have been a Slav and another a Levantine—formerly prosperous individuals thrown onto the scrap-heap, with ignoble and ruffian faces—a negro and a Chinaman, and six characterless females, human debris who might perhaps have had freshness and grace when young, but whose dismal display was reminiscent of flaccid meat in a butcher's shop.

The domestic personnel having been suppressed with good reason, Jim and the whores assisted Madame with the cold victuals and champagne that the mistress of the house had them bring out of the cupboards. She counted the bottles as they went past with a vigilant eye. A hundred francs apiece!

The champagne corks popped, and the foam poured into gilded goblets, in vain. The refreshments were installed on low tables. Inconsequential remarks were exchanged.

Such lugubrious entertainment almost put the band to flight right way, but, as a good hostess, Madame Laurent, opening the pianola, started up a java. The loud and sprightly tune spread its fairground gaiety, the unexpected tumult of its rhythms. The dance wept away the atmosphere of embarrassment. The initiates resumed amusing themselves with one another under the benevolent eye of the bawd. Their couples

---

[17] The line is from the popular comic opera *Le Pré aux clercs* (1832) with music by Ferdinand Hérold and words by Eugène Planard, although it was quoted in numerous other works.

swayed and shook to the cries of the negro beating time to the music. Léa and Fredd, enlaced, imitated them. They were relieved to recover their suburban insouciance, abandoning themselves thoughtlessly to the vertigo of the movement as if to the gravity of a rite.

A blues, with its cadenced swing, having succeeded the turbulent java, Michelle followed the example in the muscular arms of Lili Brontier. "That," she declared, when the piece ended, while clapping her hands to command the reloading of the disk, "gets one going." As the first bars were repeated, she took hold of the ardent meager body again, pressing her flexible form against the bony framework.

In a corner, Simone had isolated Jim, and, taking her inseparable sketch-pad from her pearly handbag, she drew his powerfully-muzzled face in three-quarter profile while palpating it. "The head of a true Imperator!"

Disdaining those games, the three augurs, on whom the fate of the nation was in part dependent, had collapsed along with the weary Marquis d'Entraygues onto the cushions. They were chatting while Fredd and Léa, reinforced by two habituées, came on command to answer their requirements. Ronchard and Max, still cool, only responded in monosyllables to the philosophical remarks of the pontificating Lebeau. With a condescending detachment, Max watched Simone pursuing the conquest of Mr. Jim and Michelle provoking that of Lili Brontier. As for d'Entraygues, he had dozed off.

With a broad gesture, Ronchard enveloped the hall in which the couples were whirling to the sound of the phonograph. The noisy tunes had been succeeded by the melancholy of a Hawaiian waltz. The distant guitar strung out its nostalgic notes, sometimes traversed like an echo by the mewling of a plaint.

"A truly documentary soirée," proffered the fake Henri IV. "You can attest henceforth, my dear Lebeau, that, compared to the Mysteries of the Fortifications, those of the Bois have been magnified immeasurably. As for what's happening before our eyes, it's mere child's play, in sum, which poses no challenge to the deep-seated honesty of our mores. We're investigators here. And, truly, we're not doing any great harm, are we?"

He administered a heavy slap to Fredd's naked buttock. The latter replied with a hard shove. "Watch it, you! You have the caresses of an elephant!"

With all the elegance of a Saint-Valentin, Madame Laurent judged that the time had come to play cards. She proposed a little game of poker to "the Messieurs." At that word, the Marquis pricked up his ears. The others, now bored, acquiesced. Aided by Jim, Madame Laurent opened a folding table, and placed a basket of chips on the green baize.

"That's it!" said Ronchard. "A nice game of poker, now, while we wait until the ladies"—he pointed at Madame Lourdal and Madame d'Entraygues—"have finished."

But each of them, in her own fashion, was just beginning. Shrugging their shoulders, Lebeau and Max de Laume, the most directly interested, turned their backs. Pretending not to see anything, and judging that they were thus acting as superior men, on whom such vague contingencies could have no effect, they swallowed Ronsard's coarse joking politely. At a certain level of wealth, as at a certain point of immorality, baseness, stupidity and boorishness are automatically attenuated. *Hey presto!* Nothing remained, in their eyes, on the part of Ronchard, but common sense, authority and finesse, and on theirs, philosophical serenity.

Through the acquiescence of the celebrated journalist and the future academician, the eloquence of the metallurgist then plunged, torrentially. It drowned out on occasion, in order to make itself heard, the shrill orchestra that sprang forth untiringly, with the scraping of strings and blasts of brass from the mahogany box where "Chicago" had replaced Lamb/Polla...[18]

---

[18] The latter reference is presumably to the song "Drifting," with words by Arthur Lamb and music by W. C. Polla, which was very popular in the early 1920s. "Chicago" must be the

It was a music of delirious savages, its epilepsy beating the measure of the Danse Macabre, the disordered agitation of all those poor beings penned, like beasts, in the all-purpose hall: a music grinding at the same hour in a hundred thousand other more-or-less similar places throughout the world, cradling with its knell, in all those decomposing societies, similar specimens of the same elite.

Suddenly, piercing screams rang out. One of Madame Saint-Valentin's performers, intoxicated by cocaine, had attacked the Chinaman, who had driven her back with a brutal punch: hence the nervous crisis.

"What's up?" asked Lebeau.

"Nothing," declared Madame Laurent, while Lili Brontier helped the negro to carry out the party-pooper, in convulsions.

Nothing. A madwoman.

"Without a moral press," Ronchard went on, "a press that stigmatizes debauchery and attempts to raise a dam against the wave of pornography in the process of overflowing from books into the theater, we're doomed. Lust threatens to cover everything with its miry flood. If we don't put a stop to it, we'll end up making people abroad think that it's an accurate depiction of our mores. Now, I take you as witnesses that that's false!"

"You can talk!" said Léa, planting a kiss on his mouth.

"Enough, whore! In literature as in everything, it's time to reestablish censorship. Today, people dare to attack, via the Comité des Forges,[19] the Minister Cibéron, because he supports national politics in the Ruhr. Where will we be tomorrow?"

"At the railway station!" said Fredd, rancorously.

Fred Fisher song first published in 1922, and later made famous by Frank Sinatra.

[19] The Comité des Forges, established by a group of ironmasters in 1864, remained a powerful lobbying organization until the Second World War.

"Peace, poultry! We don't need you anymore. Go away."
Bombastically, he went on: "Cibéron's not firm enough. We need a good tyrant, a Mussolini, for the upcoming elections. France, Messieurs, wants to be governed..."

But Madame Laurent was thinking about her stock-in-trade. In honeyed tones, she cut the thread. "The table is ready for poker. If one only plays for an hour, it's not worth the trouble. I've set out the chips."

They sat down.

"Is a thousand francs enough...?"

IV

"I'm glad to see you," attested Pierre Lebeau.

Standing in the middle of his office, he squeezed and patted Annika's hands, which were still feverish, in his moist paws. He was a trifle congested, having lunched with Ronchard—famous cuisine, but heavy! The sight of Annik cheered him up.

Slightly tipsy, he enquired: "Entirely better? The change of hairstyle suits you very well."

A few days confined to bed, and then to her room, with her head bandaged, had sufficed for the injured woman to recover from the shock and for the wound to scar over. Of the latter, all that remained was a red path on the forehead at the hairline. She hid it under a colored headband attached to her dress.

He admired her: svelte and robust. From the two visits he had made to her studio to obtain news of her, he had carried away the obsessive memory of her body, of its contours revealed by the clinging suppleness of her nightgown, a communicative fire of desire, in which he had felt a pleasure mingled with embarrassment. The presence of Paule and Madame Broussat the first time, and of Mademoiselle Hardy and Amédée Jacquemin the second, had prevented any allusion to that which silence or speech concealed in them.

He lifted up the brown curls of the silky fringe.

"It's fading rapidly!"

"The mark, yes—the memory, never."

The bitterly emphatic tone struck him. Until now, before having seen her in bed, he had never wanted to see her as anything other than a collaborator: a subaltern employee whose entire character as well as her extreme intelligence, much more than the situation, had kept him at a distance. Lebeau was one of those mediocrities whose pretention takes umbrage at any superiority, especially on the part of a female. Simone

61

Lourdal, with the intelligence and recognized talent, would have seemed intolerable to him but for the special distractions she facilitated for him. Simone, scenting a danger in Annik's personality, had been able to limit the risk. It was thus that he had, reluctantly, abstained from any overly pressing gallantry.

That discretion, Annik, misled by her own sentiment, had taken for the homage of a certain inclination: Pierre had always coveted her; she had no doubt of that! Thus, gradually, as much by the reaction of a loving nature, weary of an attitude for which she had initially been grateful, as by a need for combativity against often-divergent opinions, a reversal of roles had taken place. She wanted to convince him, and to conquer him.

It was only necessary—incapable as she was of loving anyone without holding them in esteem—to clear up rapidly, after the Lourdal matter, the anxiety caused by Mérette's revelation...

She had an expression so grave that he was astonished.

"What rancor! Come on—since the blow wasn't aimed at you..."

"It's no less odious for that.

"So I've been able to inflict a reprimand on the imbecile. There's no excuse, that's understood. The law of the strongest may well be the ultimate rationale of societies, but its application requires more tact in consequence..."

"It's not the arm I resent, it's..."

He dismissed the declaration, preoccupied with the one that he wanted to make. They were not here to discuss politics.

"Never mind that, excitable child; talk to me about you, your plans, your intimate life..."

He chided her humorously for the face she pulled, her eyes shining. He had taken her hands again, and drawn her, with a singular expression, toward the profound leather sofa. She allowed herself to be drawn, saying: "I don't have any plans. But what about you? What's become of Madame Lourdal? You haven't seen her for some time?"

He made an abrupt gesture, as if to expel the intruder. "No. What can that matter to you?"

Their thoughts rose up within them, distant and observant. He sensed the opportunity to lie, to sacrifice, with an apparent abandonment, the former mistress…given that he could reutilize her services later.

"You know very well that Simone is no longer anything to me, or to her husband, but a friend. For a long time, I swear. Not even a friend…a comrade…" He emphasized with a snigger: "An *old* comrade."

She confronted him with a dubious gaze.

"Simone, beside you," he attested, "with her wrinkles and her fat—she doesn't compare! Listen, I need a new sentiment…younger, more ardent. Oh, if you wanted…" She sketched a denial. "Let me put my arms around you! It's so good! I have so many things to say to you…"

She divined his hidden agenda, and felt a numbing warmth—but the image of Rosa suddenly unfolded before her, in those same arms, so forcefully that she reacted.

"What's the matter with you, my love? Do I displease you? I need a heart that loves me, a pure heart like yours…" Annik struggled under the audacious hands. "Let's love one another," he panted. "Life is short!"

She pulled away with an abrupt gesture. "No, leave me be, I beg you. Let's work…"

He made a gesture of annoyance, and went back to his desk, furious. In a detached tone, he said: "As you wish. Not much for you…this, perhaps…" He was sitting down again, holding a file out to her. "The Jalavat affair—you know, the abortionist. I've taken a few notes; you can review them, type them. There's material for a good article."

She nodded and went silently to her corner, near the window.

In an instant, the lid of the machine lifted and the paper threaded, she was at work, hitting the keys rapidly with nervous thrusts. Beyond the copied words, the vision absorbed her, harassed her. That girl, her skirts lifted…and now…the butt of

63

the gossips of Yvelines, her enlarged belly beneath her stretched dress, denouncing her…then, soon, the sad birth, the intruder to care for, in rancor and abandonment...

She stopped, her heart oppressed. The authoritarian voice enquired: "Is there something that doesn't work?"

It was a voice whose slightly hoarse masculine accent she had loved until now, but which had whispered into the humble ear of Rosa the same song! The voice of an actor, in which she discovered the artificial tone in the unoriginal phrases, the oratorical invective "Against debauchery, and those criminal mothers who..." A false virtue, in which she believed she distinguished, along with the dissonance, the seeming derision.

Frankness carried her away, and also a sudden fear that the quotidian visage, which she had thought she knew, was a mask, and the real Pierre a boor disguised as a philanthropist.

"You're going to think me very stupid, but this Jalavat case…the report of the examining magistrate tends, for lack of proof, to leave out of the case by heaping all the blame on the mother. As if, in the abortion of which there is question, the midwife, certainly a seller of filthy drugs, and in any case murderous advice, weren't the guiltier party, after the..."

She looked straight at him, waiting. Suspiciously, he prompted: "After?"

"After the father. For the individual wretched enough to refuse to recognize a child he's made..."

He frowned, cut to the quick even though he did not suspect for a moment that she might be aware of his annoying adventure…that chambermaid and the consequences...

In a mocking tone, with heavy irony, he said: "I've always heard it said that only the maternity is certain."

She stared at him, surprised by all the boorishness that the mocking objection veiled.

"In any case, you've often said the contrary in the *Appel*."

"What one thinks and what one writes…! It's like electoral manifestos."

"I knew you were a skeptic, but not to that degree."

He saw that his frankness was harming him, and took a step back.

"So be it! Let's reason. In order to recognize a child, it's still necessary to be sure..."

"Oh," she said, "if the examining magistrate had taken the trouble, in this case, he would have found no lack of evidence against the presumed father..."

He immediately thought about the recent attempts, the supplications with which Rosa had pursued him. In a changed voice, his expression harsh, he said: "We're in the presence of a case of abortion; let's leave it at that. The research of paternity isn't incumbent, thank God, on the law! And where would we be, if, after having offered herself, the presumptions of any loose women were sufficient to be believed! Any physician will tell you, in any case, that one can scarcely place any more faith in vague proofs of continuity of family feature, such as a similarity of fingerprints or the aleatory measurement of a conformity in the bone structure—go search for all of that in a nursling!—than in the attestation of a fleeting resemblance, always contestable, or he more or less interested statements of the mother, who might be nothing more than a whore. You've done your law, in any case. *Is pater est quem nuptiae demonstrant.*[20] Outside marriage, there's no qualified father, because no father is recognizable, or even presumable. It's the child and the child alone that can be recognized. And it requires, for that act of faith, not only the confession but the credulity of the responsible party."

She listened to him, retrenched within herself, "trying out his article."

He continued: "Why not, while you're at it, a law against seduction? That would be jolly, when even the jurisprudence of rape is on shaky ground. For want of life, you know your classics well enough, damn it—enough Rabelais and La Fon-

---

[20] "The father is he whom marriage indicates." The principle was adopted from Roman Law into the French Code.

taine to know that one can't thread a needle, no matter how stiff the thread, if it moves. So?"

He suddenly blushed, as much at the suggestion of the image as the disturbance by which he saw Annik gripped, at the brutality of the evocation. It was the first time he had departed, in his speech, from calculated reserve. The vision of other embraces, at the hazard of surprise…the whiteness of flesh lubriciously uncovered, on that same tempting sofa…the scorn that he had for all women, and, at the same time, the desire that clawed at him, for this one…all of that rose into his mind, with the violence of a transport.

He lost all restraint and all consciousness, and marched toward his need, his hands extended. He had before him the age-old prey, the white beast that the Male possessed in the depths of caves.

She stared at him, stupefied.

"Yes, it's stronger than me! I want you! I've wanted you for two years! I didn't dare… Today, since I've seen you in bed…"

"What?"

She had stood up, so astounded that she did not know whether she was about to allow herself to be taken, consenting in the depths of her being, or whether she was about to push him away and claw him with horror. He was holding her head, searching for her lips. He was talking like a madman, in jerky phrases.

"Annik…my little Annik…give me your mouth…your body…you'll be my pleasure!"

Ready to open up to gentleness, she reacted violently against outrage. He was holding her tightly, but she turned away, revolted, and, refusing her lips to the voracious kiss that sought them, she stiffened herself, with an energy of which he had not thought her capable. She had grabbed the hands that were already groping at her corsage, and twisted the barbaric wrists forcefully.

He seemed to wake up, heavily, as if sobering up. She hissed at him with hateful sarcasm: "Brute! Brute! Let me go! You disgust me."

In a second, the imaginary person by which her credulity had been pleased had collapsed. There was no longer anything but two enemies present, the eternal antagonism of master and slave. Liberated, she contemplated with horror the execrable tyrant of all the ages, aroused by that fit of sexual folly: a monstrous, injurious Priapus, if he imposed himself...

That, a man? No, a hunting ape...the ancestor, in the depths of the prehistoric forest...

He no longer frightened her. Under the threat, however, she was trembling all over in her civilized pride and the re-vived instinct of origins....

The employer who had helped her, the individual to whom she had been attracted? She was astonished no longer to find anything of that in the rag that now collapsed, uncertain-ly, onto the sofa. Pierre Lebeau, frightfully humiliated, did not know what to do next.

She sat down at her table and sorted her papers. After a minute she heard a snore. She looked, with the amazement of almost having loved him, at the misshapen puppet. When she had finished her tidying, she prepared a letter: let him look for another secretary!

Then she stood up and put her hat on.

At the sound, the sleeper opened his eyes, crestfallen.

"What are you doing?"

"I'm leaving."

"Stay, or I'll never forgive you!"

"Too bad. What do you expect?" she jeered. "I'm not Rosa..."

"Don't understand!" The evasive gaze vacillated under the pointed accusation. "Rosa? What's this story?"

"You've forgotten her already?"

"Don't understand, I repeat."

He stood his ground, with a hostile expression.

She simply replied: "Write to Yvelines. Mademoiselle Rosa Blanchard, former chambermaid of the Morevals. She'll refresh your memory. Adieu."

He seemed to be hearing the name for the first time. She turned round. "She'll give you news of your child at the same time."

He was nonplussed for a few seconds, and then, choked by an anger that rang false, he shouted: "You, too? It's abominable! I forbid you..."

Too late; the tacit admission had escaped, irrefutably, from his embarrassment, as from his indignation. Annik was now convinced: Rosa had not lied.

She was on the threshold, only succeeding in mastering herself by the force of her scorn. Behind the open ventilation flap, the silhouette of a domestic was visible. He was listening.

Worldly convention got the upper hand. Pierre Lebeau bowed, correctly.

In a banal tone, Annik said: "*Au revoir*, Monsieur."

Behind her, while suppressing a smile—*There's been a squabble this time!*—the domestic, who accompanied her, closed the main door behind her.

Lebeau, enraged, slammed his door. *Stupid creature!* It was less her refusal that he was holding against her than her meddling in the Rosa business. How the devil had she known? A few paces back and forth ended up calming him down. He felt strong, with all his social armor, and concluded, shrugging his shoulders: "*Bon voyage!* Let them f... off elsewhere!"

Annik, on the staircase, would have wept nervously if the sensation of the grotesque had not overwhelmed that of revolt. Those congested features, those lustful eyes... She burst into jerky laughter. If Pierre Lebeau had seen himself! The hideous expression continued to pursue her: the exact image of a hog, which so many men concealed. She raised her hand mechanically to her forehead.

A nausea revived the pain of the recent blow, adding to the resentment that she still retained against the order of things, the dolor of observing that she had followed a false route on the road of love. The sacred path extended into the distance, deserted.

Annik suddenly felt so solitary that the tears, this time, erupted. She saw then that she was in the street, and that surprised passersby were turning to look at her. She wiped her cheeks and reflected. A sensual mirage had gilded, in her eyes, a bed of mud. A small chagrin and a great lesson. She had been deceived; that was her fault. Let the experience serve her! She envisaged the future with a courageous gaze. So many worries, further along!

Three o'clock, marked by the pneumatic clock, reminded her that she had arranged to meet Paule at five. She was supposed to go meet her at her place of work. A friendly face, in the meantime, would be comforting. Not having the time to go to see Mademoiselle Hardy, she decided to go to Madame Broussat's home in the Avenue Kléber.

Fortunately, she found her at home.

Annik liked her brusque common sense, the surly kindness under which the missionary in a silk dress hid the most compassionate of hearts. Widowed young, and having lost a child whom she adored, Madame Broussat had brought to feminism, for twenty years, a quotidian devotion, to which she owed the appointment, on behalf of France, as one of the secretaries of the International Council of Women.

At the same time, she administered her Refuge in Auteuil, incessantly growing, since she had combined her personal fortune with that of her friend, the painter Zélonoff, with whom she lived in perfect harmony. There was only one bone of contention between them: the persistence that he put into wanting to marry her. Having tasted her independence, however, she refused any such concession. It was a sacrifice that she judged to be vain, and she deemed convention to be even more so. Since they were both wealthy, what could it add to their quietude?

An eccentric with revolutionary ideas in politics, Prince Michel Zélonoff had, several years before the war and without any regret for Tsarist Russia, liquidated his enormous assets and emigrated. Since then, surpassed—by a thousand leagues—by Bolshevism, he congratulated himself every morning on having changed his fatherland and found happiness

Madame Broussat was glad to see Annik, whose valor she held in high esteem, but at the first glance, she said: "No zest? Let's see that scar. So, out and about already, after such a shock! The man who hit you, I'm told, has been suspended."

Annik shrugged. "They might as well have given him a promotion."

"Not worth the trouble of being the friend of a newspaper editor...no? No longer a friend? What's happened?"

"No longer even a secretary. I've just seen Monsieur Lebeau for the last time."

She told her everything: Mérette's revelation, and then the bestial aggression. She experienced, in confiding in her great friend, a veritable relief. It seemed to her that she was washing away a dirty stain."

"A fine gentleman!" exclaimed Madame Broussat. "It has to happen! For myself, I've always thought that it stinks! This Rosa, you know—she shouldn't torment herself. The refuge at Auteuil is there, unfortunately."

"Yes...I'll write to Mademoiselle Hardy this evening. And by the way, I'd be very happy to introduce Mérette to you. She admires your work and wants to meet you in consequence."

"That's the case, or never. I, too, my child, will have pleasure in meeting your teacher. I already like her, through you."

The painter came in placidly, with the tread of a gentle giant. He made a contrast with the vivacity of his companion. Like her, however, he exuded simplicity and health, with his flax-blue eyes, his large blond beard, turning gray, and his broad shoulders. He kissed Annik's hands, and Madame Broussat's.

"You'll see," said the latter to Annik, and then said to Zélonoff: "What do you think of Pierre Lebeau?"

"A bandit!"

But Madame Broussat uttered a cry: "There's a good idea!"

Behind Zélonoff a new arrival appeared. His face brightened as he recognized Annik. Affectionately, he exclaimed: "If I'd known..."

"Amédée," said Zélonoff. "I forgot to announce you! We ran into one another just now outside the Théâtre Populaire, where he'd come to give a lecture, and I dragged him out here to subject him to the torture of the cubist demonstration."

Amédée Jacquemin protested, sincerely. Although preferring a les summary kind of painting—less "synthetic," as Zélonoff put it, than that of "volumes"—his tastes were too eclectic not to admit that every form of art, like every form of life, evolved. Excesses even appeared to be an inevitable condition of progress: ruptures of equilibrium beneficial in themselves.

"Stagnation, the dead hand, is the ultimate danger of every school," he pronounced in his warm voice. "It's by leaps, by revolutions, that one advances, and when a movement is concluded, whatever it might be, it decomposes. The immutability of Nature is the most fallacious of paradoxes: an invention of leaden backsides, riveted to the past..."

Annik rediscovered, in listening to him, her habitual pleasure. Instinctively, she made a comparison. How had she been able, even momentarily, to prefer to that free and charming mind the narrow conceit of Pierre Lebeau? Was it the slightly rustic build of Jacquemin, his heavy expression, in spite of his tender gaze, or the thin smile in the Socratic beard that had made him seem less attractive? Today, at the repugnant memory, she appreciated more fully the charm of his bounty, which was nevertheless alloyed with strength...but a strength that one sensed to be generous and disciplined, not the despotic violence to the assault of which she had just been subjected, and of which she still retained the fright.

Meanwhile, Zélonoff, a slow but tenacious mind, returned to the point of departure, and questioned in his turn:

"Explain to me, Mesdames, why Sieur Lebeau was in the dock…and may Annik excuse me if I spoke too frankly." He turned toward Jacquemin and added: "You, too, my dear, for perhaps you heard me...and you, too, I think, are a friend of that…"

"An acquaintance at the most," the député specified. "My mother praises him to the clouds, because of a service he once rendered her, but you know that my family's ideas and mine…"

"Yes," said Madame Broussat. "Night and day."

"And Mademoiselle Raimbert knows that I've never shared her admiration for her…employer." He added an ironic nuance to the word, envious of the support that the journalist had given Annik in her debuts at the Palais. He would have liked, for his part, to be useful to her, and even to associate himself with her endeavors. Did not the important situation he held at the Bar put him in a position to help a talented young advocate more efficaciously than anyone? Thus, to his hostility against a man he held in low esteem, Amédée Jacquemin added the unformulated rancor against a perceived competitor.

Annik pleased him, in every respect. Without an accredited mistress, and thus far without having felt the need for one, so much did his occupations take possession of him, he had sometimes thought, since he had made her acquaintance: *What a delightful companion she would make!* He had not gone so far as to think: *What a wife…,* knowing her ideas about free union, and never yet having envisaged marriage for himself, doubtless for want of having encountered a woman who might have corresponded to his tastes. In opposition to current opinion, and like Annik, he could not imagine how anyone could marry without being in love. Bourgeois in his origins and education, however, in spite of the sincere impulse that had driven him toward socialism, he could not conceive of a wife under the features of an independent woman—not to the point, at least, at which Annik affixed her determination, as well as her pride, to being and remaining one.

Often, in the course of their conversations, he had brought their concepts into confrontation, and they had always ended with the conclusion of Annik mocking him: "You! You admit equality in theory, but fundamentally…!" It was not without a certain bitterness that he heard the amicable reproach beneath the mockery. "You're like all the rest…a proprietor!"

A proprietor! When, on her suggestion, he was preparing the proposition of a law so bold that it would overturn the Code completely, in the matter of its provisions regarding filiation!

He had looked up at the young woman, astonished to see her face abruptly turn red: her unexpected reflex action in response to the word "employer."

At the same time, Madame Broussat consulted Annik with a glance, and the latter nodded her head.

"Yes, speak! Your husband and Monsieur Jacquemin are sufficiently my friends to be enlightened, definitively, as to the character of"—she spat out, with a hint of bitterness directed at Amédée—"my ex-employer."

Brought up to date by Madame Broussat—"Well, would you believe it!"—the two men reacted in accordance with their temperament.

Zélonoff rubbed his hands, laughing, and said, with a feigned nuance of comical esteem: "Well, what a satyr!"

Jacquemin was silent, frowning; his face was stern—his "bearish expression," as Annik often called it. The seduction and abandonment of Rosa revolted him less than the insult to a being that he suddenly saw differently, facing him…a troubling being, whom the evocation of brutal, filthy desire reclad, by repercussion, with a new attraction of femininity. At the idea of the attempted outrage, a pain traversed his heart. Thus, with a lacerating revelation, he realized, by the vision that he could no longer set aside, that he was in love, and jealously.

Annik, astonished by his mutism, looked at him without understanding. Ignorant of sensual pleasure, and having not yet sensed the mysterious current established between them, she did not perceive the sentiment, let alone the complex sensation, to which Amédée was prey, nor the sudden deformation to which, in his mind, the natural purity of the creative act—the most normal and most beautiful of all human acts—had been subjected at that moment. By the dolorous expression on his face, she could see that he experienced the same indignation as she did, but she was so far from divining the true cause of it that she was pained by the silence in which she seemed to have retrenched himself sullenly.

What was he thinking? Did he imagine that, by some coquetry, she had provoked...

As much by virtue of a need for amicable justification as the protest of her self-respect—for, always straightforward, she could not bear anyone to suspect her personal rectitude, and she affirmed: "If I was able, in any way whatsoever, to allow him to believe..."

He finished the sentence with a question mark in which there was a reproach: "In your sympathy?"

Discountenanced, she analyzed herself. It was true. Had her thought not inclined in favor of the man who was not worthy of it? At the same time, she weighed Amédée's words, and their veiled meaning. What did they signify, with their hint of mockery? She searched his eyes for the commentary, and was surprised and touched by it.

The fugitive image of possession, the very rancor of his last words, had given way to a radiation of irresistible tenderness. She rediscovered the straightforward gaze whose amity she knew, and, without displeasure, discovered there the torment of a confession, the anxious ardor of a plea. She smiled without speaking. The spark, from one heart to another, had just passed: the magnetic exchange...without them being able to distinguish as yet, in their uncertain impulses, what flame was latent there ready to burst forth.

"Ring, Zélo," ordered Madame Broussat, "and ask for the port. Yes, yes—we're going to have a tranquil drink."

"It's just that my sister's expecting me."

"Ta ta ta! For once, I have both of you, and I'm holding onto you."

Annik gave in. She felt good, in that welcoming house, in contact with those friends, the best and, fundamentally, the only veritable ones she had, outside of the maternal affection of Mademoiselle Hardy.

Gladly, Amédée imitated her. They refrained from launching themselves with any precipitation into the obscure march of their thoughts; they even avoided looking at one another. Seemingly indifferent, and yet already profoundly complicit, they abandoned themselves meekly to the nascent intoxication of life. It was an incomparable moment, in which, from their two existences, one alone was formed, already weaving, thread by thread, without them even suspecting it, the unique pattern.

On one of those large oval sheet metal trays, the old-fashioned convenience of which Madame Broussat loved, the glasses stood around plates of gateaux, their tulips filled with gilded wine. Zélonoff, standing in front of the piano, touched the keyboard with one finger and sang in his hoarse voice. A cotton-wool sky extended, and a warm breeze blew through the moans and appeals.

The painter translated:

Is it night, or is it day?
The shadows might be advancing or retreating...
The doves are circling in the dusk...
My heart is heavy: is it love?

V

"Over there," said Madame Broussat, pointing between the trees at a white ceramic pavilion, "is the infirmary: a pretty little gallery in the sunlight, well-furnished, with six beds, and disinfection and operating rooms at either end. That's where we'll put Rosa. We'll go in a little while—there's only one patient there. Beyond that is the school, or, if you prefer it, the nursery...but I can see our deputy director coming out of it, the good Madame Germinet. The playroom is in the same building.[21]

She indicated a tall woman with white hair, an intelligent expression and curt gestures, who came to meet them and bowed.

"Madame Germinet, Mademoiselle Hardy, who will soon be bringing us a new boarder. You know Mademoiselle Annik. Would you like to show them the house while I got say *bonjour* to our little society? Until later..."

She avoided, as much as possible, group visits and the collective introduction of her refugees: on the one hand, a curiosity beneath which there was too much indifference, and on the other, humiliation, even in the presence of a sincere interest. She preferred to see them on her own. She questioned them about their health, their mental state, and their activities. With a word or a smile she knew how to put them at their ease; she consoled and comforted them.

---

[21] This is the first passage from "La Femme in Chemin" to be adapted into *Le Compagnon*, but it comes from the middle of that earlier story; in that shorter version it is Paule who is being shown round the Refuge, not Mademoiselle Hardy (who does not appear in the earlier story) and they are being shown round by "Madame Zélonoff," who has not refused to marry her partner.

"How well-appointed it is," said Mademoiselle Hardy. "What calm, what repose—it's a true refuge!"

She congratulated herself for having come. Such endeavors might have reconciled her with humanity if, even at the worst hours of her laborious existence, always at odds with stupidity and ignorance, always battling against prejudice and hatred, she had not conserved, vivaciously, all her faith in the future, in spite of everything! A hunted beast, Rosa would find a shelter here in which to lie low. Once she was a mother, and the intelligent vigilance of these women, and their cares, would quickly make her once again a being content to be alive.

"How many boarders can receive your hospitality?" Annik asked Madame Germinet.

"Twenty. No more, unfortunately. It's always full. I would need a house three times as large, and several houses of the same sort per quarter..."

"It's difficult to find such a place," said Mademoiselle Hardy. "Look, Annik!"

The main building, an old Louis XVI residence, opening its rows of windows over the park, contained the bedrooms—every inmate had her own—the large dining-room, the drawing rooms converted into workshops of couture and fashion, and the kitchen, it which everyone took turns to work. A vast lawn with green spaces sowed with groves of acacias and chestnut trees served as a recreation field for the children, and between the clumps of verdure, the bright facades of red roofs of the annexes were visible. A white-haired gardener was raking the paths.

"That," said Madame Germinet, "is the only domestic in the house. He and I make up the entire administrative staff! Madame Broussat insists, quite rightly, that each of the unfortunates who come here should take part in the common labor. We only receive, for preference, the very young, you see. We have girls of fifteen here who are already mothers; there's even one of thirteen. She's in the infirmary—she gave birth to a stillborn daughter yesterday. Our oldest is seventeen—look!

That tall blonde who is watching the children, and whose own baby—there she is!—is rolling her hoop. But before seeing the school and the infirmary, would you like me to show you the accommodation of the Refuge?"

As they went through the large house, Annik marveled once again at the benefits realized by her friend. The orderliness of the property and the air of welcome and peace above all reflected from the walls and the faces, testified to lives in the process of transformation, in the tranquility of hope. Everywhere, from the kitchen to the workshops, people were working good-humoredly. A frank expression brightened the eyes, whose gaze was direct. Sometimes, before opening a door, a song could be heard through the partition wall—the chorus of some traditional song, of which Madame Broussat had taught them the facile rhythm herself, and the melancholy or gaiety of which was as healthy as the native air and poetry of old. In several rooms, little bouquets of flowers or a green branch evoked a horizon of gardens and woods.

"You have no idea," Madame Germinet affirmed, in the directorial study, pointing to her files and ledgers, "how quickly the clean soul reappears from beneath the dirt of misery and vice—unless, of course, social prostitution has imprinted the indelible defect too profoundly."

"Social prostitution is the right term," said Mademoiselle Hardy. "Under the colors of order and health, society is, in fact, the great procuress. That is what throws all the poor wrecks that you're striving here to refloat, defenseless and devoid of veritable education, first into the arms of men and eventually into the gutter."

"If you could see them when they come in! Well, when they leave again, they do so truly bound for a new existence."

"How many succeed in it?"

"The majority. We find them places, employment, even husbands. They only leave when they have somewhere to go. They go with their children whenever they can, and when they can't, we ensure the existence of the little ones until the age of seven. You've seen their dormitory; there are forty beds in it—thirty-seven of them occupied, at present."

"Private assistance! Necessarily better than the Assistance Publique," muttered Madame Hardy, "which is a Ministry like the rest, primarily occupied with bureaucracy."

"That's right. Here, at least, the mother can always follow and find her child. We also have orphans in that number. For almost all of those, we're able to find parents—and good ones, often better than real ones. We have an understanding, for that, with the Oeuvre des Enfants Recueillis."

"I know it!" said Annik. "That's Madame Ambrat's Oeuvre." For the benefit of Mademoiselle Hardy she explained: "A friend of the Blanchets, your neighbors in Versailles. Blanchet is one of Amédée's oldest comrades. He mentioned him to you last week, if you remember."

But Madame Germinet deflected the conversation. "Here's Madame Broussat. She can finish doing the honors better than me... These ladies have seen the house; only the annexes remain."

"Thank you, Madame Germinet. You're not tired? No? You've seen the entry registers and the files? What a charge-sheet against masculine criminality, eh? Let's go see the infirmary. We'll finish off with the school."

"It's an entire program in miniature," said Mademoiselle Hardy, emphatically.

"Oh, our school is very basic. We teach the little ones to sing in chorus; it's a good commencement of discipline. As for the bigger ones, whether their mothers take them or we find them an adoptive home, we teach them to read and write. Then, too quickly, they leave us..."

"Oh," said Annik, "if only you could follow them, the little folk. They all need mothers like Mérette and you. For, in spite of the admirable work of the primary teachers, the lessons of school, without the example of the family..."

"So true!" sighed Mademoiselle Hardy. "Instruction is only one part of education—the superficial part. And morality, which is the foundation of it, remains, for the majority of men—and, it must be said, women—a mere string of words."

"Yes," said Madame Broussat. "Fine words and vile actions! Traditional or innovative, doctrinal or secular, there's a long distance between the religion of the lips and that of the heart."

"That," said Mademoiselle Hardy, with feeling, "is because secular morality is very young and religion is very old. From crowds accustomed since time immemorial to worship idols, one can't expect a fervor for ideas between one day and the next. It's a long road...as long as that to Tipperary..."

They had reached the threshold of the infirmary building. A nurse coquettishly clad in white was waiting for them.

"A student," whispered Madame Broussat into Mademoiselle Hardy's ear, "and the mother of a little girl."

Annik had gone on ahead with the nurse, through the disinfection room and into the ward.

"Mademoiselle Mirat—that's our nurse's name," said Madame Brousset, lingering by the autoclave, "is very satisfied now with her lot and her maternity. She's the daughter of a good family, who believed in the promises of a good-for-nothing. I knew her before her pregnancy. Our doors opened to her when the others closed, that's all. She has no regrets. She knows that when she leaves us, she'll be able to earn enough to meet her needs thereafter as a nurse—enough to live, at any rate, and bring up her child. And in that regard, let me make one remark: there isn't one of these involuntary mothers who hasn't fallen in love, with a kind of pride, with her baby! Some, who would have strangled it at the first wail if they had been abandoned to themselves, are today hanging on the baby's every breath! Oh, if only all cradles, whatever their circumstances, were surrounded by the consent of mores and the assistance of laws, if only maternity were honored in such a way that every birth were welcomed with celebration, I could shut up shop. We're suffering from a falling birth rate, but the State is the first to drive people to Malthusianism, if not to abortion!"

"Which doesn't prevent it—O logic!—from repressing the latter as murder. I've never understood why someone who has been impregnated unwillingly shouldn't remain at liberty—theoretically, of course, as I don't approve of any form of suicide—to give birth or not to an embryo that only truly begins to live at the moment when it begins to breathe. The child in the mother's womb should be entirely under her jurisdiction, so long as it is only animated by fetal existence."

Less liberal in her thinking, Madame Broussat observed: "You're going a bit far! But I'm not astonished by hearing Annik's boldness from you. She's had a frank schooling. I might have known her for three years, and will love her forever, but I'm not yet fully accustomed to her medical student's language."

Mademoiselle Hardy shrugged her shoulders. "You're all the same in my opinion. Science, with its exact terminology, is better than hypocrisy, with its mystery and its danger. If, from the age of reason—and a child begins to reason early—adolescents were taught the how and the why of things, especially those on which the perpetuation of the species depends, there would be no more shameful departures or maladies. There would be one sexual morality, the normal and the healthy; a religion, instead of superstitions. What harm Catholicism has done in deforming antique nudity with its figleafs and veils! When I think that our textbooks of natural history depict the organs and fecundation of flowers, but draw a curtain over the secret of human life...! Well, what do you think?"

"Yes, it's idiotic," said Madame Broussat.

"The first time I talked to my pupils about these grave questions—it was at Yvelines, fifteen years ago—the parents came to reproach me, grossly. I even heard one of them say to me: 'You must be inane or perverted.' And the school inspector called me to order. Result: in our bourgeoisie, the boys, when puberty torments them, go to seek information in the brothel, and their sentiment of women is henceforth soiled. As for the girls, they begin their sexual initiation with one another, and the boys finish it off. In the country, at least there's the example of nature; in that respect, the animals provide better lessons than humans."

The two women looked at one another, moved by discovering one another so quickly, and having become friends so completely.

"You're preaching to a convert."

"And in the meantime," observed Mademoiselle Hardy, "we've lost Annik."

Madame Broussat opened the door to the ward. "Here she is...."

She and the nurse were standing to either side of the only occupied bed, in which a bloodless little face was lying, hair scattered over the pillow. They were listening to the child chatter; she was relating, with a frightful unconsciousness, how she had been perverted by a brother as a little child in the promiscuity of the familial hovel. Afterwards, as a servant in the home of a wine merchant, at the age of eleven, having acquired the habit of amusing herself with her employer in the cellar, she had ended up falling ill, she did not know of what, in the stomach...

"It was from then on that, instead of playing with me gently, as usual, he laid me over a barrel and made me very ill."

As Mademoiselle Hardy and Madame Broussat rejoined her, Annik asked: "But no one had ever told you, then, that playing like that was very bad, and that what happened to you might happen?"

The girl looked at her naively. "Yes. Maman, once, when she caught me playing like that, for fun, with my brother. But as I saw her moving much more, with Papa, I didn't believe..."

"And now," said Madame Broussat, authoritatively, "will you believe me?"

"For sure, Madame. I was too afraid, when they opened my belly."

About her stillborn child she did not care; she only retained, in spite of the anesthesia of the chloroform, the terror of the operation.

She sighed: "Oh la la! Before I start again..."

Annik drew away, pensive. An indignation, even more revolted than the similar one she read in the faces of Mademoiselle Hardy and Madame Broussat, had gripped her and impregnated her completely: a flood of bitterness that swept through her, penetrating her once again with all the physical horror re-evoked. She wanted to chase it away, and at the same time, she saw once again the troubled moment, and the repulsive face of Lebeau, leaning over her.

She thought aloud: "That child had revealed the name of her employer, though; he deserved to be prosecuted!"

"We would have done so, even though he has a wife and children," said Madame Broussat, "but when I began my little investigation, he was on his death bed. Some accident...hazard sometimes sorts things out."

"No!" said Mademoiselle Hardy. "I agree with Annik; such crimes require a more exemplary punishment. If there were any justice..." She pointed at the school, at which they were arriving. "Fortunately, there's the future!"

The troop of little boys and girls were taking their recreation on the lawn.

"Let's hope that it will put a stop to it! The troop of fatherless children that we recruit is increasing every day. Today, they're still rejected by family and disinherited by the harsh guardians of bourgeois society, watching their strong-boxes! Inheritance, the promoter of idleness and exploitation! Let it be abolished for everyone. When I think that only yesterday, in the Sénat, an imbecile majority dared to exclude natural children from the benefits of family allowance—although they're good for conscription and taxation! What meanness! Patience...we'll triumph. They'll end up changing the laws, these intruders!"

Annik smiled at Mademoiselle Hardy. A vigorous faith was seething within her, with the energy of the springs that are the sources of rivers. At the spectacle of the children growing up here, a robust and healthy seed-bed in spite of the inevitable failures, she felt a fever of hope. In confrontation with legitimate filiation, the only one patented and recognized, natural filiation would stand up as an equal.

She herself would be the first to set an example. She would love freely, in accordance with her choice, and she would bring children into the world to whom she alone would give her name, as she would truly give them life. She would proudly apply the law that would one day be passed: the law to whose elaboration she would push Jacquemin. She did not doubt the necessity; equity would sooner or later be recognized and applied.

"A child," she concluded, "ought always to bear, officially, the name of the mother. Thus will disappear the prejudice against those whose birth certificates handicap them with the designation 'father unknown.' Only afterwards, in the derivatives of the certificate as on the certificate itself, will the father's name be recorded—obligatorily whenever possible."

Madame Broussat, whose age, more resigned to accomplished facts, objected: "Even if the child is natural or adulterous?"

"Especially."

"Then beware of the blackmail of investigations of paternity. Some time will pass before a better-made society has given enough pride and resources to the mothers of tomorrow to be able to do without men. Don't you think so, Annik?"

"Oh, I don't absolutely insist, for my part, that the name of the father should be recorded. That's Monsieur Jacquemin's idea. A masculine idea, although he's one of those who believe more in the paternity of education than that of blood."

"Matriarchy, then? Well, three cheers for matriarchy. It's not my worthy Zélonoff who'll contradict me. If it's true that there was once a time when uterine parentage took precedence, we'll be returned to the point of departure!"

"With the addition," remarked Mademoiselle Hardy, "of all the baggage accumulated by past experience." Her eyes had brightened, and her tone became more pronounced. "Progress! It's necessary to be blind to claim that there's a closed circle in which humankind turns, always passing through the same places. No, the road that goes toward the future isn't like the symbol of dead religions, the serpent swallowing its tail. It doubtless turns, but it rises as well; it's a spiral. We sometimes think, because of the parallelism of the coils, that the same path is being trod: wrong! We've advanced; we're moving up!"

They took a few paces in silence alongside the bay windows of the school.

With fervor, the old schoolteacher envisaged, in her reverie, the steep slope climbed since the ancient civilizations: Asia with its Amazons and its queens; Egypt, in which women were equal to men; Greece and Sparta with their citizenesses; Athens with its courtesans; and finally Rome and its matrons, an entire period of prehistory and history, all the way to the chivalric times of the Cours d'Amour...

Afterwards, with the invasion of Catholic modesty and hypocrisy, which extinguished the pale light of the dawn of Christianity in a shadow even more barbaric than the one the heavy-fisted hordes rolled in from the North, had come the era of slavery. European women had fallen into the negligibility of African women: a long imprisonment, over which the revolutionary sun had taken eighteen centuries to shine.

Since then, the march had accelerated. In less than a hundred years, the Declaration of the Rights of Woman and the Female Citizen formulated by Olympe de Gouges in the wake of the charter of the Rights of Man,[22] had resounded so

---

[22] *Déclaration des droits de la femme et de la citoyenne* (1791) by the playwright and activist "Olympe de Gouges" (Marie Gouze, 1748-1793) was an early classic of the feminist crusade. The author, a vocal opponent of all kinds of slavery and a passionate advocate of the rights of illegitimate children, who practiced what she preached in the matter of free love, was guillotined during the Terror and assassinated all over

profoundly throughout the entire world that everywhere, except for the Third Estate of France, the horizon had abruptly broadened before the prisoner. Had not half the world, consecrating the idea for which a sacrificed *avant garde* had battled and striven, with their ideas as well as their persons, given the former minor rights of equivalence and equality?

In England, Switzerland, Denmark, Iceland and Finland women were electors, municipal councilors and members of parliament. Germany, Czechoslovakia, Austria, Hungry and Belgium had given them, as well as the vote, access to governmental functions. In America, where thirty-six states had already summoned women to the ballot box before the war, Federal law had consecrated, since 1920, the definitive victory of feminism. In Europe, only the Latin countries persisted obstinately in their routine...

Mademoiselle Hardy was saddened by the fact that the most retrograde was still the one from which the generative spark had sprung. In vain, the immense labor of French women during the war, in every kind of employment, had sustained the efforts of the soldiers! The beneficiaries of 1789, the bourgeoisie with the well-stuffed bellies, had limited themselves to throwing derisory bones, before 1914, in response to their exceedingly equitable demands and their hunger for justice: voting rights for consular and commercial tribunals, and eligibility for municipal councils. A fine ticket! Inept renditions of old songs, good at the most for the unbreathable atmosphere of café concerts, obstructed the passage, solidly barricaded, in addition, by a gerontocracy at bay...

---

again by Jules Michelet—a stern Republican but no feminist—in his History of France. An unfinished play in which Olympe de Gouges features as a character, debating politics with Marie Antoinette, was used at her trial, ludicrously, as evidence of secret Royalist sympathies. Her final essay condemning the Terror, "Une Patriote persécutée," survived her death.

Tenderly, she enveloped Annik with a hopeful gaze, as she walked in front of her with an alert step. The sun gilded her silky curls and brown neck. Annik, so grown-up!

"Fundamentally," said Madame Broussat, summarizing their conversation in her own fashion, "the wound, in all of that, is Holy History! Mademoiselle Hardy is right. The Biblical legend, with its absurd fable of original sin, is reprehensible with its serpent. That invention of a malevolent God, who tempts and who punishes has always revolted me. The Tree of Evil? Even if we admit that Eve alone was guilty for having bitten the forbidden fruit first, she has paid sufficiently since, for a curiosity for which man has not found himself at fault. The lost paradise? What a fine catch, anyway, for the angling of souls! Paradise? But it's on earth, within us! We seek it in the devil, and we have it within arm's reach, our Eden!" She smiled at Mademoiselle Hardy. "In the meantime, while we wait for Eve to bring Adam back to it, send me this Rosa as soon as you can. Her bed is ready. We'll expect her."

VI

Yvelines. Rosa in prison after infanticide. Am at Hôtel Poste. Come. Mérette.

"How horrible!" cried Annik, throwing the telegram she had just received onto her work table. "We live enclosed in our own prison of flesh, knowing nothing of others...and what does one knows of oneself?"

The poor girl! At the very moment when she was about to reach firm ground, where she would have been able to recover her footing! A few more days, and the house at Auteuil would have opened to her like a haven of mercy. Mérette's letter must have arrived immediately after the imbecilic murder...

Annik immediately made her decision. She would not leave Mademoiselle Hardy in difficulties or the criminal to abandonment. She was in haste to know, and, if needed, to be useful. This Rosa, whose savage act filled her with as much sadness as anger, would need a defender—who, without diminishing the crime, would be better able than her to find if not justifications, at least reasons for reflection, and to show pity.

She packed her traveling bag in haste, and suddenly remembered that she was due to meet Amédée that afternoon. There were no more questions between them, since a glance had sealed the pact of tenderness, of Jacquemin and Raimbert; they were a man and a woman who pleased one another. They let themselves go, meekly, to the flow of the hours.

Their complete intellectual sympathy had been supplemented by the mysterious physical magnetism. Without thinking about tomorrow, except as a long fête traversed together, they were enjoying the present as a tacit communion. They had not yet exchanged either the words that engage or the kiss that decides, but the words and the kiss rose a little further every day from their hearts toward their lips...

"I have time to call at his home. I'll warn him."

She took the Metro and arrived at the Boulevard Raspail as the elevator was going up. She ran up the six flights of stairs. The concierge, with whom she had left her bag, had not seen the député go out. He was not at home, though. Recognizing a familiar face—for Annik had come to lunch several times with Madame Broussat and Zélonoff—the old cook-housekeeper, Madame Danvois, attested: "Monsieur is at the Palais Bourbon, where there's a meeting of his group. Monsieur will be desolate!"

Annik's face allowed it to be seen that she was no less so. How could she get a message to him? She only just had time to get to the station if she wanted to get to Yvelines before nightfall...

"If Mademoiselle has something to tell him...?"

"Yes—we were supposed to meet this afternoon at Monsieur Zélonoff's, in order to go see Monsieur Roussot..."

"Roussot?"

"He'll know. He's the director of the École des Beaux-Arts. It's necessary that Monsieur Jacquemin be informed before midday that I'm obliged to depart immediately for Yvelines, and not to expect me—and that he's not to worry; it's for a legal matter. I'll write to him this evening..."

Such disappointment was legible in her features that the cook immediately said: "Mademoiselle mustn't worry. Monsieur ought to be accessible by telephone; I'll inform him."

"Thank you, Madame Danvois."

With a kindly smile, the worthy woman watched her go downstairs. Perhaps better than her master, she was aware of the sentiments he bore toward Annik. Madame Danvois had no need of any power of divination for that diagnosis; she merely observed daily witnesses in her role as a domestic, the presence of whom is often given insufficient thought.

In the taxi that took her to the Gare Saint-Lazare, Annik reflected. She experienced more than one disappointment, by virtue of not having seen Amédée, in addition to the petty chagrin caused by the regret of a pleasant day lost. The missed

visit? The great painter whom she wanted to meet, whose bitter talent she admired—especially his latest work, the astonishing fresco *Les Maréchals passant sous L'Arc de
Triomphe*...yes, undoubtedly...but most of all, the pleasure of
being together, Amédée and her...the intimacy of their understanding...

She would have liked him to be the first person to whom
she talked about what had happened. She would have liked to
hear his reflections, his advice...

The hubbub of the station, the distraction of the platform,
the carriage and the departure, enveloped her. The route previously followed, down to its smallest details, the shiny curve of
the Seine, a château with a Louis XIV fronton, between the
poplars, the brutal panel of a billboard advertising *Moto
Benzol* dishonoring the peace of a meadow, sprang forth from
her memory simultaneously at the same time as the fleeting
landscape...

The suburb of Yvelines,[23] the ruins of the old ramparts
framed by mildewed houses—the entire vision of the little
town abruptly rose up within her, along with her youth: a
stranger forgotten, it seemed to her, in the continuity of
things...a distant phantom of a little Annik she could no longer
remember having been.

She did not find Mademoiselle Hardy at the Hôtel de la
Poste.

"She's just left for the house of Monsieur Seuriot, the
butcher, where Rosa was working, in the Place Georges Clemenceau..."

"Clemenceau?"

"Yes, the old Place du Marché."

---

[23] Yvelines is nowadays the name of a département, formed in
the 1960s from part of the former Seine-et-Oise, which has
Versailles as its administrative center. The location called by
that name here appears to be the village of Rochefort-en-
Yvelines, which has a market square surrounded by linden
trees like the one described.

"Oh yes, I know..."

The Place du Marché, its centenary linden trees, framed by the market-halls with slate roofs, with their flocks of cooing pigeons! And at the corner of the Rue de l'Échaudé, the shop with the green shutters where she had lived, as an etiolated urchin, in the maternal skirts... *A la Confiance, chez Raimbert*... There had been no Place Clemenceau then; that was long, long ago...in the days when Rosa and she were at school, before the deluge...the red deluge of the war.

Except for the new plaque on which she read the name of Perd-la-Victoire,[24] sarcastically, she found the old square identical, with the lindens in flower surpassing the roofs. She searched the corner of the Rue de l'Échaudé with her gaze for the familial abode, but saw nothing but a blood-red façade where the name Seuriot was displayed in white letters, and which displayed, suspended from hooks, joints of brown-tinted meat, beneath swarms of flies.

Nostrils pinched, she went in, her heart tightly gripped. Mademoiselle Hardy saw her, and embraced her.

"Thank you for coming. I knew that you'd agree to defend her."

Annik gazed, dazedly, at the unrecognizable walls, the glazed door to the back room in which she had been born. An insipid odor had grabbed her by the throat: the taste of death that everything here exhaled, including the fat man with the cleaver stuck in his belt, whose belly swelled an apron stained with dark patches.

"Mademoiselle Raimbert," Mademoiselle Hardy said, introducing her. "Advocate in the Court d'Appel de Paris. Yes, the daughter if the former owner..."

---

[24] Georges Clemenceau, President of the Council during the Great War, was hailed thereafter as the "père de la Victoire" [father of the victory], which cynics, dissatisfied with his post-war politics, scathingly amended to "Perd-la-Victoire" [Lose the Victory].

The butcher sketched a surprised bow, and with a coarse laugh, said: "Mademoiselle is at home."

Then, satisfied in being one of the important characters in the drama that had impassioned Yvelines, he recommenced, for the twentieth time, the story arranged in his own fashion. Ready to vomit, Annik forced herself to listen. A frightful melancholy was mingled with her nausea.

"I took her on, didn't I, to work in exchange for board and lodging, as is only fair. In her condition, she couldn't hope for anything else. And, well, there's no lack of work here...so I said to her: 'Eat, my girl...you're having to work for four, it's the least you can do to eat for two...' Meat, I have plenty, don't I? With the heat, more gets spoiled than gets sold. In spite of that, for some time, I saw that there was something up with Rosa. She sat there like a dumb animal, looking at I don't know what, with her full plate in front of her. Her cheeks were thinning as her belly was fattening. The bigger it got, the more cares she had, because of the malevolence of folk. The kids followed her in the street, throwing the litter from the gutter at her. One day, she disappeared to give birth...it was Thursday...and then, yesterday, Sunday, she went to the Mairie saying that she'd killed her baby...by hitting it on the head with a shoe, that innocent! If that's not unlucky... They found it, its bones pulped, behind a hedge, yes...but the demoiselle is very pale. Would you like to drink a glass of something? Brandy? It will do you good...or a little sloe gin?"

Annik refused precipitately. She dragged Mademoiselle Hardy outside the cage of asphyxia, and took a deep breath of revivifying oxygen.

"How good the air is," she sighed, "when it isn't soiled by that stink!"

"And now," said Mademoiselle Hardy, "the most painful part remains to be done. Let's go to the prison. I told Rosa that I'd see whether I could get you for her advocate. Perhaps they'll permit you to communicate with her before her transfer to Rouen."

Although Yvelines, a small town, counted more than two thousand inhabitants, it only possessed, by way of judiciary apparatus, a brigade of gendarmes, whose Maréchal des Logis, after having consulted the Maire, gave Annik the necessary authorization.

The prison consisted of a narrow shed annexed to the gendarmerie, which only obtained daylight through a loophole with a grille overlooking open country. The sub-officer, gallant for such a well-turned-out defender, came to open the door himself. Without the warning of the former schoolmistress, he would never have believed in the possibility of a "fumelle" in an advocate's robe.[25]

On perceiving Rosa on the plank bed, which, with a wooden bucket and a pitcher, gave the whitewashed cell the aspect of a guard room as well as a dungeon, stopped short. Yes, it was an animal that she had before her, wedged against the wall in grim immobility. Her head buried in the protection of her arms, she must be asleep, unless she was weeping silently...

She called to her and touched her. "It's me, Annik! Annik, your school friend, your advocate."

Nothing. A bundle of rags that allowed itself to be shaken.

Speaking softly, and then imperiously in the face of that disconcerting mutism, Annik talked and talked, until, having become maternal and persuasive again, her voice was finally able to penetrate that heart of stone.

Rosa ended up turning to look at her. She lifted her head. Bleakly, she listened. She propped herself up on her elbow, her head still inclined toward the wall, with the same revolt, a kind of stupor made of incomprehension and rage.

---

[25] "Fumelle" is a variant of "femelle" [female], but even the unmodified version is usually only applied to animals, not humans, and the vowel substitution adds a further hint of contempt.

A ray of sunlight and a patch of blue sky shone through the bars. Instinctively, the Verlainean melody sang in Annik's mind: "What have you done, you there, with your youth?"[26] And, making herself more affectionate still, she leaned over the meager bed.

"What a misfortune, my poor Rosa! You had paid too much in suffering for the mistake of having believed in the promises of a wretch for me to reproach you today for your past stupidity. But what you've just done! Your child, your flesh! You didn't have the right. The moment he was breathing, he became sacred."

Rose seemed to return from the depths of her obscure soul, as if from a gulf.

"Of course, I'd have done better to get an abortion, like the jeweler. She receives nothing but salutations. And I'm here..."

"You're here because, by crushing your baby's skull with a shoe, you've committed a crime...a monstrous crime...against nature."

"And all those who were killed in the war? At least they weren't dying of starvation before being crushed by a shell."

You could have raised him...educated him. It's with education that men are ameliorated...that one prepares for peace..."

"You don't say!"

"Think, Rosa...a mother...killing her child, instead of loving him, pampering him..."

"With what? Bone-deep poverty?"

"By working."

"One has enough trouble staying alive oneself."

"Later, he would have helped you, consoled you He would have been your compensation..."

---

[26] The line is from "Le Ciel est par dessus le toit" in *Sagesse* (1881), reflecting on the two years Verlaine spent in prison after shooting Arthur Rimbaud during a quarrel.

"The poor are the family of dogs. As soon as they're grown, they don't know you anymore. My mother? Oh, I could cry! As for Papa…still searching..."

"You have no remorse? All the same, Rosa, an inoffensive creature, a little life, palpitating! It's horrible. How could you do something so cruel?"

"I don't think any more of it than when I killed lambs for the butcher. Why don't you ask the father how he had the courage to deny him? He ought to be in prison too, or there's no justice!"

"And who is the father?"

"You know full well, since he sent you."

"Me? You're crazy. I've come to defend you."

"You work for him!"

"I don't any longer."

"Makes no difference. Now, I've had enough. *Bonsoir*."

Rosa lay down again, her back turned, her head against the planks. Annik gazed with more alarm than hostility at the tall girl with the stringy hair and the pale skin, whose hands had lashed out to smash the little skull. Nothing remained of the little scamp with whom she had once rubbed shoulders for a year, and whom Lebeau...

She sensed, before the obstinate face and the eyes that had no more tears, the futility of speech. To speak about duties, the meaning of life, to that savage peasant who could see no more evil in murdering her newborn than drowning a kitten… one might as well try to soften a wall! Time alone could wear away that hardened heart.

Dolorously, Annik withdrew.

She would have a difficult task! Far from chilling her, however, the prospect stimulated her surge of feminine charity and human pity. She was as close to Rosa's heart, in the comprehension of her misery, as the other was distant from everything that she, Annik, incarnated in the eyes of the murderess: injustice and inequality. Rosa felt that what she represented was the image of the caste that had exploited her, in her very flesh, and, having reduced her to crime, was punishing her mercilessly. Impotently, Annik suffered in her good will.

"Well?" asked Mademoiselle Hardy, taking her hands.

"It will be hard."

After a bleak meal at the Hôtel de la Poste's *table d'hôte*, where they had to submit, along with stringy veal, to the politeness and consideration of the notary and pharmacist, both unmarried, there was, fortunately, an afternoon train available. The return journey to Paris was long, in spite of the presence of Mérette as far as Mantes, where, by means of a connecting train, the teacher could resume the route to Versailles and her school immediately.

One sole idea—the pleasure of seeing Amédée again—succeeded in soothing, like a balm, the irritation to which Annik was prey, her rancor against ill-made life: that enormous, infinite Stupidity in which the majority of beings struggled as in a dark bottomless well.

The grilles of the Metro were closed. She was hailing a taxi in the Place du Havre, in front of a brasserie, when her gaze fell upon a couple sitting before glasses of beer at a corner table.

"That's odd," she murmured.

She had just recognized Louis Martinet, her sister's fiancé. The date of the marriage had been fixed for the end of the month.

And Paule thinks she's loved exclusively!

There was no error; it really was the broker, with his heavy face, a hybrid of Moor and Catalan, his provocative moustache and his paunch. An arm around the waist of his companion, he must be whispering some dirty joke...the woman was laughing with a lewd and satisfied expression. Not young, and pretentiously dolled up...with her dyed hair, she must be pushing forty.

She was a milliner who had aided Martinet at the beginning of his career, Lise Bertah. They had once lived together, but had come unstuck long ago. He was in the process of consoling her, telling her that fundamentally, he loved no one but her, and would continue to see her...

They got up, and tenderly inclined together, moved off at the pace of a couple tranquilly going home.

She followed them with a long gaze. Tell Paule? She would, but only to be at ease with her conscience, for on that score, there was no doubt: Martinet could have all sorts of relationships, and all vices, but Paule would not stop until she had got herself married. Misunderstood self-interest? Yes, for one thing—and also, although she denied it, an attraction, perhaps unknown to herself, toward the fat man with the rude musculature? Had she not had her own moment of aberration when she had thought, without displeasure, about Lebeau? A memory that revolted her, threw her entirely toward Amédée.

She took refuge in that thought, as in the warmth of a nest.

The next few days passed quickly. The hours, in a rapid flow, carried her down the slope on which, with a sensation of delight, she felt herself sliding. He accompanied her to Rouen, where Rosa was to be tried, and introduced her, as one of his associates, to the President of the Court of Appeal, whom he knew.

They even visited Rosa together, without being able to get anything out of her except the same hateful grievances. Neither the idea that she had committed a revolting action nor the sentiment that some sign of repentance might be to her advantage had penetrated her furrowed brow, in spite of Annik's persistence. Annik did not lose hope, however, of convincing her before the autumn, the probable date of the Assizes.

Annik and Amédée were no longer apart. Delicately, and under the pretext that she was rendering him a service, he had passed a few files on to her. He had two secretaries, but they were no longer sufficient for his work. Parliament, the Palais... If she would consent to work for him, he would be very happy...

He knew her umbrageous pride well enough to have no doubt that she would have refused, especially now that the question of love had come up, if she suspected that it was a kindness aimed more at the woman that the advocate. Now, certain of not being unnecessary to him in the preparation of his speeches, she went to his home every morning, to open the mail and supervise the typists.

The delayed visit to Roussot's studio, toward the end of June, was the decisive treaty of the union. With Zélonoff, joyful at being the godfather of their affection, they met in the Rue Bonaparte, in the great courtyard of the École des Beaux-Arts.

Annik delighted in going through the old buildings, their arches, passages and arcades, the long corridors linking the constructions of various epochs together. It was almost a miniature city, with its gardens and enclosures. She would have loved to be one of its inhabitants, to see the pupils—men and women—going by, with fine features and keen gazes.

"An excellent métier!" she said to Zélonoff. "Recomposing and creating life, with its beauty and it ugliness, inseparable from one another."

Amédée approved, although inclined by taste to a form of art that selected and idealized more. They arrived at the Director's immense studio, in the green heart of pathways bordered by ivy, beneath tall trees; Jean Roussot was smoking a cigarette on the threshold.

He came to meet them, holding out his hand, with the cordiality of an old master in whom the artist, at the end of his glorious career, had remained simple. He was only proud of being the son of humble Breton artisans, and of his works. At sixty years old, he was so alert, with a short body and eyes sparkling with wit, he only seemed fifty.

On going in, Annik did not know where to look, before the mass of canvases displayed and piled up: vigorous sketches with brutal reliefs, and, sometimes, in search of indications, shading whose grace was captivating. At the back, dominating all the scattered labor, was the enormous fresco of the

Maréchals, raising its triptych, ten meters broad and five high along the entire extent of the back wall.

Roussot noticed the excited gaze of the young woman, struck by the same mute admiration that she had experienced when she had discovered at the 1920 Salon, in the midst of the noisy crowds, that gripping evocation of the war and its hideousness.

"Yes," said Roussot, "it's still here! The Sorbonne, for which it was painted, didn't want it. Subversive, it appears. It's just as well it didn't cost me my job. If it weren't for my brother, those Messieurs of the Bloc would have sacked me.[27] Reform number one!"

The elder brother, Pierre Roussot, was one of the veterans of radical socialism, a député for Paris, and several times a Minister before the war. Jacquemin, knowing that parliamentary wolves only eat one another when they cannot reach an understanding—and that Pierre Roussot was too old a wolf not to make people listen to him—protested: "They wouldn't gave dared!"

Roussot shrugged his shoulders, and pointed at the left-hand panel of the triptych. "They dared to do *that*!"

That, assembled in a terrifying synthesis, was all the ignoble dementia of the war. In the foreground, there were women in mourning with tortured faces, bending down over a heap of cadavers filling a broad trench. From living freshness to the putrefaction of death, the flesh offered, in the dirt, the

---

[27] The right-wing Bloc National, elected on a wave of nationalist sentiment following the end of the Great War, came to power in 1919 and was still in power when *Le Compagnon* was written; Margueritte had no way of knowing that it would be defeated in 1924. Raymond Poincaré, President of the Council for much of that time, and Alexandre Millerand, the socialist President of the Republic forced into co-operation with the Bloc, are replaced in the novel by "Cibéron" and "Vilfaux," although Poincaré is cited by name with reference to his earlier activities.

mud, the pus and the blood, all the decompositions of the palette. Above was a sky of smoke and fire, in which, through the conflagration of a battle, a howling crowd was stampeding. Assault-lines were scythed down, pulped; damned souls were writhing in mephitic layers of gas and the jets of flame-throwers; there were iron squalls of monstrous shells...the entire formidable turbulence off funereal chaos. Finally, in the distance, the blue cloud of reinforcements was arriving in close-knit battalions, melting, melting and melting in a continuous flood, a vertiginous fall, into the whirlwind of the furnace.

Like all those who were not blinded by a prejudice of métier or a windfall of repulsive profits, the painter, too old to be conscripted in 1914, had rapidly fallen from the somber enthusiasm that had initially transported a people believing the catastrophe to be inevitable to the conviction that the war had been nothing but an operation of international finance beneath a cover of patriotism.

He had since had but one desire: that it should conclude with the most rapid peace on satisfactory terms—and when he had acquired the conviction in 1919 that it could have finished two years earlier, in 1917, returning Alsace-Lorraine to France, if, instead of following the sentiments of Lloyd George, Presidents Ribot and Poincaré had preferred to believe, with Italy, in the bad faith or impotence of the offers made by the Emperor of Austria—a rage had never quit him, against all the makers of human sacrifice.

It was then that he had painted, after his first picture, the other two. In the center was the re-entry to Paris of the allied armies. The Arc de Triomphe, gigantic, opened its porch over the procession climbing the Champs-Élysées, pressed on one side by the frozen swell of spectators: idlers with delighted faces, pinched and titillated whores, the surface and the underside of the great City piled up pell-mell, entangled in a fever of curiosity and ecstasy; and on the other side, between nurses, the dense and sinister host of the blind, the wounded, the sick and the convalescent: a Court of Miracles agitating stumps and brandishing crutches, faces corroded and stitched, eyes full of reproach and hatred. Then, emerging from the gate of glory, after the file of the deputation of the Mutilated, the head of the procession: Maréchal Foch in blue horizon, and Maréchal Joffre in his old uniform—cavalcading conquerors, Foch elegant and arrogant, the baton of command resting on his thigh, Joffre embarrassed by his own and clinging to the reins, afraid of falling...

Behind them, with the bands and the standards, was the profound mass of the foreign armies, and then the French, preceded by Maréchal Pétain, the veritable orchestrator of that return: an undulating mass whose lines were lost in the distance, in the Avenue de la Grande-Armée. Only the first ranks were composed of living soldiers with grave appearances; they were followed, as far as the eye could see, by an interminable and macabre column: the dead! All the dead, lined up for an endless review, their heads white skulls with hollow orbits...

To the right, the triptych displayed, rising from the height of the bare parvis, where crowns of faded flowers and disjointed pearls were heaped up, the Arc again, with its monumental orb. From the raised slab, the Unknown Soldier was emerging: a skeleton so tall that—with his arm extended toward the assembly route where the Maréchals of the last war were descending from their autos in order to mount their horses, and where other armies and other Maréchals could be distinguished, preparing for a new entry—he was almost touching the summits of the pillars. Turning his tragic vertebrae to the East, it seemed that his gesture was exorcising the future. With all the force of his example, he was crying to future wars: "Halt! You shall not pass!"

Annik and Jacquemin, upset, exchanged glances. They understood one another, in the depths of their souls. In spite of his disapproval of a painter who did not borrow the force of his symbolism from cubism, Zélonoff considered Roussot respectfully. Taking a step back, he pointed at the celebrated work.

"After that, my dear fellow, you can be tranquil. If Nationalism isn't content, the nation is with you, and humankind into the bargain. That page will immortalize you."

Roussot muttered in a surly fashion. His sincere modesty did not like praise, nor work that had gone cold. The imperfections leapt to his eyes. He opened a folder, showed a few new drawings: Sodom and Gomorrah evoked, in Parisian costume, mores as old as the world, the entire modernized saraband of the epochs of decadence, after a social upheaval.

"Sketches for another triptych...yes, just as vast: *L'Après-guerre*. The bamboula of the profiteers...women, even young women, in dance halls after emerging from the hospitals and factories...the lies of the salons, the general need for filth and orgies, alongside the veritable feminine ideal: an ideal of bounty and tenderness...you see! And to finish off, in the last panel, Adam and Eve reconciled, naked in primitive simplicity, going hand-in-hand toward the future city..."

Annik listened ardently, her fingers enlaced with Amédée's in a confident grip. Roussot, without suspecting it, had just cemented the alliance between them. More narrowly and more surely than a golden ring, the community of their faith united them in their reciprocal choice.

Zélonoff considered them slyly from the corner of his eye. Outside, while Roussot escorted them back to the main courtyard, he hummed, cheerfully, the Slav tune whose words he had translated for them one evening in the previous month: *The doves are circling in the dusk...My heart is heavy...is it love...?*

The memory ignited in their eyes, which instinctively sought one another, the same glint. Now, in the souls that had been incubating it day by day, the double flame sprang forth, setting the commencing road and the common tomorrows ablaze with its gilded light.

VII

In spite of the desire that haunted him, and which he had not dared to pursue ostentatiously, Amédée still hesitated before the definitive words and gestures. It was not because he did not sense an equal attraction between them, but he perceived that with Annik, the act of love had an importance that he had never thus far measured with any other woman.

No assimilation was possible, he was sure, with those young women who were only virgins by definition, or who, still being semi-virginal, were only curious to cease to be. What Annik reserved really was the nuptial gift, the offering of an intact personality.

The son of the bourgeoisie that he remained, in spite of himself, had a scruple—not a reservation, for he was smitten to the point of taking his entire responsibility joyfully, as valuable and as certain as if it had been written in the registers of the civil estate and countersigned by the municipal authority. However, precisely because he knew full well that the virginal Annik would also offer herself without reserve, and even with a will so deliberate that she would take pride in her free will, he invested a delicacy in leaving her mistress of her moment. He was sure that the moment would come, and soon.

On leaving Zélonoff they had arranged a rendezvous at Versailles, where the député had a case to plead, prepared by Annik, and in which he wanted her to assist him.

After the hearing, concluded at four o'clock, having the entire evening before them, they had the idea of going to surprise Mademoiselle Hardy.

"We could also go to see the Blanchets," Amédée proposed. "It's a priceless opportunity, since you're curious to get to know them. I'd be happy about that entry to friendship myself, for I'm sure that you'll like them as much as I do.

The school's widely-spaced new buildings, with a courtyard planted with old trees, opened on the Avenue de Paris.

The classrooms were empty; they arrived after the end of the school day. Mademoiselle Hardy, who was in the process of pruning her rose bushes, cutting off the faded flowers, uttered a joyful exclamation on perceiving them.

"This is a nice surprise!"

As much as she had been hostile to Annik's project when she was thinking of Lebeau, she rejoiced in the inclination that had finally drawn her toward Amédée. With a man like that, there was every chance that she would be happy.

She put a certain coquetry into showing the député around her school and her apartment at the back of the second floor: humble provincial furniture, but whose neatness shone and whose old-fashioned charm rendered it pleasant. In the dining room, a large aviary enclosed canaries. At the sight of the old lady, the little yellow bundles showed off, leaping onto the slender bars an opening their beaks, chirping. Even their minuscule eyes were appealing.

She asked about the great affair. How was Rosa?

"She's still in the same state: revolt or prostration; a rock from which the softening spring of tears has not yet gushed forth."

The trial?

The date' had been fixed for the twenty-first of October. Lebeau had learned that Rosa wanted to bring his name into the case.

"He's furious," said Annik, smiling, "that I agreed to plead. He's sent me threats via his editorial secretary, one of my former comrades at the *Appel*—and terrible ones! If I have the misfortune to identify him, if I even permit myself the slightest allusion to him, he'll destroy my career as an advocate—not to mention a counter-charge of slander and blackmail."

"I'll be curious to see that," said Jacquemin, tranquilly.

"Oh, even without you I'd have no fear. With you..."

She took his hand. With him, she would be insouciant about the end of the world.

Satisfied, Mademoiselle Hardy enveloped them with her limpid gaze. Both of them, sensing with emotion the tenderness that bathed them through that freshness of soul, rendered her their affection with the same impulse. She held her arms to Annik, who threw herself into them, filially.

"And me?" said Jacquemin, when their grip relaxed. "With your permission?"

Gauchely, he came forward. She embraced him, too, like a son. It seemed to Amédée, in rediscovering the trace of Annik's lips on the aged cheek, that he had just exchanged the first and most solemn of kisses with her—a kiss that bound them together for the future with the consent of the woman she called Mérette, and who had been her real mother, her family...

"You're going so soon?" groaned Mademoiselle Hardy. "You don't want to have dinner with me?"

"Not today," said Annik. "We'll come again, and soon."

Egotistically, she was in haste to find herself alone with him. She would willingly have sacrificed the visit to the Blanchets for a walk in the Park before returning to Paris, but they lived practically next door—a tall Louis XV gate with an arched top and mossy tone vases.

"It's pretty," she said, as they went in.

Framed with centenarian chestnut trees, the ancient building at the back of lawn had a grandiose air, long and low with its mansard roof. Pink geraniums were flowering in all the windows, punctuating the ivy.

At the foot of an acacia in flower, they perceived a seated young woman reading. She was clad in a bright dress with bare arms. There was a baby carriage beside her. At the sound of the bell announcing a visit, she looked up at the same time as the master of the house appeared on the threshold of the French windows. He recognized his friend Jacquemin at a distance, and waved his arm joyfully. They had been comrades at the École Normale and, having remained friends, had found themselves during the war, after the first Champagne offensive in 1915, lying fraternally side by side in hospital beds, into which the hazard of the evacuation had thrown them, Blanchet as an infantryman and Jacquemin an artilleryman.

The introductions having been made between the two women—"Mademoiselle Raimbert, advocate at the court, my associate...Monique Blanchet"—the two men walked arm in arm back and forth along the broad pathway between the lawn and the house. They chatted gaily, as old friends whose relationship had been tightened by the ordeal.

Monique, with her striking blonde beauty and the frankness that emanated from her entire being like a living flower, had immediately conquered Annik. In spite of everything that Amédée had told her about her: her adventures after having quit her family, what he judged to be her somewhat excessive conception of individual liberty, for a bourgeois young woman—which had rendered her sympathetic in Annik's eyes in advance—Annik divined, on seeing her, that between the judgment of the stupid, hypocritical and malevolent world and that dazzling young woman, whose happiness had not numbed her personality, there was the abyss that, for sincere souls, separates Lies from Truth.

Monique showed off her son, sleeping in the carriage—fifteen months old! The little face, pink and chubby, radiated health. She was proud of him. Maternity had calmed her, decked her as if in armor with strength and tranquility. Between her husband, whom she loved, so tender and so fine, and the children, whom she adored, her entire existence, once so precarious, was held, henceforth equilibrated, in stability.

Instinctively having confidence in Annik, and also savoring a proud contentment in showing off her daughter—one month old!—she took her into the nursery. In a crib with a white mosquito net, watched over by Georges' old maidservant, the minuscule ruddy heap stirred, uttering a willful wail.

"She's thirsty," said the old woman.

Monique consulted the clock whose tick-tock on the ripolin-covered wall regulated the cares of hygiene.

"She's right, almost to the minute. Fortunately, the nurse is here. Excuse me!"

She unhooked one of the shoulder straps of her tunic dress, uncovering her bosom, and the firm roundness of a beautiful breast, with its network of blue veins. The milk inflated the white skin and the taut nipple. Gluttonously, the little leech began to suck. Monique watched the voracious lips and palpating hands with an ecstatic joy, while Annik, moved, marveled at that sacred exchange, that flow of life, which, in the happy mother and the satisfied child, seemed only to be animating a single being...

"Do you know," she said, as she was walking back with Amédée toward the château, the pompous mass of which was looming up in the green frame at the end of the avenue, "that the example of Monique proves that there's only one thing in the world that counts... Oneself, one's happiness, when it's worth the trouble, and when one has had, as she has, the good fortune to find it..."

"And the determination to hold on to it..."

"She's paid rather dear to enjoy it in peace! How many others have done as much, without settling, and live forgetful and considered! As for the opinion of imbeciles..." She swept that aside with a gesture.

Happiness! She too had it there, beside her, and she would be able to hold on to it, preserve it from the assaults of others. A presentiment ran through her: she would have to struggle, against everything that she would confront of prejudice and ancient forces. But the energy of love, multiplying that of youth, would carry her, serene even in profoundly troubled times, toward her destiny.

She knew that she was not ignorant with regard any of the mystery that for the young women of old thickened around the great role of the woman and the mother; but she also she knew that, with regard to the "revelation"—that of the creative act that pleasure often did not accompany—she was completely ignorant. Bizarrely, singing within her was a reminiscence of "Hérodiade," the ritual syllables of Mallarmé's poem—"I

107

am expecting something unknown"—while she replied, distractedly, to Amédée's questions and remarks.[28]

Without noticing it, they had reached the fate of the Place d'Armes, having mechanically climbed the slope that leads, via the vestibule of the Escalier des Princes to the exit from the gardens. The sun, setting in a cloudless sky, spread over the majesty of Versailles the softness of an impalpable golden powder.

"It must be beautiful in the park," she murmured. "We could walk for a while."

"I was about to propose that. We could even have dinner afterwards at the Réservoirs. The most beautiful time, in this incomparable décor"—he indicated the expanse of the Parterre d'Eau, and, beyond the balustrades of the Orangerie, the view of the Etang des Suisses, framed in the emerald of the woods—"is the end of the afternoon. When the light dissolves the broad lines slightly, and, becoming less ardent, caresses the spacious order of the landscape..."

The same embarrassment gripped him, as they advanced past the symmetrical designs of the box-trees, the beautiful lichen-corroded vases and the green-tinted statues toward the solitude of the park. By way of diversion, he pointed at a descending staircase between the flowerbeds.

"The three rose marble steps!"

The bitter odor of African marigolds mingled with the satined perfume of heliotropes. They imagined that they were respiring all the poetry and all the melancholy of the past. It floated around them like a great luminous shadow, with the memory of its passions and it glories, the vanity of what it had been, and was no more.

---

[28] Stéphane Mallarmé's poem "Hérodiade" was written between 1864 and 1867. Like the novelette by Gustave Flaubert with the same tile, which formed the basis of Massenet's opera, it is based—very loosely—on the Biblical myth of Salomé, here given the eponymous name (the equivalent of the English Herodias), and John the Baptist.

The advice of being happy, which seemed to emerge from the magnificence of the location and the splendor of the daylight, suddenly combined, with the reminder of the death of all present footsteps, the imperious appeal of life. The illustrious phantoms, and the anonymous crowd that had suffered and played here, whispered to them until they vanished, that time gathers everything like fruit.

Everything spoke of the brief season, and the immense peace of nature, into the crucible of which winter falls and spring resuscitates. Forgetfulness, which alone, and in spite of the immortalizing bronze and marble of life, would have reigned in that necropolis if they had not reincarnated their vision of the past in their thoughts, incited everything to vanish. They were alive! They were alive! Instinctively, they put their arms around one another, savoring the fleeting moment in all its plenitude. They were walking with the same rhythmic cadence, magnifying the moment and all the certainty of the future, of the long, long route of their love.

The Labyrinth, the Colonnade and the Jardin du Roi saw them pass by, absorbed in their desire. She relaxed against him, as if modeling his movements. They did not see either the rectilinear flight of the hornbeams, or the stagnant pools in which the sky was mirrored in the lacework of foliage. Blue, green and gold, the evening was just one immense bouquet, into which the powerful scent of the earth rose like a breath. They had passed the Tapis-Vert and its last strollers and plunged into the deserted pathways along the Grand Canal.

One might have thought that it was the edge of the world. The grass had invaded the trace of the royal paths, which were only delimited by the awning of high foliage and the ranks of the centenarian trees. Between the ligneous columns of the trunks they had the impression of penetrating, at each further step, into the gloom of a living temple.

The call of a bird sounded. Above the undergrowth, sulfur-colored butterflies were fluttering. Flax-blue bindweed was invading the bushes.

He bent down and offered Annik one of the wild flowers. "In memory of this stroll."

She extended a hand, which he took and kissed. Then, drawing her to him, he said: "Help me. We'll gather a bouquet." Beneath the boyish tone, the voice was tremulous.

"That's it—throw them to me."

She had sat down on the moss; he did the same. He ran an avid gaze over the whole of the elongated body, the shiny legs whose skin was alluring beneath the silk, the breasts uplifted by a palpitation, the mouth whose lips parted, consenting.

"Annik…," he begged.

She let her head fall onto his shoulder.

"My darling..."

Their lips came together.

"I love you…and you? Do you love me?"

Leaning over her face, he drank in passing the emotional *yes* that she pronounced. He gripped her more tightly, intoxicated to be holding her in his arms.

"How happy I am! How I love you! Do you want to be mine? Do you want that?

Her only response was to pull him against her.

"I've desired you for a long time," he stammered. "But I wanted to be sure that you… My love... My wife..."

The communion was consummated delicately...

When Annik opened her eyes again, she seized Amédée's lips again with a violent instinct. With the pain that she had experienced, the sensation had been mingled of a pleasure so intense that it was more than joy, and, at the same time, an infinite gratitude, an intoxicated lassitude...

"My darling," she murmured, "I love you, I'm yours…all my flesh and all my mind."

Fervently, he repeated: "I love you, I'm yours."

As she stood up, a crumpled bindweed flower fell from a pleat in her skirt. Amedée picked another for her. "In memory of this moment..."

She kissed the frail corolla.

Together, they experienced the same pride: that of having celebrated their free union, in the face of nature, in accordance with the religion of their hearts.

PART TWO

To reach the truth, it is necessary, once in life,
to deconstruct all the opinions that one has
received and to reconstruct anew, from the
foundations, the entire system of one's knowledge.
Descartes.

I

A week later, Paule's marriage took place.

Laborious negotiations had preceded it. The rage of possession that was devouring Martinet—let him first get rid of the "loose woman," and then they would see!—did not prevent him from handling the matter in his own way. Tranquil with regard to his lover, the existence of whom Annik had discovered and the recriminations for which he had striven to appease that evening, the fat man had taken his precautions for the future.

Ceding less to Paule's insistence than to Annik's arguments—the interest that he had in his wife contributing, by means of the work she loved, to the prosperity of the household—he had consented that she could continue to exercise her art. On the other hand, as he was marrying her without a sou, he had demanded that communal property be reduced to acquisitions. Thus, he preserved his present wealth, intending, in case of divorce, to dissimulate future gains. In the meantime, he got his hands on half of what the musician might earn from a métier of which he had control and a life-interest.

In exchange, although posing as a freethinker who laughed at "mummery," he had consented to the marriage taking place in a church—a petty low mass, of course, on leaving

113

the Mairie. He did not intend to hang about. Paule, who wanted the red carpet, the beadle and the organ, was obliged to resign herself to that. In spite of Annik's disapproval, she had held absolutely to the religious consecration, which she considered indispensable.

"You can say what you like—for me, marriage remains a sacrament..."

"Fine when you were still a girl at the Annunciation! But you never practice..."

"I beg your pardon! I still go to mass from time to time..."

"The Sunday when you have a new dress! It's like the mania for wearing white, with a little crown, for everyone to look at you!"

"So what?" Paule had protested. It seemed to her that a marriage veil was like that of the first communion: the uniform with which, on those ritual occasions, a woman could not dispense without disgrace.

"But since you don't believe in anything!"

"I believe that it's not worth the trouble of having maintained my virginity if not to have the social benefit..."

"At least that's logical! It's absurd, but it's logical! And it doesn't make you sick that people, while looking at you with a dirty smile, are thinking about the victim who'll bleed after the altar? Personally, I find that custom only good for savages. There are things that don't concern anyone else. The Mairie, if necessary—if one believes, like you, in the utility of social formalities—but without inviting anyone. Two witnesses, the registration, the signatures and *bonsoir!* In your place, I'd be content with that."

But Paule, obstinate, this time in concert with Martinet, had sent invitations to all the relatives she could. And since she had obtained that along with her sister, Monsieur Amédée Jacquemin, député of Paris, would be a witness, Martinet had, for his part, let fly with the President of the Chambre Syndicale des Joailliers, and had unearthed a provincial uncle who was an honorary notary. The prospect of a few days of celebration in Paris had enticed the man of law.

Annik and Amédée retained a melancholy memory of that day. The shocking exhibition, the mocking curiosity of the guests, all in jewelry and couture, lined up at the Mairie and the church, as if at a theatrical performance, and the hubbub of lunch at the Restaurant Gillet, where three other weddings were already belching their racket and songs in the neighboring rooms, all rendered the pious souvenir of their own union dearer.

They had continued to keep their separate apartments. Amédée often slept at Annik's, and for the rest of the day she installed herself, as if in residence, in the Boulevard Raspail. She arrived in the morning and supervised the secretarial work, leaving Madame Danvois, of devotion she was aware and whose competence she appreciated, total control of domestic affairs. Gratefully, the excellent woman cooked tasty little meals for them; they were not great eaters but gourmands.

Vibrating in unison, in the concert of the senses, they experienced a perfect harmony. Annik, happily, thought of nothing but pleasing him. She was ingenious in the small attentions that complete the attachment of a man by delighting him. He always found his worktable tidy, decorated with flowers. Small trinkets and pictures appeared to cheer up items of furniture and walls. Well-tailored garments and elegant cravats, carefully chosen, renewed Amédée's wardrobe, giving him a new look, by which his friends were gradually struck, as by his joyful expression.

Only one momentary discord—for everything was immediately cleared up—had put a slight shadow between them: the question of money. Amédée, divining that a pretty young woman, even the most reasonable, would be forced to economize on the eight hundred francs a month that Annik had consented to accept when she became his secretary at the end of May, wanted them to have a common purse.

"Since we've given ourselves to one another complete-ly," he had declared, one evening when they were talking about the high cost of living, "I don't want you to have any worries of a material nature. What I have belongs to you. It's not a present that I'm giving you but a restitution. With what you have, you can't live as I'd like you to...more broadly..."

She had interrupted him, and said, affectionately: "I have no need of anything, I swear. If I were short, I'd be the first to say so, quite simply. Don't go on. Thank you..."

Before his disappointed gaze, she sought to analyze her-self, and admitted: *It's odd, but the idea, between us, of the slightest...oh, not argument...no, but even the slightest con-versation about money, embarrasses me, almost offends me. Why? I don't know... Pride? Excessive independence? Per-haps...*

She saw that he was chagrined, and regretted having of-fended him. She kissed him.

"Try to understand! Oh, I know that there's nothing in your mind but delicacy and generosity, but what do you ex-pect? I have that modesty. Is it stupid? I don't think so...well, we'll talk about it again, as soon as it's necessary. That I promise you. Don't worry!"

Without any ill humor, he had withdrawn his proposal, with the imperceptible vexation of being misunderstood, and also of sensing in her, for the first time since he had possessed her, of a corner of the soul in which she was retrenched. He would now have liked, as he had united her with his labor, to be able to associate her with everything that interested or af-fected him. Although, fundamentally, like her, he only at-tributed a relative value to money, he managed without dis-pleasure the portfolio constituted by his father's fortune—an income of fifty thousand francs, three-quarters of which he had inherited, incessantly increased by the fees he received from the Palais.

Annik's collaboration contributed to a measurable degree in augmenting those fees, by virtue of the care she put into the preparation of his briefs. In a matter of months, she had taken her place beside him, and it had been noticed in the wake of two cases that he had asked her to plead. That of Rosa, who had fallen gravely ill with typhoid fever, had been postponed to the April sessions.

The change in Amédée, rejuvenated in his thirty-five years, was so evident that his mother, on returning from the vacation that she always spent in Auvergne, at the Château de Moreval, perceived it immediately. The bourgeois Madame de Moreval, an austere Catholic who did good deeds, as she would have administered the knout, had, in remarrying for reasons of interest an equally rigorous Protestant, conserved intact her protective and finicky tenderness for the child of the only man she had ever loved.

"Don't you think," she had said to her husband, "that Amédée is in a phase of transformation?"

Monsieur de Moreval had agreed all the more readily because he had remarked, in *Comoedia*, where the musicienne had had it inserted, a notice recording, with Paule's marriage, the decorative names of the witnesses: "Annik Raimbert, advocate of the Court, younger sister of the distinguished harpist, and Monsieur Amédée Jacquemin, député de Paris, one of the masters of the Bar..." And the cunning stepfather had sought information in the field. He had known for some time that "young Raimbert," a schemer whom Lebeau had been obliged to send packing, was prowling around the worthy Amédée...

"I saw that months ago. I told you. I fear that she's got her hooks into him!

Monsieur de Moreval, a great dignitary of the National Bloc, judged Jacquemin, with his socialist ideas, doubtless to be a simpleton, but dangerous. He had been meditating for some time a marriage with a distant young relative, Antoinette Cesson, the daughter of the ship-owner, whose millions had been multiplied tenfold by the war...

Cesson was certainly—in the company of a few influential parliamentarians—under the threat of criminal charges arising from some tedious story of a bankrupt finance company, but with his relations, the alliance remained highly honorable. And by captivating his son-in-law to some degree, she would be able to attenuate the toxicity of his ideas.

"We need to clarify this matter!" he declared.

He had the stature and stiffness of a wading bird with a plucked head, having no chin and a long beak for a nose.

Every time he saw his parents from then on, he was the butt of their allusions, insidious to begin with and then direct. He spaced out the encounters, judging it more prudent to break off than to clash blades, refusing a couple of dinners, especially the one that Monsieur de Moreval hosted on the thirty-first of December every year for the family reunion, and when, this time, Antoinette Cesson had been invited for him. A telephone call at the last moment—"Urgent affair!"—had informed his desolate mother. "I'll be back tomorrow; I'll drop in to embrace you."

He found the household united in Monsieur de Moreval's study, and assumed a defensive stance, warily.

They tried to disarm him by talking about banalities to begin with—information to be obtained from the Court about the eternal affair of the Asiles du Soir versus the Compagnie Laitière, which had lodged an appeal.

Then Monsieur de Moreval slipped in, affectionately: "You were keenly missed yesterday; we had the whole family."

"I regretted it, too."

"It was charming," said Madame de Moreval. "Antoinette sang delightfully. She's an artiste..."

"And a true one!" said Monsieur de Moreval, supportively.

Silence.

She added: "The voice, when it has a nicely timbre, is worth as much as any instrument."

"Including the harp," fluted the wading bird.

Silence.

Judging that the comedy had gone on long enough, Amédée got up to leave.

Then, raising the stakes, because she sensed the full extent of the danger, the mother held him back, putting her arm around his neck.

"It's bad that you don't confide in us! I know full well that your private life, and even your public life, belong to you. You're old enough, from every point of view, no longer to have to give an account to us, but we can still talk heart-to-heart. A mother always has the right to worry about her son's future. There are even instances in which it's a duty."

He questioned with his gaze the hard face whose tenderness could not succeeded in warming the ice. What was she trying to say?

She sensed his recalcitrance, and detested, through the mocking force of his mutism, the foreign force whose influence she blamed. Poor boy, duped in his sentiments! Especially by an interested cleverness...

She attempted to be flexible, and indirect.

"Certainly, my dear child, you're free. And I know your heart and your intelligence well enough to be certain that you've only placed your affection discriminatingly. You've never mentioned to us—by virtue of a discretion that I thought praiseworthy at first—your...liaison with this Mademoiselle Raimbert, but we know about it. I love you too much not to keep track of your life, too distantly for my liking. At first, we believed it to be an unimportant caprice for you, as for her. We know that the young...person is independently minded. And we also know that she's charming..."

Monsieur de Moreval coughed.

"Do me the justice," she continued, "that as long it appeared to us to be a question of a passing encounter, I respected this whim, as for your preceding adventures..."

Amédée extended his arm. "I will not tolerate, Mother, your establishing any comparison..."

"But..."

"Mademoiselle Raimbert is indeed independent and charming, but she is not the 'person' you believe. A whim? Make no mistake: I consider Annik not as my mistress but as

119

my wife. And if I have not asked her to marry me, it's because I knew for certain in advance that she would refuse me her hand..."

"That hasn't prevented her from according you the rest!"

Monsieur de Moreval had a grating laugh. With a gesture, however, his wife cut it short. It was for her alone to conduct the discussion.

"And that is precisely what frightens me. You are, for that..."—she searched for the least insulting word—"demoiselle, the dream match. And not only is she letting it escape, but saying fie to it! There's something shady and incomprehensible underneath that."

"You can't understand. Mademoiselle Raimbert is obedient to motives the morality of which is antithetical to the one that you and my stepfather are accustomed to respect. And Mademoiselle Raimbert's motives, being sincere, are, at least for me, as respectable as those that lead you to suspect her. Of what? Of a calculation? She is disinterest itself. Of some indignity? Annik is honesty incarnate!"

"Honesty! A young woman who has a lover!"

"Which proves," observed Monsieur de Moreval, ironically, "that honesty, like everything else, varies in accordance with the angle from which it is considered."

Amédée shrugged his shoulders. Convince his parents? No, it was impossible; he knew that. He had anticipated this scene. It had been fatal from the day when, with their scheme to marry him to the Cesson Shipyard millions, they had perceived the place taken by Annik in his existence.

He judged it preferable to demolish at a stroke, and forever, the scaffolding of their project. Divining from their reticence, however, some vile supposition about the woman he loved, he affirmed decisively: "There is nothing for which to reproach Mademoiselle Raimbert, and if the day should come when she does me the honor of consenting to render me entirely happy, by accepting my name, don't worry—I shall marry her."

That determination on Annik's part to remain independent, which he sensed piercing even the abandonment of their love, was, in fact, a nascent preoccupation on his part. He was beginning to imagine that by attaching her to him legally, he would possess her, not to a greater extent, since they no longer had any reason, good or bad, to live separately, but even more completely.

"You'll marry her…you'll marry her!" muttered the old woman, choking.

At the same time, Amédée glimpsed a disdainful grimace on the face of the wading bird.

"And why not?" he snapped. "I suppose that I'm of an age to do without your consent!"

"But my child, since you love that…"—she searched again—"emancipated woman, it's not my place to cause you pain by informing you of the rumors going round about her. Inform yourself!"

"Calumnies! It's sufficient to live, even decently, on the margins of Society, as you call it, in your grandiose meaning of the word, with reference to the poor petty circle in which you move, for all anathemas to be thrown at you, and all mud. Your mud!"

"You think so, my dear chap?" Monsieur de Moreval put in. "But we're not in one of your public meetings here. Your mother will tell you…"

"Yes, I beg you, let me."

Amédée looked at his mother sadly. What inventions was she about to set out? His stepfather, as he swelled up, tugged his sleeves with the satisfied gesture that was customary to him, during his rare oratorical interventions in the Sénat against moral license, after having drunk a sip of sugar water.

He then passed his tongue over his lips, doubtless remembering the particular lust with which he secretly documented his indignations on a weekly basis at a house in the Rue de Richelieu.

Madame de Moreval put on a show of hesitation.

"Speak, Mother!"

She took the plunge. "It's you who are forcing us. Did you know that Mademoiselle Raimbert, before being your secretary, was Monsieur Lebeau's?"

He defied the insinuation with a direct gaze.

"I knew that."

"And do you know why he dispensed with her services?"

"I do know."

"That's impossible! Or else, my child, you're not merely an innocent but a simpleton, or depraved. Your Mademoiselle Raimbert, after having attempted all coquetries in order to get Lebeau to marry her, used insistences so…provocative that he ended up throwing her out in disgust. She's avenging herself by trying to plead a case of blackmail against him! We know all about that, you can be sure. That Rosa, whom we were obliged to sack when we perceived that she was pregnant— and we can congratulate ourselves today for our severity!— it's your Annik, your wife, as you call her, who suggested to her that she pin it on Lebeau. She's the one who, after the infanticide, imagined that fable of paternity. She believes that she can take her vengeance thus, just as, in declaring to you that she doesn't want marriage, she's got you to bite. And today she has you on the cheap. Marriage—we would, of course, have been able to prevent you from committing such a folly. She's taken the initiative, and let the shadow go in favor of the prey."

An indignation so convinced animated the harsh features that it brought a hint of red to the ordinarily pale cheeks.

"Is that all?" Amédée demanded, coldly.

"Isn't that sufficient for you?"

Bitterly, he quipped: "I must be difficult! Not only is that sufficient for me, but, if you want my opinion, it's too much. Lebeau, of whom you've just served as the echo, is going too far—and that risks costing him dear. You can tell him that, if you see him before I do,"

His complete calm ended up irritated Monsieur de Moreval. He sniggered. "What's the point of more preaching,

Caroline? Your son is decidedly incapable, in morality as in politics, of listening to reason."

She, judging that she was not beaten yet, begged: "Promise me one thing, Amédée. It's possible that I'm mistaken, that I've been deceived. It's possible, on the contrary, that the future will take charge of removing the scales from your eyes. If I'm wrong, I'll be the first to admit it. You'll know that I've only talked to you like this in your own interest, and you'll forgive me. If events justify my fears—as I believe they will—know that you'll always have in me the recourse of an entire affection, an affection which, in spite of our differences of opinion, has never faltered. Who knows—you might perhaps be the first to realize, one day, that your old Maman was right, and regret not having listened to her. In any event, we've told you what our conscience ordered us to tell you..." She sighed. "To think that you might have been so happy, that you might at the same time, have fulfilled all our desires, if you had wanted to found a family with the woman who was waiting for you...who might, perhaps—who can tell?—continue to wait for you..."

"Oh, yes—Antoinette Cesson."

He started to laugh, after having been, several times, on the point of leaving and slamming the door. An effort of comprehension for mentalities so different from his own, a residue of filial deference for the old woman who had once been his Maman, and who still remained today, after all, his mother, had caused him to suppress his indignation and disgust. He congratulated himself; better to avoid a painful rupture. In a melancholy fashion, beneath his feigned good humor, he measured the abyss that had been hollowed out between the generations, and the full depth of the one between his mother, his stepfather and himself, which the turbulence of recent years had excavated further.

"*Au revoir*, Mother," he said. "I'll charge you with a second commission, this one to the address of Antoinette Cesson...or rather her millions, which I shall *never marry*. Advise her, when she returns to Deauville, to choose a responsible editor from among her flirts. She must be sufficiently informed, by now, as to their advantages. She sings well, indeed, but she…dances even better, one of her partners in the tango informs me."

"What a pleasantry! It's unworthy!"

"You think so?" And, returning Monsieur de Moreval's irony: "Which proves that slander, like everything else, varies in accordance with the direction from which one considers it. Meaning no offense, Monsieur le Haut-Commissaire…I beg your pardon, Monsieur le Grand-Officier…one never knows by what title to address you!"

"Call me colleague, my dear député," said the senator, with a sickly laugh. Although he detested in his stepson an adversary whose political concepts appeared to him to be not merely utopian but a treason against the interests of his class, he conserved a kind of consideration for his success and his talent. There was also the opportunism of the fraternity between parliamentarians, in which the majority ultimately had a mutual understanding, like thieves in a fairground. Monsieur de Moreval had seen too many ministerial conspiracies not to hope that Jacquemin's socialism might one day—he was young!—lose its color as it aged, like that of so many others. Let him only come to power, like Vilfaux!

With the philosophy of a heron, cunningly lying in wait, patiently awaiting the thrust of the beak, sometimes standing on one foot and sometimes the other, Monsieur Moreval concluded, once the door had closed: "Let's wait and see!"

II

When he saw Annik again at lunch, Amédée could not conceal a preoccupation from her.

Madame Danvois had, however, striven to put together a meal worthy of the great day: the first of the year! Roses from Nice put a ray of sunlight onto the embroidered tablecloth, and Asti was foaming in the glass from which they had taken turns to drink "to Year One!"

Amédée had taken care, in mentioning his conversation with his mother, to leave out everything concerning her, but Annik knew him too well, down to the subtlest nuances of his expression, and his very thoughts, not to divine that they had talked about nothing but her, and in what sense.

"Really? They said nothing about me? Not the slightest malevolence? Swear?"

He smiled, with the frankness that he was incapable of avoiding, and which was the very bedrock of their mutual confidence, the foundation of the reciprocal edifice of their love.

"Yes," he confessed. "A heap of slanders."

"Tell me."

"Lebeau can't get over his humiliation. You can hear the grudge he has against you from here. I've warned him to shut up, or that he'll have to deal with me."

"I'm strong enough to defend myself!"

"Of course," he murmured, vexed.

"And what is he saying?"

He shrugged his shoulders scornfully.

"But what?"

"The opposite of the truth."

"That!" She laughed, and more heartily still on learning about the pseudo-blackmail of the paternity.

"Be careful!" Amédée advised. "It's the weak point of the case. Rosa's accusation has no basis except for her word...no evidence, or even presumptions. If you bring

Lebeau's name into the case, as you intend, you run the risk of indisposing the judges, who are men. He's powerful; he'll make arrangements to pass himself off as the victim of an aggression."

"On my part!"

"On that of your client. Bad for the verdict."

"So?"

"Hmm…he's guilty, and he's afraid. Perhaps it would be better to have him for you in this affair, than against you. Who knows? In exchange for a promise to leave him out of it, perhaps one could negotiate something favorable for Rosa…"

"The jury doesn't take such considerations into account."

"The jury, no—but the Avocat Général… And depending on the charge-sheet…Tartuffe himself affirms that he makes accommodations with Heaven. He might have even more influence with…the god of the Place Vendôme. Solmou is a friend of Lebeau's…"

"Do you know," she said, "what disgusts me about politics, which could be so pure, so beautiful…?"

"What men have made of it?"

"Exactly."

"Touché."

"They're not all like you. Which doesn't prevent you, too"—she wagged her finger at him—"from having your slight tendency to make bargains. It's necessary to believe that it's a professional flaw."

"Every profession has one."

She protested: "A profession is what one makes it. I promise you that as an advocate…"

"Bah! You remain, under the robe, what we all are, under our suits…"

"Oh, no! Women are more idealistic! You'll see that gradually, sincerity—for without men, we'd be less habituated to lying—generosity and feminine softness will bring progress to every order of ideas. Even into your dirty politics, when we have the vote."

In the same way that he resented, in spite of himself, her independence—for in rational terms, he admitted it as a just principle—she unconsciously resented his absorption by a métier in which ambition was poorly compatible with love. Often, in the evenings, he was sorry to have to leave her. Oh, to live in the intimacy of the studio, where they often dined nowadays, on a light meal that she took pleasure in preparing. To be able to prolong the conversation, and the caresses! But a meeting that he could not put off, a promised speech... It was necessary for him to tear himself away from the arms that would have been so glad to retain him...

An involuntary grievance, on Annik's part, because she had always taken an interest, in spite of their Byzantine nature, in the complicated appearances to which, in every party, the division of groups gave the political fleet. In socialism alone, toward which Jacquemin had gone in the times when it had been unified under Jaurès, and in which she situated the future, what a conflict there was of good wills, what a disintegration of efforts! Outside the party, the radical socialists, the republican socialists; of the old party, the independents—of which he was one—and the ex-unified, orthodox rebels against soviet dictatorship, whom the communists, for their part, excommunicated... On the one hand, the four principal groups, disposed to reach agreement; on the other, the sectarian clans, a destructive ferment or mysterious leaven, one never knew... All of that ravaged by individual interests and obscure hatreds...

"It's not astonishing, my love," Annik often said, "that three-quarters of the electors are disinterested in your kitchens! The odor that rises through the ventilation shafts, whether it comes from the right or the left, is nauseating. One ends up telling oneself that whoever is holding the handle of the frying pan, they're only interested in their own fricassee! That's Madame Danvois' reasoning. 'What does it matter to Ministers that butter costs twelve francs? Their plates are full!'"

Actively, while Amédée, agitated by the first fevers of the electoral period, still fairly distant, was constrained to mul-

127

tiply his excursions, Annik made her way to the Palais. Her real juridical science and her lively talent for speech-making, was winning her a small notoriety that as growing every day.

From the very start, she had put all the gallants in their place, graying side-whiskers or smooth faces, like those of old dogs, as well as young, who were more pressing and more polite. As she was desirable, however, with her young breasts, and her wig neatly perched on her short brown curls, and as she also had a pleasant manner and a witty repartee, she had immediately been adopted. Annik Raimbert? An original!

Only the women, cantankerous competitors—even if they were young and pretty, they were no more facile—criticized her. Annik Raimbert? A poseur!

Eventually, success having arrived, and especially once the rumor of her liaison with Jacquemin—today's leader and tomorrow's Minister—was spread around and confirmed, opinion was established: Annik Raimbert? A clever one, with whom it was necessary to reckon.

She was under no illusion regarding the reasons for that success: the occult protection of Lebeau, and then Amédée, had served her more than her work. And, even today, she knew full well that only the fact of earning enough to live on shielded her from difficulties. It was an inextricable swamp in which, without support and resources, she would have struggled or sunk, like so many others less favored by circumstances and less determined...

Those were observations for which her rancor against injustice and inequality would have provided a durable aliment even if, every time she thought about it, the odious memory of the first of May, of the brutality of which, for want of the vanished scar, her entire being retained the trace, had not entertained her combative energy.

She had not, moreover, abdicated any of her beautiful, valiant faith, constantly at the service of the weakness, and soon the despair of Paule. Between her and Martinet, on the very night of their marriage, there had been a savage rupture: a rupture of the hymen so brutal that the patient had found nothing therein but a horror, henceforth insurmountable, of her husband, and, in consequence, a rupture of the union. None such, even those that assemble a linkage of interests over time, can endure against carnal repugnance.

Martinet, having only revealed to his wife's virginity the intense pain and humiliation of legal rape, had striven in vain to awaken her sensuality. Unable to succeed in that, as soon as his desire was slaked and unworried any longer as to whether his companion's might correspond or that she might feel a visible repulsion, made the decision to turn his back, or on his heels, cheerfully. For him, Paule fell to the rank of a domestic object, while Lise Bertah became superior again, for "love-making."

After a few weeks, neglecting his wife—"a dead end!"—he had become reaccustomed to his former outlet. Paule, relieved at first, and then with a black neurasthenia, had found herself alone again. If only she had a child! A consolation for her distress, a deflection of the aspirations with which her heart as swollen. But her lord, from the very start, had had clear ideas about that: "A child! When one doesn't have the income! A child! Why not several! The grain of the wood of the bed is all right for those who don't know what they're doing! Drunkards and destitutes!"

Annik? But, affectionate as she was, she had her life. Paule did not know who to turn to. There remained her métier: concerts, that exalting, although hard career…but that was a constant source of scenes with her husband. He found the vulgarity of it unbearable.

The appellation of Martinet, under which, since her marriage, Paule performed, and which, from the very beginning, he had wanted to attach to her like a stamp of ownership, he now did not let a day pass by without reproaching her, with spiteful envy, for its fame. What would become henceforth of him, Martinet? Dogshit?

Not a day went past, either, when he did not demand a rendering of accounts. The salary of the smallest lesson and the earnings of the most lucrative soirée were the daily ransom of that surname, the excise duty. "The law," he sniggered, at her complaints. "The law? I'm above it. I took you without a sou. It's your contribution to the household expanses..."

It was thus that what was bound to happen had happened.

One afternoon in May, after two months of hell,[29] as she was beginning to think again about Lili Brontier, at the exit from a performance at Gaveau's when she had played Mozart and Grieg superbly, Paule had met a young industrialist introduced to her by Zélonoff: Roger Jouves, a former aviator and now a manufacturer of electrical devices, of Jouves, Chabaz & Co.

Still quivering with her success and emotion—for she threw herself entirely into the consoling intoxication of the music, and was now unable to play without putting her soul into it—she had been sensitive to merited compliments and sincere admiration. Roger Jouves had proposed that they should all—with Zélonoff, Madame Broussat, Annik and Jacquemin—go to take tea in the Bois, and she had accepted gladly, moved by one of those impulses that seems to come not from unreflective decision but from Risk, the master of destinies.

---

[29] This date implies that Paule's marriage took place in March, but that seems inconsistent with the imminent statement that Paule discovers her pregnancy in February, having presumably conceived in December, given that this happens before Rosa's trial in April (presumably of 1929, within the implicit time-scheme extrapolated from *La Garçonne*). The confusion arises because of the interleaving of the *Oeuvres Libres* story of "La Femme en chemin," with the new material, amending its chronology in the process. The inconsistencies are never sorted out completely, but the best compromise in trying to make sense of the chronology of the final version is to ignore this assertion and assume that Paule was married in the autumn (of 1928), and that she met Roger in November, not May.

Two weeks later, she was Roger Jouves' mistress. The stranger of that evening incarnated, without her being astonished by it, everything that she had lacked until then: past, family. In being born to pleasure and, in the same abrupt blossoming, to love, Paule was reborn to life. Roger was henceforth the quotidian haven, the horizon of all her hopes. He permitted her to tolerate even the stifling presence and the finicky despotism enthroned in the home to which she returned.

Annik, with an impotent sadness, had seen her suffer. She had spared her the futile and wounding reproaches, "You wanted it!" and "I told you so!" But since Paule had now realized that marriage, when it is only a business contract, can become for some individuals the worst of tortures, her experiment was complete. Let her not hesitate to reclaim her independence! Divorce him!

After first, Paule had hesitated. Liberty, yes, but also a living to earn again…a dilemma. Life, so rude thus far, had ground her down, worn away every spring. Neither better nor worse than her bourgeois sisters, she felt weak, her legs cut off, before the necessity of setting off once again, alone, into the unknown.

Loved, and in love, she discovered another potential future. She was ready to resume the march lightly, sure that Roger would not let her down. Annik, to whom she then confessed her passion, became even more pressing. She could not admit, in her horror of lying, that Paule could remain silent any longer.

"Understand," she repeated, "that deception isn't sleeping with someone else—it's the dirtiness of doing it without saying so. Now, you must—*must*, you hear—tell your husband the truth…"

"Yes," said Paule. "At the first opportunity…"

The two sisters formulated a plan of liberation and orchestrated the means. Annik always came back to the same conclusion: "It's necessary, for your divorce to be rapid, and even for it to be possible, to reach an agreement with Martinet."

An unexpected event arrived to anchor Annik's conviction, at the same time as it threw the dithering Paule back into uncertainty. At the beginning of February she had to yield to the evidence: she was pregnant.

"No mistake?" asked Annik.

"I've seen the doctor. Three months."

"What does Roger think?"

"He's crazy with joy."

"That's because he's no longer thinking about you. The child, in your situation, complicates matters. However, it's necessary not to recoil. It's necessary to tell your husband immediately. He won't hesitate, and with good cause, knowing that the child isn't his, to leave you the responsibility of raising it..."

"It's just that..."

"That isn't Roger's opinion?"

"On the contrary; he's harassing me to take action."

"Well?"

"It's just that...listen, Annik. How long does a divorce take, if it's agreed, at a minimum?"

"Three or four months..."

"Perhaps a year."

"That depends on the good will of your lord and master."

"And won't that child, even if I divorce, legally bear my present name: Martinet?"

"Yes, unless your husband legally disavows paternity."

"Ah!"

A doubt was so visibly tormenting her that Annik pressed her: "What are you thinking? Explain."

Paule ended up confessing: "It's just that...well, Roger has to spend a few months in Japan."

"You'll be divorced; you can go with him."

"Impossible. A voyage too tiring for two, and too costly. Oh, it torments me not to be able to go with him. I'm afraid. Of what, I can't tell. Not that he'll drop me, no—of that I'm sure. But something worse…an accident…" She seized Annik's hands and gripped them feverishly. "The sea, perhaps? I'm afraid. What if he doesn't come back?"

A frightful vision dilated her pupils: a ship sinking, the cries of drowning men…

"You're mad," Annik joked.

"No, I have a kind of presentiment. Then I wonder whether it might not be better to be patient, to a wait…"

"Martinet will learn soon enough, at the first glance, what you can't hide for longer than a few more weeks…"

She blushed. "That's not what worries me."

"What?"

She turned her head. Annik understood. "You've taken precautions, with him?"

"Yes."

"Oh, Paule…"

Annik contemplated her with amazement. She was weeping now, ashamed. Everything within her was adrift…she no longer had any courage, or will.

"You've done that?"

"One defends oneself as best one can."

Her sobs redoubled. Annik did not feel that she had the strength to console her. So, this was her sister, that poor being exalted momentarily by the egotism of passion, and immediately fallen back again into the mud of servitude. A monster of baseness and duplicity? Not even that. A victim of oppression, whose laxity had picked up, for protection, the only arms she had. Annik felt sorry for her. Paule was no more responsible, on reflection, than a Rosa. The brute killed, the civilized deceived. Crime or fault, was it not, fundamentally, the same reflex?"

Spring came without Paule having made a decision, entirely absorbed by Roger's imminent departure. The two sisters did not see as much of one another. The younger had not forgiven the elder for conduct that revolted her. She did not love Paule any less because of it, but, wounded in her moral religion, she could no longer succeed in holding her in esteem.

Her talent as an artiste did not justify, even if it partly explained, her disequilibrium as a woman.

With the approach of the Assizes, the days passed so quickly, and were so full, that they deflected her further from that adventure, as from her customary occupations. Entirely given over to her secretarial labor and the preparation of her plea, she no longer had time to see either Mademoiselle Hardy or Madame Broussat.

The only pauses in the whirlwind were the hours of oasis—evenings, too rare, spent with Amédée. She had resolved, in order to lose less of their sweetness, and to gain on the overly short mornings, to live almost entirely, albeit discreetly, with him. She had not yet moved in, but she had prepared her place, as sedentary cats do.

Both of them adjusted, with a very tender joy, to that quotidian accommodation which nocturnal solitude in the communal bed tightened with a corporeal bond in the union of souls. Gradually, they penetrated one another, adapted themselves to one another, submissive to their reciprocal influences.

She had been obliged, not without resistance, to resign herself to following his advice with regard to the trial. Rosa's interests demanded it imperiously, as Annik had quickly realized. Lebeau under silence was a possible acquittal, or at any rate, attenuating circumstances. During the last journey she had undertaken to Rouen, in passing from the Court to the prison, the Avocat Général had let her hear a few covert words...

There was nothing that could compromise the impartiality of the façade, the cold reserve of Justice, of which the smooth face of the magistrate, with dignity, put on a show, but an impression that was unmistakable: a glance, an intonation... The god of the Place Vendôme has accommodated Themis to his sauce. Let her not depart from generalities, and the case was better. If, instead of defending, she attacked, she would find arrayed against her—she was certain of it—the society of men, in league in its entirety, around Lebeau.

That iniquitous counterfeit of equity, after having filled her with a cold rage, initially discouraged her. Nothing to be done against such a fortress! She would only succeed in sacrificing Rosa, first of all, in a futile assault. Mademoiselle Hardy, consulted, advised her to yield. As an advocate, her first duty was to save her client. Only the end was important; let her resign herself to the means! Amédée's common sense completed her persuasion: a capitulation that had been, for her, a veritable crisis of conscience.

She had had no difficult convincing Rosa of the necessity of the strategy. The illness had sapped that grim soul of the somber obstinacy of the beginning. She was no longer anything but a poor drifting wreck—devoid of remorse, for she remained in the same incomprehension of what she had done, but she spent hours weeping even so. She was a murderer murdered, in her animal solitude of neglect, her utter disarray before the terror of punishment. She trembled during her insomnia at the idea of the Court of Assizes, and the threat of the day after.

Annik found her feverish, her hands limp. She drank, as a sedative, the counsels of prudence.

Finally, the solemn day arrived. Annik, apparently self-controlled, was nervous. Amédée, claimed by the Chambre for an interpellation that could not be put off, accompanied her to the station, desolate. He would have liked to be able to comfort her with his presence. Since the beginning of April, she had often been weary, without cause, and those fatigues worried Amédée. He confided her to Mademoiselle Hardy, who was absolutely insistent on attending the trial; no one anticipated that it would last more than two days.

"If the session finishes soon enough, I'll be in Rouen before midnight. You won't be pleading today. I'm absolutely determined to hear you."

She thanked him with her gaze. She would have preferred, in spite of her pleasure in feeling him by her side, to be alone, but did not tell him that: an instinct of personality, freer in his absence to affirm itself, and, at the same time, a sentiment of modesty, a fear of being inferior to what he might expect of her.

They met up that evening in the hotel room where she was waiting for him, still tense because of her effort of concentration and determination to follow the interrogation and the depositions. She was hopeful; Rosa, with her expression of a haggard beast, and her stammering responses, had stayed within the agreed reserve, and the jurors did not seem malevolent. Why should they not be as pitying, with their human common sense, as the Avocat Général, with his social common sense?

"Do you know," she confessed, opening the window, "I'm stifling! To what do I owe that effect? I have butterflies in my stomach, like an actress about to go on stage...it's so similar to the set of a theater, that huge room with its tall woodwork and its bare walls, with the accessories of its clock and its crucifix, the spectators on the benches...on the side of the courtyard, the public ministry and the jury; on the side of the garden, the defense, the gendarmes, the accused. And at the back, arranged like puppets, the judges, for whom the play is being enacted. Fortunately, I know my part. It makes no difference that there's a terrifying comedy therein..."

Her heart was beating when, after the speech for the prosecution, she stood up in the great silence. She searched with her eyes for Amédée and Mademoiselle Hardy, sitting in places of favor, on the chairs piled up behind the President. Delegated to observe, Madame Lourdal, beside the *Appel*'s judiciary reporter, was wearing a reseda straw bonnet, with a large myrtle-green bow.

Then, returning to Rosa, Annik no longer saw anything but her, and the objective: to discharge the poor creature from the responsibility for the crime of which she had only been the blind instrument.

She spoke in a voice that was initially faint, but immediately became firmer, as soon as the automatism of doubling had been succeeded, ardently, by the full possession of her lucidity. It seemed to her at the start that there was another self in her, reciting a learned lesson, producing the effects of a conventional handle, but the anguish was quickly effaced, and the explosive conviction took possession of her luminously resplendent being.

Surprised, at first suspicious of the unusual intervention that the female Parisian advocate constituted there, and then interested by the grace of the woman, the jurors listened attentively. The captive audience sometimes approved, by a movement, of the touching arguments, the eloquence of the passionate dialectic, under which the judges, immobile or sometimes letting their heads slump, seemed to be doing off with their eyes closed.

Rosa, shrunken, was no longer anything but a back shaken by sobs. She had her head in her hands and never ceased repeating: "My God! My God!"

The speech resounded in the general emotion.

"Oh, Messieurs, what a difficult task yours is! I understand your revulsion before this monstrous crime. For a mother to kill, to trample, her child! And yet, what if for that inexpiable act, there were reasons that, I certainly don't say excuse it, but perhaps explain it? Do you not tremble, in your soul, as administrators of justice, at the idea of perceiving one day that you might have saved by your generosity a poor being that you instead have thrown into the mud and anarchy by an implacable verdict? Yes, certainly, this woman is guilty, but she did not know. She told me herself, on the day after her murder: 'I've bled so many beasts in my life!' That child with which she was charged, since the father did not want it, she did not spare any more than a goat-kid. Remember, I beg you, that she was in the habit of killing for the butcher...

"Ask, members of the jury, ask any combatant whether death is as hard to deliver the second time as the first. They will all tell you that even the best, at length, are hardened to it.

"I would be the first to tell you to condemn, and with all possible rigor, if you had no one before you but a conscious criminal, but does not everything here—the repentance of that unfortunate, whom malady has further exhausted and who has almost died of chagrin, the depositions that have demonstrated her desperation, as the object of rejection and derision, and finally, the very moderation of Monsieur l'Avocat-Général's speech for the prosecution—plead attenuating circumstances? A hand stronger than hers, members of the jury, armed her in the shadows, and pushed her hand. There is, behind her, the seducer who hides, and the law that protects him!

"What! You will strike her alone and give amnesty to the accomplice—what am I saying?—the instigator of the crime? Have pity, members of the jury, for an unfortunate who was taken as a virgin and who did not want to be a mother, one whom harsh destiny and cunning male desire threw into the eternal trap! She has been punished enough already by the remorse hat is crushing her. She has woken up in the night of the soul!

"Poor woman, you have destroyed a life that you believed to be yours, and you have struck yourself! But another, more criminal than you, is escaping his responsibility.

"Have pity, I implore you; it is a woman who asks you that on behalf of one of her lamentable sisters. This one has suffered already and she is only twenty years old. Twenty! Perhaps, members of the jury, you have daughters of that age who are waiting for you patiently, dreaming of their fiancé! Rosa had no father to protect her! In the name of our fortunate and beloved daughters, I ask you for mercy for this poor woman."

A murmur, a few bravos—but Annik could no longer distinguish around hr anything but a confused whirl. She collapsed rather than sitting down, putting her hand to her heart…

When she recovered consciousness, the distressed faces of Amédée and Mademoiselle Hardy were leading anxiously, over her pallor.

"I don't know what came over me," she said. "A dizziness…"

She smiled at the crowd that surrounded her with sympathy, shaking her hand.

"Certain acquittal," affirmed Mademoiselle Hardy.

"Attenuating circumstances, at any rate," Jacquemin corrected. "You were admirable!"

It was a moment of hope in which he did not suspect, any more than Annik did, that a greater hope had just been born, announced already, in the utmost secrecy of her flesh, where a new life was obscurely revealing itself.

III

Rosa had been sentenced to five years hard labor.

"What a hammer blow," Annik had sighed, when the sentence was read out.

Amédée had explained to her that the Court, in spite of the evident indulgence of the Public Ministry and the dispositions of the President, had been bound by the responses of the jury, which had judged in accordance with masculine and social laws. In obtaining attenuating circumstances, she had obtained a considerable personal success—but Annik retained from her failure, along with the vision of the bewildered Rosa being led away by the gendarmes without her appearing to take any account of it, a sadness and a bitterness.

A prompt diversion, however, absorbed her imperiously.

She was soon convinced of the origin of her bouts of malaise. Another life had been installed within her. A mysterious presence was dwelling within her. At first Annik had only felt, with the temporary fits of nausea, and astonishment into which as much preoccupation entered as joy. Accustomed to free possession of herself, that entrance of the future, into her thought as well as her flesh, filled her with a reverie...

What would it be, that embryo, in which Amédée was revived at the same time as herself, and which, distinct from them, would later transmit in its turn the spark by which the torch of the generations would be reignited one after another? Boy or girl? Which would she prefer? With a proud quiver of her entire being, she placed her hands on her belly, whose fecundation nothing yet revealed, and imposed her will on the present minute and the future hours. It was hers; it would be hers, that soft fruit that her substance, by itself, was in the process of forming, cell by cell.

It was an idea that rapidly restored all her delighted strength. She no longer felt her fatigue. A satisfying radiation emerged, so visibly, from her lively gestures and her newly-brightened visage, that Amédée was struck by it. He rejoiced in rediscovering, in his beloved, the lover whose occupations had taken possession of her in recent weeks. Then, Annik continuing to be animated by an increasing activity, he did not hold it against her that she was not thinking more about him, but living satisfied, in spite of their separate and dispersed existences.

She had not told him yet about the great event. She kept her secret jealously, in anticipation of everything that her revelation would cause to surge forth between them, of inevitable modifications, and new sentiments—and perhaps dissents? Instinctively, Amédée perceived the profound transformation in her, and was irritated because he could not determine the cause.

For a long time he had been unable to understand, since they loved one another more every day, her obstinacy in wanting, not merely to conserve her studio on the Place Saint-Sulpice—he admitted that she ought to keep it as a professional domicile, for her consultations—but not to spend, as yet, every night in his own apartment.

For one thing, it was inconvenient, those perpetual comings and goings in search of the most trivial objects…a dress, underwear. She was not, conclusively, either living in her own place, or with him. And above all, constrained as he was to go out so frequently, it was difficult not always to find her here when he returned, ready to listen to him, to surround him with her tender, judicious understanding…and with her arms, such beautiful arms, knotting their embrace… The nights when he did not feel her asleep by his side had become dolorous to him.

Married, they would have been able to be more constantly, more completely together—but to his pleas, she had always replied: "Later! Let's wait!" Why would she not agree, at least, to install herself definitively in the Boulevard Raspail? Madame Danvois? The gossips? Since he did not care about that…!

A scene—the first, after twenty reproaches, always eluded with a pleasantry and a caress—gave body to the grievance. They were idling, still in bed in the apartment, when Annik suddenly threw back the sheets.

"*Zut!* We promised Roussot to go to the private view at the new Salon..."

"Will it amuse you to see that cortege of officials, with Vilfaux at the head?"

"Yes—and their faces in front of the first two panels of *L'Après-Guerre* and Zélonoff's *Rues*. I only just have time to go get dressed, if I want to be at the Tuileries by eleven. We'll meet up at the entrance, shall we? Near the Grand-Bassin, where the children push their toy boats..."

He consented, sulkily.

"What needless trouble you give yourself, with this partly double life. It would be much simpler if we were married."

"I don't see what marriage would add to our affection..."

"Nothing—but to our tranquility, a great deal."

"You're not happy like this?"

"I could be more so..."

She came back to the bed, where he was lingering, in a bad mood. Taking him by the shoulders, she shook him, laughing. "Bourgeois! Dirty bourgeois!"

He grumbled: "You're not being serious. Let's talk, in good faith. You know very well that I think exactly the same as you about marriage and its social value. I don't care about the convention of a Monsieur in a tricolor sash linking you in the name of Society with a stammered reading of the articles of the Code."

"Indeed!"

"Yes, yes, you're right, that's understood. And I even concede that we're united all the more solidly because, having proved, without the permission of Monsieur le Maire, our perfect understanding, we know that our happiness will last, or as long as we want, as much as we..."

"So?"

"So, since we're certain of the profundity as well as the duration of our sentiments, what is stopping you becoming, officially, my wife? We wouldn't love one another anymore, that's agreed, but we'd leave one another less frequently..."

"There it is!"

"You want to work to make life better for future societies? Begin by making it easier for me. Let's work for the future, agreed—but without complicating the present in the process."

"Do you think it's necessary to your happiness that I be called Madame Jacquemin? Look at Madame Broussat and Zélonoff—they're happy as they are."

"What a comparison! She's a widow and fifty years old. As for Michel"—he shrugged his shoulders—"For one thing, he's an artist, and for another, he's a Russian! Yes, it's necessary to my happiness that we march side by side along the same route, at the same pace. You've realized the paradox of living like a bachelor and having it accepted by everyone that you live like a bachelor, in an epoch and a milieu in which young women who don't submit, at least in appearance, to social rules, are still considered as whores."

"Convention! Which doesn't prevent them, anyway, from running around as they please!"

"That's true. But conventions, whether you like it or not, are the bread we eat and the air we breathe. You observe fifty conventions yourself every twenty-four hours, and submit to them with good grace. You don't even notice them...and even though some of the bread isn't tasty and there's a more salubrious air, you eat and breathe like everyone else, and it doesn't do you any harm. Given that marriage between us would only be a formality, and would have the advantage of juxtaposing our lives more closely, what serious inconvenience do you see in it?"

She listened to him, becoming serious.

He concluded: "If you really love me, you won't refuse to come and live under my roof and help me in my public life. My name isn't dishonoring to bear, so far as I know!"

She tried to evade the issue by joking again. "Ask your mother whether she wouldn't like it better if I kept my own!"

For the first time since they had known one another, he made an angry gesture. "Leave my mother out of it! I don't care anymore about the opinion of my family than the hypocrisy of society. It's only a question of you and me. Either your ideas about social reform and future happiness are only cerebral theories, or you'll heed the impulse of a generous heart!"

Piqued, she retorted: "It's not in little things but in great circumstances that it's important not to compromise with one's conscience. I don't want to marry, my dear husband, because I want to remain your equal, and I intend to demonstrate, by our example, that the formality in question is unnecessary to life perfectly united..."

"United! You're very generous! And perfectly! You're not difficult. Example: I come home the day before yesterday, exhausted, after three meetings. Madame isn't here! Pretext: work at home in the morning. Another example: it's ten o'clock, and here you are, obliged to gallop once again to the Place Saint-Sulpice. It's idiotic—there's no other word for it. If you really loved me..."

"*If* I love you?" Annik's visage softened. Only the last word had touched her. Instead of two egotisms at odds, and two wills in confrontation, there was no longer anything in the face of a beloved man, but a loving woman. "Hold on!" she said. "If that's all it is, it can be arranged." She bowed, with mischievous ceremony. "Although I have the honor of refusing you my hand, I won't refuse to move my wardrobe, one of these days, and become, definitively, the mistress...of the house. All the more so..."

"All the more so...?"

But, in spite of his persistence, she fell silent. And, kissing him with an impetuosity that cleared his frown, she darted at him, as she ran away: "Later. This morning, I don't have the time!"

When they arrived at the Salon the officials had gone and the halls were already half-full of the privileged crowd. They recognized the habitual public of miscellaneous grandees, swelled by the small society of the exhibitors: artists and their families, professional and occasional models, standing anxiously beside their canvases. A stir among the idlers, or the assembly of a group, signaled the successful works.

"Can't see a thing," said Annik.

"One doesn't come to the private view to see," Jacquemin observed, "but to be seen."

"There you are!" The tall figure of Zélonoff emerged from a bewildered group around his five panels of rutilant inextricable architecture. He had just perceived his friends. "Let's not stay here," he said, good-humoredly. "One hears too many stupidities."

However, save for a few exclamations of indignant criticism, a dubious silence reigned at the spectacle of a novelty so hermetic: admiration, real or feigned, or the simple dread of emitting a compromising judgment of any sort...

"Have you seen Roussot?"

"Not yet—we've only just arrived."

"Magnificent! What a scandal! Vilfaux turned his head as he passed by, with an expression of disgust, as if he couldn't look at the work or the painter. I wouldn't be surprised if there's a new Director at the École des Beaux-Arts soon."

As they approached the room where *L'Après-Guerre* was, the crowd became denser. There was an audible hubbub. The name of Roussot was running around, amid interjections and laughter.

The unfinished triptych, of which only the first two panels, *Les Mercantis* and *La Gynandre* displayed their rude satire on their own partition, had burst like a bomb in the amazement of the private view. With disapproving expressions, even Roussot's friends had fallen silent before the sarcasms of some and the bilious criticisms of others.

An audience of all the profiteers of peace and war, and all the females in the evil of stupidity or hypocrisy, reinforced the jealous exhibitors. They were spreading the rumor—false but reported as certain—that Roussot had just sold his famous previous triptych, *Les Maréchals*, for three hundred thousand francs to a Danish buyer acting on behalf of a German merchant: news that completed exasperating the envy of comrades, from the most celebrated to the most obscure, and the chauvinist phobia of the society figures.

"The private viewers!" groaned Zélonoff. "Shiny on the outside and putrescent on the inside!"

Along with the cubist painter, only a few fervent pupils of Roussot's dared attest their comprehension aloud. Annik and Jacquemin were already familiar, not only with *Les Mercantis* and *La Gynandre*, but the powerful sketches of their preparation, a selection of displayed their audacious elliptical lines and patches of raw color on the other side of the partition. They rediscovered their emotion intact.

Les Mercantis! The fat profiteers, with their porcine jowls, their fresh butter craniums, their symbolic bellies, and the thin ones, with their raptorial beaks, the muzzles of hyenas and jackals; the band of base pleasure-seekers invading, in a brutal rush, a dazzling restaurant where women naked beneath fine robes were already at table, among the wines, the meats and the pâtés, in a profusion of fruits and flowers, sparkling with diamonds and pearls, in the fake daylight of electricity.

In the foreground, emerging from the shadow, was a cohort of barefoot, lice-infested individuals with savage gazes and clenched fists: ageless men and women, ragged children, mouths open, raising themselves up in order better to desire...

In the background, above the luminous décor of the orgy, was a bloody cloud in which one could distinguish the flow of blast furnaces, the bristling of factory chimneys: monstrous cannons spitting out black smoke, from which fell over the entire canvas, like ruddy moths, a rain of fragments of partly-burned banknotes.

La Gynandre, similarly, displayed in a drunken saraband all the debauchery by which Paris, simultaneously Babel and Babylon, had been infected during the war, and which, from factories and hospitals, cheap hotels and open boudoirs, had overflowed unstoppably into the streets. The canvas was one immense dance hall with multicolored lighting, where gynandrous women in short skirts were agitating with dancers of all races and all uniforms in an epileptic pell-mell of couplings.

To the right, separated by a display window, Life and Death were standing, side-by-side. Hand in hand, they were watching, one with eyeless orbits and the other with the fixed stare of the blind, the tumult of unleashed instincts, the entanglement of bodies shaken by music, like a spasmodic undulation...

Above, striping the whole upper section of the panel, there was a long gray wall of brothels, with the red light of lanterns, above a regiment of numbers. A central breach displayed the nude troop of the prostitutes, a bleak herd of pale livestock crushed beneath the earthy landslide of a pullulating mass of soldiers...

In the first row of the spectators, a gray-haired lady was waving her feathery hat and emitting gurgling sounds like an outraged turkey. It was Madame de Saint-Valentin, with whom Simone de Lourdal, red with indignation, was joining her sighs in chorus.

"It's ignoble!" declared a harsh voice, very loudly.

Amédée shivered; by the timbre, he had recognized Monsieur de Moreval. Annik perceived the wading bird at the same time as Lebeau's former mistress.

The senator took as his witness the stout Reichmeyer, a hairy, flat-footed bear. "Come on, my dear chap, you're an art-lover, whose collection is worthy of the Louvre..."

"You can say that again!" hissed Zélonoff. "Ten fakes for every genuine item."

"Let's go," said Amédée, who did not want to get into a public argument with his stepfather.

Annik, who was hungry, complied. "It would have amused me, though, to hear his stupidities!"

Squeezing Reichmeyer's arm, Monsieur de Moreval directed at him the fire of a few heartfelt phrases: practice fire, with a view to an imminent speech that the deregulation of mores—he had been discussing it with Ronchard the day before in the Rue de Richelieu—rendered necessary. He was in haste to regale the Sénat... Each of his interventions, in his capacity as the President of the League Against the Danger of Kiosks earned him noisy applause, under which his stupidity could not discern the ridicule.

"If things go on like this, France is nearing her end, and a shameful end!"

"Perhaps you're going a bit far," suggested Reichmeyer, in whom the buoyant commerce of the Grands Magasins du Tout pour Rien maintained optimism.

"No! Such is the fate of countries dishonored by debauchery! Has not antiquity—to which it is always necessary to look for our models—demonstrated that, with Rome? *Populus Romanus!* The strongest, the greatest of peoples! What vanquished it? Arms? No—lust! Lust, the mother of population!"

"Most certainly!"

"Tacitus and Juvenal were only too prophetic..."

"So, then," said Reichmeyer—who owned several Roussots, and in matters of painting always liked prices going up, "the picture they painted of mores was accurate?"

"Undoubtedly."

"Can one, then, reproach the painter—when all his life testifies, as Roussot's does, to artistic honesty—for the resemblance of the picture? Either the painting is accurate, in which case it's necessary to congratulate him for his courage, or it's slanderous and it's necessary to tear up his canvases."

"Slanderous or accurate, it presents the same danger! There are things that one ought not to say. It's a crime against the fatherland to depict one's country in such colors!"

"Even if they're veridical?"

"Especially! The foreigner, my dear! You're not thinking about the foreigner! What will he think of us? At least let's hide our flaws, if we can't destroy them. Monsieur Roussot, believe me, is a bad Frenchman."

"Perhaps," conceded Reichmeyer, impressed. He was Jewish, originally from Poland.

"Monsieur de Moreval is always right, simpered Simon de Lourdal, butting in.

She was in on the secret of Reichmeyer's desire and was striving, with regard to various Ministers and highly-place individuals, to expand his red ribbon into a rosette. She was counting, in exchange, on a subsidy for the *Appel*, not to mention a large credit for herself at the Tout pour Rien. Importantly, she introduced: "The Comtesse de Saint-Valentin."

The senator bowed deferentially after estimating the necklace and earrings. Then, satisfied with a larger audience, he went on: "It's not only a question of exactitude, in any case; it's a question of art. Ask Madame Lourdal. Now, what is? An idealization. One can, in unveiling that which, personally, I believe it is better to hide, remain decent. Look—the proof! Those charming nudes, signed by Simone, in which pleasure and vice are wittily suggested..."

Madame Lourdal uttered a modest "Oh!" for form's sake.

"But yes, yes! It is—how shall I put it?—stimulating, troubling. Roussot's nudes, by contrast—look!—are treated with a brutality that disgusts. The style, my dear—in the social interest, of course—the style is everything."

Reichmeyer sensed that style, in his own interest, required him not to persist, and when Simone Lourdal and the Comtesse moved away toward other friends, he whispered to the senator: "Speaking of the social interest, I need to confide an idea to you. What would Madame de Moreval say if, to the *Oeuvre des Asiles du Soir*, we were able to add, to the three quarters where your wife has opened her admirable dormitories, the *Soupe Populaire?* A few friends of mine have some

149

capital at their disposal at present. I can't think of a better employment...

With a sideways glance he sounded the ossified visage, and congratulated himself. *A bite!* With the promise of donating his collections to the Louvre, the twenty-five thousand francs pocketed that morning by an intermediary friend of the Minister of Commerce and the two hundred thousand sacrificed to bring the *Soupe Populaire* to the boil, it would be diabolical if he did not catch on the wing, from one Ministry or another—Hygiene, Public Education or Commerce—the "satined decoration" that was preventing him from sleeping...

IV

Since the previous evening, Annik had completed the transfer of her personal effects from the Place Saint-Sulpice to the Boulevard Raspail. The change of residence had not been complicated: three trunks and some parcels. Linen and familiar trinkets, plus a little box of books, a few philosophers and poets: her Renans, *L'Avenir de la Science* and the dear *Souvenirs*; the enchanter, Anatole France; Camille Mauclair's *De l'amour physique*; Jean Finot's *Préjugés et problème des sexes*.[30] She had reduced it to a strict minimum, leaving her professional library, furniture and paintings in the studio.

"*Adieu*, walls! *Adieu*, good table! *Adieu*, my bedroom!" she had said, caressing with her gaze or her hand the life of things that had been mingled for years with her own. She attributed to them an existence of their own, in her conviction of universal life, quivering even within the appearance of insensibility. She had reached the point where she was often prone to recite, silently, the beautiful verses of Gérard de Nerval, one of her favorite distant friends:

> *In the depths of obscure being lives a hidden god.*
> *Fear in the blind wall a gaze that spies on you;*
> *To matter itself a word is attached,*
> *Do not make it serve some impious usage.*[31]

---

[30] Jean Finot's sociological tract was published by Alcan in 1910.

[31] These lines are misquoted from "Vers dorés," in *Les Chimères* (1853). The last three lines cited are the penultimate triplet of the sonnet, while the first is a slight variation of the next line in the poem, which has "*Souvent*" [Often] rather than "*Au fond de*" [In the depths of].

"I'm leaving you now, but I'll come back almost every day."

From the threshold, before closing the door, she had embraced the vast room. A happy stage in her labor and her independence! But also, hours passed, a slight melancholy at the moment of setting out *en route* again, on the next stage of the journey...

She was only expecting happiness...but she knew that nothing new is founded without difficulty and without struggles. Thus, she felt a comfort in leaving behind her, like a lifeboat solidly anchored on the uncertain sea, the redoubt where she had hoped, loved and worked. The idea that she could find here, several times a week, along with the personal space where she would receive consultations and visits, a refuge always open to her necessary self-collection and frequent need for reflection and solitude, was very pleasant.

No less pleasant, at any rate, was the idea of installing herself completely in the quietude of a stable abode, of sharing, henceforth without reserve, with the man she loved, the diversity of days and the unity of nights. He had, within twenty-four hours and without her suspecting it, fitted out for her, beside the room with the big bed, a secretarial office, in order that she could be at home, whenever she wished. A toilet, separate from the bathroom, was attached to it.

"Darling!" she said, touched. "But, you know, I'll hardly ever be there..."

That evening, they had refused dinner with Madame Broussat and Zélonoff, who had a box for the Ballets Suédois.[32] They took a child-like pleasure in savoring the intimacy of their new closeness, celebrating the inauguration of their common life like a festival.

---

[32] The *Ballets suédois* was an *avant garde* company formed in Paris by Rolf de Maré, which performed various innovative pieces between 1920 and 1924. It was the height of fashion when *Le Compagnon* was written; the author could not know that it would soon be disbanded.

Wearily, Annik had sunk into the profound leather arm-chair that was the only comfortable seat in the study. She was reading under the beam of the electric lamp, the reflector of which Amédée, seated at his desk, had raised. He had gone back to work, opening a heap of reports and pamphlets sent by the America Chamber of Commerce. Since the war, he had been planning to visit the United States, traveling from New York to San Francisco and Chicago to New Orleans, desirous of getting to know—after England, where he had once so-journed—the great nation of business, the all-powerful finan-cier of European reconstruction.

A hazard—or an instinct?—caused him to raise his eyes as Annik dropped her book with a sudden expression of ma-laise. She put her hand to her heart, and so pale was her hand that Jacquemin got up anxiously and ran to her.

"What's the matter?"

"Nothing," she said. "Don't be alarmed."

"You frightened me."

"Oh, my stomach hurts. Let me go..."

"I'll go with you..."

"No, no, I beg you. I'll come back."

She reappeared a few moments later, her features drawn, but smiling. He questioned her with an indecisive gaze. She kept quiet, simultaneously gave and mischievous.

"What is it?" he demanded, his heart beating rapidly.

He contemplated her at length, and read the mute re-sponse to his avid interrogation.

"Do you think it is?" he stammered.

"I'm sure of it. Yes…now I'm sure."

"Oh! That's wonderful!"

He was transported by joy. At the same time, everything that he had locked away within him, since their last conversa-tion—objections, wishes, pleas, and also nascent rancor at the determination she had manifested—took form at a stroke.

"In that case, darling, no possible hesitations now. It's necessary to resign yourself to becoming my wife. You must, for the sake of that which is mine, as well as yours... Think about it. Henceforth, if you hesitate, you'll only have bad reasons for opposing me."

"But..."

She perceived the astonishment on his face, and above all the pain, on divining what she was going to say to him again. Driven by the profound impulse of her conviction, however, she asked him: "Why no more hesitation? What has changed?"

"You, an advocate, can ask me that, tranquilly? When you know the prejudice, idiotic but powerful, that still militates in our society against natural filiation..."

"Exactly! Since we, personally, mock those prejudices! Since we can give our child the education and also the financial security that will shelter him from those idiotic prejudices, powerful as they are... Isn't it up to us to set an example?"

He shrugged his shoulders, annoyed. "Let's not get carried away. It's not in a generation that the stage can be accomplished. Our children will live in a society manifestly similar to ours. In that society, can you guarantee that our son—our daughter even more so!—won't risk, one day, in spite of his education, having to suffer?"

"Don't you admit that one can suffer for the sake of an idea? Then again, have you not put forward a proposal for a law that..."

He cut her off. "Yes, yes! But from the deposition to the vote...we and our grandchildren might die beforehand! Remember that, for divorce, it was necessary to wait, after the Restoration, the July Monarchy and the Empire, for another twenty years of the Republic! Let's be pioneers—I want that—but let's not disarm ourselves at the outset."

She continued with all her valor: "On the contrary, we'll arm ourselves! Every consciousness that awakes, today, is a suffering being born. Our children, whose minds we shall have formed from the first breath, will suffer less tomorrow. By liberating them even before they draw breath, and showing them the right road as soon as they open their eyes, what strength we'll give them! I'll turn your argument back on you: now, no more hesitation is possible!"

He sighed. "Little Annik, exalted heart! Be careful! Unjust as it is, this society is, for generations yet to come, the one in which our child will have to live. You don't have the right to allow him to be born illegitimate."

"Ah! Allow me to laugh! So, your mother's son, you've rediscovered your heredity, your spiritual patrimony!"

"And the time is ripe! The other day, when I pressed you to consent to our marriage, I was, it's true, only thinking of me; I was speaking as a man. Now, after the immense joy you've given me, now that I *know*, now that our son is here, already present, I'm speaking to you with the authority of a father. I want him to enter into a veritable hearth, a stable family. He'll only be more pampered by everyone—his parents, his grandparents, our friends..."

Annik could not hold back her tears.

He took her hands. "You understand, Madame Jacquemin?"

"No. I don't understand at all. It's all this social baggage with which you're embarrassing yourself that, even at the risk of causing you pain, I want to spare, from the very outset...*my* child! Oh, no, no! Let's not prolong this futile and painful argument. Less than ever, Amédée, must you count on my acceptance. For more than ever, henceforth, I need my legal independence with regard to you. Don't worry—think about it. What can it matter to you, since we always act in good accord? Have I not consented to live entirely with you henceforth? Here, I'm yours, outside of my working hours. Today above all, when the greatest good fortune has come our way, oh, my darling, don't torment me anymore! Only think, like me, of the joy of reincarnating our love, of prolonging it, in a little being. Tell me—am I not right?"

Tenderly, she had taken his head, imposing her persuasion upon him. She sat on his knees, her arms around his neck, pressing herself against him affectionately. She listened to his heart beating, silently following the train of his thought. She

155

sensed that it was calmer, but, in spite of everything, divergent. She did not try to dig any deeper.

She lightened her tone: "And then, you know, it's necessary not to oppose me—it's a craving!"

She said to herself: *Little by little, I'll convince him...*

Softened by the contact, in which their desire was inevitably reignited, she soon ceased to reflect...she was no longer concerned with determination, or affirming which of the two of them was right. She closed her eyes, relaxed as if by an anesthetic, at the approach of voluptuousness.

Annik had taken over the direction of the household, only leaving the employment of the food budget to Madame Danvois. She even consented to occupy herself with Amédée's business and to advise him in the management of his fortune. She was only obstinate on one point: that of ensuring her upkeep with her own personal resources.

The days and weeks passed by, May and then June. Although, by tacit agreement, they had excluded from their speech any allusion to the sore point—her determination to remain entirely independent—the discord weighed upon them. It floated over the evenness of the hours like a stormy sun over a plain.

They often spoke about the future, the host of projects that her pregnancy, as yet invisible, stacked up on the imminent horizon. If it were a son, they would call him Claude, after his Jacquemin grandfather. A daughter? He would have liked her to have Madame de Moreval's name, but at the first desire he had manifested, Annik had been unable to hide her repugnance. While comprehending the antipathy she nourished against his family—an antipathy of which he was sure—he regretted, in his unconscious traditionalism, that rift between the two families, and that his mother could not be loved by his wife.

"A daughter?" Annik had said in order to avoid the collision. "And why not call her Claude, too? It's no less pretty in the feminine..."

As the months went by, Amédée became more somber. He was wondering how to bring Annik round to the marriage before the birth of their child. He lost sleep over it. Annik followed, dolorously, the labor that was talking place within his thoughts.

Constantly, in the afternoons, the obligatory absences of Amédée, in the midst of the political struggle, left her alone. She abandoned herself then, in spite of the diversion of work—consultations, the Palais—to her preoccupations. She foresaw, as the deadline approached, and inevitable hard combat. She tried, by seeing her friends more, and renewing contact with her sister, to react against that tendency to pessimism. At the same time, in the attempt to escape her obsession, she devoted herself to her professional duties with a more quotidian application.

The Salle des Pas Perdus saw her on a regular basis. With a briefcase stuffed with files under her arm, she strode over the floor tiles, always busy, saluted from all sides. Consideration had increased! She noticed it in the broader smiles and the deeper nods of the wigs. She replied to them with distant good grace. *Oh, if they didn't find me attractive...and if they didn't know that I was Amédée's companion...*

She would have liked to attribute her success entirely to her talent.

She confessed that to him after winning a case when he inquired—it was always the first question they asked one another when they came in—how her day had gone.

He reacted reflexively, with a vivacity that pained her. "You're asking too much! Men are men. If your métier causes you disappointments, why exercise it? Nothing's forcing you to do so!"

She had looked at him in astonishment. What ill humor! His expression revealed, perhaps unwittingly, more than it said. But what could he find to resent in such a normal employment of her faculties and her time?

157

She limited herself to replying: "Nothing forces me, it's true—but the same applies to you. Could you conceive of life without your work?"

"It's not exactly the same thing."

"Not the same thing? Why not?"

The announcement of dinner cut the conversation short, but she conserved a shadow of it. Not the same thing? She sought to distinguish his hidden agenda. The sentiment of a man that the roles of husband and wife, in association, are essentially different, enclosing each of them, by custom, in their own employment? Evidently. Even the most liberated, then, were possessive egotists, like all the rest!

She did not go any further, unable to suspect that the celebrated advocate looked with a jaundiced eye on her practicing, and succeeding in, the same profession as him. No, of that pettiness—frequent, however, in household whose members exercise similar métiers—she sincerely did not believe him to be capable.

She took advantage of one Thursday when the Chambre was in session and she was free to re-steep herself in the amity of Mademoiselle Hardy. Mérette welcomed her with her habitual joy. On finding her so good, she reproved herself for having neglected her when she had no need of her.

"How is your pregnancy going?"

"Very well."

"I've been longing to see you," said the old spinster. "Here, except for my little ones, I live in a hermitage. Without the Blanchets, I wouldn't see anyone."

"How are they?"

"Hmm—I believe that recently there's been a slight rift between them."

"Oh!" said Annik, incuriously, primarily anxious as she was about her own troubles. "I thought perhaps I'd call in to say *bonjour*. It's two months since I last saw them. I don't know where the time goes."

Since her first visit, linked in her memory with the unforgettable anniversary, she had become friends with Monique

158

and had established a frank sympathy with George Blanchet. They had seen one another often, had dined with one another. "The spectacle of their union is a joy to behold," she had even said, last time they had dined in the Boulevard Raspail.

She remembered Amédée's melancholy "Yes." He had added, with a sigh: "They're *entirely* happy. Marriage has been successful for Monique..."

When she reported that remark to Mademoiselle Hardy, the latter also sensed the disguised reproach therein.

"Still the same mania, then—marriage?"

"More than ever."

"I understand it a little better now, you know. It's difficult for a man, even one as intelligent and good as him, suddenly to dismantle the habits of thought and feeling that have held sway for so long. It's all very well to be as advanced as he is in theory, but when one has to put it to work, its different..."

"Oh, I understand it, too—and I feel sorry for him. Yes, I'm the first to suffer from the chagrin I'm causing him. But what can I do? I haven't promised him anything. On the contrary, I've always declared, for as long as he's known me, that I'd never marry. The laws are too badly made."

"Since you live together and he'll recognize your child, let him say fie to the rest!"

"You're touching the most sensitive spot there. The recognition! I tremble when I think that it will be necessary, before I give birth, to bring up that subject. I put it off every day. He'll have to resign himself to it, though."

"What's the problem? You're worrying me..." Mademoiselle Hardy put her hand on her heart. She was very pale.

Annik looked at her tenderly. "How well I know, thanks to my métier, the legislation to which we're subordinate, even in free union! Listen to this, Mérette! *Law relating to the protection of natural children*. Once the Code gets mixed up in protecting them, it is, *naturally*, against the mother! *Article One*—oh, I know it by heart—*The parent who is the first rec-*

ognized shall have paternal authority, and, in the case of simultaneous recognition, the father."

"Only the father?"

"Yes."

"The father—I understand. But first, forgive me while I make a note, for the little book I'm writing, my *Practical Code for the Usage of Women.* It's frightful, our ignorance of juridical matters! Me first, as you see! The essentials of the Law—that's an elementary notion that ought to be taught in schools, instead of a heap of unnecessary things![33] Don't you think? The law relating...good...since when?"

"The second of July 1907."

"Thank you. With the consequence that if you want to conserve the right to bring up your child as you intend..."

"I'll be forced to ask Amédée only to recognize him after me."

"He'll never agree."

"Yes he will."

"You think so?"

"He can't refuse it to me. To remain mistress of the education of my children is the most important reason for my refusal to marry!"

"I fear that he might refuse, in his turn. Think, my dear child, of the chagrin and humiliation of a man, a father, constrained to enounce the first of his rights...a privilege, if you wish, but whose usage makes the law as much as the law! I can just see him at the Mairie, registering your child, as he'll want to do, and allowing the inscription: *father unknown!*"

"He can recognize him the following day."

"Think about it! What an abdication! You're asking the impossible—it's too cruel."

---

[33] In fact, it had been proposed in 1887 that *Droit usuel* [the essentials of the Law] should be taught in primary schools, but the plan never made it into law and in 1905 it was scrapped, the subject being restricted to secondary schools.

"But Mérette, it's for that liberation that you've worked, sacrificing your entire life! That which, while remaining a spinster, you've dared to teach me, the daughter of your heart, ought I not, no matter how cruel the struggle might be, try to accomplish that?"

"Yes. But what resistance! Before Amédée agrees to efface himself from a task that he's capable of fulfilling almost as well as you..."

"I know that. Amédée, whom I adore, doesn't merit that suspicion. A just man is paying for the iniquitous. Oh, if he'll only realize that a fatality surpasses us, that the woman whom he loves is obliged to defend herself, even against him... Tell me, am I not right?"

Mademoiselle Hardy enveloped her tenderly with her beautiful blue gaze, the limpidity of which was saddened, and only offered doubt.

"At any rate," Annik sighed, "we still have time. It's not due for another five months... Until then..."

"Try to live without making yourself suffer, darling. There's no plant as rare as happiness! Fundamentally, I believe, it's not on either marriage or free union that it depends. Madame Broussat is right; it's on us. You're tormenting yourself with this child you want to be yours alone, and which is dividing Amédée and you in advance. And Monique and Blanchet, in spite of the beautiful children that now unite them..."

"Oh yes...Monique! Tell me..."

"You know that the principal household income, even though Blanchet has his own fortune, comes from the interior design studios founded by Monique when she was Mademoiselle Lerbier: *Le Chardon Bleu*..."

"So?"

"Well, she had entirely discharged responsibility for them, while retaining ownership, to her secretary, the Russian, Mademoiselle..."

"Tcherbalief—Claire Tcherbalief, who has married Baron Plombino. Zélonoff knows her."

"And as the latter no longer occupies herself with the company, where she has put some steward in charge, *Le Chardon Bleu*, in spite of its fashionability, is failing. Monique wants to take over the direction again. Blanchet is opposed to it. Hence the quarrels.

"You see," said Annik, "the inconvenience of alienating one's liberty!"

"Oh," said Mademoiselle Hardy, "they adore one another. She'll give in."

V

Paule and her lover had just unknotted their embrace on the ravaged bed.[34]

Exhausted, as if after a furious struggle or a vertiginous voyage, they remained motionless, lying on their backs. Finally, he opened his eyes and touched her hand. She shivered at the contact.

He smiled on perceiving, beneath the gilded thicket of fine hair, the pink flush of her face. The torso projected its cups, full and firm. One knee bent, the other was extended to show off, with the design of the hips, in the noble planes of the belly, the maternity that had been visible for some time.

He contemplated her with the profound gaze in which gratitude softened pride, and flashed the complex expression of which she loved so movingly that she suddenly sat up, throwing an arm around his neck, and, with her head on his shoulder, murmured passionately: "My own!"

But today—a more languid fatigue, a preoccupation returned?—Paule was meditative, her gaze distant...

Mechanically, he asked her his habitual question, the one that his entire loving being was obliged to launch untiringly, like a sound, into the mystery of the soul that he thought he had subjugated, but which instinct regripped if it did not feel itself perpetually retaken.

"What are you thinking?"

Sure as he believed himself to be of the unreturnable gift of his mistress. Roger knew that love is not a property that can

---

[34] This is the point at which "La Femme en chemin" begins, although a few retrospective paragraphs relating the history of Paule's marriage and affair with Roger and filling in the background of Annik's character are moved from the first few chapters of the earlier story back to earlier points in *Le Compagnon*.

be acquired once and for all, but so precarious and so precious a wealth that it needs to be merited by an incessant purchase...

She sighed. Immediately, he regretted his maladroit interrogation. He could guess all too easily what unique thought was absorbing Paule's reflection at that moment, at the same time as his own chagrin: their last rendezvous before long months of obligatory separation, and the imminent parting...an *au revoir* as heart-rending as an *adieu*!

She turned onto her side and put her arms around him, as if she were hanging on to the sole support of her existence. Without saying anything about the principal torment—because she had sworn to be strong—she spoke, nervously:

"I think I ought to go home. Home! That prison camp in which I have nothing of my own, except the hope of our little Ginette..."

She wanted a daughter, and to call her Gi. With an instinctive gesture, she had lifted up the sheet to veil her nudity. Since her pregnancy, outside of the times when everything was abolished in the vertigo of their caresses, she had recovered a modesty in love, less by virtue of the relaxation of her Catholic hypocrisy than a sentiment of complex coquetry: a delicacy that reconciled her, inconsequentially, to the amorality of the double deception.

Under the veil with which Paulette had coiffed it, along with her hat, when she undressed, the clock spelled out, in the silence, the silvery chimes of the hour: four...five...six...

"Six o'clock," she repeated, sadly.

"Already!" said Roger.

She stretched her limbs.

Sitting on the edge of the bed, she pulled her stockings on. She had already put on her finely drawn chemise, whose pink color went so well with the whiteness of her skin that Roger, still lying down, pulled her toward him in order to kiss the roundness of her softly satin-clad shoulder.

"No, leave me be now. I'll be late."

She stood up with a brisk movement. He copied her. Life, with its monotony and its mediocrity, immediately gripped them again, at the same time as the uniform of custom, the livery of servitude. They had never experienced its heaviness so painfully—and at the same time, an increasing anguish strangled the necessity of their speech.

With all their will and all their courage they had promised one another not to sadden their last conversation before the inevitable departure with futile regrets. Even more than Roger, Paule was determined. And the less she wanted to say, the more involuntarily she showed it. What did the voyage she dreaded so much reserve for her? He had, of course, promised to return in September, the anticipated time of the birth, but she could see nothing except darkness, the perilous sea, her hostile house, her jeering husband…all the somber uncertainty of the future.

A specialist in matters of banking, as well as an industrialist open to the newest methods, Roger Jouves, long before meeting Paule, had meditated going to develop relationships with the Japanese formed under the previous Mikado by a Chabaz resident in Osaka, and who had been able to establish important outlets for the firm of Jouves and Chabaz on his return. At the same time as a retail business dealing in all kinds of electric gods, Roger, in association with a few friends in banking, had thought of founding an agency of lading and commercial credit in Osaka, when the Societé Centrale opened in Paris. That would enable the operation of a vast exchange of merchandise, and hence—with capital, probity and skill—the possibility of a magnificent fortune. Certainly, there were risks! Was that not necessary, in order for success to have its full amplitude, and its full price?

Now, what had been, thus far, just a project, had materialized, in the brutal surge of actuality: the separation, the *adieu!* Suddenly, the mirage vanished. They were before the ditch—an abyss, Paule foresaw, in the nervousness that she could not overcome.

"A drop of port?" he said. "We need to finish it."

She listened to the descent within herself of those words devoid of precise significance, which nevertheless burned her like an acid. *Finish...finish...* She saw the sea extend, limitless, a boat fleeing, with the cherished face, and disappearing...

Roger knotted his cravat in front of the mirror. He perceived her distressed features therein. With a bound, he was beside her, putting his arm around her, consoling her.

"Since it's for our happiness! Since you're as sure of me as I am of you...since it's necessary...and since, when I return, the divorce..."

"I know," she stammered. "I beg your pardon...but it's stronger than me."

Tears pearled in the corners of her eyes. She made an effort to get a grip on herself, stamping her foot.

"It's idiotic. We swore that we wouldn't talk about it, but regardless...

She tried to regain control, dabbing her tear-stained cheeks with her minuscule handkerchief, soon soaked, and accepted, from the hands of the desolate Roger, one that he had just taken from his chest of drawers and was holding out, unfolded into a vast square. She tried to smile.

"I could dampen half a dozen like that," she said, "if they weren't such coarse cloth. Only good for blowing the nose! You could at least have given me one of those I bought you!"

"They're preciously packed away in the trunk, next to your perfume...and look, here's your photo!" He opened his wallet. "You see, I'll never stop thinking about you."

He finished drying her swollen eyes with little kisses.

"The thought of you, and me...it's the thought of you and our future Gi that will be my comfort every minute. You'll accompany me. It's because of you that I'm departing confidently, and thanks to you that I'll support the absence valiantly. Your image will defend me against solitude and ennui."

She shook her head. And without even thinking about the counter-insurance that she had taken, with regard to her husband, and of which she was resigned, at some stage, to make the settlement, she said: "You'll have your distractions...the voyage, your work...and then, a man has more courage."

He looked at her with an affection so tender that she was moved by it, even though, through the compassionate expression, she detect a kind of internal satisfaction at the idea of impending action and the unexpected, of effort and adventure. Her heart was suddenly bitten by a sharp jealousy.

"Swear that you won't forget me! And those villainous women who look like little mechanical dolls...I have a horror of them, with their submissive attitude and their hooded eyes..."

She captured him entirely with a possessive gaze. He was so handsome, with his tall, slim stature, his clean-shaven face and his slightly long brown hair combed back to reveal a high forehead, frank and energetic. She sounded the light in his chestnut-brown eyes, so magnetic, which were going to pose on other feminine faces.

He laughed brightly, which reassured her. She savored his oath, as if she herself were without reproach.

"You can be tranquil, darling. There's no longer any room in my heart for any other woman. You're here, here, and here..."

He sketched an expressive gesture, touching successively his forehead, his heart and...lower down.

She shivered, laughing. "A funny sign of the cross! My sweet, I, too, have you in my blood. That's what gives me the strength to wait for you...and to struggle. For I dread being all alone in the house, with that vile man!"

"Would you like me to stay, if you fear that something...? I'd prefer to abandon everything than to..."

She read Roger's anxiety in his face, and, in order not to torment him with a graver preoccupation, said: "Bah! We'll carry things through, Annik and me. Leave without any anxiety; when you come back, I'll free myself..."

A few moments later, a door to open, and she would leave first, alone...

They would each go in a different direction, toward their destiny. He was leaving Paris that same evening, bound for Marseilles on the evening express. In their equal horror of separations that the waiting prolongs on station platforms, amid the bustle and the indifference, until the supreme disarray of the adieux, they had preferred to exchange the last kiss in secret, in Roger's apartment, in the sweet intimacy of their privacy.

They contemplated one another silently. She fell into the extended arms. At that supreme moment, no more than at any other time, was there any consciousness within her of her duplicity, but the instinct of a light heart flying successively, with the same terrible sincerity, back and forth between her pleasure and her interest.

"My lover, my life," she begged, "don't forget to write to me every evening, as I shall write myself. Let every post bring me a true journal—at Annik's address, as agreed? A dispatch from Marseilles, and one from every port of call. And afterwards, at regular intervals, in order that I can be patient while awaiting your letters..."

He looked at her, at the tears in her eyes, and responded *yes, yes* to every instruction. Then, seeing that, in spite of the stiffening of his will, he was about to be overtaken by sobs, she had the presence of mind to cut it short. She enveloped him one last time with a brief, total contemplation, in which, at the same time as she enclosed him passionately within herself, she hurled at him, as a viaticum, all the ardor that she was experiencing at that moment. And, precipitately, she left...

It was only on the staircase that she felt herself buckle, as if, in quitting him, she had lost all her strength. It seemed to descend within her, something dead, into oblivion...

"All the same," said Annik, dropping the newspaper, "Lebeau's exaggerating."

Almost every day since the opening of the Salon, the *Appel* had mounted a campaign against *Les Mercantis* and *La Gynandre*. When it was not a piece by Lebeau, it was a nauseous article by the art critic Simone, flagellating "the impudent" on behalf of the Virtue of French Womanhood.

Amédée suspended above his coffee cup the little spoon with which he had just stirred in his sugar.

"Another article against Roussot?"

"As ever! Listen: *Let not the Director of ordure think himself safe because justice has not yet been done. Jean Roussot, in trying to tarnish the good renown of France, in the eyes of foreigners, by means of an abject depiction of our mores, is merely guilty of recidivism. Has he not tried already, with is famous triptych of the Maréchals, to sully national glory? His pretention of plying the moralist, when he is merely amusing himself picking up gold in the mud, is what sickens me most in this tragic farce!*"

"Damn!" said Amédée. "That is, indeed, a bit strong! But for anyone who knows Roussot, and his disinterest, it's idiotic."

"Listen! It's not finished: *Woe to the Profiteers of Lust, who have the audacity to cover their merchandise with the flag of ideas! It is up to the government, while waiting to pluck up the courage to drag this public malefactor into the courts for outraging morality, to apply other sanctions. I am told that numerous complaints have already been lodged at the Ministry of Public Education as well as the Court. Will this hooligan of the paintbrush be left free to continue any longer his official poisoning at the École des Beaux-Arts? Let him be expelled before the prosecution is launched. We hope that the Ministries of Public Education and Justice, and the President of the Republic, will not allow themselves to be intimidated any longer by the consideration of a certain relationship. Let Monsieur Vilfaux, a member of the Académie des Science Morales et Politiques, forget political compromises in order to remember his moral obligations!"*

"Bang!" exclaimed Amédée. "Straight in the stomach of Pierre Roussot! If it's not you, it's your brother!"

He had fully digested, as a dilettante, that bowl of bile. In his opinion, such attacks, to which he knew that Roussot was, in any case, insensible, falling from such a pen, aroused nothing but scorn.

"We've arrived!" he concluded. "Everything becomes clear. That violent frenzy, incomprehensible at first—for, after all, the boor is intelligent...crapulous if you like, but intelligent—has but one aim: to attack, via the younger brother, the elder, against whom Lebeau is standing for office in the IXth. This time he's shown the tips of his ears...there's the doorbell. Are you expecting someone?"

"Yes, Madame Broussat and Zélonoff. All three of us are going, in fact, to visit Roussot. I forgot to tell you...I knew that you weren't free."

"What?" he joked. "No Palais today?"

She sensed the sarcastic intention, but simply replied: "No, only my consultations in the Place Saint-Sulpice, after Roussot. No Palais."

"Fortunately, you have your friends to distract you—otherwise, you'd be at a loose end."

Thanks to the entrance of the painter and Madame Broussat, toward whom she went with open arms, Annik was able to pretend not to have heard. She nevertheless perceived, like the prick of a pin, the dart of the observation, and, beneath the light tone, the weight of his increasing hostility against her activity in their common métier.

"The *Appel*," said Zélonoff, pushing the newspaper away with his foot like a dirty rag. "You've read the Lebeau? What a filthy individual! Funnily enough, I'm going to see him this evening. I accepted an invitation to dinner at the home of the Comtesse de Saint-Valentin."

Annik remembered the name from having read it in recent society columns. "You're placing yourself well, Prince!" she mocked.

He bowed, humorously. "I ought to tell you that this Comtesse—Belgian nobility, it appears—is a curious woman. Between parentheses, a rather old picture, although in painting, she's in the swing. She bought my latest canvas—for next to nothing, and hasn't yet paid me. One encounters All Paris in her salon. Today there'll be Ronchard, Reichmeyer—*Tout pout Rien!*—and…you'll never guess…the Morevals, my dear. Who else? Solmou, the Minister of Justice, the Lourdals, and—naturally—Lebeau..."

"What a salad!"

"Russian," said Zélonoff. "I rather like these mixtures." With a broad smile addressed to Madame Broussat, he added: "Not every evening!"

"You're alone, then?" said Annik. "You can dine with us. Monsieur Zélonoff can come to pick you up.

"Agreed," he said, after having consulted his companion with a glance. "You don't know, Mesdames, what a comedy you're missing by depriving yourself of going into society occasionally."

"All the Comtesses de Saint-Valentin resemble one another," declared Madame Broussat, "and so, in consequence, do all their diners. When you've seen one..."

"The imagination is sufficient for me to vomit in advance," said Annik, getting up.

"Always excessive!"

Amédée had uttered the observation so softly that its tone only retained amity, but the reproach struck her regardless. She looked at him sideways. How resentful he must be, to be able, in spite of himself—at least, she supposed so—to take every opportunity to exhale his bitter rancor.

"You're leaving me, then?" he said, escorting the visitors out and kissing Annik.

She took advantage of the fact that they were already in the antechamber, and swiftly stepped back into the study. "But you're going out yourself?"

"Not immediately."

"What! You have a meeting at three."

"I don't have to be here until four. Between now and then, I have work to do." He indicated the heap of letters, files and books, fearsome in spite of their careful ordering.

"Do you want me to stay?"

"No need. I'm used to doing without you in the afternoons."

"You're never here"

"And when I am, you're not."

"How could I know?"

"What do you expect? If it's not one thing it's another: the Palais, your consultations, your friends. It's a fact. Go, go—it's of no importance. I'm just making the observation."

She kissed him hastily. She was torn between the desire to offer her excuses to Madame Broussat in order to keep him company and the regret of not going to offer Roussot their sympathy, at an opportune moment. She made her decision.

"Until this evening. You'll find me here when you get back."

No, she was not going to yield to a caprice that was of no significance in itself, if it was not pregnant with danger: a new threat, doubtless confused, but which she saw, apprehensively, gradually taking form.

A surprise awaited her at the Beaux-Arts. They found Roussot in the middle of moving house. Sickened by the violence of the attacks of which he was the object, he had sent his resignation as Director of the École to the Ministry of Public Education the day before.

"Yes, my friend, I've had it up to here! Oh, I know what they'll say. I can read tomorrow's piece by Lebeau in advance: *This gesture if apparent disdain is really only prudence....Jean Roussot is putting on a show of thumbing his nose at the pub-*

lic authorities by resigning from a post from which he was about to be ignominiously sacked...a clever feint that will not fool anyone...etcetera, etcetera..."

"How sad, all the same!" Annik exclaimed.

"The swine!" muttered Zélonoff.

"Leave it be," said Roussot. "I had a chain around my neck; now I'm free."

Pipe in mouth, he was presiding serenely over the arrangements. He was in haste to clear out his studio, strewn with large packing crates.

His friends helped. Zélonoff, in his shirt-sleeves, had immediately set to work. The immense room seemed empty, with its walls completely bare, since the removal of *Les Maréchals*. It had been sold, not to a Danish dealer, but to the celebrated antiquarian Silgemann, acting surreptitiously for Reichmeyer, who was clever but prudent, as long as his rosette had not appeared in the *Officiel*...

"Everything they're saying!" exclaimed Roussot, spitting philosophically after a well-drawn puff of smoke. "What a heap of cretins! In any case, the first result of their campaign has been to allow me to sell anything I wish! The sketches for *La Gynandre*! I could have made a thousand instead of five hundred, and they'd have gone. My two large panels, of course, I'll keep. I'll exhibit them again, later...when I've finished the third. You know—Adam and Eve, the march toward the future city! Then they'll see, if they want to see. In the meantime, *bien le bonjour*—there's salubrious air on the Maures coast. You don't know my little corner? Cork-oaks, pines, the sun, the sea...and a studio big enough for brushing triptychs! You'll have to come to see me. Paradise! For three years, since I found the place, I've been saying to myself: you must be mad to spend half the year in Paris! So, now that nothing's keeping me here any longer..."

Zélonoff, who could not imagine that one could live anywhere but the Avenue Kléber, exclaimed: "Quit Paris! But that's insane! First of all, you still have to defend yourself..."

Roussot pointed to a half-burned piece of paper, with which he had lit his pipe. "The prosecution? It's gross. No, I don't believe they dare! My brother told me yesterday that Solmou, in response to the insistences of several Societies of Decency, said: 'Legal action? You know that the painting will be acquitted. No one is convicted nowadays for things like that.' And it's a fact that, if one were condemned for things like that, it would be necessary also to put in prison, logically, all those who served me as models! That would be far-reaching..."

"That's true," said Zélonoff. "All the same, we've seen funny things in the last ten years. The war gave us such a rude shock that the lees are rising to the surface everywhere..."

Annik left him in the company of Madame Broussat. She had asked Roussot for permission to embrace him. She was more emotional than he was about the astonishing adventure that had overtaken him. What Phariseeism? Everything, as soon as she thought about it, excited her anger. The impunity of the grandees responsible for the Slaughter, that of the ambitious and the incapable who had prolonged it militarily, that of the profiteers at the rear growing fat on public ruination, whose paunches the ill-made peace had finished rounding out... At the top, a fury for lucre, a vertigo of depravity; at the bottom, a lassitude, a spinelessness, of having submitted to so much, and suffered so much...a rancor still contained, but growing... And the clique of the Private View believed, with its fit of fake virtue, that it was deceiving anyone? What derision!

The necessity of exteriorization, of responding to the two visitors with whom she had a rendezvous, had secured her the habitual diversion when she left the studio in order to go home rapidly, to get there before Amédée. Her penchant for perpetual examination always yielded to her innate appetite for action.

The evening was agitated, entirely, by her narrations and those of Madame Broussat, the fire of which Zélonoff came to stoke at eleven o'clock. He related, in brief and truculent terms, the amusing farce of his dinner and its aftermath: ladies in the salon, gentlemen in the smoking room, naturally.

"There's no other word for it by farce! No! Ronchard, omnipotent, discussing armaments with Cesson, inflated by his naval orders..."

"Cesson?" said Amédée, smiling at the memory of the Antoinette proposal. "He must be radiant at his acquittal."

Prosecuted for the distribution of fictitious dividends in one of the numerous companies he had founded during the war, the case against shipping magnate had just collapsed.

"But the funniest thing was Reichmeyer bowing down before Solmou and Solmou before Lebeau. No, it's true, you would have laughed. The *Tout pour Rien* courting, with his spine bent, the master of the Grande-Chancellerie, donor of officers' crosses, and the *Appel*, chest swollen, reprimanding the master of the Court, reluctant to bring charges... Solmou's eyes, Jovian in listening to Reichmeyer, and that amicable smile, in listening to Lebeau. A fine affair, in sum, for the Minister, this Roussot business. One gives Holy Water to the *Appel*, whom one believes to be powerful, and one encourages a dirty trick against a political adversary..."

"That will teach Pierre Roussot to get mixed up in reconstituting the left-wing bloc against the Bloc National!" said Annik.

"But what surpasses everything, which Flaubert would have found most *hénaurme*,[35] is the rascality of Lebeau. He confessed—yes, my dear, confessed in front of your stepfather and me—that he hasn't even set foot in the Salon! He's talked about the picture without even having seen it! I exclaimed: 'At least, that way, you're impartial!' And do you know what he had the cheek to reply to me?"

Zélonoff imitated the hoarse voice: "'Certainly. I don't risk being influenced. The opinion of Monsieur de Moreval,

---

[35] *Hénaurme* is a literary term, copied from Flaubert by other writers, used to indicate a hyperbolic exaggeration of *énorme* [in this sense, monstrous].

from whose authority no one dissents, was expressed in the presence of Madame Lourdal. That suffices for my religion. There is, in any case, but once voice, Prince—except that of Soviet cubism, of course'—that was for my benefit—"in recognizing that *La Gynandre* is the ultimate in obscenity. And Moscow, happily, no more than all the Roussots of the world, has not yet been able to impose its dictatorship on us…'

"'But *La Gynandre*,' I put in, 'isn't Pierre's; it's Jean's.'"

"Then he looked at me pityingly. 'Everything is connected, in politics as in art. Today, there must no longer be any but one France, that of the Victory. By combating, on all the battlefields that I can reach, those who risk lessening her prestige, I'm accomplishing a duty of public salubrity…' And *zimbalaboom!*"

Amédée laughed. "The devil! He already said that the day before yesterday at the Salle Penthièvre. It's a chorus!"

"Would you like to know what I think?" said Madame Broussat, sickened. "Ronchard, Solmou and Lebeau equal Battage & Co.[36] On everyone else's back, unfortunately!"

"So much the worse for the sheep," Annik opined, "if they allow themselves to be shorn. They have only to change shepherds."

"We're working for that," said Amédée, with an involuntary yawn that gave the signal for departure.

"You're tiring yourself out too much!" said Annik, a few days later, one morning when Amédée was complaining of a headache. "Send everyone packing today. Your elections, you elections! They might as well have been brought forward. They're not until October! Two months of campaigning! Take your vacation like everyone else."

---

[36] The term *battage* [beating or threshing] has numerous meanings in different contexts, one of which is similar to the English "drum-beating" in the sense of vulgar publicity or rabble-rousing.

"Like everyone else? Do you think my electors are idle? The workers don't have vacations."

"But the Chambre does. You can take a week or two off. Since you don't want to go too far, why don't we go stay in Versailles for a while? We love it so much. And it's so good at the Trianon! You'll have Blanchet and I'll have Mérette—not to mention Monique."

He had allowed himself to be convinced, all the more easily because he saw it as a means of persuading her. The change of scene, the intimacy recreated in its entirety by the long days spent side by side...perhaps he would succeed, more easily, in triumphing over her stubbornness, in making her go back on a decision that could not have been definitively made...

They enjoyed, like a bath after harassing labor, the green daylight of the solemn pathways in the abandonment of the park. Behind the artificial plaything of the Petit Trianon, with its melancholy English garden, and the décor, falling into ruins, of the Hameau, where Marie Antoinette played milkmaid while the monarchy crumbled, they had discovered a corner, the majesty of the Grand Trianon. Le Nôtre's designs were still visible,[37] as in the times of the Sun King, with their starry intersections, but everywhere nature had regained the upper hand, with its invading vegetation and its profound undergrowth.

They undertook a pilgrimage to the holy place. The bushes were still thickening their virginal verdure along the colonnades of the temple. The same blue bindweed was flourishing in the same place. Why, at the memory that their thoughts tried piously to revive, could they not find themselves as completely happy as before? Why, far from completing their communion, did the infantile presence that had now revealed itself in Annik's womb continue, so contrary to their initial hopes, to deepen the misunderstanding between them?

---

[37] André Le Nôtre (1613-1700) was Louis XIV's landscape architect, who designed the park of the Palace of Versailles.

The sage influence of Mademoiselle Hardy, and her appeasing philosophy, did not succeed—to her great despair—in helping them to understand one another better, in spite of their reciprocal desire for concessions. Annik put all her instinct of conservation, as Amédée put all his atavism and domination, into not giving way: a latent antagonism from which, without having the simplicity of confessing it, they suffered as much as one another.

A visit to the Blanchets, in which they arrived unexpectedly in the middle of a dolorous scene, completed the anchorage of Annik's resolution, at the same time as it excited Amédée's rebellion.

"Oh, you've arrived at a good time!" Georges Blanchet had cried, on perceiving them at the far side of the lawn.

Already, several times, Annik had had the sensation that the Blanchet household was falling into complete discord. Mérette was right, there was more than disagreement; there was tension, and it was dramatic! Only the respect for politeness had prevented Monique and her husband from drawing them into the argument on previous occasions. This time, the cup was full; the bitterness was overflowing.

"I'll make you the judge, old man," said the professor, taking Amédée by the arm and placing him between himself and Monique. "There...you're up to date: still the story of *Le Chardon Bleu*. Monique, under the pretext that the business is going downhill, and that she can't find anyone to replace, as is necessary, Madame Plombino—who, between ourselves, has chucked it in—Monique is absolutely determined to take over the direction of the business. If she intends to occupy herself with it seriously, our intimate life is finished. For a start, she'll no longer be able to nurse..."

Instinctively, Annik had sat down next to her friend, and kissed her with a tenderness that she would have liked to be comforting. Personally, she took her side against her husband. It was Monique's right to work, if she wanted to, and from the moment that it was the surest means of protecting her interests....

"Don't falsify the case!" said Monique. "You know very well that my milk is diminishing, and that it will be necessary to wean Sylvestre.'"

"At any rate, she'll no longer be able to occupy herself with her children…and, naturally, it goes without saying, with her husband. *Le Chardon Bleu* is such a large enterprise that it will absorb all of her time, fatally…."

"Three hours a day in the afternoon? Since Mademoiselle Hardy has found me an excellent deputy…"

"She says that! But soon it will be another two hours in the morning, and three in the evening…all of life spoiled! Why do we need so much money? Sell the business. You have an offer of five hundred thousand francs. Today, it no longer brings in more than twenty thousand, so you'll increase our income and ensure our repose…"

"Yours."

Blanchet went pale. "I've lived without your fortune. And since we've been married, we've been living on my earnings as much as your income, haven't we?"

"Oh, Georges, it's wrong to interpret it in that way. I'm only saying that, in trying to prevent me from working, you want to have me to yourself all the time, without reserve…"

"And without division."

She went pale, dolorously. "You don't admit that I can, in the hours when your own métier absorbs you, desire to take an interest again in my own?"

"I admit it—but then I'm forced to observe that the new elements of interest that you have in your life, your son and your daughter, are no longer sufficient for you."

"Louise, who brought you up, is capable of looking after the children during the hours when *Le Chardon Bleu*…"

"There's an order of service in which a maid is not as good as a mother."[38]

---

[38] There is an untranslatable pun here, *bonne* being used to mean both "maid" and "good"—hence Monique's reference to a joke.

"What a joke! At the ages of Georges and Sylvestre! No, there's an entire order of service in which children have no need of having their mother for a domestic. Don't change the subject."

"In the final analysis, am I the father or am I not? Am I the master of the organization of our life as I intend it to be?"

"The father, yes, Georges. The master, no. It's necessary to come to terms with your slave." She stood up and excused herself. "Forgive me, my dear friends—and come and drink a glass of orangeade. It's necessary to pay no attention. It's been like this for three weeks. It's as if he were crazy..."

Blanchet sniggered so insultingly that she lost her temper.

"You exasperate me! Well, tell them, then, if you dare, the true reason for your opposition! But I warn you, be careful! Nothing, since I love you, authorizes that degrading supposition! If you lower yourself to confessing it, I..."

Annik stopped her threatening gesture. "Be quiet, Monique! Have pity on yourself..."

"Does he have pity on me?"

They were all standing up. Blanchet, beside himself, cried: "Either you obey me, by renouncing this absurd project that will be, whether you want it or not, the beginning of our separation, or..."

"You be quiet, too!" ordered Amédée. He had taken his friend by the arm, drawing him away in order to make him listen to reason.

Annik and Monique watched the two men move away: Blanchet gesticulating, Jacquemin lecturing him, with a hand on his shoulder.

When they had turned the corner of the avenue, Monique threw herself into Annik's arms, in distress. Then, when she had wiped away her tears, she spoke.

"Oh, the past! The past! Georges is good, he knows that I love him, uniquely. And the idea that, with the *Chardon Bleu*, I might be led to see old acquaintances, to be tempted again... The imbecile! To suffer from that which is no longer...that

180

which has never been... I've known that torture already...another, less generous than him, inflicted it on me. Oh, Annik! Men, even the best, when they love, and above all when they sense that they're loved, are tyrants. And when they don't love, they're brutes. What should I do? What would you do in my place?"

Annik looked at her, sounding the nature of that being, tender and pure in spite of her previous torments, in the depths of her heart. Did she have sufficient energy to accomplish what she believed to be sage and just? Was her weakness before love greater than her revolt against marital power?

"I wouldn't give in," she murmured, "but you, my friend, will yield."

Monique sighed profoundly. "It's just that in your case, Annik, Amédée knew you when you set out *en route* with the same heart. Life had not yet touched you with its bruises! Oh, what wouldn't I give to be able to start again, like you! Perhaps today, I'd have more valor..."

"No one has entire mastery of their life, my friend." And yet, Annik was thinking: *What a lesson, for directing mine!*

"Who knows," said Monique, "whether, if, like you, I were independent and without regret for any error, I'd even be married? You're going to be a mother. You too, in spite of your convictions, will give in..."

Annik embraced her without making any reply.

"Let's sit down," Annik said. "I'm beginning to get a little tired."

Having set out early, they had reached Roquencourt via
the Porte Saint-Antoine and the edge of the forest of Marly.
She was bearing her maternity lightly, coming and going, as
alert in the seventh month as on the first day.

She had never visited what was left of the ancient château. Curious about all the souvenirs of History, she wanted,
during the long walks that were still permitted to her, to push
on as far as the esplanade where the small palace, located between the Grande Cascade and the immense Bassin des
Douze-Pavillons, once respired deeply through its four facades
its funnel of woods.

She was surprised to find an entirely flat table. A rubble
of grassy earth was already filling in the place where the expanse of water had once been. A desert field leveled out the
rest. A few birds were singing in the park, which had become
woodland again. And over that vanity of a name, no longer
recalled even by ruins, there was solitude, sterile abandonment...

"One can see that the Revolution has passed this way,"
she said.

"Followed by the black band,[39] which has torn everything apart."

She was astonished that the people, sovereign in their
turn over the royal domain, had not resuscitated it by means of
buildings useful to all: laboratories, agricultural exploitations,

---

[39] The *bande noire* [black band] were asset-strippers active
during the Restoration, who bought up land and châteaux
cheap in the wake of the 1789 Revolution, breaking up estates
and demolishing most of the buildings.

retirement homes, vacation colonies...instead of shooting grounds for presidential usage.

"It's astonishing, don't you think, the extent to which we've remained monarchical? Progress is slow."

"I didn't make you say that," observed Amédée, swiftly. He was following his own train of thought, obscurely but tenaciously.

She understood the allusion, and smiled imperceptibly. "All the more reason for those who can to move forward!"

"Not too rapidly!"

Mechanically, she bent the blades of grass with the tip of her cane, rummaging around the tree trunk on which they were sitting. She continued, without responding. Following her usual strategy, she was avoiding the argument. The later the better; every day that passed was their happiness.

He sought another means of reaching her, returning to the subject that had almost caused the scene toward which all his reason and sentiment were pushing him to burst forth between them the day before.

"Yes, not too fast!" he repeated. "Or a day comes when one is obliged to retrace one's steps. That's what Blanchet said to me yesterday."

"With regard to what? You asked him for advice? Let him occupy himself with his wife, and more intelligently! That would be better."

She had stood up. They continued walking.

"How nervous you are as soon as you think that anyone is standing in your sunlight! No, I haven't talked to Georges about us; it was him who confessed to me that if he was unable to allow his wife to go back to work, it was because she had once gone too far, and that he feared, for their happiness, the rediscovery of a certain environment..."

"Monique regrets her past errors sufficiently for him to have confidence in her today."

"You're aware of my sympathy for her..."

"It doesn't prevent you from putting her in the wrong!"

"Exactly—and it's about Monique's tranquility that Blanchet is thinking, as well as his own. He's right."

"Naturally!"

"Not because he's a man, but because in this case, given his wife's past..."

"Her past! One would think, to listen to you, that she's the only one to have been married with a past. What about his? Does she reproach him for it? It's irritating and stupid on Georges' part. Such suspicions! From him, who appears so intelligent! Retrospective jealousy is the most stupid kind."

"One can't do anything about it."

"On the contrary, one can do a great deal about it. If women didn't make an abstraction of the past of the men they love, there wouldn't be a single happy one among them. Not even me."

He leapt at the opportunity offered. "Oh, when one isn't tormented by one thing, it's something else. It's Monique's past that worries Blanchet, but it's our future that preoccupies me. How easily you could ease my chagrin with a word, if you wanted to!"

She squeezed his hand tenderly. "Your chagrin?"

"Yes, my profound, profound chagrin! You know that full well."

She sidestepped, saying, in a falsely cheerful tone: "You no longer love me?"

"Oh, I love you too much—and you don't deserve it! Listen to me, I beg you..."

She sighed, resignedly. "You want that? Speak, then, since you're so determined. And then we won't come back to it. After all, perhaps you're right. Wounds that one allows to fester risk becoming too serious."

"First of all, you were scornful of me yesterday, with regard to my allusions to your determination to work, to exercise a métier ten times more absorbing than the one that Monique wants to take up again. I've been aggravated sometimes, on finding myself deprived of you, when it steals from me the hours when I'm at home and would love to have you with me, but I'm not egotistical enough to demand that you deprive yourself of a pleasure, of which not the least part is, in any case, that of affirming your independence..."

"And of making myself useful to everyone, in the measure of my capabilities..."

"Ambitious woman! You're asking too much...useful to everyone!"

She smiled. It would be quite sufficient, wouldn't it, to be agreeable to only one?"

"No, Annik!" he protested. "It's not only of myself that I'm thinking. It's of the little life that's about to be born. Your silence, your determination not to face up to the decisions that it's necessary to make—that's what causes me pain...."

"But darling, since we adore one another, since we live for one another, since the one who will soon arrive can bring us one joy more...oh, dread that fate might give you veritable reasons to be unhappy..."

"I have them. Being able to understand why the wife of my life, my companion of every hour, that being who is mine, who says she loves me, refuses me the joy of giving my name to the mother of our child..."

"You're back to that! Well, so be it..." She pointed to a bench that was nearby, a vestige of mossy stone. "Let's sit down there, and let's burst the storm, in order that our sky can become blue again. Why are you so stubborn in that petty social satisfaction to which I'm not only insensible but actively hostile?"

"Because we live, whether you like it or not, in a society, and I want the mother of my children to be respected and honored by that society."

"Since I don't care about that..."

"I don't want imbeciles to be able to telephone me, or to meet us, while inviting me alone to lunch, as Plombino did yesterday."

"What can that matter?"

"It irritates me, and it embarrasses me. There are people useful to my affairs that I no longer see, either because I can't go to their homes on my own or because their wives refuse to come to our home. If you were a mistress, they'd be able to call you Madame Jacquemin and put on a semblance of believing that we're married, but everyone knows Mademoiselle Annik Raimbert, advocate. To close the eyes isn't possible for those hypocrites. Whatever you say, it's a source of constant friction."

She smiled. "If it's my presence that's the cause, and you're suffering from it, I have only to return to my own home."

"Annik, that idea is unworthy of you."

"Since I'm putting you in the wrong!"

"You know very well that there's a better solution, but you're avoiding it, mischievously."

"Don't get upset, my darling. Yes, I'm teasing you—forgive me. But then, seriously, I don't see any remedy. You know that I don't want marriage, now less than ever, since I'm going to have the responsibility of a young soul to form..."

"We'll form it together!"

"Undoubtedly, and as long as your advice is good, I shall follow it, believe me."

"After all, the child is as much mine as yours!"

"No, not as much."

"What!"

"Is it you that it's kicking in the belly? Whose kidneys it's pressing to the point of making you scream? Confess that if it's yours as much as mine, its presence doesn't weigh very heavily upon you thus far!"

"Oh, obviously—but I am, after all, its father. It will bear my name, since, if I can't do better, at least I shall recognize it at the same time as you. It will grow up in our environment. Then again, whether or not you're my wife, you know full well that I'll have all the rights of paternal authority—and in consequence, your obstinacy is not only absurd but intolerable!"

"Calm down, and try to listen to me without anger, so that I can tell you, my dear love, my entire thinking."

He assumed his firm face.

"If I were capable, you understand," she said, and emphasized the words by repeating them: "if I were capable of not believing in a higher duty, I swear to you, on the head of the child I bear, that I would marry you immediately. Can you who know me, really believe that a limited obstinacy..."

"You suppose that you're marvelous because you don't act like other women!"

"Then you don't really know me."

"You're obstinate in making me suffer needlessly. I want you all to myself, and you refuse, as if you don't trust yourself. You're taking your precautions for the future."

"I don't distrust myself; I love you, completely. But I know that two people can't be made into one, in spite of all the love in the world. We have two bodies—which is to say, two different organisms—which have personal reactions. You're a man, which is to say, a being who is strong by virtue of being free. Married, I'd no longer be anything but your wife—which is to say, a weak being, oppressed by your laws."

"That's why a wife must have a man who loves her, to defend her."

"Not at all! That's why all the efforts of new women ought to tend to liberate them from men, in order no longer to count on anyone but themselves."

"Pride is leading you astray."

"Perhaps! Nevertheless, I believe that the sentiment and the faith that are guiding me have nothing to do with pride. I only want to extract my children from the matrix in which I nearly remained stuck myself...to make them into true men and true women, capable of edifying a better society, in which the great prostituted words, liberty, equality and fraternity, would cease to be mere words. Understand me! Understand me...to inculcate into those brains in formation a new ideal...a horror of injustice and violence...a hatred of war...a disgust for money..."

She fell silent, prolonging her dream.

"Marriage wouldn't prevent you from raising them as you wish."

"Yes it would—because I wouldn't have any legal right! Admit that if something displeases you in their education, and you wanted to impose your will on me, what means would I have of opposing mine to it? None."

"You're being irrational. Married or not, my rights over our children would be the same."

"No."

"Yes!"

"No...and we're arriving at the great sacrifice about which I haven't thus far dared to talk to you, but for which it's necessary for me to ask you now..."

"Shut up, Annik! Shut up! You're mad...insane!"

"You don't know what I'm going to say to you."

There was a sob in his voice: "Not to recognize my children!"

The storm burst. With his head in his hands, he wept convulsively. Before that touching despair, tears overcame Annik. She put her arms around him.

"My love, my dear heart, don't cry, I beg you. I love you; trust me. No, that's not what I wanted to say to you, no, no. I would be so cruel, so stupid, no. If you knew how I suffer from your chagrin! Oh, how I'd like to satisfy it. It's hard, you know, to want, scorning one's egotistical happiness, to do better than others!"

She had taken his hands, and pulled them away from his face. He was obstinate in keeping his eyes closed, but gasped: "Yes, yes, I'm calm; I'm ready to listen to you. What more do you have to ask of me?"

She no longer felt the courage to speak, to increase his pain. An infinite fatigue overwhelmed her. She remained lacerated by having seen him cry like a child.

"No, nothing, it was nothing important. I'll tell you later. Later..."

"Why not now?"

"I no longer want to. I'm tired, weary..."

"You don't love me enough!"

"You're my life, and you can take mine; it's yours."

"Then be truly my wife!"

"If I were the only one at stake! My life, yes, but the life of my children, the future, I can't give you. That's not a plaything. It's all of human happiness that mothers bear within them. Thus far, they haven't been able, haven't known how to preserve it. Admit that, since the birth of the world, they've abdicated, that they haven't yet succeeded in killing in you the idea of war, they who have children in their skirts until adolescence!"

"Let them raise themselves up higher, then, before claiming to raise others!"

"You're reproaching us for your fault! That's why those who have reflected ought to inform those who don't know yet, to cry out to them: you will only have completed giving birth when you have fashioned the moral being as well as the physical being!"

"Until they're capable of doing so...!"

"You'll see, you'll see. In every country, now, female educators are emerging. And shall I abandon the struggle? No one—that, you see, in spite of you, in spite of me, I don't have the right to do."

Centuries opposed, with their dense night, the feeble light of day, the rise of the slow dawn. Paternity, with its apparatus of age-old primacy, its reign confirmed by laws and customs...and suddenly, looming up before it, Maternity, demanding an equal place, identical rights!

"Confess it, then," she said. "Reveal your entire thinking, honestly. Your intelligence and your heart would be with me, but for the old man..."

"Oh, I don't know anything!" he cried. "Perhaps it's only a reflex that pushed me, yesterday, when I approved Blanchet...a reflex that's pushing me, in begging you not to say a definitive no. I feel, on making appeal to my will, that we can live as happily married as unmarried. I'm sure that a child raised by us, in accordance with your ideas, would grow up

189

tall and strong, like a fine plant. But you see, one can't remake cities or individuals overnight. Be careful that your generosity, by virtue of a hatred of iniquitous rules, doesn't fall into excess in the opposite direction. Be careful, in trying to avoid the future suffering of beings that you don't know, you don't make the man you love suffer unjustly today..."

"Darling," she said, putting her arms around him in a spontaneous gesture, "Do you think that I'm not torn by it myself? And if I didn't have the absolute conviction that our suffering might be fecund, that a better future might be born of it, do you think that I'd inflict it on myself? You love me and I adore you. Let's try to continue living, I beg you, as we have lived thus far. Who knows? Later...when the children are grown up..."

"Grown up! Oh, then..."

"What do you mean?"

"Who can tell what the future has in store for us? It's now that it's necessary to have pity on my suffering, not later!"

Annik perceived a danger, and fell silent.

He threatened: "Great dolor, like great joy, is a rupture of equilibrium that can't last forever.

"So...let's wait!"

He sensed that she was digging her heels in, and made a gesture of impatience. He was not ready for resignation. He was, however, experiencing more bitterness than irritation— and also a vague hope that life, stronger than individual obstinacy, would bring about some modification of its own accord, still possible... They went back in silence, she upset, discontented not to have had the courage to talk to him about the inevitable sacrifice, he with a heavy heart, thinking about the distance that such a brief interval, from one year to the next, from the dazzling park of Versailles to the tenebrous corner of the park of Marly, had put between them. The communion of their flesh, knotting the mysterious fruit! And in the very bond of the tightly-bound bodies, the dramatic conflict of their minds, disputing the child to come.

PART THREE

Human beings will be happier when they are more just.
Jean Finot, *Préjugés et Problèmes des Sexes.*

I

Thanks to Annik's enveloping tenderness, Amédée, in spite of his preoccupation, had resumed a happy expression. He often teased her: "Only a month and a half to go... Only a month... Let's take advantage of it, for afterwards, when the little mystery within you is born, you'll see whether I'll take my revenge for the miseries you've made me endure!"

She laughed. He had ended up convincing himself that only Annik's condition motivated her obstinacy. Having recovered her equilibrium, she would consent, before the child of their flesh, to the inevitable legalization. Full of pride, he said at every opportunity: "My son!" and embraced Annik affectionately. He did not see her eyes darken then.

Soon, the electoral battle was in full swing. The apartment was a continual coming and going of men shouting and gesticulating. When they chanced to be alone, Amédée read her his speeches, commented on his program. He ran rapidly through the post that she had carefully sorted, in order to filter out the anonymous letters full of threats and filth.

It was so turbulent and so tiring that she took advantage of it to ask for permission to go to take up residence, until she gave birth, at the Trianon. She could no longer bear the agitation of the frantic hours, whereas at Versailles, with Mérette...

Cowardly with regard to the torturing scene, she pursued her plan: to leave him impotent before the consequences of the action.

"You'll escape every time you can...and then, with the telephone...as soon as I feel the first pains, I'll send word to you.

He had accepted, not suspecting anything. He understood that all the noise and movement, in which she could no longer participate, was bound to overtax her at a moment when, for her, things could not be too calm.

At Versailles, she arrived at the school in the middle of recreation. Mademoiselle Hardy was strolling in the courtyard with her associates. The girls were playing, running around in all directions. As she headed toward Mérette she noticed a little blonde girl, scarcely seven years old, all alone. Sitting on a heap of stones, the child looked so sad that Annik went over to her.

"What are you doing, my darling?"

"Amusing myself."

"With what?"

"With nothing."

At the same moment, Mademoiselle Hardy' voice made her turn round. "What a surprise!"

The child stood up as the headmistress approached.

"Moping again! Leroux! Let Louise Marchand into your game! Go on, my child, go on..." She explained: "She's an unfortunate child. Broken home. The father's a drunkard. The mother, in order to shield the little one from the scenes, wanted to send her to her grandmother, who adores her, but with that brute..! Result: a lost childhood. Louise Marchand never plays..."

"Poor mite!"

"Let's go upstairs. You'll have a cup of tea? You have time?"

"All the time in the word. I moved into the Trianon this morning, until you've found me a good sanitarium."

"What? What are you saying?" Anxiously, Mérette opened her eyes wide. "What about Amédée? What's happening?"

"Don't worry, Mérette—we're in accord. The apartment had become impossible. Chaos! Whereas here..."

"Good! He'll come for the birth?"

"He believes so, but I'll only tell him after the registration."

"And your recognition? Father unknown, then?"

"For a few hours. It's necessary, since it's only at that price that I can obtain paternal authority."

"You haven't dared talk to him about it, then, since our conversation?"

"Oh, I haven't had the courage. And then, an accomplished fact is easier to bear than the anguish of seeing it accomplished. We'll see..."

Mademoiselle Hardy shook her head. "How many torments still to come!"

"What's the point of understanding one's duty if one flees from setting the example?"

"That's true. But what if he refuses, thereafter, to give the child his name?"

"Impossible, as I know him. And then, neither one of us would die of it. Inheritance? But beyond a certain figure, all fortunes ought to revert to the State. Would I have worked if I hadn't been poor? Anyway, my name will be as honest to bear as his...I'll see to that."

"How much determination you need to follow your path!"

"You're the one who's given it to me."

"No, it was within you. A preachy old spinster, that's all I am. I've recoiled before action. You, you're the Pioneer, your faith overturns all obstacles."

"Aren't I right? For if I'm mistaken...if I'm wrong to cause so much suffering, to the man I love and to myself..."

"No, Annik, nothing great is ever created without pain. One only advances with bruised hands, groping..."

"Into the darkness!"

"Toward the light!"

The ringing of the telephone, aggressive and tenacious, broke the silence of the apartment. It was lunch time. There was no secretary. Madame Danvois, out of breath, arrived from the kitchen.

"Hello!"

"Saxe twenty-one twelve? Monsieur Jacquemin?"

"Yes, that's here. Monsieur isn't in."

"Oh. Tell him, then, that Madame has just had a little boy..."

"Oh! Did everything go well? ... Oh, good! ... Good, I'll make a note: twelve, Rue de la Paroisse, in Versailles... Monsieur will be very pleased ... Hello? ... Hello?"

The person at the other end of the wire had hung up. Avid for details, Madame Danvois listened for a few moments longer, disappointed.

At the same time, the nurse whom Annik had charged with making the call went back into the room, where the latter was waiting, feverishly, having taken the responsibility for her action!

"Well?"

"He wasn't there; I left a message. Do you need anything? I'm going to lunch.

Pale, Annik gestured to indicate that she was all right. After a night of intense pain, she had given birth at four o'clock in the morning. Now that her son had been certified and registered, the essential thing had been done. She sighed, exhausted.

Mademoiselle Hardy had insisted on aiding the physician and the nurse, upset by the tragic spectacle: the howls of the patient, the writhing of the body striving to expel its burden, blind gazes turning without knowing where to pose their suffering...then the anesthesia, that kind of death from which life was finally born, in the whimper of a plaint... And it had to be Annik, the first person she had ever seen paying such a ransom of maternity!

Sent away by the physician in order that she could rest for a while, she had come back at eleven o'clock, but without

Monique, with whom, in the company of the physician, she was supposed to go to the Mairie for the formality of the registration before Amédée could be informed. Blanchet had forbidden his wife "to play that dirty trick on Jacquemin." She had been obliged to obey. The director of the sanitarium had replaced her.

With a light hand, Annik caressed the sleeping infant, who had just been placed beside her, and suddenly began to weep: a collapse of will-power...a release...solitude... It was all of that, but above all—in spite of the fact that Mademoiselle Hardy, departed half an hour ago, had promised to return immediately after lunch—a profound sentiment of abandonment. She thought about mothers who were surrounded, pampered. Around her, there was no family, no mother, no husband... No husband? *Didn't I want one? Oh, poor human soul, how many somersaults, how many struggles, to overcome your ancestral habits, your prejudices, your errors! I'm escaping, and it's that escape which is causing my torment...*

She turned her head, gently, to look at her son. "You'll see...you for whom I've already suffered so much...you'll see how difficult it is to be content with oneself!"

She reached for the piece of paper under her pillow and re-read it.

Amédée-Claude Raimbert, born of... Father unknown... As long as Amédée forgives me! Oh, I'm not taking his son away from him, I'm only taking my part, that which is truly my due...

His son? What would have become, without me, of the blind seed, the mysterious atom of which we don't even know in what measure it combines with the fecund cell! My son...

He wouldn't be breathing without my breath! I've vivified his feeble lungs when he was nothing yet but an inert mass in my womb! There he is, born, and I no longer count

No, no! What I've done is just...

Amédée had not been informed until mid-afternoon, when he had telephoned Madame Danvois from the Chambre to find out whether there was any news before setting out. Although he had three meetings that evening, he was looking forward to going to Versailles in between times in order to embrace his invalid, whom he had not seen for two days.

"A boy? And everything went well? ... Quickly, pack my bag. I'll call in to pick it up... Monsieur Blanchet? He telephoned as well? ... He wanted to talk to me immediately? ... Because it would be too late afterwards? ... All right."

No suspicion had awakened. He was so happy that he could have burst into song. Everything, he had the conviction, was about to be settled.

"Boulevard Raspail, quickly!" her ordered his driver—one that he had hired for the elections. He made his arrangements at a whirlwind pace...what he needed to sleep at the Trianon if he could not stay in the Rue de la Paroisse. But why the Rue de la Paroisse, since everything had been foreseen and arranged at the hotel?

The auto, no matter how rapidly it was traveling, did not seem to be advancing. It was a long road that separated him from his wife and son. An emotion of gratitude toward the one who had given him that joy suddenly softened him. What did he look like, that little form that emerged from her? What unknown seeds, what heredity, did that parcel of flesh contain? Father? Mother? Which would predominate in the little man?

He was so absorbed that he did not notice that the auto had stopped. The driver had to get out and inform him. His heart was beating rapidly when he rang the bell. On hearing his name, the nurse assured him that he had a beautiful son, very good, that Madame was as well as could be expected, but that it was necessary, for twenty-four hours, in order for the milk to rise, to avoid tiring her. He should let her speak as little as possible!

As soon as she saw him, she could not hold back her tears. He took her hands, caressed them, kissed them fervently. He spoke to her in a soft voice, as if to a little girl.

Words so tender, a caress so soothing, only weakened Annik's will further. She made him a sign to pick up the child.

196

He lifted him up at arm's length, with touching awkwardness. He contemplated him avidly, embarrassed and important, as if, suddenly, he were carrying the world.

He leaned over, in order to lie him down next to Annik, but she stopped him.

"No. Keep him and sit down. I have something to tell you."

"It's necessary not to talk, the nurse said."

"Yes..."

"No, my love. Besides which, I'm in haste to go to the Mairie to register the birth of this little fellow."

"Exactly. Listen to me."

"Shh!" he said, placing a finger over his lips.

"His name is Claude-Amédée..."

"That's understood. Ring so that he can be dressed..."

"Wait! You only have to recognize him. He's already registered."

She gazed at him, with all her dolorous love, and held out the birth certificate.

"What? Wait until I put the baby back to bed."

He did not understand yet. His brain was immobilized, like a stalled engine. At the first glance at the paper, his thoughts abruptly started moving again.

He went white, the sheet of paper trembling in his hands.

"You've done that!"

"Forgive me. Listen! Let me explain..."

He motioned to her to shut up. The dropped birth certificate fell to the floor. Amédée clenched his fists, tottering, like a victim struck by a sledgehammer, on the point of collapse.

She did not know, before that stupor in which a rage was growing, what words to find to calm him down.

Suddenly, sensing that all self-control was abandoning him, and that he was about to commit some act of savage violence, he ceased swaying, ran to the door, with a great gesture that swept it open, and ran away, like a madman.

The week that followed was, for Annik, full of alarms. In spite of the supplicant letters, into which she put every persuasion, and the urgings of Blanchet, who was now trying to make him see reason, Amédée had not wanted to return to Versailles. Pretext: the electoral battle. Motive: a hateful humiliation.

"You ought, however, to recognize your son."

"No point. She wanted him; let her keep him."

"Be reasonable! You love her, and you'll love him. Anyway, you're the father. And since, once recognized by you, it's your name that he'll bear..."

"Why didn't she tell me in advance?"

"She claims that you'd have refused."

"I don't know."

"So? I'm not saying that she was right, obviously, since I forbade Monique to be a witness, and tried to warn you. But today..."

"No, no!"

"Yes, you'll do it—you must. Pride? A bad adviser, in the final analysis. I've reflected a great deal since the arguments I've had these past few months with my wife. Fundamentally, Monique, in wanting to work, was in the right, more so than me. New women, new mores, my friend! It's necessary that we resign ourselves to these dolorous but inevitable conflicts between their young independence and our old authority. In sum, what's separating you here, you and Annik? A question of words. Is she, yes or no, for you, the true and the only possible companion? Yes. And what is she asking of you? A simple concession of form, since, fundamentally— which is to say, in the sense of the education your Claude is to be given—you're in accord. Give her the platonic satisfaction she's requesting of you. After all, she loves you better, and perhaps even more, than you love her. You remain the stronger."

On the evening of the day of that conversation, Amédée went to the Hôtel de Ville for the counting of the votes. The ballots piled up...Jacquemin, Jacquemin, Jacquemin... His election was now certain. A joy was reborn in his saddened heart.

For a week he had not returned to Versailles! A letter from Annik, received during the day, was in his wallet, alongside a photograph of little Claude, which Blanchet had sent him. The rancor, insensibly, was beginning to calm down. An obscure need for tenderness began to labor within him again. Although he affirmed no pleasure in the idea of seeing Annik, an emotion invaded him at the thought of seeing their child again.

He took out his watch. Midnight...

Although the calculations had not yet been concluded, everyone was congratulating him; he would appear at the head of his list. Suddenly, he made his decision. He would go to Versailles, thus avoiding the wait until the announcement of the results.

In the Rue de la Paroisse, however, the door was closed; he was not able to see Annik until the following morning.

When the nurse introduced him, and he perceived that thin face on the pillow with the drawn features, which was smiling at him with such a sad and weary expression, his heart was constricted, and with difficulty repressed an impulse to leap forward.

As if she had seen him the day before, she questioned him about the elections and expressed her happiness at his success, which the morning newspapers had announced. She did not want to talk to him about the child, not knowing what his dispositions were. But it was time to feed him; instinctively, or out of habit, the baby woke up and started to wail.

"What time is it?" she asked the nurse.

"Another five minutes. I've prepared the bottle."

They were alone; he was still avoiding looking her in the face. "You're not nursing him?"

"Impossible at the moment; my milk makes him ill."

"Why?"

She shook her head. "No reason. But I don't want them to pass him on, because I hope to be able to recommence in a few days. In the meantime, it's making me ill."

He went to the crib, looked at the little fellow, who, with his eyes closed, was moving his mouth in search of the absent teat, picked him up, and placed a long kiss on his forehead.

"Thank you," she murmured. "Thank you, my love. It's not against you...you'll see...you'll see..."

He had put the child down again. He came to the bed and soothed her: "Be quiet—not now, later. I'll watch him drink, and then I'll go to see my people, and I'll come back this afternoon...."

Without saying a word, Annik took Amédée's hand and pressed it to her lips.

Three months later, the Boulevard Raspail.[40]

Sitting tranquilly beside the cradle of her sleeping son, having swatted away with a mechanical gesture the fly that had landed on the wrinkled face, Annik recapitulated with the precision of perspective the changes wrought around her by the passing of the squall.

She no longer knew how she had lived, between her departure for Versailles, to the moment when she had finally been able to return, with Claudinet, to the pleasant house.

Agonizing hours, mentally as well as physically, with the quartering torment—hours so far in the past today that she had almost forgotten, along with her bestial cries, the torment of the soul from which she no longer retained anything but a great appeasement, the pride of having suffered in order to give birth.

The book that she had set down, pensively, on her knees, allowed the card that she was using to cut the pages to slip out when she opened it again. She picked it up: the announcement of Claude's birth.

Amused, she re-read it: *Mademoiselle Annik Raimbert and Monsieur Amédée Jacquemin have the honor of informing you of the birth of their son, Claude-Amédée...*

What a scandal! She laughed at it again. The stone had fallen vertically into the frog pond—and how much croaking it had provoked! They had received, from opposing camps, a voluminous correspondence of insults and congratulations, letters from strangers and anonymous ones. The unusual notice, published by the press, had caused a great deal of discus-

---

[40] This sentence implies that it is now January, but subsequent temporal references move the schedule back by at least a month. Again, the inconsistency probably arises from the patchwork pattern of composition.

sion. Journalistic hacks had prolonged it with reaching extrapolations.

A few days after a violent scene between Madame de Moreval and her son, in fact, a spiteful article signed *Vindex* had appeared in the *Appel*. It scourged the "insolence" of the "challenge," the insult to marriage and the family, in a style so pompous that they had recognized the eloquence of Monsieur de Moreval.

War had then been declared between the rebel son and the indignant parents. The sack of reproaches emptied by Madame de Moreval exhaled such a stink that Amédée, sickened, had beaten the retreat, leaving them free to pour out their maledictions from the height of their tower.

"You will never see me again," he had informed them, "until you have recognized your error."

"Poor fool! You're the one in error!"

"*Adieu.* I'll await your apologies."

"Never!"

"Never, then."

The clarity, as well as the dignity, of that attitude had filled Annik with an emotional admiration. She sensed all that Amédée's courage must have cost him, and strove, by the surge of her affection, to bandage the wound.

It was a deflection of bitterness, which, for the time being—as Annik's intuition had immediately realized—had turned away from her in order to direct at the Morevals, a rancor of which he could not as yet be healed.

The hostilities had not lasted long, at least in a sharp sense. Annik sensed them nevertheless, rumbling away beneath the wheedling that, for several days, the old woman had been undertaking. She had written a long letter to Amédée, in which she admitted that her good faith had been taken by surprise. While deploring the form that he had though he ought to give his union with "Madame Raimbert," she inclined before the latter's rectitude and merits. She would gladly see her son again. They would not talk about the past, and, in the meantime, she begged him to kiss her grandson.

A new danger that she would have to ward off! Amédée had been so happy about that prompt repentance that she had been anxious. He had agreed to have lunch the day before at his parents' home in order to seal the pact of reconciliation. He had only given her brief details of the ceremony. What did he think, fundamentally? After his own lack of confidence, might he not be hiding something?

She wondered incessantly what his good humor and his apparent calm were covering. In spite of his capitulation to the irremediable and his duty done—he had recognized Claude before returning to Paris—was it possible that he had become happy again without any reservations? She did not believe so, but hoped, by means of delicacy and unflagging kindness to complete the work of time. Amédée's wound would close eventually, and then, with his existence busier and more ab-sorbed than ever...

The elections had almost swept the Chambre clear of "ignorance and stupidity." Paris had re-elected Pierre Roussot, defeating Lebeau. From time to time, therefore, justice was served! The Cibéron dictatorship had been succeeded by a Ministry of the left, orienting the country toward an era of international peace and European reconstruction. With the Ruhr evacuated and accord in the matter of Reparations finally achieved thanks to the ultimate agreement of the Allies, there was talk of the departure of President Vilfaux: *submit or re-sign*. But Amédée knew the man and was in no doubt: he would submit.

As for the *Appel*, it continued its shady politics, in the service of Ronchard and the steel coalition, half-reactionary and half-progressive. A renowned député of the Basse-Seine, the sycophant had only paid five hundred thousand francs for his mandate. As for Lebeau, he consoled himself for his par-liamentary setback by beginning, with an eye toward the Académie, a campaign on the low birthrate, the patriotic and philanthropic character of which added a further entitlement to those he had acquired by his previous campaign against "the Tide of Lust."

Reichmeyer, having obtained the rosette, had abandoned the *Soupe Populaire* and resold the *Maréchals* to America for six hundred thousand francs, while Jean Roussot serenely completed his *Après-Guerre* triptych in the sunlit calm of La Galliarde, a beach lost in the forests of cork oaks and pines on the slopes of the Monts des Maures.

Annik promised herself that in the next vacation period, if Amédée carried out his long-postponed project for a voyage to America, she would go with Claudinet to spend August and September near the painter, in Saint-Aygulf. That was the nearest town, on the coast. She would rent a villa there with Madame Broussat and Zélinoff. And perhaps Mérette, who had been fatigued for some time, would consent to accompany them, in spite of her dread of the heat...

She rejoiced in the idea of convincing her old friend. It would be pleasant to bask in the sun after he had labored for the entire year—for now, she said to herself, the halt was over; it was necessary to become an advocate again, and make up for lost time!

She got up, with a smile at the child who was snoring softly, his hands clenched, and laid a tulle coverlet over the crib. Then, going to the mantelpiece, she opened a file that she had placed there when coming from the study. She had just begun to riffle through it when Amédée came in on tiptoe.

He knew that the baby went to sleep after each feed, the times of which the mother had fixed with medical exactitude. At the sight of Annik, her head bowed over the papers, the confident expression that illuminated his face—he had come to kiss her before going out—faded.

"Leave that!" he said. "Jacquet will sort out that business." Jacquet was one of the secretaries that had been filling in for Annik since September.

She looked at him in surprise. "But it's not for you, it's for myself that I'm working!"

"You might have said something to me! I hoped that now you'd be able to abandon—oh, not entirely, of course, but for some time yet—at least part of your occupations. Is the baby not absorbing you sufficiently, already?"

Annik sudden felt her throat tighten. The truce was over! So long as she had remained at the rank that Amédée's dream had assigned to her, effaced in the role of the little Maman and the good housekeeper, that had been fine! But now that she was manifesting not even a resolution, but a desire to get back to work...

Calmly, she observed: "You know very well that, in spite of my desire to nurse Claude myself, and in spite of the diet I've imposed on myself, I no longer have any milk. It's not for my pleasure that I've been obliged to commence, a week ago, with sterilized teats. Fortunately, Amélie is neatness itself: apparel, feeding bottle, nothing to criticize; she'll substitute for me marvelously."

"Another idea of yours! A good nurse..."

No! A good milk cow! Everyone to his or her own métier. That of mothers is to feed their babies when they can, not to sell to the rich, because they're poor, the milk of which their own children are deprived. It's true! Of all the exploitations of woman, that's the one that seems to me to approach her most closely to a beastie, as they say in Yvedon."

"Then you're still determined to keep your Amélie?"

"Yes, since Madame Broussat vouches for her! Do you see any problem with that?"

He hesitated, and then said: "Not in the least, given that our friends affirm that we can be tranquil. Although, between us, the conditions of recruitment at the Auteuil shelter..."

"Do you have something better to propose?"

He hesitated again. "No, since it's done. Anyway, you doubtless wouldn't have wanted her..."

She nodded her head perspicaciously. "Because it's your mother who suggested her to you? Yesterday, wasn't it, when you had lunch with her? What solicitude, the first time you returned there! Why didn't you say anything to me?"

"I didn't attach any importance to it."

He looked at her tenderly. Maternity had completed, after love, the blossoming of the plenitude of her figure. He admired her. His prejudices never held for long in confrontation with that gilded gaze. In compensation, they only came back more forcefully when he ruminated his grievances alone. He retained in his heart the humiliation of being obliged to resign himself, whether he liked it or not. Dispossessed of paternal authority, he had not yet forgiven Annik for that defeat, in which cunning had triumphed over his will. He was meditating a revenge, counting on her lassitude, and an acquired taste for familial habitude, for an accommodation to her veritable role: that of the mother of a family, doubled with that of his aide and secretary.

Suspiciously, Annik enquired: "And who was your protégée?"

"A middle-aged woman. A widow who had a situation, and misfortunes..."

"Say straight out, a formerly wealthy person!"

"Not exactly, but almost..."

"Then no thank you! I'd rather have a young and simple girl. A former pauper! At least I can do her some good, while directing her as I wish."

He rubbed his hands, with a knowing expression.

"I bow to you, Madame Authority! Ah! Your son's awake!"

She threatened him with a comically extended fist. It was the latest tease, not malevolent but nevertheless revealing, that he had invented. "*Your* son!" He never called Claude anything else, in front of Annik.

The child whimpered. She lifted up the tulle—but the regular respiration had resumed already.

"Your father is shamefully susceptible!" she attested.

"You find that much more accommodating," he said, kissing her. "*Au revoir!* Oh, I forgot—I won't be dining in this evening. Jacquet's just reminded me that I have a banquet—the friends of Jaurès.

"Good! I'll take advantage of it to stay for dinner at Paule's. She's alone, and she's not very well, in spite of the success of the weaning. No news of Roger, naturally! He's at sea. So she's tormented, after that extended voyage. And as it's not going, but hasn't been called off, with Martinet..."

"If only she'd followed your advice!"

"It's good sometimes, then?"

He did not want to admit that he was beaten. "Oh, one can always see clearly on behalf of others!"

III

In the nervousness in which the absence of news had plunged Paule, a panic dread was agitating her, between the ardent hope of imminent liberty with Roger's return, and disgust of the slavery accepted by her sluggishness. Alone with Martinet, with no other refuge than her cherished letters from Japan, she had been obliged to submit to the new assault of ignoble desire. Reassured as to the consequences—the harm's done, eh?—the husband treated himself, without stinginess, for a pleasure that no longer risked any cost. Bleakly, she could no longer see that adipose mass, with rude fists and red hair.

Paule, in her bedroom, where Annik and she were both installed next to Gi's little cot, was finishing her last complaints. Brutally, the vestibule door slammed. She recognized the heavy tread, trembling.

"It's him..."

Martinet came in, grumbling. "You weren't expecting me?"

"No," Paule stammered. "You told me...you can see...I invited Annik..."

"Madame Advocate. How nice...too honored..."

He rang. Fine, the maid-of-all-work—for although he earned a good salary, the broker deemed that, with Paule, she was sufficient—showed her long bony face of a barren mare.

"Set another place at table for me, my girl. And let's sit down!"

The soup swallowed, not without pouring a glass of wine into his bowl—"That cheers you up!"—he deigned to explain his change of program and, at the same stroke, his bad mood.

"Damn it! I didn't expect to find myself here this evening. Does that bother you, eh? It disturbs your little conspiracies?" He cut himself a large slice of boiled beef, covered his plate with vegetables, and then passed the dish. "I had one of those runs of bad luck today. First I lost a little pearl for which Véron, the jeweler in the Boulevard Bone-Nouvelle was giving me four thousand francs. Yes, Mesdames, four thousand francs down the drain. And I needed it tomorrow to pay a bill for four hundred francs. Then Lermot, who had invited me to the restaurant, and whom I was supposed to pick up at home at six o'clock...in bed! A fluxion! Then I said to myself: I'll go surprise Paule. Rather than stay out, I'll go have dinner at home. I'll be more comfortable, and it won't cost me anything."

He omitted to add that, in this instance, Lermot was, in reality, Mademoiselle Bertah, who, suffering from a bad headache, and having gone to bed with a sedative compress and all the lights extinguished, had refused inflexibly to let him in.

He scratched his head, annoyed by the settlement due tomorrow, the loss of the pearl and the four-hundred-franc gap to plug. The housekeeping budget? Insufficient. Paule complained incessantly of being short. Take the sum out of his bank account? His avarice suffered from that hypothesis. But had not his wife received, the day before, five hundred francs of a delayed payment, for a few musical performances? That was what he needed! That money would sort everything out.

He intercepted with authority the dish of vanilla cream the Fine brought, and, instead of taking the lion's share in advance, gallantly offered it to the two women. Paule looked at him, surprised. What had got into him?

He was not lapping noisily the large plateful with which he had gratified himself, having taken back and then emptied by turning it upside-down, the dish whose passage through Paule's and Annik's hands he had watched with regret.

"This cream is excellent!" he declared. "Mustn't say that to Fine, who's intolerable enough as it is! The great lummox will think we can't do without her! One of these days, as soon as we've found someone more agreeable, I'll throw her out."

"She likes Gi so much, and she cares for her so well."

"That's not a domestic's business. The mother's there for that. If you weren't out all the time playing the harp...and the flute!"[41]

Paule raised her eyes to the ceiling, and Annik drummed a scornful finger on the tabletop. He reflected that he had made a false step; one doesn't catch flies with vinegar..."

"Oh, you're free, evidently. Your sister repeats it often enough: the rights of women...and soon the citizeness! Me, I don't hold with all that...but in the end, I recognize, you have a métier, and it's only just that you exercise it, since it brings money in."

He scratched his head again: a habitual gesture when he had something on his mind. Paule trembled. He folded up his napkin, introduced a hundred-franc note into the embroidered envelope and suddenly launched his attack.

"Do you know what you'd do if you were kind? You'd give me the four hundred francs for tomorrow's bill."

"But..."

"You can. You've got five."

"It's just that..." She hesitated, and paused.

He assumed that it was the habitual acquiescence, and, as Annik and Paule got up from the table, he placed his hand amicably on his wife's shoulder, while Fine opened the glazed door of the drawing room, without delicacy.

"Fine!" he ordered. "Fetch the *fine*!"[42]

He underlined the joke—which he reserved for evenings when he was in good form—with a broad laugh. Paule curled up in the Louis XVI wing chair—gilded wood and silk, signed Dufayel—which was, in her husband's eyes, the sign of supremacy and bourgeois elegance.[43]

---

[41] In Parisian argot, the verb *flûter* signifies heavy drinking, or bingeing in a more general sense; it will become clear eventually that Martinet is making a pun of sorts.

[42] In this sense, brandy.

[43] Les Grands Magasins Dufayel was a vast and pretentious department store in the Rue de Clignancourt, which became

Annik, pulling up a stool, sat down at her sister's feet. She wrapped her arms around her knees, and covered her with her inclined body, like a rampart.

Monsieur Martinet strode back and forth with the swaying gait of a caged bear. When Fine had deposited the tray with the bottle and the small glass on the sideboard, he served himself generously.

"No higher than the rim!"

He replaced the cork as if he were screwing it in, and used his fingernail to draw a line on the label at the lowered level of the liquid.

"That way," he sniggered, "one is tranquil."

Paule shrugged her shoulders. "Fine never drinks."

"So she says! But the butcher's boy, or the grocer...with women, one never knows."

"Thanks on their behalf," said Annik.

He disdained the mockery. It was not a time to argue. The four hundred francs first. He swallowed his glass of alcohol in a single draught, and clicked his tongue in satisfaction. He only lacked, to complete his digestion, one of those old pipes... He took it out of his pocket, with a packet of Maryland, and a contraband lighter, of which he was proud. Paule didn't like the smoke, of course, but why should he deprive himself for so little? He drew voluptuously to the tobacco, which ignited, and blew out a few puffs, his eyes half-closed. There! One could go...

He planted himself in front of the wing chair.

"It's agreed, then, my dear. You'll give me the four hundred francs, eh? You'll still have a hundred francs to amuse yourself.

Paule, fortified by Annik's presence, summoned up her courage, and said: "Don't count on it. I've already spent the money."

---

prosperous selling furniture and household goods on credit. It went into a steep decline after the Great War, but was still a going concern when the present novel was written.

"What do you mean?"

"I mean that even if I wanted to give you the money, I couldn't."

She responded to his surprise, already rumbling, with a resolute coldness, replying to his addressing her as "*tu*" with a distant "*vous*."

"You've spent…without telling me…"

"Exactly."

Suffocated by so much aplomb, he stammered: "And may…may one know how?"

"A couturier's bill, overdue for a long time. I can't dress myself with what you dole out for the housekeeping. A dress for my concerts costs more than five hundred francs…you know that very well."

He knew it. But he also knew that he was the head of the family, and therefore the master: the master of disposing of the money belonging to his wife, and also the master of deceiving her. She was his thing and his property.

He cried: "Oh, of course! Madame sticks five hundred franc dresses on her back to go play the beauty before a heap of smooth talkers! And Monsieur slaves away all the time to pay the household debts! I don't give a damn, personally, about your harp and your bare arms!"

With the disappointment of the expected recovery, a rage was mingled. It was as if he had had the money in his pocket. But what was even more irritating was the coolness of the replies, the calm insolence of the revolt. He enveloped his wife and his sister-in-law with the same hateful gaze. For these bees that Paule had in her bonnet, the métier that she practiced in order to create uncontrollable resources and to extend her tether, it was Annik who was partly responsible. He judged—his hope recovering—that it was a good opportunity for a sortie that these females would remember.

"Gently, gently, my beauties!"

They had risen to their feet. Paule, disdaining the outrage, had taken Annik's hands; she felt stronger thus.

"If you think you can get away with that, you're wrong! First of all, henceforth, accounts! I was wrong to give you leeway. A book, undated every day! Receipts: what I pay out and what you earn. And expenses…it's too easy to hand out five-hundred-franc bills! And then, the liberty—finished, since you abuse it! You'll submit to me, in the future, all the offers you receive: private lessons, fees, the lot! That'll teach you to hide things from me!"

He burst into triumphant laughter. "And that, as Madame Advocate can tell you, is my right! It's the law! Shrug your shoulders…it won't do you any good to struggle. Tied up and sealed!"

"You're forgetting," Annik said, "that Paule has the right to use her own income without your authorization."

"Yes, but not to spend it on baubles. In a household, it's like on a ship. There's one who steers it—that's the captain. And the captain, is Bibi…"

"Until the day the contract ends," replied Annik.

"Fu…uh!" hissed Monsieur Martinet. "Excuse me, Monsieur doctor in law? Are you, perhaps, talking about divorce? *Benissimo!* Let's go! I know the deal. For a divorce, as for a marriage, it takes two who say yes. Then it can be unstuck. If one says no, it sticks! No means of extrication. Or there have to be reasons…and the judge weighs them up. Ha ha! I don't say, if Madame gives them to me…and she's in the process! Have to see! In the meantime, she can do without, in my opinion, the defender. If the cap fits, wear it! Paule's turned upside down enough as it is. You'll do me the pleasure of leaving her alone, and to begin with, of not setting foot in here again. And with that, *bonsoir*."

Annik had stood up, haughtily. Martinet pointed at the door. "Go practice law in your député's house—as much as you please, with him. But here"—he slammed his fist down on the sideboard—"obedience!"

He pirouetted, singing: "*In life, you mustn't worry—and me, I just don't care!*"[44] And he went out, strutting.

"The filthy beast!" sighed Annik, revolted

Obedience! Obedience! The best and the worst alike had nothing but that word in their mouths! The key word of marriage, sentencing the slave, without remission, to jail. She put her arms round Paule, who was sobbing nervously: a release of contained emotion."

"I'm going with you. We'll take Gine."

"I beg you to wait for a few more days. Next week, Roger will be here, now that you've waited so long! Abominable as that scene was, perhaps it might not have been useless. Who knows whether the idea of divorce might germinate more rapidly? Have courage. We can see one another elsewhere. Tomorrow, any time you like, in the Boulevard Raspail. Agreed?"

"Agreed."

They hugged one another.

---

[44] The words are taken from a song written in 1921 by Maurice Chevalier, who rapidly made it popular.

IV

Scarcely had Paule closed the door of the apartment on her sister than she perceived Martinet. He was waiting for her on the threshold of the drawing room.

"I'm going to bed," she said.

"Stay."

He was twisting his gnarled fingers, embarrassed. He regretted his anger. Also, that stuck-up Annik was unbearable—whereas with Paule, one could reach an understanding. She must have a few more sous put aside. He adopted a mild tone.

"You mustn't hold it against me; I'm wound up. Without your sister, coming to bother us…! It's the loss of that pearl that caused everything, you see. I thought I could count on you to settle the account tomorrow morning. I would have given the four hundred francs back to you, you know."

She looked sat him in amazement. Unconsciousness? Bad faith? Resolved not to start the argument again, however, she smiled bitterly and moved away with a gesture. He grabbed her by the wrist and forced her to sit down. She wiped away her tears, pulled in her shoulders, and waited.

"You're weeping? There's no reason to. A real fountain! No…my word, one would think that I beat you! It's not serious. Dry them up, my girl."

He tried to raise her lowered head. Paule resisted.

"Leave me alone."

Instead of letting go, however, he put one hand on her shoulder, and used the other to force her to show her face. Her eyes were shining with a feverish gleam. Her cheeks were burning beneath the pearly furrows.

A strange sentiment stirred within him. He was not touched by her dolor. On the contrary, he experienced a pleasure in seeing the unhappy woman suffer. He found it a new expression, which excited him.

She recoiled violently. "Leave me alone—you're vile!"

Abruptly, with the sudden fury of the weak, who tolerate everything until the moment when they explode, unexpectedly, not caring that she was undoing in a single minute an entire year of calculations and resignation, she cried: "Poor man! You think that someone has turned my head? It's you, and you alone who are the cause of the fact that I long ago ceased for feel for you, I won't even say affection, but gratitude... Affection, yes, perhaps I would have had it once if, after having offered to be your wife, you had not brutalized me immediately, if you had shown me a little tenderness. But I've not only served, from the first night as the drain for your needs; every day, for four years, you've treated me as a domestic—as your housemaid. It would be nothing, that slavery, with someone that one loved..."

The dear, distant visage appeared through the one she execrated. She wrung her hand. "Ah, love! Love and you! Your grossness...your baseness...your rapacity! There's only one love that stirs in your entrails—that of money."

"But I married you without a sou!"

"I earn as much as you do today, and I don't know, myself, either what you buy and sell, or what you spend outside—but you know, to the nearest twenty francs, everything I bring in. And perhaps, without that, it would have been a long time ago that you'd have invited me, to use one of your amiable expressions, to go and play the harp—and flute—elsewhere. Don't worry! That's what I'll end up doing."

She fell silent, exhausted.

He bowed. "As you wish. The door's open; no one retains a bad mother by force. Go—I'll keep Ginette. And while you're at it, take Fine with you. Two mouths less. All profit."

She sensed, beneath the sarcasm, that he was saying what he thought. Go without Gi! At that idea, her blood ran cold. The noose was strangling her, brutally. Her excitement had died. She remained devoid of strength and a voice.

"My turn, if you'll permit? I won't respond to an ingrate. Only know that if I don't have the good fortune of pleasing you, there's no lack of others to render me justice. You haven't always spit on the loaf! Ginette is here to prove it. Love and me, my girl, go very well together. Just ask..."

"Lise Bertah?"

Instead of reddening with vexation, as she had hoped that he would—for the only courage that sustained her in the repugnant argument was now the glimmer of light at the end of the tunnel: the glimpse of divorce and the salvation of Gi—he swelled with satisfaction.

"She loves me. It's the truth! So much—it might surprise you, but it's the way it is—that she has but one dream: to marry me! We'll see, we'll see..." Then, reflection taking effect, he added: "But wait a minute. How do you know her name? That's funny. Who is it that's informed you so well? Speak!"

She saw his fist clench, menacingly. Perhaps, after all, a complete explanation was preferable, if she could not avoid it. Although she was out of breath, she summoned up her determination, and extended all her intelligence toward the goal.

"A letter fell out of your pocket, which I read before putting it back."

"When?"

"Six months ago."

"And you kept it to yourself, tranquilly? It appears that it doesn't bother you much! Thanks for the consideration! It's true, then—I don't count any more than that, for you?"

She made a gesture of repulsion.

"That's funny!" he murmured, looking at her suspiciously.

Until then, he had retained the conviction that, whatever she said, she appreciated him physically. Attained unexpectedly in his marital security, doubt took hold of him. For her to renounce, so deliberately, an association such as theirs and a company such as his, there had to be something abnormal underneath it. What? A secret? What secret? First, find out, in order to make her pay dear—and to find out, use cunning...

He played the wolf in sheep's clothing.

"Well, it's necessary to play my part. I can see that you won't miss me. That's my fault. At least, since we're talking about separation, people can, when they part, part without hatred. They've been companions; they can remain friends. I repeat, fundamentally, I'm abrupt, but not malevolent. You want a divorce? You can have it. Ginette? As long as you take charge of her maintenance...and I can always see her...eh? You see, with me, there's a means. It's only necessary to talk reasonably. But that isn't all. Someone doesn't leave a shelter cheerfully without knowing what will become of them. It isn't to live with your sister that you're planting your hearth there. I'll wager that you know where you're going?"

"I haven't thought about it yet. But I'm sure that Annik..."

"It's not in the roost of her study that you can lodge yourself with Ginette. Come on, my pretty—as I used to call you back in the day—a little confidence! Because I've been stupid, all the same, not knowing how to keep you. If it's going wrong for me, it's only what I deserve. But if I haven't been able to be a good husband, from now on, you won't have a better friend than me. Confide in me—come on, talk. And if you love someone else, well, you'll have your liberty."

Liberty! Roger *en route*...a mirage dazzled her. The sea extended, luminously. The future opened up. She only saw, in the hypocritical expression of her husband's smile, the gleam of promise. And, ingenuously, she confessed...

Well, yes, she did love someone else. In the same way that he had an affection for Lise Bertah, she had fallen in love with a younger man. He had surrounded her with attentions and tenderness. He had been able, gradually, to conquer her. He had left Paris six months ago...a long voyage on business, to Japan. He was about to return.

Entirely devoted to the sincerity of her confession, and the alleviation she experienced, she was not following the repercussions of her revelations on the adverse face. She responded, without thinking, to the questions posed.

Rich?

No, but earning a good living.

His name?

Scarcely had she pronounced it, spontaneously, than she uttered a scream.

Her husband had fallen upon her, first raised. She moaned under the shock. He had seized her by the throat, and was strangling her.

He saw the eyes revulsing, the face reddening...and re-laxed his grip.

"Slut! Don't hope to die. Liberty—no! Blows. Between ourselves and these four walls. As for going gallivanting around with your putrescent sister, twelve o'clock's chimed on that. Forbidden to see her. Understood? As for Ginette, you're not worthy to bring her up. Tomorrow, we'll find her a nurse in the country. It's healthier. She'll have fresh air! And you! You! Instead of making music outside, you'll make it here, if that suits you...but without your harp, and without anyone, even Fine, hearing you! Fine, anyway, is in the dustbin. I've seen enough of her. With her and Gi gone, you'll be more tranquil polishing my shoes..."

She cried: "No, no! You can't take my daughter away. You don't have the right!"

"The right? The Right? Consult the advocate. Is Gi my daughter, yes or no? A father has all the rights."

"Gi isn't your daughter."

"What are you saying?"

"I'm saying that..."

Like a madman, Martinet had raced toward the room where the child was asleep. Paule, leaving her sentence unfin-ished, ran after him in order to hold him back, but he reached the cradle first. He was about to take hold of the innocent—who, in spite of the noise, was still asleep, rosy, breathing evenly....

Then Paule, throwing herself upon him, bit his hand.

Marinet saw red and, changing his target, expended his fury on the face and breast of the enemy. Stunned, her eye swollen, Paule fell onto her bed. She was lying there, semi-conscious, her legs dangling. Her dress, pushed up in the struggle, displayed shiny calves in silk stockings, and, above the roundness of the knee, a glimpse of the satined whiteness of the thigh...

Irresistibly, he launched himself.

Mingled confusedly with the image of Paule, amorous, in his need for rape, was the image of the humiliated lover. There was not only the sadistic excitement that Paule had aroused a little while before, at the spectacle of the tearful face—the attraction of a new grace in pain; there was also, and above all, the revenge of the deceived husband, the pride of the male taking back his female, the instinct of stolen property, returning to his possession...

A blind mass, he satisfied his lust on the supine prey.

Paule had lost consciousness. The child, woken up, howled, while, with gasps and moans, Martinet crushed and crushed the inert flesh, to which sensibility gradually returned...

V

"Where will you lodge her if she leaves 'the conjugal domicile,' as the Code puts it?"

"What?" Annik paused in chewing the piece of toast that she had just dipped in her milky coffee. Already dressed to go to the Place Saint-Sulpice—her files to review, all her work in suspension—she stopped and looked at Amédée, perplexed. With his hat on his head, he was buttoning his overcoat.

"A hotel is unsuitable. Here, impossible…so? My studio—I can't see any alternative."

"What about your consultations?"

"Ah!"

He took off his hat and overcoat again, and sat down. He reflected. Yes, good idea! "Do them here. We'll only have one study. It's more practical."

He could already see her, deprived of being able to exercise her métier comfortably, more sedentary, and—who could tell?—soon absorbed, in the Boulevard Raspail, in the movement of his own affairs. Thus she would become again, in his shadow, the perfect quotidian collaborator…

Not divining the calculation, she conceded: "Indeed, yes…in the meantime. There's no other solution… Come in!"

Madame Danvois showed her fearful face. "It's Madame's sister! With the baby, and the maid."

Annik ran out.

When the hubbub of the initial explanations had calmed down, Paule, sitting with her daughter on her knees, related the entire drama to Amédée, while her sister gave instructions.

"You, Madame Danvois, take charge of Fine. Amélie, take the baby to your room, with Claude. Put him in the basket. Has she been fed? No, of course not. At nine o'clock, then, in five minutes, sterilized milk, like Claude. The spare feeding bottle. That's it."

And, filling her own cup while Amélie took the whimpering Gi away, she forced Paule to drink a few sips.

"Don't worry. We were just talking about you, Amédée and I...everything's arranged. I'll install you in the Place Saint-Sulpice."

"What about your—you papers, your meetings?"

"Here...but what about your things?"

"Everything left behind, in my mad rush!" She went pale. Everything! Including, in her small desk, Roger's letters, including the last dispatch from Colombo, announcing the good crossing.

"That's crazy! It's necessary to get Fine back right away. Since your husband has gone to his office, go back with her, pack your trunks, get your letters and come back directly to the Place Saint-Sulpice at eleven-thirty. I'll sort my stuff out, arrange somewhere for Fine and Gi to sleep...you can have my divan. And we'll bring everything I need here when we come back for lunch. Do you approve, Amédée?"

"There's nothing else to do...yes there is! A medical assessment of the injuries. Poor thing! He's marked you, the brute!" Her neck was still showing the traces of the strangulation, and there was a bruise on the right cheek. "Take care to telephone Dr. Gibon. The precaution is indispensable, in case your Martinet refuses a consensual divorce..."

Three hours later, when Paule, in distress, rang the doorbell at the studio, Annik uttered an exclamation: "What's happened now?"

"The letters! He's found them, taken them. My little desk was broken open, the drawers on the floor...and the hiding place empty."

"He's got you."

"What more can he do."

"Everything that his malevolence inspires him to do. How can we tell?"

Paule, in complete ignorance of where she stood in regard to the law, declared, confidently: "You're here. With you, I'm not scared."

A singular change had taken place in her. Trembling the day before at any possibility of taking action before Roger had returned and she could hold him in her arms, alive, she found it almost satisfying, on thinking about it, to have the situation clarified in this fashion. Merely in sensing the release of the link that had riveted her yesterday to her horrible despot, she was breathing more easily, seeing the Gordian knot already cut... In ten days, Roger would be here, and with Annik's advice and Amédée's support...

The sight of the studio changed into a nursery, and the trunks that Fine was helping to bring up, completed the diversion.

"I'll be all right," she said. She indicated a place in front of the bay window. "I'll put my harp here. Fortunately, it's remained since my last matinée at the Salle Gaveau, for the next concert...otherwise, it would have been necessary to get another beating, in order to see it again..." She counted on her fingers. "In a week's time...Tuesday... Between now and then I'll have received the dispatch from Suez. I'll play concerts, the Mozart concerto...my green dress...what do you think? And two days later, Thursday, Roger disembarks at Marseilles!"

Life was beginning to arrange itself, more comfortably than she could have believed.

"I didn't want to inconvenience you. Mademoiselle Hardy or Madame Broussat would have liked nothing better than to take me in..."

"You're not inconveniencing us at all," Annik replied

It was agreed that Paule would have lunch in the Boulevard Raspail and dinner at the studio, where Fine, happy to be in charge, would organize everything: feeding-bottles and walks for Gi, light meals for Madame.

Zélonoff, with his gruff generosity had demanded that Paule accept a loan—"Yes, it's understood that it's a loan!"—

of ten thousand francs…the unexpected windfall of a *Poppy Field* acquired by the Comtesse de Saint-Valentin. She had already bought a *Pear-Trees in Flower* and a *Neuilly Fair*. Zélonoff assumed—and was not mistaken—that the Comtesse, taking his pictures on trial without paying for them—"One can only judge the effect after a few days"—was selling them for twice what he asked to worldly art-lovers inclined to the provenance: *Collection of the Comtesse de Saint-Valentin*. She won't get any more from me," he concluded, stroking his beard.

Annik had been glad, in that circumstance, not to have to make an appeal to Amédée's good will. It was as well that he had not thought of it first…

Occupied with her own installation in their apartment, which had suddenly become too small, she had advised Paule to wait for Roger's arrival in order to attempt anything with regard to Martinet. It was still too soon to have news of him…

She began to regret having consented so rapidly to the expropriation of the Place Saint-Sulpice. Where could she arrange her files, in a corner of her own? Where, above all, could she hold her consultations? She had transformed the little room adjacent to her bedroom into a studio, but the space was too narrow for her to be able to both work there and receive visitors. There remained Amédée's study.

"You can take it when I'm not using it myself. It's a matter of making a schedule, that's all. What do you expect— we'll cope, by inconveniencing one another slightly. As for clients, a common waiting room. Madame Danvois can sort them out, and if, by chance, I need the big room, you can use the small one…unless we can adapt the dining room to a double purpose?"

"The secretaries are there all morning with the typists, who are still tapping away there in the afternoon."

"Bah!" he said rubbing his hands. "It will work out…things always work out. You'll see."

By the end of the week, however, she judged that it had worked out as badly as possible.

Fatally, given the layout of the apartment, there was only sufficient room for one workplace. There was no means of accommodating two without the second becoming a peripheral encampment, and suffering. Was that what he had wanted? At first she could not believe in the malevolence of such a hidden agenda. No, he had only seen it as a temporary expedient, while Paule found an apartment or set up home with Roger after his return. Her mistrust vanished on reflection. She even chided herself for having had the momentary suspicion.

Paule's joy contributed to her reassurance. Liberation had returned all the old insouciance to the woman in love; the black birds of her presentiment had flown away; there was no longer anything but clear sky, illuminated by hope. Again, she had set off at full tilt toward the future.

The suddenness of the rupture with her evil past caused her to feel an infinite intoxication. The amity with which her sister surrounded her and Amédée's solicitude, contributed to the soothing the present moment. She resumed her luminous blonde complexion. The bruise of the punch to her face had faded to pale blue, already almost invisible under face powder. She had resumed her ritual gestures: the little mirror raised to eye level, the powder puff dabbed over her cheeks with a light gesture, the touch of rouge placed on the contours of the lips by the finger.

On the eve of the concert, however, she became anxious again. No dispatch. And the *Paul-Bert* must have left Suez...

On Tuesday morning, she was gripped by an anguish.

"Something's happened," she said to Annik. "Otherwise, I'd have had news."

"He must have written the address badly. I'll surely be able to bring you his letter this evening at the Avenue Kléber, since we're dining at the Broussats' before the concert.

Paule insisted on waiting all day with her sister. She became increasingly nervous as the time approached for her to get dressed, and the necessity of appearing on stage, of putting on an act before the curiosity of an audience, even sympathetic. She left Annik at the last possible moment and came back to collect her. She was almost in tears before her disappointed face.

"Nothing?"

"Nothing."

Paule stamped her foot. In the taxi, throughout the journey, she repeated: "I won't play...I won't be able..."

The insistences of Madame Broussat and Annik calmed her down. She had been stupid to be anxious... The dispatch would come tomorrow... And this evening, after her success, she would be glad to have shaken off her neurasthenia... With such a talent...!

"You can play this one for your friends: Fauré's *La Sicilienne*!" Zélonoff enthused, in his Slavic accent. "It's ravishing, ravishing!" He pronounced the word lasciviously. "And you're as pretty as an amour! That emerald satin dress suits you so well! What a line, with your beautiful bare arms!"

The arrival of Jacquemin, and his enthusiasm, brought a good humor that Madame Broussat, which an amicable agitation, strove to maintain. The dinner was cheerful. And from the Avenue Kléber to the Salle Gaveau, the auto into which all five of them were crammed sped so rapidly that Paule found herself hurled, without having time to think, from one distraction to the other.

The pieces to interpret? Yes, she had them all. The harp? It was there, ready to be transported into the corner with the green plants, not too close to the footlights. The special life, the hallucinating absorption of the wings, took possession of her. It was a total forgetfulness of everything except her entrance on the stage. As usual, she shook the hands of her comrades: singers and pianists. A glance at the program. "You're on, Lambersac!" The applause rang out, at the end of each piece; its rumor swelling as the doors opened.

That will be mine, Paule said to herself.

Mechanically, she smoothed her eyebrows with a moist finger, checked her face powder and rouge. She heard, without listening to them, the fragments of conversations going on around her.

A violinist with short hair said to Lambersac, who was mopping his neck with his wadded handkerchief: "Have you seen *Le Temps*? These accidents are frightful. Another steamer blown up by a floating mine..."

"Where's that?"

Her heartbeat accelerating, Paule lent an ear.

"Before the entrance to the Suez Canal. A ship coming back from Japan, I believe..."

She did not have time to hear any more.

"You're on, Madame Martinet," said the stage manager.

"And as she hesitated, haggard, he shoved her, repeating: "You're on."

Abruptly, she found herself on the lighted stage. Was she about to faint? Her harp! She marched toward it like an automaton. She did not hear the bravos. She could not see the noisy auditorium, opening like a gulf of shadow. She had to play three pieces: Fauré's *La Sicilienne*, a *Madrigal* by Gaubert and, with the flautist Albert of the Opéra-Comique, Mozart's *Concerto for Flute and Harp*.

Mechanically, *La Sicilienne* unfurled its light theme. In a strange state of dissociation, Paule accomplished the habitual gestures; the sounds flew from the harp as if the strings were touched by fingers others than her own. It seemed to her that she was dead, and, at the same time, that she was playing in a dream, in a desert...

At the final notes, when the murmur of satisfaction rose up, consciousness returned to her, and an atrocious dolor clawed her. She passed her hand over her brow. It was necessary to play, to play again! She believed, at the first chords of the *Madrigal*, that her torture would never end. The motionless body and the anguished face had the rigidity of a statue. Only the harmonious arms appeared to be alive, rising and falling along the quivering strings, to the tender rhythm of the bucolic piece.

A tumult of tragic visions was seething in her head: the ship struck by a muffled impact, the panic of the passengers and, little by little, the great cadaver of wood and iron, vibrating to the last breath of the engines and tilting in the water...

She had no doubt that it was the *Paul-Bert*; she imagined Roger calling for help, Roger leaping into the lifeboat, Roger thrown into the sea, Roger clinging desperately to some piece of wreckage...

When she had bowed, after the *Madrigal*, and Albert came on for the performance of the third piece, she wondered whether she might be going mad. Those rows of faces, fixed like the dolls in an Aunt Sally booth, the dazzle of the chandelier, the heat...

She passed from a sensation of fire to a chilling frisson. Her head burning, her hands icy, she succeeded nevertheless, by a desperate effort, in mastering her nerves...

Suddenly, the Concerto having concluded, her arms fell, inertly. When she bowed for the ovation, she tottered. Albert only just had time to catch her, and draw her, unconscious, into the wings.

The stage manager appeared almost immediately, calming the emotions. A simple malaise, for which the artiste apologized.

Annik, Madame Broussat, Zélonoff and Amédée, arriving in haste, surrounded with their affectionate anxiety the sofa on which Paule, supine, had just recovered consciousness.

Now she was sobbing in Annik's arms. In vain, Amédée reassured them: there was no proof that the sunken ship was the *Paul-Bert*; there were several shipping lines serving the Far East. It was necessary to seek information, to be certain, before getting into such a state...

Unfortunately, Lambersac and the violinist had gone. No one had an evening paper. Madame Broussat and Zélonoff insisted that she go home. She was exhausted, in need of rest...

But she shook her head. Go home! They couldn't possibly think...

"I'm going to look for a paper. I have to get one."

"Futile—everything's closed."

"No, no—at the Gare Saint-Lazare. I want to know. I'll go mad with anguish if I have to spend the night like this."

"Well go with you," Jacquemin affirmed. "But even if it is the *Paul-Bert*, hope remains, even so. Go home and sleep— that would be best."

Sleep when Roger might be...she saw him, pale, his eyes crazed, his mouth open but no sound emerging... He sank, returned to the surface, inanimate, and disappeared again. But no! Roger wasn't dead! He had been picked up in time, in a lifeboat. Boats had come, in response to the wireless mayday call, had organized the rescue...

At the Gare Saint-Lazare, Amédée got out in front of the kiosk. "Wait in the car."

Anxiously, Paule followed him with her eyes. He opened the newspaper.

"Well?" she shouted at him. "Tell me, quickly..."

Amédée got back into the car. "There are no details. It's been announced, in fact, that the *Paul-Bert* has touched a floating mine, but that's all.

She had grabbed the paper, and was trying to read, but although the auto was illuminated, she was trembling so much that the letters were dancing before her eyes.

"Read it, Annik!"

And, as the words crushed her heart, she murmured: "I knew it. I was sure. I had a premonition. I told you about my dread, my conviction. Roger's dead—I can feel it. Oh, what a catastrophe! So much the worse: I shall die, too. Not even thirty...too bad. I'll have had a poor little life..."

She was no longer listening to anyone; she was hallucinating.

Annik took her to the Boulevard Raspail and made up a bed for her in the studio.

All night long, the voracious sea unfurled around her. Her wet hair was plastered to her cheeks. Splashes of water slapped her. She was drowning, with Roger.

VI

She ended up, at daybreak, falling asleep. She was stunned. Annik hardly slept herself, awake at first light. A wan wintry glow was beginning to appear. Sadly, she calculated at length with Amédée the tragic tomorrows that lay in store for the unhappy woman.

"Oh, if only she hadn't made that stupid marriage! Only one consolation remains to her—her daughter. And who can tell now what tortures that Martinet has in reserve for her, with regard to that consolation. Husband and legal father, he's the master twice over. Poor Paule! She can only suffer from it! Confess that the law is badly made…and that if women knew better…"

"They'd marry less? Perhaps. But confess, too, that not all men are like Martinet. Free union has as many inconveniences—even worse than those of marriage, when a woman falls brutally, from the hearth to the street, and it's necessary for her to struggle in abandonment and poverty alone, with children……"

"If they all worked, like me…"

"Even by working. Free union! Free union! First of all, it's not always possible. For the poor, yes, because, fundamentally, if they're rude, they're good. In any case, they aren't hampered by as many prejudices. But in the bourgeoisie! For us, with our liberal professions, undoubtedly, it can work—but in every case where the man depends on society… Think: the University, the Army, the Civil Service…there, no common life possible, if one hasn't accepted the *conjugo*…."

"The yoke!"[45]

"Well, yes."

"You see, then, how right we are in working to break it…."

---

[45] The pun linking *joug* [yoke] to *conjugo* does not translate.

He sighed. "A heavy task! It will be very difficult even to make it more flexible..."

He said no more. But the obsession was there, boring into him tenaciously. She could see it clearly. Only long habituation...

She returned to Paule. "How sorry I feel for her. How I'd like to be able to give her a little of my courage, to struggle. Fortunately, there's still something, apart from Gi, that might attach her to existence..."

"Her art?"

"Yes. And also the need to support her daughter. She has a métier that she loves, and that's already something."

"It doesn't bring in enough yet."

"We'll help her."

"Of course."

"And then, forced to work, she'll end up pulling herself together. Obligatory work for all, and remuneration in accordance with effort—there it is, the great law of tomorrow. When women are able to live without the support of men..." Forcefully, she repeated: "Work! If you knew what a sentiment of strength and pride mine gives me..."

"I know," he sighed.

She kissed him affectionately "Would you, too, like to hold me in dependency? For me to knit, while I watch Claude's teeth grow! When all of us, mothers or not, are capable of filling a table without you, my fine Messieurs..."

"A charming future!"

"Oh, it will never prevent people going to bed together!" she added, laughing.

"Marriage will have had its day, then."

"A fine misfortune."

"And the family, too."

"The family is like love, my dear. It can't die. There'll be another form of family, in which all the children are natural, when the State will care for them a little more than it does today. And there'll be another form of love, which will be no less beautiful for being free..."

"The skies of the future hear you! In the meantime, to-day's is funereal."

He stood up and opened the window. "A sky of mud!"

Annik sighed. "Poor Paule! She hasn't moved yet. What an awakening!"

A sky of mud! Amédée's intonation resonated for a long time in Annik's ears.

Since the bleak morning when the newspapers had brought the confirmation of the disaster, she sensed the narrow December horizon weighing upon her, enveloping her like a heavy shawl. *Year One*, so cheerfully commenced, so sadly completed for Paule.

It had been necessary to abandon all hope. The *Paul-Bert* had gone straight down, in deep water off the Egyptian coast. Without being able to put the lifeboats to sea, there had only been time to send a mayday. Merchant ships and an English warship had only been able to rescue a few passengers. The list was published. Roger was not on it. In fact, his name had appeared on that of the lost: *Roger Jouves, 32, industrialist of Paris*.

That inscription, on the immense anonymous tomb, Paule had initially refused to believe. He was alive! He might have been picked up be some sailing ship. She gave her illusion a delay of expectation.

When two weeks had passed, her feverish excitement faded. She did not get out of bed if there was nothing to do. She had an ashen complexion, and a few gray hairs at the corners of her temples. She dressed in black. As obstinately as she had hoped, she plunged into her desolation. To the vague suppositions with which her sister continued to tempt her, she put an end with a "What's the point?" so conclusive that Annik fell silent.

Annik knew that there are no words to soothe certain wounds. Paule's was so deep that she did not manifest any sentiment at the announcement of the petition for divorce launched by Martinet, to which Annik had immediately replied with a counter-petition.

She had feared briefly that, in spite of the influence of Lise Bertah, interested in trading her casual relationship for a grappling hook that she would know how to manipulate, the frightful individual, in order to avenge himself on Paule, might refuse her liberty. She rejoiced no less on learning, from the advocate charged with Martinet's interests, that he had also launched a suit for the disavowal of paternity. She did not admit, in her sense of justice, as in the logic of her ideas, that Gi should bear any other name than that of her mother.

By contrast, the anxious Paule was alarmed by that new threat.

"Have a little backbone, then! Don't you feel that everything in that bourgeois kitchen is repugnant? That, the family! No: saucepans numbered according to fortune, in which each is simmering its sauce of heritage on a low fire!

Fortunately, to comfort her when she was too sickened, there was Claudinet, whose fourth month had begun insensibly to model delicate features in the red clay of his initial visage. He resembled her.

"Your complete portrait!" Amédée never ceased repeating, with a hint of reproach.

"No, he already has your gaze..."

They leaned over the blinking flower of the little eyes, and, envious in her turn, she said: "The gaze is the most important thing; it's the soul." At least, it was by that route that it was visible, when, without thinking about it, she placed herself at the window...

Resolutely, Annik had gone back to work. She had resumed her consultations, and returned to the Palais.

With a melancholy resignation, she could read Amédée's thoughts quite clearly now. Not only was he exasperated that, by working, she was depriving him of a part of herself, but who could tell whether the very community of their professions, and especially the fact that she might shine in hers, alongside him, might be a quotidian element of irritation?

One the first of these points, soon after leaving the Place Saint-Sulpice, she was obliged to open her eyes. A visitor who had come to see him was introduced in error to her study. He had reprimanded Madame Danvois so severely that the disproportion was obvious.

On another day, she was receiving, in his absence, in the large study. Having come home unexpectedly, he had been obliged, while waiting for the departure of the important client, to install himself in the small drawing room. That evening, his ill humor had caused an argument between them for which he was still bearing a grudge against her.

She had reflected. There was nothing to do but separate their studies again. The opportunities for friction—disagreeable, evidently, but it was necessary not to exaggerate—would disappear of their own accord. Paule was too narrowly accommodated in the studio. Annik resolved to find her an apartment large enough to accommodate both her sister and her métier.

An extraordinary hazard came to her aid at the opportune moment. Directly beneath her studio, in the Place Saint-Sulpice, an apartment whose tenant, an army officer expecting a provincial posting, fell vacant.

"What if I were to rent it—do you think—darling?"

Her proposal, so natural, redoubled Amédée's ill humor. He had rejected it with a: "No! Everything will gradually sort itself out here. As for Paule, she can find something else, close to us..."

She was not duped by the latter amicability...

In the second week of January, on his return from the Chambre, he was opening an evening newspaper under the studio chandelier, when a news item leapt to his eyes.

"Look," he said, passing her the article. "Read that."

It was piece on female advocates, with regard to the imminent Assembly of their syndical Association. It announced the probable nomination of Annik Raimbert for the vice presidency.

"My compliments! You're moving quickly. After the case of the bank employees that I let you plead and, I must admit, you probably pleaded better than I would have done..."

"Not better, my love. Differently, with my woman's heart..."

"Solidarity! Familiar tune. But no...I don't want to wound you. On the contrary, it's another eulogy. Now you're reaping the honors. Why didn't you tell me?"

"It was only a possibility...and very uncertain. I didn't want to talk about it too far in advance. I don't believe it, anyway. Personally, as long as nothing's definite..."

"Don't worry—it will be. And I'm delighted by it."

"Really? Thank you, darling!"

"Why wouldn't I rejoice because something good has happened to you? Since it's deserved!"

He was so evidently sincere, and, far from being resentful of this new success, even showed, once the surprise had passed, such affectionate pleasure that she blushed at having been able to think, momentarily, that there might be any mean sentiment on his part. She felt sufficiently encouraged to confess to him, this time at the risk of annoying him, of a decision that she had made.

"Listen. You might perhaps scold me, but I need to tell you about a decision I've had to make without talking to you about it. It's about the studio. Things can't go on like this—it's impossible, with those three women..."

"One of whom isn't very big!"

"But who wails a lot. No kitchen, the water tap on the stairs... So I've seen the tenant of the downstairs apartment. He's being posted to Orléans. In a week, the apartment will be empty: five rooms and a telephone. We've reached an agreement. It was necessary to settle it immediately, for the owner. There's no lack of potential tenants, as you can imagine. I have a meeting at ten o'clock tomorrow for the transfer of the lease."

He was astounded. "You've rented it? Without consulting me?"

"I didn't have time."

"You didn't waste any!"

"Indeed. Are you annoyed? Why? Paule couldn't have found anywhere better—and it will return my studio to me. I'll be able to clear my papers out of your way—and my presence…as an advocate."

"What!"

Such disappointment was painted on his sullen face that she sensed the full impact of the shock. The scaffolding of sly, tenacious hope, felled at a stroke!

"I would have preferred…," he declared.

"To keep me?"

"Isn't that natural?"

She laughed. "At any rate, I can't think of a more flattering tribute. But darling, the Place Saint-Sulpice isn't far away, you know, and if the advocate's leaving, the woman is staying. Isn't she the one you prefer?"

They dined together that evening facing one another, without gaiety. Once the routine returned of their distinct offices she congratulated herself on her clear-sightedness. Every day, she appreciated the results of her resolution more: separate métiers, but the parallelism of which remained close enough for them each to follow their own while helping the other…

Thus, she had escaped the dangerous enterprise, conserving intact, along with her personal income, the guarantee of her independence, the maintenance of her personality.

And Amédée, for his part, got used to it. After all, what had he lost? Nothing. He gained additional tranquility, and confessed that Annik was right.

After her success in the case of the female bank employees, more high-profile cases came to her. Attracted by her reputation as a good advocate as well as her notorious feminism, women in difficulties with divorce or bad business dealings entrusted their cases to her. She thus began to bring in a significant income, which permitted her, thanks to a few advance honoraria, to furnish Paule's lodgings with a charming simplicity.

Feeling that she alone was capable of taking on that responsibility, and glad to do so, as well as lightening her sister's burden, Annik had taken out the lease in her own name. One of the five rooms, contiguous with the antechamber—the former drawing room—had been linked by a staircase to the studio. Thus, with Fine assuming—as well as her other task—responsibility for the door, she benefited from a waiting room and a domestic presence: an indispensable amelioration, with her enlarged circle of clients.

In the other four rooms, Paule declared herself to be at ease. "I've never been so well off!"—an observation made with such a bleak expression that Annik's pleasure was almost entirely spoiled. The little dining room, amusing in its rustic quality; the studio where the harp was enthroned; the bedroom in bright cretonne with its bathroom; the sewing room, the domain of Fine and Gi, with a tiny kitchen, adequate for their bird-like appetites: the younger sister almost envied, for herself, the nest in which the elder, broken-winged, continued to live her phantasmal existence, like an automaton.

Paule was insensible to everything, except for the living resemblance that her daughter offered to the dear departed. Thanks to Gi, it seemed to her that Roger was not entirely dead. She could still see him as she had the last time, on the threshold of the *adieu*, or when they were extended on their bed and he was laughing at some mischievous remark she had made. The hallucination was so strong that she sometimes thought that he was caressing her fine hair, or kissing the soft skin beneath her ear. Sometimes, he was by her side, and they were walking along the street together.

"I know very well that it's all over now," she said to Annik one morning—her sister had come to force her to go out, to breathe the air in the nearby Jardin du Luxembourg, where the buds of spring were showing their tips on branches that were still black—"but I can't get used to thinking that death has taken him from me entirely. I sense that his soul is close by...that it continues to live..."

"Yes," said Annik. "In Gi's little breath."

"And also," Paule murmured, "in another form, almost palpable. At times, it seems to me that I'm touching him. I only have one softening in my chagrin, which is the thought that he had a very brief agony, and that perhaps he wasn't even aware of it...that he's there, near to me, present. He always has the same appearance, his confidence, his strength. He no longer leaves me."

A blue sky extended over the flowers beds, doubled in the mirror of the fountain. There was an eruption of renewal after the ice of winter. The pathways were full of strollers. They were moving at a brisk pace, their cheeks whipped by the keen air.

Paule sighed. "Life! What a mystery! You remember my presentiment? Perhaps it had to happen like this? Perhaps I didn't deserve to be happy with him, while he was alive? But no, no, he's not dead. I wouldn't see him beside me, I wouldn't hear his voice, if he were dead, as you believe people die! Otherwise, nothing of us would survive!"

"Who knows? On that subject, no one can have any other certainty than a sentiment. And I understand yours, my darling. Why would I try to dispute it, since it consoles you? Perhaps you're right..."

Materialist as she was, she was reluctant to darken with a doubt the glimmer that had risen in Paule's soul. Another life! Certainly, on condition of only meaning by that the mysterious prolongation of forces in the unknown in which the brevity of human existence is situated...

Personally, Annik reduced herself to a brief individual spark. Soul and matter were born and died together: a magnificent product of nature, which a slow education, the legacy of centuries, civilization after civilization, had improved; a spark of the great vital fire, whose very precariousness gave it an incomparable value. What folly it was, in consequence, not to make those brief instants throw off all their light! Not the thick and smoky flame of the senses, but the noble, pure clarity of the intellect, which the senses fueled.

Paule had discovered that too late! Poor Paule, a victim of her social formation, and, in her lack of individuality, so subservient to the laws of men that she was attaching herself to the domination of a shadow! But first, it was necessary, whatever the cost, to separate her from her tyrannical past.

The petitions for divorce and disavowal of paternity followed their course. Paule had only obtained a derisory alimentary pension—legal alms—which Martinet's rapacity was obstinate, at every due date, always to pay belatedly. Behind his ferocity, Annik sensed Lise Bertah's lurking. A spider lying in wait, that one would not cease until she had sucked dry the fly that had so stupidly thrown himself into her web.

It was a lamentable adventure from which Paule, all her calculations gone awry, emerged miserable and alone, and furthermore, with a humiliation and disturbances with which Annik could not succeed in reasoning: Gi, a nameless bastard, denied by Martinet and rejected by the Jouves family.

Discreetly, the advocate had made approaches to the child's grandparents. She had been surprised to find them informed, in spite of their denials and protests. Some testamentary letter of Roger's had, undoubtedly, been confided to his family before his departure, and which they must, Annik carried away the clear conviction, have intercepted and destroyed. She would never forget the odious memory of that visit, those faces contracted at the first word, those lips sealed as if by purse strings, those eyes aiming the pistol gazes at her...

"I'm not a thief," she had declared, in vain. "I haven't come to ask you for anything. I'm limiting myself, out of politeness, to informing you. Roger Jouves' letters, of which Monsieur Martinet doubtless intends to make use in his lawsuit, leave no doubt as to the filiation of little Ginette. I thought that the veritable family ought to be warned in advance of the public scandal."

"The scandal, Mademoiselle, is that such attempted blackmail should be possible. Who can guarantee the authenticity of these letters? Be warned, at any rate, that we shall defend ourselves. Of course, if certain proof existed—a testament, for example, made by poor Roger—and honorable family like ours would do its duty. But there is nothing at all in his papers, and as nothing has been found, either, in the notary's office..."

Sickened, without replying, Annik had left. She could still hear the shrill voice of Madame Jouves, and the sarcasms of her older daughter, a fat married woman, defending the inheritance. Fortunately—and it was the sole thought that could calm her disgust—Gi, an adulterous daughter, was not, any more than Claudinet, a natural son, suffering that bile...until she was of an age to understand.

A new and unexpected catastrophe arrived to complicate matters. Martinet's advocate advised Annik, in a telephone call, that his client was withdrawing both his suits.

"What's happening?" she asked, stupefied.

"Would you like to have a chat, shortly, at the Palais?"

She arrived in advance of the meeting, and learned, with anguish, of the death of Lise Bertah, carried off in a matter of hours by an infectious influenza.[46] Martinet, finding himself alone, had naturally returned his thoughts to Paule—a deflection of his chagrin rather than a slaking of his vengeance. He had stopped the legal procedures, intending to retake possession to his wife and daughter.

---

[46] At this point, Paule's story, which has already been altered in its chronological order by the timing of Roger's death, which happens much earlier in "La Femme en chemin," diverges sharply from that of the earlier story, where there is a subplot involving Martinet and Lise Bertah's blackmailing of Paule's friends in order to buy back the compromising letters, but in which Lise does not die and the divorce case takes its course, with Paule retaining Gi as a slight consolation for all her woes.

"He's obstinate. Nothing to hope for."

It was the whim of a brute, which had amazed Annik and terrified Paule.

"What can I do?"

"Go to earth, disappear, and hide—you and Gi—in some obscure corner."

"Otherwise?"

"He might do anything. Force you to go back, to submit to the leash, take away your child. The law is on his side, and the gendarmes."

Immediately, in concert with Amédée, Annik made preparations for a departure for the Midi. She had sent a telegram to Jean Roussot.

A dispatch from the painter the following evening reassured her: *Awaiting your sister and daughter. Lodgings found.*

She was preparing to take Paule the good news when Amélie sent Fine in, panic-stricken.

"What is it? You're frightening me."

Sobbing, the worthy woman narrated the drama. Assisted by a Commissaire de Police, Martinet, who must have been on watch since the previous day, had accosted her as she was turning the corner of the Rue Bonaparte and the Luxembourg. He had displayed papers, exciting the passersby, crying abduction.

"He made so much noise that people were ganging up on me. The Commissaire wanted to take me to the police station. Then, while I was explaining, Monsieur Martinet snatched the pram off me. A taxi was waiting at the gate. He got into it with the baby, and when the Commissaire let me go and the crowd realized what was happening, there was nothing! The taxi had gone and the pram was empty. I shouted in vain. There was no one there."

Annik reflected. The Commissaire? An accomplice. Martinet, untouchable.

"And Madame?"

"I went upstairs straight away. She's gone out...she had a séance with her friends...what are they called? The occultists...the ones who summon spirits..."

Paule received the blow full in the heart. All steps taken were futile. In vain, Annik had tried to approach Martinet. He had, with sardonic coarseness, told her to mind her own business. He was free to take back his daughter from an unworthy mother, and also free to confide Gi to a good nurse, in the country, in the interests of her health. Where? That was no one's concern but his.

Amédée, for his part had seen the Public Prosecutor and the Prefect of Police, in vain. It was doubtless lamentable but there was no need for them to tell the eminent advocate that Monsieur Martinet, in acting as he had done, was exercising unassailable rights granted to him by the Code, as a husband and father. It remained for Madame Martinet, for her self-defense, to have recourse to the courts...

"The courts!" Annik exclaimed, beside herself, when Amédée had finished reporting his visits. "What a joke! Paule can do nothing—nothing!—to defend herself. Her divorce petition? That could drag on for years now! And perhaps end in failure! In the meantime, that brute has Gi and won't let her go."

"That's certain," said Amédée consternated. "Fair as the judges might be, they'll find themselves tightly bound by the bandages of the law! It's as if one were to say to a mummy: stand up and walk!"

"You see, darling, how right I was to want to fight on behalf of all those who suffer! Do you understand me better now?"

He squeezed her hand tenderly. He shared her revolt, and her faith.

VII

They lived, for the next few days, in the same dramatic atmosphere. Martinet, pressed with questions, had only decided to give news of Gi after a provisional injunction in which he had won his case, fundamentally. His daughter was with an aunt of his, a farmer's wife in Sologne. She was well—and now let them leave him in peace!

Annik was in despair at being unable to find a solution. Perhaps there was one? If Paule consented to take back the leash, and then to provoke some violent scene before witnesses... With the old certificate of injuries provided by Dr. Gibon, that might hasten, as well as her return to liberty, the release of Gi. But would she have the courage to imprison herself in that cell again?

She found her sister playing the harp, seemingly absorbed, and unreactive. Annik sat down, looking at her in surprise.

After a few moments, Paule stopped.

"I'm playing for him," she said, simply. "He's there."

She pointed at the large armchair in which she usually sat. Sadly, Annik contemplated the empty space in which the seer was incarnating her dream.

Paule explained: "Without Roger, I'd have killed myself. But he's forbidden me to do that. I asked his advice again jut now, about Gi. Look! The paper and the pencil are there, on the side table. You can read it..."

Her heart constricted. Annik leaned over the page on which Paule had written, feverishly, under the imperious dictation: *Don't worry about Gi...submit to destiny...*

"You're resigned, then?"

"I'm obedient..."

The tone of conviction and the submission of her faith were such that Annik dared not persist. Of these mysteries, whose darkness enveloped her, and which opened for Paule their luminous shadows, she was sufficiently intelligent to deny the existence, on the pretext that she could not perceive them. She understood that the profundities of the metaphysical unknown, to which her reason set a limit, attracted Paule with the vertigo of their gulf. On the table, beside the pad in which his sister scribbled communications from the beyond, there was a volume by Allan Kardec.[47]

"You see! That's my consolation. One feels better, at the thought of raising oneself up into the order of supernatural forces. I know now that Roger's soul is protecting me. Isn't that so, my love? Yes, the perispirit survives our body. Nothing dies; everything is transformed and purified."

She was speaking so tranquilly, in her concentrated exaltation, that Annik got up without raising the question of a return to Martinet's house. After having kissed her, however, she changed her mind and sounded her out.

Paule made a gesture of horror, and then said, reflectively: "I can't do anything without consulting Roger. I'll ask him, and I'll tell you after lunch... No? That's true, you're going to Versailles... This evening, then. And depending on what he decides..."

Annik, in the train that was taking her away with Amédée, was still astonished by the breakdown that her sister had suffered. Her misfortunes—oh, certainly! But also, what an instinctive need for servitude! Yes, poor, poor serf, always thrown from one master to another, ready to liberate herself from her real chains by forming imaginary ones!

She leapt down lightly onto the platform, smiling at the blue sky. Almost a summer sun!

---

[47] "Allan Kardec" (Hippolyte Rivail, 1804-1869) was one of the most prominent pioneers of the French occult revival, and the popularizer in France of "spiritism"—the French equivalent of the Anglo-American spiritualism (which required a different name because the latter term already had a distinct meaning in French).

"Oof!" she said. "It gives me pleasure to breathe a little, to have a change of air. With Mérette and Monique, at least one can understand one another!"

They called at Mademoiselle Hardy's residence first, but she was at the Blanchets'.

We were just talking about you!" cried Georges.

He pushed forward an armchair. The circle under the old acacia was enlarged. The beer was so cold that a mist was forming on the crystal of the tankards. Annik gave them the sad news, and the devious step that she had suggested to Paule.

"In truth," said Monique, "in her place I'd make the attempt. Not to the extent of the definitive submission, of course. Obedience is on condition of being consented, out of tenderness, like mine." She smiled at Blanchet. "For he's ended up by reckoning with me, the tyrant. I can announce to you that I've just sold *Le Chardon Bleu*."

Blanchet, looking at her affectionately, did not conceal his satisfied expression.

Monique protested: "It's not worth the trouble of puffing yourself up, Pacha! Ask Annik whether she would have given in. Fundamentally, I'm nothing but a stray lamb, bleating for the fold. I was born to be a normal wife, very submissive. Your dream, Messieurs."

"Long live the fold!" observed Blanchet.

Monique indicated the two men: "Your enemies, Annik. Oh, they won't admit it, but fundamentally, they see themselves as nothing but shepherds, with a big crook!"

Blanchet smiled. "What do you expect? With all the respect that I have for feminism, it's necessary in every household that one of the two should lead. Why you, rather than us?"

"I return your observation to you!" protested Mademoiselle Hardy. "Why you, rather than us?"

Annik picked up the ball, teasingly. "Because we're your inferiors, eh? Say it?"

"Beware," said Amédée, "if Annik's pitching in."

But Blanchet, amused, said: "Inferiors? In fact, the majority of scientists affirm..."

"Donkeys!" Mademoiselle Hardy put in.

"Ha ha! They even demonstrate, with strong supporting evidence, that the inferiority in question, not merely from the physical viewpoint, is congenital, and that..."

"Congenital! Because you've raised woman for the usage of your pleasures, in the weakness of gynaecea and harems, in the inaction of boudoirs, in the cage of kitchens..."

"Pardon me. Those 'donkeys,' having put on their spectacles, observe that measurements of the cephalic indices..."

"Monsieur le Professeur will excuse a humble schoolmistress, but he knows as well as I do what assertions of that sort are worth. Science today, heresy tomorrow! One hardens the body as one tempers the soul. A hundred years of Swedish gymnastics, and the modern young woman will be as strong as the maidens of Sparta. Physical equality? Content that with the African women who are carrying burdens under the tropical sun at this very moment."

Amédée twisted the point of his beard with an ironic moue.

"Oh, I can see you coming!" said Annik. "Come on, trot them out, your famous lines from de Vigny: *The companion of whom the heart is unsure...the woman, a sick child a dozen times impure...*"[48]

Amédée recused himself, not without having observed: "Impure, no. Let's say...fatigued. At least a few days per month...not to mentions a few weeks before and after...what seems to me, thus far—Monique and you won't contradict me—the feminine mission *par excellence*."

It was Monique who replied, with a sudden gravity. "Yes, *the mission*. To create life, not merely with the temporary contraction of a spasm, but for months, with our blood, with our flesh, with our agonizing pain! Isn't that a service

[48] The lines are from "La Colère de Samson" (in *Les Destinées*, 1863) by Alfred de Vigny.

great enough to compensate for a few hours of immobilization? The physical inferiority of women? Get away, with that slander! It's a rumor that men have put about—a false rumor, that is becoming increasingly so. A matter of corporeal education and social prejudice."

"Bravo!" cried Annik. "Besides which, there's one fact that surpasses everything else."

"What's that?" said Blanchet.

"The law of environment. The new economic world that is conditioning us. A different humankind is in preparation, in which work, reconciling the sexes in the common necessity, will be the universal rule…"

"Obviously," the philosopher conceded. "For equal responsibilities, equal rights. But then, let's get rid of all the porcelain dolls who spend their lives making up their faces and pinning on their nails—not to mention the claws—and thinking of nothing but betraying us. All the Simone Lourdals…"

"You're right!" Annik exclaimed. "I'm ashamed of being a woman when I think of them. But be fair—whose fault is it, Messieurs, if your companion's heart is unsure? Is a man's heart any more so? And is it not inappropriate for that master of egotism and infidelity to want to reproach his slave for the vices of which he has provided the lesson since the world came into being? Delilah—but that's the work of Samson. Wait until the future has enfranchised the eternal minor. We'll see then what she's capable of doing!"

"She'll always think, and directly, through the abdomen," mocked Blanchet. "Oh, pardon me! It's not me who makes the claim, but one of your favorite authors, Mauclair, if I'm not mistaken."

"You're not mistaken," Annik admitted. "Which proves that the best of men have difficulty ridding themselves of their prejudices. And with what do men think, then? Sophisms, all that, against the truth. Yes! You alone have the monopoly on masterpieces…there are no female geniuses, in the order of the sciences, or letters…but is Madame Curie the equal of her husband or not?"

"And Madame de Noailles?"[49] Monique put in. "She's the foremost poet of the modern era."

"One could cite hundreds of other names," added Mademoiselle Hardy. "That's not very many? Give us two thousand years of study! Wait! Just give us, henceforth, the same education as men…yes, yes, with courses in cooking as well, if you want…and while I'm formulating wishes, begin, at primary school, by abolishing the stupid barrier between boys and girls."

"Coeducation?!" said Annik. "Why not?"

"You, Madame Headmistress," mocked Blanchet, "will end up getting yourself sacked for encouraging minors to debauchery."

"Pardon me—to simplicity and health!"

"You don't see, then, that Blanchet is pulling your leg?" Amédée concluded. "In sum, I believe you're right. There is not, in the human couple, any superiority to the advantage of one, nor inferiority to the detriment of the other. The brain has no sex. There is equivalence; there ought to be equality."

Annik thanked him, with a gaze in which triumph was kneeling…

They would have known an unalloyed joy, if Paule's misfortune were not darkening their sky. Happy in sensing that Annik was happy. Amédée was savoring, without afterthought, the free life that he was enjoying in that marital exist-

---

[49] Anna de Noailles (1876-1933) was a leading figure in contemporary salon society, who was acquainted with the entire literary elite of France in the early decades of the 20th century. She published numerous novels and collections of poetry; the book contemporary with the present novel, which included both prose and verse, was *Les Innocentes, ou La Sagesse des femmes* (1923), which might well be the work that Monique has in mind.

ence, in spite of the difference in surnames. Sometimes he teased her about it, showing her letters addressed to "Monsieur et Madame Jacquemin," and prospectuses addressed to "Madame Amédée Jacquemin," but she shrugged her shoulders and smiled.

They had bought a small car, which he amused herself driving, after a few lessons given by Zélonoff.

"She has road sense!" the painter had declared.

"And a sense of direction," Amédée completed, with tender malice.

"Is that a reproach?"

"An observation."

"You drive the chariot of State. Leave your servant the modest eight-horsepower."

He had rubbed his hands. Being myopic, he was delighted that she served him as a chauffeur. Both of them, on coming back from the Palais or the Chambre, took a child-like pleasure in taking their toy out of the garage and going in search of some inn with good cuisine on the banks of the Yvette, the Marne or the Oise. They kissed Claude before leaving. Carried in Amélie's arms, he waved his arms in a gauche gesture, punctuated by an "A-houa," which signified *au revoir*. Then they set off in a carefree fashion, and on the return journey, beneath the splendor of constellated skies, savored, along with the nocturnal freshness, that of their re-tempered love.

Happiness gradually relaxed them and enveloped them, a charm taking hold of their interwoven common habits, which, without them perceiving it, insensibly wrapped them in the softness of a clinging garment. Often, now, she had to make an effort in the morning to go to the Place Saint-Sulpice to work. And the Palais, with the inconvenient timing of the hearings, frequently obliging her to have lunch alone before midday, would have begun to appear to her, sometimes, as a fastidious chore, if she had not summoned up all her courage and determination.

Inopportunely, Amélie had left her in order to marry a former *maître d'hôtel* who was employed as a concierge in a neighboring building.

"Madame will understand...a stable place...a worthy man..."

"Do you love him?"

"We understand one another."

"All right, then! Since you're happy with that..."

Amélie had blushed. "I beg Madame's pardon...but marriage is surer...and since he's prepared to take my daughter...oh, it's not that she's badly off at Madame Broussat's, but later, he'll adopt her. That way, the little one will have a name..."

"She has yours."

"That's not the same thing, though..."

Annik had not tried to dissuade her. Yes, the beaten track was sometimes easier. She thought with a commencing mildness about the abdication of women whose existence was not too rudely disrupted in its quietude, and, without approving of their idleness, understood their desertion a little better...

A whiplash brought her upright again.

Her consultations having finished for the day, she was about to go down to see Paule and embrace her when Fine, pale with emotion, came to find her.

"Madame has just had word from Monsieur Martinet. The child..." Sobs cut off her voice.

"What? Gi? Bad news?"

Fine howled: "She's dead! If God permits...!"

Annik hurtled downstairs. With a somnambulistic gesture, Paule held out the letter from her husband.

Infantile diarrhea...unexpected misfortune...buried at Cointrey, Sunday...

The words blurred. Annik forced herself to read on to the end. He had been unable to warn her in time. He had arrived too late himself. A plea followed, which only unconsciousness could have formulated, that Paule come back. She would rediscover her place at the hearth...

Silently, Annik interrogated her sister. Stooped, as if curbed beneath the fatality of her lot, Paule was looking straight ahead, without a tear. Finally, she murmured: "I knew that she was going to die. It's the punishment..."

She picked up the notepad, and pointed to a page striped with black lines.

"Roger said so,"

"And now?"

Paule turned the uncertain gaze of eyes the color of slate. "I'll resume my lessons. I'll try to work...I'll do as Roger would wish...

With all her impotent will, Annik contemplated the human wreck. It was her sister, that poor woman for whom all responsibility henceforth was incumbent on her, in the measure to which it pleased the man who regulated her conduct from beyond the world with his sovereign authority. Far from refusing that new charge, it gave her a surge of energy.

Briefly, she thought of asking Amédée to take Paule in; Fine would take care of her, and simultaneously replace Amélie with regard to Claudinet. But her sister begged her to leave and let her stay in the Place Saint-Sulpice.

"You understand? Here, I live with Roger. We're at home."

Annik consented to that all the more willingly because a Breton woman, sent by the local dairy, who had good references had just presented herself. She liked her, in spite of her face which seemed carved in wood.

"Maria Kerdalec? Well, Maria, come and see the child..."

"A true Jesus!" the Breton woman had exclaimed. "I'll look after him well."

That heartfelt exclamation had convinced Annik. She confided Claude to her.

She rarely went out any longer, except for her professional occupations. The circle of existence had narrowed to intimate friends. In the midst of the agitation of Paris, she lived in her happiness, as in a Charterhouse. She had even ceased to take umbrage at the visits Amédée made, with increasing frequency, to his mother.

After three attempts, Madame de Moreval had been obliged to yield to the evidence. Neither Antoinette Cesson nor young Thorot-Morizé—a cousin of Ronchard's—with whom she had cleverly contrived encounters, with the best of motives, would supplant Annik. A true friend, the Duchesse de Rosseille—a young American who had bought, along with her title, a senile husband, and whose provocative glamour Amédée had noticed in the days when she was Miss Eyrik—had also offered herself in vain: a game of conquering a notorious political figure as much as the attraction of pious rescue.

Beaten on that terrain, Madame de Moreval had resigned herself to making other advances. There was no question, of course, of entering into personal relations with Madame Raimbert—"Your companion would be the first to refuse that, would she not?—but it was simply a matter of Claude...

"You understand. Months ago, you told me that the child is delightful. It's only natural that I be allowed to kiss him some day. The innocent isn't responsible for...for...in sum, that which is now the past. Bring him to me. A mother can't refuse a grandmother the pleasure of knowing her grandson..."

Pressed, Annik had not said no. She sensed that the concession to the legitimate sentiments of a father and an old woman who loved her son would please Amédée. There was no danger that Claude, so small, would feel the malevolent lips posed on his forehead. He was incapable of understanding the words that might emerge. And later, when his intelligence awoke, she would be there to neutralize the venom.

"You, my love, who hardy knew our mother," Amédée had said to her, "can't understand the sentiment that I feel toward mine: indulgence, as if for an aged child, a certain respect for her narrow but rigid worship of tradition, and also an instinctive tenderness for that decrepit flesh, the only poor, frayed link that attaches me to the familial chain..."

"Yes," said Annik. "I can appreciate, even though the chain, for me, commences with Claude and you, the fact that

252

yours is lost in the past. Mine is confused with the future: it's a new family commencing—but that doesn't mean that I want to detach Claude brutally from yours. Life will do its work soon enough..."

"And death! Thank you for giving the ancestor one of her final joys..."

"The ancestor! That's the word, in these times of 197 kilometers an hour!"[50]

Pensively, they measured the stage accomplished in thirty years: the bicycle, the automobile, the airplane...Icarus flying in the open sky...then, in spite of the monstrous recoil of the war, with its reflux of barbarity, almost everywhere the quiver of a new surge, science drawing, from the depths of original darkness the as-yet-obscure but infinite forces of the movement and vibrations of light: telegraphy, wireless telephony...the vital energy captured in part, perhaps discovered tomorrow...

"You consent, then?" Amédée concluded. "I can tell my mother that I'll bring Claudinet to see her?"

"You can even telephone her, if it will give you pleasure."

"Thank you."

The first visit was recounted in detail by Amédée, who had accompanied the pram pushed by Maria there and back. He had demonstrated such gratitude, and had described the grandmother's welcome in such simple and touching terms, that she had consented to the renewal of the experiment on a weekly basis. Every Thursday, Maria spent an hour at the home of Madame de Moreval with the child. Annik instructed her that the visit should not last any longer, and that the child must not be given cakes or barley sugar.

---

[50] The figure of 197 km/h probably relates to the land speed record set by a Darracq racing car at Daytona in 1906, although that figure had been surpassed (and far surpassed in the air) by the time the present novel was published.

253

One Wednesday afternoon, on coming in, as usual, without ringing, as she passed the open door of the nursery, she heard the sound of a whispered conversation. The housekeeper—it was cleaning day—said to the Breton woman: "Of course his grandmother is right; children ought to be baptized."

Annik held her breath and listened. "So it will be tomorrow at three o'clock. Won't it, my little angel, my little Jesus?"

"Madame will throw a fit, when she finds out!"

"We won't tell her."

"It's bad enough for her to damn her own soul, without that of the child. She never goes to mass, eh?"

"Never."

"You're not baptizing him here?"

"Of course not—she might come in! No, at Saint-Germain-l'Auxerrois. That way, if ever anything happens to the cherub, he'll go straight to paradise."

What she did not add was that Madame de Moreval had promised her, in exchange for keeping the secret, five hundred francs.

Annik, astounded, almost launched forward to sack the pair of them on the spot, after having told them off. Did they even understand? She contained herself. Patience! Tomorrow! She would lose nothing by waiting. Three o'clock, at Saint-Germain-l'Auxerrois.

Abruptly, the veil had been torn. She perceived, in its full extent, the marsh into which she was in the process of sinking, and in which, without the call of destiny, she might perhaps have sunk entirely, until it was too late, until, in the mildness of her quietude, she might even have lost the strength to react.

Amédée had been absent since the day before: a lecture in Lyon. He would not return until the evening of the next day. She was glad that he was not there. He would have perceived her distress; he would have attempted to avoid the explosion.

The night was slow to pass and the hour to come. Maria had set out *en route* with her little Jesus. Annik had caressed

the child as usual, in order for the idiot not to suspect anything. As soon as she was alone, while Madame de Moreval
was expecting Claude at home, she ran to Saint-Germain-
l'Auxerrois…

A glance around: no one. The clock? Half past two...

I have time before they arrive!

She climbed the steps polished for five centuries by the
flocks of the faithful, and went into the nave. A cellar-like
light was suspended there, punctuated by the sunlit gems of
the stained-glass windows: a theatrical penumbra to which she
would have been sensible but for the sickening odor that af-
flicted her nostrils, of ancient dirt and moldy incense A few
old women, prostrated in the darkest corners, resembled heaps
of rags forgotten there. She contemplated the apse, above
which the priests of the God of Mercy had shaken the bloody
bells of the Saint Bartholomew's Day massacre, sending out
the summons to murder. A beadle who was passing by informed her. The baptismal fonts? He was just on his way to
open the grille…there was a baptism at three o'clock.

Thus, by all means, by violence or by trickery, the
Church followed its despotic design: to enslave feminine
weakness and fear eternally. Oh, without the complicity of
those makers of men…!

She remembered humble curés, maintaining their untir-
ing devotion, and their faith as well, during the war, and others, in the depths of the country, living as saints…exceptions
that confirmed the rule.

Before the altar of a little chapel, so somber that it resembled a crypt, two women were still kneeling. She would
have liked to be able to pick them up and convert them: "The
God you seek is within you! It's on your efforts alone on
which the future life, and another world, depend."

A child of fifteen went past, holding a candle bought under the porch. She lit it, in a hypnotic fashion, from one of
those already burning against a column, their ardent wick bristling in an iron triangle. The wax was melting, sizzling, with
an odor of grease. Annik shivered. Torquemada's pyres, still

burning, were in those sly flames...and all the water of all the Jordans would never suffice to extinguish them!

Tumultuously, she waited, hidden near the entrance, behind the holy water stoup. She had thought at first of waiting outside, before the battens of the door, but, on getting out of her auto, Madame de Moreval or Maria would have seen her, and beaten a retreat. Better to seize them in passing, to cry out...what? She did not know, was not even thinking about it. Her heart tensed. The door opened.

Tall and black-clad, displaying her cut-glass face, Madame de Moreval appeared, followed by Maria, carrying Claude. They stopped at the stoup; both dipped their fingers in, and made the sign of the cross...and they headed for the baptismal fonts.

Annik surged forth, and in a dull voice, said: "What are you doing here?"

Madame de Moreval took a step back. She stood there open-mouthed, frozen.

Annik repeated: "What are you doing here, with my son?"

She pointed at Claude, who had recognized her, and was agitating in Maria's arms. The Breton had been transformed into a statue.

Madame de Moreval trembled, more with hateful wrath than fear.

"He's the son of my son. I'm fulfilling the duty in which you've failed. Between a grandmother and you, God is the judge, and justifies me."

"Mam...Mam...," appealed the child, crying.

Annik had placed herself in front of him, and now advanced. "Your son has no right! Nor have you! My child belongs to me, and my duty, as a mother, is to prevent you from fashioning him in your image, of snatching him into your society of lies and murder."

The two women challenged one another, face to face, with all their being. Annik hurled into the old woman's visage:

"You'll never see him again!" Then she took Claude from the terrified Breton.

The exchange had been so rapid, its violence so contained, that it would have passed unperceived but for the piercing cries that the child suddenly uttered. He had thought, as Madame de Moreval extended her hand, that he she wanted to take him back. He clung on to the maternal neck with all his strength.

Attracted by the unusual noise as they were about to go into the chapel of the baptismal fonts, a priest in a surplice and another in a chasuble hastened their steps. The man in the chasuble had recognized Madame de Moreval. He bowed to her, like a salesman before a rich client.

"What is happening?" he demanded, formally.

Madame de Moreval explained, precipitately: "Madame intends to oppose the baptism of my grandson."

In a haughty tone, the man demanded: "And Madame is…?"

"The mother, Monsieur."

"Ah!"

The beadle and two choirboys, carrying the box of salt and the incense burner, had reinforced the reproving group. Madame de Moreval, between the bewildered priests, drew herself up to her full height, ready for combat. *What a gross creature!* But Annik, in sovereign fashion, immobilized them with a scornful stare.

"Stay with the one who pays you," she ordered Maria, who made as if to follow her.

She did not listen to the man who was stammering: "House of God... Redoubtable scandal... Pious work..." She drew away, head high.

She carried way her wealth, like a treasure. She had preserved him from the lock-pickers, and hugged him, urgently, to her bosom.

She went out without looking back.

VIII

Amédée's first movement, when Annik told him what had happened, was to run to the telephone. Tolerant, yes, but not to the point of supporting such an aggression! He was mad with rage. It was too much—his mother would see!

"Don't shake her to much," Annik interceded. "She's sufficiently confounded as it is."

"No! She has to leave us alone. We're free to raise our son as we please!"

He paced back and forth in the study, angrily, and then thumped a pile of books. "I'm going to see her!"

At the same moment, though, the telephone rang.

"Wait! It's probably one of your electors."

"*Zut!* Answer it, then."

Annik picked up the apparatus. "Yes, yes... All right!" She gestured to him, and handed over the receiver, murmuring: "It's her."

Amédée replaced her, with an expressive mime: *Let her go hang!* Scarcely had he put his ear to the receiver, however, than his expression changed, stupefied and then compassionate.

"Don't torment yourself. Perhaps it's nothing. Don't cry! I'll be there right away."

He hung up.

"They've just brought my stepfather back from the Sénat...in a very bad way. He's saying inconsequential things, and doesn't recognize anyone. Until later—I'll phone if I need to stay there for a while."

Senile: Monsieur de Moreval was senile.

The austere moralist, the member of Leagues against all kinds of license was paying the unexpected but long overdue bill for his hidden vices. Every Saturday, at five o'clock, as if he were going to his office, Monsieur de Moreval, his buttonhole deprived in advance of his *grand-officier*'s rosette, rang a doorbell in the Rue de Richelieu. The women had orders to pretend that he was a rich provincial businessman, and to treat him without undue ceremony.

As soon as he came in, Madame had him shown up to the room "from which one watches." Sometimes he had to wait. One of the ladies then kept him company, but invariably without success. He only began to get aroused when his eye was at the peephole in the partition wall. One could see the room next door, with its mirrored alcove, occupied by a couple, of which the man, at least, was unaware that he was providing a spectacle.

As soon as the game was over, the actor went out and the actress lay there. Monsieur de Moreval came on stage, followed by his accompanist. Clad in a single peacock feather inserted in his *derrière*,[51] he knelt before the soiled altar, while the two women, feigning an increasing enthusiasm, cried with admiration: "Oh, the handsome peacock! the superb peacock!" until the conclusion.

That day, the conclusion had been a brain hemorrhage. Monsieur de Moreval had collapsed beside the bed, his eyes white, babbling inconsequential words.

Panic, cries, vain remedies…until, dressed again, the senator had been set upright and steered, like a little child, to an urgently-summoned taxi. The brothel keeper, a strapping woman, had hoisted him into it. Then, discreetly giving the address, she had accompanied him, got him out and planted him in the large entrance corridor.

Monsieur de Moreval, without recognizing his monumental vestibule, only stopped repeating: "Oh! Oh! the su…su…perb peacock!" to laugh in satisfaction. On hearing the noise, the bewildered concierge had opened the door and

---

[51] Mademoiselle Hardy might have taught Annik to use accurate anatomical terminology, but the narrative voice still has difficulty.

recognized his illustrious tenant. He had been carried up to his apartment like a parcel.

The physician had shaken his head on contemplating the hemiplegic in his bed. "Nothing much to do! Cerebral congestion. If he doesn't recover in forty-eight hours…no, no, nothing to fear immediately. He might last for years like that...."

The following day, Monsieur de Moreval, his eyes bulging, his lips slack, was still muttering: "Handsome…superb…peacock." There was no more hope that he might one day resume his seat in the Sénat—a misfortune about which, fortunately, the major newspaper received orders to keep quiet.

Madame de Moreval had other chagrins.

First of all, there was the visit from the notary, from whom she had requested money. Papers in hand, he demonstrated to her that, although married under the regime of separate wealth, she only now possessed, in liquid form, 25,000 francs of her own fortune, plus 50,000 francs in six-month Defense Bonds. Monsieur de Moreval, equipped with the power of attorney that she had entrusted to him, had invested the remainder, along with what remained of his own fortune, in three businesses from which nothing had been returned for a long time. He had also lost 250,000 francs gambling on the Bourse.

The next day, a lady who did not want to give her name insisted on seeing her. She was bringing a briefcase stuffed with reports concerning Debauchery, which "Monsieur le Senateur" doubtless counted on using for his next interpellation. Pressed with questions, she had hidden nothing, and even insinuated, after the "ohs" of suffocation uttered by Madame de Moreval, that it was only necessary to assure her silence in the usual fashion… The unfortunate woman would have paid no matter what, if the second order newspapers had not spread the rumor of the scandal that very evening...

The blow had been so violent and so abrupt that she was stunned by it. Before the despair and distress of that dolor, before the face unfrozen by the fount of tears, and which, without yet understanding, was watching all the successive masks with which her husband had duped her fall into the mud, Annik, as well as Amédée, had been moved to pity. Now, having gone astray from what she had believed to be a straight road, Madame de Moreval's old age was doing penance; she had the humility of a little girl caught in sin.

Annik had not yet seen her, for fear of adding to her shame, but she had written a letter, which Amédée had taken to her, and which had touched her.

"Oh," she said to her son, after having read it, "I no longer know what is good and evil. Everything is confused in my mind. I have the sentiment of having spent my life without seeing, like a blind woman. The man I admired so much, who read a verse from the Bible before every meal!"

"Poor Maman..."

"Isn't it a crime to show oneself as one is not? I can still hear him saying to me, when he talked about you: 'Your son is dishonoring us with his concubine. I swear to you that if he'd been mine...!' And he cited his own father, from whom he had obtained his high moral quality..."

"And you believed him?"

"What do you expect? When one is at the foot of a wall, can one see over the rooftops? It's him who mounted the attack against your household...oh, what can I believe, now? Can God permit such things, even for our mortification? Your wife"—it was the first time she had described Annik as such, and her tone emphasized it determinedly—"has written me an admirable letter. Oh, I misunderstood her! She's intelligent and generous. You're truly happy?"

"I couldn't be happier."

"Then why not regularize yourself?"

"What more can the marriage of today give us?"

"Consideration..."

"That of our friends isn't lacking. And that of others..."

Madame de Moreval looked at him. Her son seemed to her to be a new being. She murmured: "Perhaps you're right. After this catastrophe, my ideas, my judgments...everything has fallen apart. And the money, too! The money! All these annoyances I'm causing you, since you've so kindly come to my aid..."

"Let's not talk about that. I'll come back tomorrow. *Au revoir.*"

Madame de Moreval sighed again. "Oh, marriage, when a woman can't defend herself...never mind! *Au revoir.* Thank Annik...ask her not to bear a grudge against me any more for...for what happened the other day...it's so far away, all that. I'd also be happy to kiss little Claude whenever she wishes..."

"Yes, Maman, don't torment yourself any more about that..."

IX

"Hey, Companion!" shouted Amédée from the threshold of the house. "It's bathing time."

Annik replied from the other end of the terrace: "Oh, no! The sun's still too hot; let's wait a while."

Lying on a chaise-longue in the shade of a tall mimosa with golden pompoms, she as amusing herself embroidering a red silk G on minuscule nightgowns: baby clothes; an entire layette destined, in a few months time, they hoped for Claude's little sister. They had decided to call her Gine, in memory of the innocent. The fresh joy had been born within them only a few days previously, and added to the luminous hours that they had been living since their arrival in the admirable region.

Dressed in white, Amédée crossed the esplanade where the flowering orange trees thickened their perfume. He picked a rose from the old well and, as suntanned and robust as the mariners whose fishing boats he had been watching since dawn, he came back to sit at Annik's feet.

"How comfortable we are here! How beautiful it is!" With a broad gesture he embraced the cork oaks and pines extending among the rocks all the way to the sea, the immensity of the water sparkling in the sunlight, and the distant line of the blue-tinted mountains.

"You approve of me, then?" she said, pausing

Rejoicing in the idea of giving him a surprise, secretly, and for a modest sum, she had bought the old farm perched on the slopes of La Gaillarde: a few hectares of woods and vines indicated by Jean Roussot, juxtaposed with his property. The furniture was simple and the walls were bare beneath their whitewash, but they were better off there—"Admit it!"—than in the furnished villa on the beach that they had initially thought of renting, and where Madame Broussat and Zélonoff were spending the vacation close by, in company with the Blanchets.

"I admit it," said Amédée. "And if you push me, I'll even confide to you that I'd like to spend my old age here! You can be sure that I wouldn't have refused my marital authority, if I had any, for the purchase."

He kissed the hand that she had left dangling.

"You're gilded like an apricot!"

Having placed her needle in it, Annik had put the cloth she was embroidering down on her knee. Her thought overtook and prolonged Amédée.

"To think that, even with separate property, like your mother, a married woman can't do anything in life without her master's consent! And that, by contrast, he... Mérette is right, you know, wanting to take advantage of her two months of repose to finish writing the little book of which she's been dreaming, her *Code pratique à l'usage des femmes*. The majority take the plunge into the lobster pot without knowing what risks they're taking. They're ignorant about everything: the world that surrounds them and the laws that rule them. Good old Mérette! If she were here, nothing would any longer be lacking, so far as I'm concerned..." She reflected. "Without her, darling, what would I have become?" On a sudden impulse, she caressed Amédée's hair. "And without you... How good you've been!"

"No...I've only reflected. Thanks to you, I've rid myself of the ballast of prejudices. I'd made mountains of them, but I perceived, on drawing closer, that they were only molehills. It's me who has you to thank."

He had taken her hands, and he squeezed them gently.

"How sweet it is, today," she murmured, "to sense that our suffering and our anxieties weren't wasted! That we're not mistaken. It's comforting, isn't it—the idea that one has earned one's happiness!"

"Darling!" He added: "I don't know, of course, whether that proves anything much from the viewpoint of our ideas. Happiness and unhappiness don't depend exclusively on social forms. We've proved, after having had the luck to find one another, that we were made to understand one another; that's all. Our free union or happy marriage doesn't make a summer, any more than a single swallow..."

"Wretch!" she joked. "Are you going to diminish our merit? Do we not all, from top to bottom, in our large or small sphere, have the value of an example? There's no action without reaction! I'm sure that an invisible equilibrium is in the process of being born from our agitations, because I firmly believe, like Mérette, that the only virtue there is in the world is that of effort. Even if we only succeed in liberating a single soul, our efforts won't have gone entirely to waste."

From one of the windows of the house, through the closed Venetian blinds, a dolorous melody rose up: Grieg's "Death of Aase."[52]

"Paule..."

Annik sighed. "That one, undoubtedly, nothing can extract from her slavery. The task is beyond my strength. And Gi's no longer there, to cross the stage on the threshold of which Paule had fallen. Fortunately, there's Claude, and there'll be Gine..."

In spite of the desire expressed by her sister—who dreaded, by abandoning her lodgings, driving away the soul from which she now lived utterly in suspension, Annik had forced Paule to come with them. The latter had renounced all work, absent to the point of not thinking that, but for Annik's delicate affection, she would have been a heavy burden on her. Amédée had insisted: "She must come! The sun and sea will be good for her..."

In spite of their pleas, however, she had immediately shut herself away. She was vegetating in obscurity, between her harp and the table laden with balls of clay, in which she modeled the disappeared faces relentlessly. She only came out of her room in order to share meals, silently. Spectral, she al-

---

[52] From *Peer Gynt*.

ways seemed to be arriving from the Beyond, and had to return there, incessantly."

Suddenly, the music stopped. There was a silence—and then a scream.

Annik ran, followed by Amédée.

"Wait," she said. "Let me go in on my own..."

He listened at the door—but Paule was talking in her weary voice, always flat. Annik soon came out again, and shrugged her shoulders.

"She was playing for *Them*, as always," she explained. "Suddenly she felt that Roger was drawing away; she turned round and saw the table on which her models were disposed. He was molding the clay, discontentedly. Then she screamed. She's just shown me the imprint, which she's surely made herself. You might well claim that it consoles her, but I think it saddens her...enough to make one weep! I've just remembered something she said to us one day: 'A poor little life!' That's it, exactly. Come on, let's get moving. Zélonoff and Madame Broussat are waiting for us now."

"And Roussot, your painter, whom you're forgetting."

"Our painter."

"Oh, as a model for Adam, you know, there are better ones than me."

She offered her lips to him. "So I can pass as Eve, in a bathing costume?"

They exchanged a long kiss, during which, at intervals, he exclaimed, lyrically: "Eve! Venus Anadyomene! Our Lady of the Sea! What else?"

She laughed. "Don't throw out any more of them."

He had put his arm around her waist, and they went down, joyfully, toward the resplendent sea.

The terrace of the Villa Mireille was connected by a landslide of mica-speckled rocks to a deserted beach from which one could perceive, on turning round, the dark green mantle of the forest on the slopes of the Maures, and, like two patched monkish habits, the slate roofs of the Roussot house and the Jacquemin-Raimbert farm.

The Blanchets, Madame Broussat and Zélonoff, seated on a bank of vegetation, had their backs turned to the sparkling water, watching out for the new arrivals. It was time for the evening recreation: the time for bathing and, in a little while, for the arrival of the mail. Beside them, under the surveillance of Madame Davois, promoted to the rank of Claude's private governess, and responsible for general child care by the seaside—was a sector delimited by blue thistles, which served as the empire of that little society. Georges, now two and a half years old, was directing the play with a comical importance. Sylvestre, at one year three months, and Claudinet, at six months, were tottering on their unsteady legs around a vague heap of sand.[53] All three seemed intoxicated, shouting without reason, excited by the salubrious air.

Zélonoff took out his watch. "Six o'clock: they're late."

"Here they come!" said Monique. She waved her bare arm. She had just seen them at the corner of the path through the pines.

"Let's get undressed, then," said Zélonoff. "I've already had a dip this morning. It's delightful."

Left alone, Madame Broussat greeted her guests. Amédée and Annik, whom Roussot had met on the way, ran in

---

[53] Within the time-scheme of the novel, these ages are not perfectly consistent with those implied earlier, when young Georges was said to be fifteen months old, and the schedule of elapsed events. The reference to Mademoiselle Hardy's two months' repose implies that the present vacation is the summer vacation, but if it were, having been born in October, Claude would be ten months old, not six months; (it is possible that "*six*" is a misprint for "*dix*"). At any rate, within the calculable time-scheme of *La Garçonne* and *Le Compagnon*, it must now be the autumn of 1930, if that timetable is taken seriously. The reasons why it cannot are discussed in the introduction to the translation of *Le Couple*, which suggests an explanation of the fact that the dates cited in that novel are blatantly inconsistent with it.

response to a rallying cry to the bamboo huts that had been installed next to the terrace, beside Zélonoff and the Blanchets. The painter, sitting on a cane chair, opened his drawing folder and took out a large sheet of paper, on which he scribbled untiringly, seizing the attitudes on the wing...

"How's your big panel going?" Madame Broussat enquired.

"Hmm," he said. "Slowly. Given the seven thousand years—by La Bruyère's count—that humans have existed,[54] and have been making progress...let's rather say, which would be more accurate, according to some, the millennia, during which Adam has been making his way...it's only natural that my painting is doing likewise..."

"Fortunately," said Madame Broussat, pointing at Monique and Annik, emerging first from their hut, "Eve is there to urge Adam on...and your brushes!"

"It's a fact," observed Roussot, admiring the two bodies, the color and lines of whose nudity was emphasized by their black bathing costumes, "that I don't have any complaints to make about my models..."

Monique, pale and blonde, followed Annik—smaller and more muscular—at her own contentedly maternal pace. The brunette slenderness of the latter had a dancing grace. She started running toward the sea.

"She's astonishing," Roussot murmured, his charcoal seemingly animated by the same movements. "What enthusiasm! See how she throws herself into the water like one of those Amazons, of whom only the name of a single warrior is known, and that of a river! And Monique behind her!"

He seemed to be collecting a feature from one, then one from the other, and combining them, with his interconnections

---

[54] Jean de La Bruyère (1645-1696) did not actually make a calculation of the time elapsed since Adam's creation, but quoted Archbishop Ussher's calculation in his scathing attack on 17th century intellectuals, *Les Caractères*.

and curves, into the design of a single woman: a thousand complex arabesques—suggestions rather than strokes—from which one unique jet was born, one clear line...

"Life is simple," he affirmed.

Madame Broussat, unused to his abridgements, looked at him.

"That seems idiotic to you? I only mean that it's necessary to penetrate its meaning. It's the Sphinx's riddle: *Guess or I devour you!*" He pointed at the men, who had begun splashing around in their turn. "But there are three, however, who seem to have discovered the key." Suddenly, he shouted at Zélonoff, who was displaying his powerful stature on a rock: "Don't move, damn it!... Isn't he beautiful, that animal?"

Blanchet and Jacquemin protested, gaily: "What about us, then? We'll refuse to pose from now on."

His note made, closing his folder, Roussot shouted; "The future city will do without you, seeds of Adams!"

"The essential thing is that it will do," retorted Blanchet, putting on his bath-robe. "*Sic vos, non vobis*—it's the age-old story."[55]

"Well," added Amédée, "it's not so bad to have worked for others."

They were now at table, all seven of them, in front of the iced Cinzano that Zélonoff, with an unquestionable authority, was imposing on the men, the women having rebelled at the bitterness as much at the principle as the aperitif.

The postman arrived on his bicycle, delighted to have made a triple strike in a single distribution.

Tranquilly, they opened their mail. Zélonoff, who had no letters, opened the local newspapers, which were brought to them from Saint-Aygulf at the same time as the post.

"I demand to speak!" he shouted. And, enjoying his effect in advance, he proceeded:

---

[55] The quote from Virgil means "thus we labor, but not for ourselves."

"*Fatal road accident. Yesterday, on the coast road, an auto traveling from Saint-Raphael to Nice crashed after Le Trayas while trying to avoid a vehicle traveling in the opposite direction. It fell into the sea after colliding with and demolishing the parapet. Two of the passengers, Monsieur Ronchard, the owner of the mines of Vingré, député of the Basse-Seine, and Madame Simone Lourdal of Paris, as well as the driver, were killed instantly.*"

They fell silent, pensively.

"Well," observed Annik, "it didn't do Simone Lourdal much good to have given the *Appel* to Max de Laume after quitting Lebeau and his eczema for Ronchard's millions!"

The frightful image of the journalist, confined to a sanitarium by an exanthematous erythrema,[56] imposed itself momentarily, in all its repulsive hideousness.

Lebeau! Annik thought, with a frisson, at the memory of the peril that she had avoided. *Lebeau condemned! And out there, in her prison, Rosa suffering his punishment...*

"The last time I saw him," Amédée said, "he was a frightful sight. A purulent wound! With his hands always gloved and his face patched with black sticking-plaster, he couldn't succeed in hiding his bleeding scabs, and his skin peeling off everywhere."

"He's in the process of sweating his fine soul," said Roussot. "He'll die of it."

"*We'll no longer go to the woods!*" sang Zélonoff. "That'll teach him, the pilferer! And now, Mesdames et Messieurs, the cheerful note: *The prosecution of the Comtesse de Saint-Valentin for selling cocaine and operating a gambling*

---

[56] Generalized exanthematous pustulosis is also known nowadays as "pustular drug eruption" because contemporary cases are almost invariably produced as a reaction to medication, usually antibiotics, but in the early 1920s, before the advent of antibiotics, it was commonly regarded as a symptom of tertiary syphilis, and contemporary readers would undoubtedly have taken that inference.

house at Villebon, has just concluded with a judgment of no case to answer. She must have influential connections. Ah! Much better! The court reports are a mine of information: *The so-called Jim, well-known racehorse trainer, has been sentenced to three months in prison for the attempted blackmail of the Marquise d'Entraygues. It will be remembered that he had slanderously accused the prominent breeder of having doped one of his horses, engaged in the Prix de Diane...*"

"According to whether you are powerful or wretched...," Blanchet mocked.

"It's curious," said Monique, "how petty all these stories of all these people seem, seen from here, and on such an evening...so petty...."

"Ha!" growled Zélonoff, after filling his lungs with marine air. "There wouldn't be so many who are, in fact, wretched, if all these people weren't powerful... The Varnish, eh, Roussot, you who've scaled them!"[57]

"Powerful, yes! And to think that they're only a handful of vermin, underneath which France is healthy and strong, and by whom it's allowing itself to be eaten away." He stood up. "They only endure thanks to our sluggishness, our shoulder-shrugging and our smiles. The day when, by virtue of proclaiming the truth, they'll be sent packing..."

"The people will crush those lice," said Amédée. "Are you coming, Annik?"

Having become serious, they went back up to their small, high dwellings. In front of them, Madame Danvois was pushing Claude's pram. Jean Roussot was walking beside her. At a bend in the path through the pine wood the artist bid them *au*

---

[57] *Les Vernis* [here translated literally as "The Varnish" to preserve the word-play], is also a slang term for those what attend the Private View in advance of the Salon, which is given that term familiarly because so many of the oil paintings, finished in haste before the deadline, have only just had the final varnish applied.

revoir, and for a moment, though the limpid evening, watched them climb up, supporting one another.

Their march was rhythmic; they were moving at an even pace, and such a force of union emanated from their harmony that Roussot, irresistibly moved, thought of the symbolism of the couple that he was in the process of painting: the eternal hope of humankind, heading, hand in hand, toward the happiness to come...

"They at least have advanced, over the route of ruins..."

Annik was walking pensively.

"And what about us?" Amédée asked her. "Anything interesting in the post?"

"Yes...I was just thinking about it. A heap of letters, as usual, but above all, look, these two newspapers." She showed him the humble sheets. "*La Voix des Femmes*, with a courageous article by Dr. Pelletier[58] on the inevitable evolution of the family. The circle growing, the child brought up, increasingly, and gradually better, by the State..."

"That's for the future," said Amédée, smiling. "It's true that every hour is bringing us closer to it. Everything is still in transition. Between now and then we'll have brought up Claude...and Gine."

"They'll see, in their turn, a vaster horizon. And thanks to us, with a surer gaze. In the meantime..." She paused. "It's necessary to think of today. Listen. This concerns you."

She unfolded a letter, also displaying the moving little sheet: *Vivre:*[59] the timid voice of those who recalled, from the

---

[58] The prominent radical feminist Madeleine Pelletier (1874-1939). The periodical cited was actually called *Le Voix de la Femme*.

[59] The author inserts a footnote here: "The organ of the F.N.B.P., 17 Rue Béranger, Boulogne-sur-Seine." The F.N.B.P. (Fédération Nationale des Banques Populaires) was, and still is, an organization promoting the co-operative model for banking organizations, founded in 1878 but consolidated into a movement after the Great War, when it took on a wider

depths of their infirmities, their sacrificed existence, when they should have been able to demand, very loudly, the full payment of the national debt; the voices of the tubercular and the gassed; the voice of the immense debris of the war, a voice made of a million groaning voices, which Annik heard resounding in her heart, amplified by the reproaches of the blind, the one-armed, the one-legged, and all the Wounded and the Mutilated who, on few sous a day, were finishing paying, with the rest of their lives, for the hour of heroism given in order that France would not die, not so that the Profiteeers could get rich; a voice stifled by the ingratitude of the Living, so ferocious that it drowned out, at the same time, even the great murmur of the orphans.

"Listen; it produced a chill. *Mademoiselle, knowing the point to which you take the frankness of your opinions, and the care*...hang on, that's too complimentary, I'll skip it...*we consider it a duty to communicate to you the reports of our recent conference on Tuberculosis and the War*...I've read it; it's unbelievable...there are three hundred thousand of them, and do you know how many beds there are for them in sanitaria? Nine hundred and ten! Listen again: *Our lamentable and iniquitous situation is so little known, in spite of our efforts. The politicians who made use of us to arrive*...that doesn't mean you...*and those who are now in power know full well of our distress, and although having proclaimed it in the Palais Bourbon, have not yet done anything to ameliorate our fate, nothing to diminish the percentage of our deaths, nothing to ward off the terrible consequences of lack of hygiene and contagion*..."

"Give me the letter," said Amédée, "and those reports. I promise you that when the next session begins..."

She hugged him. "Oh, my love, you have such a fine role! I'm such a small thing compared to you..."

"The activator!"

---

crusading role. The periodical's name means "To live"— hence Annik's subsequent comment.

"I'd like to be. So many wounds to heal, so many miseries to soothe. Yes, a great many, for which all that you can do, in spite of all your intelligence, will be very little, so very little! To live! To live better! Oh, my love, that's what we must permit everyone to do. Those who fought the war and those who, if they wish, will not fight any more. But it's necessary that to their voices, those of women—of all women—are added, and for that it's necessary that we finish delivering them from their chains. Until there's a new society, it's on mothers that all the happiness of human beings depends..."

She evoked, in the sadness of their celibacy, all those who had not dared to live, to create life...those who had withered on the vine, like sterile grass: Weakness that ought to have become Strength...all those, religious or secular, who had thrown themselves into the arms of the mystical Spouse or had been consumed in the hot flame of a vain sacrifice...Forces half-lost to fecund Energy...

They had reached the edge of the esplanade. The perfume of orange-trees saturated it with sweetness. Amédée enveloped the good companion of his route with a grateful gaze. The hope that she bore, and the one that, son of his own, was already blossoming in the eyes of little Claude, was as radiant as the magnificence and peace of the day.

Annik responded to his confidence by pointing at Claude.

"The worker of Tomorrow!"

Sainte-Maxime-sur-Mer
July 1921-July 1923.

SF & FANTASY

Adolphe Alhaiza. *Cybele*

Alphonse Allais. *The Adventures of Captain Cap*

Henri Allorge. *The Great Cataclysm*

Guy d'Armen. *Doc Ardan: The City of Gold and Lepers*

G.-J. Arnaud. *The Ice Company*

Charles Asselineau. *The Double Life*

Henri Austruy. *The Eupantophone; The Olotelepan; The Petitpaon Era*

Barillet-Lagartousse. *The Final War*

Cyprien Bérard. *The Vampire Lord Ruthwen*

S. Henry Berthoud. *Martyrs of Science*

Aloysius Bertrand. *Gaspard de la Nuit*

Richard Bessière. *The Gardens of the Apocalypse; The Masters of Silence*

Albert Bleunard. *Ever Smaller*

Félix Bodin. *The Novel of the Future*

Louis Boussenard. *Monsieur Synthesis*

Alphonse Brown. *City of Glass; The Conquest of the Air*

Emile Calvet. *In a Thousand Years*

André Caroff. *The Terror of Madame Atomos; Miss Atomos; The Return of Madame Atomos; The Mistake of Madame Atomos; The Monsters of Madame Atomos; The Revenge of Madame Atomos; The Resurrection of Madame Atomos; The Mark of Madame Atomos; The Spheres of Madame Atomos; The Wrath of Madame Atomos* (w/M. & Sylvie Stéphan)

Félicien Champsaur. *The Human Arrow; Ouha, King of the Apes; Pharaoh's Wife*

Didier de Chousy. *Ignis*

Jules Clarétie. *Obsession*

Michel Corday. *The Eternal Flame*

André Couvreur. *The Necessary Evil*; *Caresco, Superman; The Exploits of Professor Tornada* (3 vols.)

Captain Danrit. *Undersea Odyssey*

C. I. Defontenay. *Star (Psi Cassiopeia)*

Charles Derennes. *The People of the Pole*

Georges Dodds (anthologist). *The Missing Link*

Charles Dodeman. *The Silent Bomb*

Harry Dickson. *The Heir of Dracula; Harry Dickson vs. The Spider*

Jules Dornay. *Lord Ruthven Begins*

Alfred Driou. *The Adventures of a Parisian Aeronaut*

Sâr Dubnotal *vs. Jack the Ripper*

Alexandre Dumas. *The Return of Lord Ruthven*

Renée Dunan. *Baal*

J.-C. Dunyach. *The Night Orchid; The Thieves of Silence*

Henri Duvernois. *The Man Who Found Himself*

Achille Eyraud. *Voyage to Venus*

Henri Falk. *The Age of Lead*

Paul Féval. *Anne of the Isles; Knightshade; Revenants; Vampire City; The Vampire Countess; The Wandering Jew's Daughter*

Paul Féval, *fils. Felifax, the Tiger-Man*

Charles de Fieux. *Lamékis*

Louis Forest. *Someone is Stealing Children in Paris*

Arnould Galopin. *Doctor Omega; Doctor Omega and the Shadowmen* (anthology)

Judith Gautier. *Isoline and the Serpent-Flower*

H. Gayar. *The Marvelous Adventures of Serge Myrandhal on Mars*

Léon Gozlan. *The Vampire of the Val-de-Grâce*

G.L. Gick. *Harry Dickson and the Werewolf of Rutherford Grange*

Edmond Haraucourt. *Illusions of Immortality*

Nathalie Henneberg. *The Green Gods*

Eugène Hennebert. *The Enchanted City*

V. Hugo, P. Foucher & P. Meurice. *The Hunchback of Notre-Dame*

Romain d'Huissier. *Hexagon: Dark Matter*

Jules Janin. *The Magnetized Corpse*

Michel Jeury. *Chronolysis*

Gustave Kahn. *The Tale of Gold and Silence*

Gérard Klein. *The Mote in Time's Eye*

Fernand Kolney. *Love in 5000 Years*

Paul Lacroix. *Danse Macabre*

Louis-Guillaume de La Follie. *The Unpretentious Philosopher*

Jean de La Hire. *Enter the Nyctalope; The Nyctalope on Mars; The Nyctalope vs. Lucifer; The Nyctalope Steps In; Night of the Nyctalope; Return of the Nyctalope; The Fiery Wheel*

Etienne-Léon de Lamothe-Langon. *The Virgin Vampire*

André Laurie. *Spiridon*

Gabriel de Lautrec. *The Vengeance of the Oval Portrait*

Alain le Drimeur. *The Future City*

Georges Le Faure & Henri de Graffigny. *The Extraordinary Adventures of a Russian Scientist Across the Solar System* (2 vols.)

Gustave Le Rouge. *The Mysterious Doctor Cornelius* (3 vols.); *The Vampires of Mars; The Dominion of the World* (w/Gustave Guitton) (4 vols.)

Jules Lermina. *Mysteryville; Panic in Paris; To-Ho and the Gold Destroyers; The Secret of Zippeliu; The Battle of Strasbourg*

André Lichtenberger. *The Centaurs; The Children of the Crab*

Jean-Marc & Randy Lofficier. *Edgar Allan Poe on Mars; The Katrina Protocol; Pacifica; Robonocchio; Return of the Nyctalope;* (anthologists) *Tales of the Shadowmen 1-10*

Xavier Mauméjean. *The League of Heroes*

Joseph Méry. *The Tower of Destiny*

Hippolyte Mettais. *The Year 5865; Paris Before the Deluge*

Louise Michel. *The Human Microbes; The New World*

Tony Moilin. *Paris in the Year 2000*

José Moselli. *Illa's End*

John-Antoine Nau. *Enemy Force*

Marie Nizet. *Captain Vampire*

C. Nodier, A. Beraud & Toussaint-Merle. *Frankenstein*

Henri de Parville. *An Inhabitant of the Planet Mars*

Gaston de Pawlowski. *Journey to the Land of the 4th Dimension*

Georges Pellerin. *The World in 2000 Years*

Ernest Pérochon. *The Frenetic People*

Pierre Pelot. *The Child Who Walked on the Sky*

J. Polidori, C. Nodier, E. Scribe. *Lord Ruthven the Vampire*

P.-A. Ponson du Terrail. *The Vampire and the Devil's Son; The Immortal Woman*

Edgar Quinet. *Ahasuerus; The Enchanter Merlin*

Henri de Régnier. *A Surfeit of Mirrors*

Maurice Renard. *The Blue Peril; Doctor Lerne; The Doctored Man; A Man Among the Microbes; The Master of Light*

Jean Richepin. *The Wing; The Crazy Corner*

Albert Robida. *The Adventures of Saturnin Farandoul; The Clock of the Centuries; Chalet in the Sky; The Electric Life*

J.-H. Rosny Aîné. *Helgvor of the Blue River; The Givreuse Enigma; The Mysterious Force; The Navigators of Space; Vamireh; The World of the Variants; The Young Vampire*

Marcel Rouff. *Journey to the Inverted World*

Léonie Rouzade. *The World Turned Upside Down*

Han Ryner. *The Superhumans; The Human Ant*

Pierre de Selenes: *An Unknown World*

Angelo de Sorr. *The Vampires of London*

Brian Stableford. *The New Faust at the Tragicomique;The Empire of the Necromancers (The Shadow of Frankenstein; Frankenstein and the Vampire Countess; Frankenstein in London); Sherlock Holmes & The Vampires of Eternity; The Stones of Camelot; The Wayward Muse.* (anthologist) *News from the Moon; The Germans on Venus; The Supreme Progress; The World Above the World; Nemoville; Investigations of the Future; The Conqueror of Death; The Revolt of the Machines*

Jacques Spitz. *The Eye of Purgatory*

Kurt Steiner. *Ortog*

Eugène Thébault. *Radio-Terror*

C.-F. Tiphaigne de La Roche. *Amilec*

Louis Ulbach. *Prince Bonifacio*

Théo Varlet. *The Golden Rock. The Xenobiotic Invasion; The Castaways of Eros; Timeslip Troopers* (w/André Blandin); *The Martian Epic* (w/Octave Joncquel)

Paul Vibert. *The Mysterious Fluid*

Villiers de l'Isle-Adam. *The Scaffold; The Vampire Soul*

Philippe Ward. *Artahe ; The Song of Montségur* (w/Sylvie Miller) *Manhattan Ghost* (w/Mickael Laguerre)

MYSTERIES & THRILLERS

M. Allain & P. Souvestre. *The Daughter of Fantômas*

A. Anicet-Bourgeois, Lucien Dabril. *Rocambole*

A. Bernède. *Belphegor*; *Judex* (w/Louis Feuillade); *The Return of Judex* (w/Louis Feuillade); *The Shadow of Judex*

A. Bisson & G. Livet. *Nick Carter vs. Fantômas*

V. Darlay & H. de Gorsse. *Arsène Lupin vs. Sherlock Holmes: The Stage Play*

Séamas Duffy. *Sherlock Holmes in Paris*

Paul Féval. *Gentlemen of the Night; John Devil; The Black Coats ('Salem Street; The Invisible Weapon; The Parisian Jungle; The Companions of the Treasure; Heart of Steel; The Cadet Gang; The Sword-Swallower)*

Emile Gaboriau. *Monsieur Lecoq*

Goron & Emile Gautier. *Spawn of the Penitentiary*

Rick Lai. *Shadows of the Opera: Retribution in Blood; Sisters of the Shadows: The Curse of Cagliostro*

Steve Leadley. *Sherlock Holmes: The Circle of Blood*

Maurice Leblanc. *Arsène Lupin vs. Countess Cagliostro; Arsène Lupin vs. Sherlock Holmes (The Blonde Phantom; The Hollow Needle); The Many Faces of Arsène Lupin; The Island of the Thirty Coffins*

Gaston Leroux. *Chéri-Bibi; The Phantom of the Opera; Rouletabille & the Mystery of the Yellow Room; Rouletabille at Krupp's*

Richard Marsh. *The Complete Adventures of Judith Lee*

William Patrick Maynard. *The Terror of Fu Manchu; The Destiny of Fu Manchu*

Frank J. Morlock. *Sherlock Holmes: The Grand Horizontals; Sherlock Holmes vs Jack the Ripper*

Jean Petithuguenin. *The Adventures of Ethel King*

Antonin Reschal. *The Adventures of Miss Boston*

P. de Wattyne & Y. Walter. *Sherlock Holmes vs. Fantômas*

David White. *Fantômas in America*

Pierre Yrondy. *The Adventures of Thérèse Arnaud*

SCREENPLAYS

Mike Baron. *The Iron Triangle*

Emma Bull & Will Shetterly. *Nightspeeder; War for the Oaks*

Gerry Conway & Roy Thomas. *Doc Dynamo*

Steve Englehart. *Majorca*

James Hudnall. *The Devastator*

Jean-Marc & Randy Lofficier. *Royal Flush*

J.-M. & R. Lofficier & Marc Agapit. *Despair*

J.-M. & R. Lofficier & Joël Houssin. *City*

Andrew Paquette. *Peripheral Vision*

Robert L. Robinson, Jr. *Judex*

R. Thomas, J. Hendler & L. Sprague de Camp. *Rivers of Time*

NON-FICTION

Stephen R. Bissette. *Blur 1-5. Green Mountain Cinema 1; Teen Angels*

Win Scott Eckert. *Crossovers* (2 vols.)

Jean-Marc & Randy Lofficier. *Shadowmen* (2 vols.)

Randy Lofficier. *Over Here*